T0194887

Tales You Never Saw Coming

TALES YOU NEVER SAW COMING

R.M. Ahmose

iUniverse, Inc.
New York   Bloomington

R.M. Ahmose Presents Tales You Never Saw Coming

iUniverse books may be ordered through booksellers or by contacting:

iUniverse
1663 Liberty Drive
Bloomington, IN 47403
www.iuniverse.com
1-800-Authors (1-800-288-4677)

Because of the dynamic nature of the Internet, any Web addresses or links contained in this book may have changed since publication and may no longer be valid. The views expressed in this work are solely those of the author and do not necessarily reflect the views of the publisher, and the publisher hereby disclaims any responsibility for them.

ISBN: 978-1-4401-9148-0 (sc)
ISBN: 978-1-4401-9150-3 (dj)
ISBN: 978-1-4401-9149-7 (ebk)

Printed in the United States of America

iUniverse rev. date: 12/30/2009

Contents

Acknowledgement

Here, I'd like to take a moment to thank my dear mother and father, who, with happy abandon, brought me into this lousy world.

The Better Design

A report by journalists Lefty Person and Dee-Dee Day

Be advised: This tale is mainly about the behaviors of two groups of robots. However, the *people* whose brains, sweat, and tears went into making, maintaining, monitoring, and manipulating them are of some importance, too. Thus, a measure of time is sacrificed to shed light on *the sapiens*, as well, in this account. In an odd twist of circumstances, the humans in many ways proved more predictable than the "nuts and bolts" characters presented.

On the other hand, it comes to mind something said in a promo for the 1969 film, "They Shoot Horses, Don't They?" *People,* it was suggested, *are the ultimate spectacle.* So, we, the presenting journalists, leave it to you to decide whether man or machine steals the show in the drama to follow. But, again, from our perspective, this tale is mainly about the behaviors of two groups of brainless automatons.

The story opens with a view of its secondary "players," the humans. Included is a brief look at their educational and other backgrounds. From two rival institutions within the same state hale the *robot makers*. Spotlighted first is the more remarkable cadre of *engineering* professors and students, among the duo of sets. That would be the group representing LeBlanc University.

In its seventy-year existence, LeBlanc launched careers of some of the most distinguished professionals of the past half century. Its scholars excel in areas ranging from *science*-related disciplines to *politics*. Framed LeBlanc *doctoral degrees* have adorned office-walls of the most influential women and men in our nation. Enjoying the bestowed honor have been, and are, those running the gamut from corporate executives to world renowned theologians, from oceanographers to astronauts.

While new compared to its other academic *programs*, LeBlanc's *school of robotics engineering* is fast becoming nationally respected. Indeed, the professors who founded and nurture the program are completely dedicated to enhancing that recognition. Whispers abound that an elitist faction of educators, in general, at LeBlanc are given to enormous pride and pompous affect. By all accounts, LeBlanc *engineering* professors not only condone such hubris, they aspire to be *among* LeBlanc's so-called "egotistical tenth."

The avenue to achieving that status: outstanding research. Consequently, they conduct their work with fierce, almost hostile, dedication and resolve. They appear not only to aim for irrefutable success, but also in the end to be held in awe. Whether or not the professors intended it, their students seem to have adopted the same drive for achieving glory and renown.

Names and descriptions of the LeBlanc *robotics* team are presented for later reference. Comprising the five *robotics* professors are: 1) Dr. Demorest Box, *micro-circuits and wiring*; 2) Dr. Lumus ("Lu") Haxsaw, *functional programming*; 3) Dr. Glef Hortzenstal, *casing and structure*; 4) Dr. Brianna ("Bree") Quietly, *mechanical motion*; and 5) Dr. William ("Bill") Trimolke, *remote signal transmission*. Their ages span a neat fifteen-year range, from forty-one years on.

Dr. Eazl Attababy oversees LeBlanc's entire *engineering* department. While the fifty-eight-year-old is especially fond of *robotics*, he is not formally part of the team. However, with specialties in fields as wide-ranged as *architecture, integrated circuitry*, and *bionic-parts design*, Attababy often contributes useful ideas to the team.

LeBlanc's nine *robotics engineering* students all have impressive academic records. There seems no question but that each is a credit to both the *robotics* team and LeBlanc itself. As was done for the professors, the students are presented below in alphabetical order, rather than order of significance. To foster an appreciation for how "3-dimensionaal" each is, a word or two about their looks, locks and home-lives, is included. Descriptions correspond to the time that interviews were being conducted, to gather information for this report.

Ivan Api, twenty, reportedly can boast a IQ eight times his age. Two of his standout features are blondish scraggly hair and his height of only five feet, eight inches. His mom's a zoo director, his father a co-owner of several daycare facilities. Saul Caristmas, nineteen, in contrast stood over six feet tall with light-brown, curly textured hair. In relation to his height, his arms appear slightly short. His father directs a charity organization that is active the world over. The owner of several lucrative pawnshops, his mother had the far-greater income of the two.

2

Sarah Chichingski, twenty, wore her brown hair cut stylishly at medium length. Her father got rich from clever stock trades and now lectures nationally about it, for pay. *Mrs.* Chichingski is a top level official in the U.S. Federal Reserve. Tasha Heffergel, another of the four females of the student team, was also twenty. She sported long, dark-brown hair, held in place from day to day with a variety of schemes and tethers. Her mother's a surgeon, her father a retailer in expensive draperies. In contrast, Lindsey Jipper, nineteen, is a natural blond with shoulder-length hair. Both her parents were in t.v. advertisement.

Brian Noos, twenty-one, has a lot of long, unruly, medium-brown hair which falls constantly over his round face and spectacles. His mother, a former attorney, disappeared mysteriously two years prior in a boating incident. His father is an international shipper of twine and chord. He also owns and leases marina boats.

For what it's worth, Mr. Noos was rumored to be of key interest to police in his wife's disappearance. However, from what we could tell, investigators of the case made no such admission.

Mona Novapovka, twenty, has the look of a seductive, dark-haired siren. However, by all accounts she's both socially lofty *and* academically immersed. Accordingly, fellow students get little more, socially, from her than fleeting attention. Her mother's an airline pilot; her father a balloon manufacturer.

Vander Sanbo, twenty-one, is tall, blond, athletically built, with a chiseled, determined face and intense facial expression. Although unaware of it, he often ogles those with whom he chats with an odd stare. Some say it is as if he were viewing an evil presence or something. His mother is a highly successful mystery-suspense writer. His father is on the board of a toy-making corporation.

The ninth, and last-presented, student is Jon Smitten. He was nineteen at the time of this writing. Overall, the impression held by professors and fellow students was of his having been a generally wholesome young man. Stable, reliable, well-groomed, he seems never to have had a hair strand out of place. His mother works with a team of scientists who find and classify new species of birds and insects. His father owns a company that makes precision tools.

Before giving mention to LeBlanc's *rival* in the showcasing of robots, a preliminary description of the *contest* is presented. The idea for it was born in a science center/museum complex. Not just any—but the premier one within the state: the *InnerGalaxy Science Center*. Its director, a Mr. Miteus McPeak, actually proposed the match.

McPeak was aware, as many were by this time, of LeBlanc's pioneering work in a new procedure. While the storage of solar energy, in cells, is nothing new, the re-radiation of it *after* storage *is*. In other words, LeBlanc researchers were in effect capturing energy from the sun and distributing it *later*, within a specialized environment. So, for limited applications, it was like having access to solar radiation over a period beyond actual sunlight. It is perhaps foreseeable that the practice will someday be a routine matter with much more advanced production and utilization. For now, however, the LeBlanc technology is considered both novel and state of the art.

Everyone at the *InnerGalaxy*, including McPeak, took great interest in a somewhat anomalous development in their state. A mid-status, state-run college had put together a fledgling *robotics* program within *its* school of engineering. Actually the planning had been underway for years. But its quiet *start* occurred around the same time as LeBlanc's. Even then, few knew of its existence. Surprisingly, this "new" program over time received two good reviews from visiting scientists. Like many science-related happenings in his state, the miniature kudos referred to were likewise brought to McPeak's attention.

At this point, the "gears" of Mr. McPeak's "mental apparatus" began to turn. Finally, it churned out an idea he thought might gain great national press for his center. Like many other science-minded folk, he had watched on t.v., and also attended, intra-collegiate robot competitions. What if, he wondered, in his state a way was found to combine LeBlanc's new solar research with something *new* in robot competition? Of course, just the right relation between the two would have to be conceived in order to stir maximum curiosity and attention. After days of thought, he came up with a plan. He called a meeting with the relevant officials at both schools of interest.

Believing fully in the merits of scholastic competitions, McPeak proposed that a *robotics* match be held right within *InnerGalaxy*. The center would provide the area required and bear the expense of the needed props and set-up.

Soon, he announced his overall vision to a group he convened. It was of robots devised to operate from first- and second-hand solar energy supplies. Immediately, at his pause to reorder his thoughts, it caused murmurings within his audience. McPeak continued.

Since the robots could be "fed" continually without constricting electrical hookups, a much neater, less jumbled arena could be constructed. Requiring neither power-feeding wires nor remote control functioning, the machines could be programmed to operate with greater autonomy, he said.

Beyond the creation of little radiation-powered machines, McPeak stated another challenge to be met. It concerned finding the right *task* at which the two separate teams of robots would compete. This, of course, was a standard in robot contests. But McPeak envisioned a match slightly more *exotic* ("sexy," he jokingly called it) than the typical "low brow" robot endeavors.

These latter, he cited, with intentional dismal affect, include the old, run-of-the-mill, dull robot activities. Examples he gave were such as having robotic arms vie for scores in pitching balls into a net. Others, he reminded the audience, involve "awkward contraptions" engaged in "boring quests." Examples he gave, now, were of vehicular robots maneuvering across, through, and over obstacles, or avoiding them altogether. And in these, the robots were often battery-powered having only so much energy to burn in the tasks. He evoked the memory of other contests wherein strange-looking machines slogged around attached to thick electric cords.

McPeak's *imagined* robots, on the other hand, would receive energy constantly, through invisible waves. And it would be thanks to solar work pioneered and conducted at LeBlanc. Now, with this novel and fabulous technology, a whole new set of *exciting* activities of robots in competition could be devised.

When McPeak finally revealed the full scale of his vision of robot functioning, the listeners around the table sat in thoughtful silence. In a nutshell, McPeak presented this: He wanted to see robots from the university and college, respectively, compete in not one but *two* categories. The usual *mechanical* task, of one sort or another, comprised just *one* of them. In addition, McPeak suggested that the machines be required to demonstrate *learning*, i.e., category *two*. This acquiring of "knowledge" should occur alongside the robots' obligatory kinesthetic doings.

The fact that McPeak was politically well-connected gave some weight to his recommendations at the conference. But that accounted for only a fraction of the appeal his proposal generated.

As McPeak was well aware, his audience was largely composed of academic researchers. That being the case, the essentials of his scheme had two clear benefits: First was the *face* simplicity of it in the midst of a lofty objective. No aspects of the proposal seemed dauntingly unmanageable. Second, it had a quality such as to inspire a spirit of challenge. While the robotic *skills* involved were in present-technology range, it was clear that the project would require much thought and planning. In addition, the prospect of inducing mechanical *learning,* and having it displayed, always brought excitement.

The proposal's academic seductiveness and lure of excitement were one thing. But it had another attractive feature—namely, its seeming ability to garner much *national* interest and publicity. Notably, officials from *both* schools found that appealing. There were always benefits to accrue from that level of exposure. They ranged from heightened school enrollments to increased private, state and federal funding.

So far, only one group of the competitors has been highlighted, along with the school that spawned them and the man initiating the contest. Finally, LeBlanc's *rival* in the robot competition was state-financed *Hughe College*. The seven *robotics* students in the *Hughe engineering* program were under the tutelage of five talented professors. Altogether, though, their ordinary lives and circumstances contrasted sharply with those of their counterparts. They certainly were of far less financial means. Forgoing, here, a special presentation of them, the *Hughe* members get introduction as they appear in the unfolding of events in this report.

The teams were given a year to prepare for the competition. At least one local t.v. station had signed an agreement to air it. Depending on the level of publicity and interest stimulated, however, many believed coverage could go national.

As had been earlier stipulated, LeBlanc would make *Hughe* familiar with the properties of radiation to be emitted throughout the robot "work" area. The robots, you will recall, were to get their energy requirement from this source. There was nothing for LeBlanc to be concerned about in this sharing of information. Engineers were careful, in the information transfer, not to disclose secretly-held processes of *acquisition, storage and reemission*. Understandably, LeBlanc had ambitions to develop, unilaterally, their technology farther and market it wisely.

The issue of just what *physical* task the robots would undertake had been decided early. It needed to be simple—these were, after all, just robots. It needed to be entertaining—human audiences, as the teams knew, love a show. It needed to show imagination—Mr. McPeak's public *image* was on the line. As one might imagine, the choice of *deeds* assigned the machines would also influence their *designs*. Sixty days of hatching ideas, and hashing through mixtures of proposals and reformulations, finally bore fruit.

For sure, there were many matters to be considered. *Learning*, regardless of the recipient in question, often requires numerous trials. Thus the overall competition would have to involve repetitive sessions. McPeak envisioned, for maximum effect, robots performing over several meters of distance. For this application, smaller sized robots were favored—30 centimeters in height. The robotic task chosen was that of pushing and maneuvering small, three-dimensional geometric figures. By design, robots would "learn" to be more skilled in positioning these to drop into matching floor slots.

Eventually, the decision makers had to tackle head-on an issue they seemed to be avoiding. The energy absorption feature for the robots, it was known, was going to significantly damage their parts. In address of this matter, robots were to be composed of materials inexpensive and disposable. However, this decision impacted directly the plan for having the robots undergo repetitive sessions for *learning*.

The solution came from the mind of LeBlanc's Dr. Attababy. He confidently proposed robot-*memory transplantation*. After a set of robots, he explained, had its trial in performing the desired task, their *programs* would be removed. Within each program was a "memory" of the last adventure. For each robot, its collection of *memory bytes* would then be inserted into the program of its replacement robot.

It was Professor Sheila Deal of *Hughe* who expanded and refined Attababy's ingenious scheme. She did it by tying into an initially-laid requirement in the robot tasks. Her proposal was as follows:

Dr. Deal suggested that one hundred of the inexpensive robots be designed for each team. However, both sides would require only ten "pieces" of insert-capable memory-hardware. These would be the most expensive parts of the robots, so limiting them to ten-per-team satisfied cost concerns. For each team, the ten *memories*, within the first ten robots, would be reused nine more times. In total, these ten usages would correspond to each team's set of *ten robot trials*. So, again, there would be ten robots per trial, per team. This summed to two hundred robots, one hundred built by each school.

Finally, the long awaited competition between LeBlanc robots and the robots of *Hughe* was just hours away. The *InnerGalaxy Science Center* wherein the contest took place buzzed with reporters and observers. The excitement was near palpable. But, then, this wasn't to be a match of just an hour or so duration. It was to last ten days! The first two sets of *ten* robots, moving in their designated domains, would operate nonstop for five hours each day.

So, starting on that particular Wednesday at ten a.m., the machines would be set to action. Straight through until 3:00 that afternoon, they would go about the programmed tasks. Very early the following morning, the teams would remove the programs and memories from the two sets of ten "disposables." They would then insert the *memories* of the old twenty into the programs of a "fresh" twenty of the remaining 180 machines.

To present a clear picture of the events to come, the contest *space* approved by McPeak is described. He listened carefully to the formulated and reformulated proposals for the match. Finally, he worked out the following set-up with the teams:

At the center and base of a theater-like section of the science center, the robot *arena* would be built. This would be the space within which the robots functioned. For it, he designated an area three and a half by five meters in width and length. Within the rectangle, each team was assigned half its space.

Running along the length of the *arena*, at the center, were a pair of bifurcation walls. Between these was a space of 30 centimeters. This center space within the robot's rectangular arena, along with the walls at either side, separated the two *domains* within which the two sets of robots performed.

Another function of the 30cm space was that it aided students in the set-up activities. Within it, the team members could squat to reach into the arenas, over the little walls, and avoid stepping into the arena proper. In short, when the top cover of the *arena* was lifted, students had manipulation-access from the arena's center as well as from the sides.

At this base level of the assigned theater, the robot *arena* itself was set within a large space. Here the robotics *teams* were allotted respective areas (right and left) for their operations and observations. Finally, within this oval base were two raised platforms which afforded LeBlanc and *Hughe* program-monitors a good view of activities within the arenas. These program-monitoring activities will be described in more detail later, as their role in the contest becomes clearer.

No one had quite heard of anything like the match to be played out. Just as McPeak and officials of the two institutions hoped, it got the attention of everyone from the merely curious to the intensely fascinated. Robots that demonstrate *learning* in trials right in front of cameras and observers—it was thoroughly captivating.

Particulars of the match's design and objectives were well publicized. In addition to the robots, there would be small *geometric figures* to be manipulated by them. In addition to the figures, the arena floor would be interspersed with corresponding, indented, geometric *shapes*. A tally of successful matches of geometric figures with the shapes would be ongoing.

Each time a robot managed to position a figure such that it fit snugly into an indented shape, it showed on a scoreboard. Because the indentation was slight, robots were able to travel over them with ease. But when a geometric figure was placed precisely within the indented slot, a trap was triggered. In this case the figure was allowed to fall through the floor completely. The trap then resumed its former position.

The time was eleven minutes to the ten o'clock hour. The admitted spectators, reporters and cameras were all in place to witness and record initial hours of the first event. With the earlier arrivals of successive groups, McPeak tirelessly repeated aspects of the contest design. At three p.m. sharp, he emphasized and reemphasized, power to the robots would be cut off. Other science-related activities may continue or be started, but the *robot show* would be over until the next day.

Six minutes before the top of the hour, LeBlancs and *Hughes* made essentially the same checks. Their focus was mainly the two *inner* sidewalls running along the length of the domains for each group. Thirty centimeters in height, same as the robots, it was the two sidewalls of each domain that aided the robots' learning. For each domain, all along the two walls were indications of where shapes in the floor were located. These indications were in the form of data transmissions via radio-waves.

Robots were programmed to receive diagrammatic information from the walls and match it with those of the floor. Over trials, they were expected to show increasing skill in nudging the little geometric figures around and fitting them in place. These plastic *cubes, hemispheres, prisms,* and *bars* were initially placed at the back end of the domain. The result was that, in the first session, most of the floor was left free for robot exploration.

Right down to the last two minutes before "zero," the LeBlancs appeared cool and confident. Quietly, they discussed the nine sets of ten *replacement* robots their team had created. As was the case with the *Hughe* team, their remaining *ninety* were stored in a special place at the center. Tasha Heffergel responded dryly to a private concern of two teammates. She spoke low:

"There's no way Mr. McPeak would allow that kind of crap to go on. Why in hell would he go to all the trouble of setting all this up, if he was going to allow any kind of tampering?"

Ivan Api replied: "Oh, no, I don't think he'd be *part* of it. But can't you just imagine the *Hughes* wishing to gain access to *our store*? This is, goddamn-it, *cutthroat competition!* I believe they'd do anything to win out over us."

Heffergel sneered at Api and shook her head. "You're a cynical little bastard, aren't you? Everybody's either overly lax or all about dirty tricks, in your book. If we don't trust McPeak, we shouldn't have gotten in this in the first place. So, how about you and Brian just relax and let this thing play out. We're *going* to outclass the lowly *Hughes*. Besides, we'll have our eyes on them the whole time. You know the rules: no team here without the other."

"I just couldn't bear to lose to them, Tasha," declared Brian Noos. "I just couldn't stand it if they found a way to cheat, and win! We're the *elite*; they are…garbage!"

Squinting, Heffergel replied. "*Je-sus*. What the hell did they *feed* you when you were little? The folks of *Hughe* aren't *garbage*. They're just, compared to us…*inferior*. …Shh! Quiet—both of you. McPeak's about to announce the start-up."

Just as Tasha had advised, the science center director made the final repeat of his introductory spiel. Yet again he referenced the two educational institutions involved. Once more he ran through the names of the team members while cameras were trained on them. With greater emphasis than before, he focused on the twenty robots standing motionless inside the 1.5 meter tall glass casing. As he reiterated, the ten on his left were LeBlanc *robots*; those on the right, the *robots of Hughe*.

With thirty seconds left before start time, McPeak re-explained the object of the contest. He pointed to the little figures placed at the rear of the two domains. Showing handheld replicas of them, he noted that each had a side or diameter of about 10 centimeters.

He had cameras zoom in on the bisected floor space of the robot arena. On the audience's big viewing screen could be seen the indented areas wherein the geometric objects were to be fitted. Finally, cameramen heeded his request to get a close-up of the two sidewalls of each domain. All along them, glowing in electronic display were the geometric shapes indicating the floor-locations of each shape.

Robotic Competition
Session I

At exactly 10:00 McPeak pulled the switches to start the stored solar energy supply for the robots. To the enthrallment of all audiences, the machines began to show signs of "life," twitching, turning slightly. The exaggeratedly large L-shaped arms of each robot practiced independent up and down movements. Their little hand-like pads were positioned a space apart such as to allow light seizure of the figures, once found. In a repetitive gesture, the robots just slightly widened and narrowed the space between their arm extensions. They appeared to be practicing for programmed feats. Ever so gradually, they rolled to and fro on their tractor-like wheels and spun around left and right.

For months before this contest, both teams had tested their one hundred robots in short-time trials. In these, they used batteries capable of powering the machines in exercises lasting up to fifteen minutes. At that time, they practiced sensor-detection of the applicable geometric shapes, both at "head" and floor level. The teams also tweaked the robots' abilities lightly to seize the three-dimensional figures. Both teams had reason to believe their machines were up to those tasks in competition.

For optimal distinction of the robots, each team selected a color scheme. The LeBlancs chose an elegant *platinum* exterior. Of course, it was all gild, since it covered the same light, inexpensive casing used by both teams. For their robots, the *Hughe*s chose a dour and dignified smoke gray. This only moderately heat-resistant paint cost much less than the silver flecked platinum of their counterpart. Nevertheless, the toned-down radiance of the *Hughe* robots gave them a staid, business-like aura. They seemed ready to perform without glitz, dazzle and façade.

As with human sports figures, the robots wore conspicuously painted numbers. These ranged from "1" to "10."

So, this "first generation" of the robots impelled, seemingly cautiously, within their respective boundaries. Arena-mounted and overhead cameras recorded every move. Having the floor to themselves, they wandered around tentatively, stopping on occasion to get sensory input. The latter emitted from levels both head and foot, as earlier mentioned. Outside of their awareness, of course, the little machines' internal functioning was being closely assessed. Such vigilance occurred on the two sides of the floor semi-circling the robot arena and assigned the teams.

Seated at one of the three robot-monitoring computers on the *Hughe* side was Professor Bertram Suggs. Although still filled with the same level of nervous excitement that had gripped him all morning, he appeared calm. Dr. Suggs spoke in low voice to the student, Doris Cokespoon, sitting to his right:

"We got a real good start, Doris. Thank *Jesus-Lord-God* in *Heaven*! I've had nightmares for the past week, wherein McPeak threw the switch and our robots failed to energize. And the whole place erupted in laughter."

"Oh, my *God, Professor*," responded Doris. "That would have been just…unbearable."

"I'd have fallen over dead right from this chair," informed the professor. "But, Doris, *we're in the game…we're in the game*. Look at those *babies*, doing what they're programmed to do. They're taking their time, getting to know the environment.

"Look at that! Every once in a while one of them finds a *geo-indent*. And look at ol' *Number 4*, sidling along the wall. Sooner or later, that one's going to find an *info center*." The latter of which Dr. Suggs spoke was also termed, by both teams, an "IC."

Professor Suggs eyed the actual robot, and alternately its computer image, with pride. Again speaking low, he gave a mock address to the #4 machine. "You keep going, you sweet baby, find that *IC. God*, I'm lovin' this! That's it. Keep going. Yes…yes. …Who loves you, baby—*who loves you!*"

"Oh, *Professor*," chimed in the student to his left. "Number 9 is finding its way to a wall also!"

"Hallelujah!" exclaimed the professor in a whisper. The alerting student, Dominic Ratroprekocius, pleased with his discovery, yielded his seat to a waiting student. He then joined five fellow *Hughe*s kneeling along the length of the *arena* glass—on the *Hughe* side, of course.

Again, each team had a wide space marked off, at the front and sides of the robot *arena*, from which to view their machines. They watched through the arena's glass cover, which kept the robot-feeding radiations contained within. As explained, just beyond the front of the "robot cage" was a slightly elevated platform with computer setups. Here, on the right and left sides, team members monitored computer programs *and* viewed real events from a "raised" vantage point.

Among the spectators of the robot show were visiting faculty and students from both LeBlanc and Hughe. Respectively, these latter had special seating sections among the science center audience. For all viewing the spectacle, every twist and turn and roll of the robots was fascinating stuff. But, of course, it was especially so for those seated there representing their school.

Glancing subtly around at the LeBlanc visitors, team member, Jon Smitten, caught a glimpse of the *school of engineering* program-director. He nudged teammate, Mona Novapovka while speaking:

"I see Dr. 'A' finally arrived," reported the student *sotto voce*. The reference was to Dr. Eazl Attababy.

Mona responded in a whisper: "I guess he finally tore himself away from that *private conference* with Mrs. Jipper." In saying the latter, Mona glanced over at teammate, Lindsey Jipper, who was attending fervently the robots. "Boy, it's like they say: the apple doesn't fall far--."

Smitten, chuckling, got the implication. He then spoke: "If Lindsey's as great a *whore* as you say she is, I wonder why I've never gotten with her?"

"I'd say," Mona answered, "it's because you have at least to *try, virgin-boy*. I don't think they call you 'Smitten the Kitten' for nothing. You can't *meow* your way to the *goods* in this world."

"What the hell are you talking about, Mona? What are you trying to say?"

"Jon, you're too meek. You can't expect girls to wait to catch you alone at *lab*, hop up on the diode table, and, just like that, give you an *LCD event*."

Smitten responded testily: "Don't get me started repeating what they say about you, *Miss Lock- Drawers*. I just happen to--. ...*Oh, hell*—look at Number 3! It's standing at yet another wall IC!"

Mona focused abruptly on the machine in reference. "Oh, yes!" she delighted. "That little son-of-a-bitch looks like a good candidate. It may be one of the ones to pass on a *learning memory* to the next generation. And keep your eye on Number 6. I believe we've got another *study-freak* in that little can of gears and nuts."

Ivan Api had just come from computer-monitoring of his team's robots. Now he joined Novapovka, Smitten and the other *up close* observers. He wore an impish sneer as he spoke:

"Hey, have you *electron-heads* been taking any note of what's doin' on the other side?"

Sarah Chichingski fielded the question: "What the hell are we—halfwits? Damn right we're casting glances over there. The *robots of Hughe* are moving a little slow—just like the minds of their creators. This contest is going to be a *cakewalk* for LeBlanc. ...Just look at *our* boys...goddamned *Trojan Warriors*, every last one. That's ten little platinum *balls of fire* you *robot junkies* are watching."

It was true—what was said earlier. The *robots of Hughe* were already showing the notable movement flaw, that is, less energetic, than that of the LeBlancs. As the *Hughe* team suspected when they first noticed the discrepancy, the fault did not lie in the robots *proper*. The machines had been very carefully planned and constructed. They were, in fact, very well suited mechanically for the assigned tasks. Instead, the drawback they were experiencing was centered in the *energy receptor* of each robot. The LeBlanc team had simply outdone them in designing an apparatus for maximum energy absorption.

Both the *Hughe* professors and those of LeBlanc knew that the energy factor alone, however, would not decide the contest. The reasons were multiple. One, the difference in *vigor* observed between the two sets of machines was not all that great. Two, much of the robots' successes in performing the tasks would depend on the strength of the *robotic programs*. Three, victory in the contest would hinge ultimately on the quality of memory passed to each successive robot "generation." This was true provided all other considerations were not too unequal. And, four, there exists, almost always, an *unpredictability factor* in these cases, which might work to the advantage or disadvantage of *either* team.

During the five-hours of Session One, there were many sets of audiences. Individual members of all observers watched for whatever time-segment was appropriate for them. Cameras, however, were always rolling and recording scenes within the arena on the great screen.

At three p.m. the *InnerGalaxy Science Center* director turned off power to the robots' domain. He had been in and out of the forum, just as fascinated by the movement of the little machines as everyone else. According to prearrangement, McPeak had the only key that allowed power to be turned on within the robot area. In addition, the latter was provided a securing mechanism which only McPeak could disarm. Now, at seconds after the hour, the robots were almost smoking hot but perfectly still. By design, they would remain motionless and undisturbed until the following morning. Over those hours of dormancy, the robots would have ample time to cool off.

When the *robotics* students arrived at 9:00 a.m., their excitement was near that of anticipating a wild spring vacation. Before their eyes, McPeak "remotely" lifted the glass encasement of the robot arena. The sight and sound of it had a very *advanced science* appeal. In fact, though, as everyone knew, it was just a combination of simple *electronics* and *hydraulics*. Now the LeBlancs and *Hughe*s, as scheduled, began the task of delicately removing their respective robots.

The *robots of Hughe* were blackened and blistered at their painted surfaces but "yielded" to access of their programs. On the outside, the LeBlanc machines appeared a lot paler and duller of color. And it was clear upon opening them that, like their counterparts, the heat devastation was massive and irreparable. Of course, this was expected as only the *program* interiors of each robot were insulated from the heat.

Diligently the teams went about the technical processes that were their morning obligation at the center. One was that of removing the score of "first generation" programs and *memories* from the first twenty machines. In turn, 20 *second generation* robots were outfitted with new programs containing *memories* acquired by their "forebears." Very carefully, both teams checked the energy absorption apparatus built in each new robot.

By 9:45, the center's robot-viewing auditorium was filling with similar clusters of robot enthusiasts as the day before. LeBlancs and *Hughe*s still went about their private conferences and setup activities. The robot scoreboard, located a ways beyond the glass *arena*, listed "0" for each of the numbered robots in either domain. That was because, in the day prior, none of the machines had made any scoring "inserts."

If, on this day, any of them "dropped" a geometric figure through a slot, two things would happen: First, its corresponding number on the board would display (and tally) the success. Second, the robots internal program would also score a "hit." In the latter, the robot received a sort of circuit-based *reward* for achieving a programmed goal. This acted as an incentive for the machine to repeat the activity for which "payment" was received.

Robotics Competition
Session II

At the throw of the power switch, the second generation of the little machines began to crank up. With verve, they lurched and twitched, seeming to flex mechanical "muscles." Whirring around inside their glass domicile, the robots moved without the initial hesitance of their predecessors. This was because, as their creators had hoped, the new set of twenty was equipped with a benefit. Within their *memories* were the sensor experiences of the generation that came before them. As before, however, the LeBlanc set displayed a little more zest.

For this new group of robots there was an important difference in the arena. While before, the *geometric objects* were stacked inaccessible at the far back end, they were now placed randomly throughout. The little rolling machines, then, "knew" the arena's floor and walls from memory but had to get acquainted with the little *figures*.

Far from creating a problem or being an alien factor in the challenge, this new feature accorded with the robots' built-in predisposition. In short, they were built to detect and manipulate the "*geobjects*," as the 3-dimensional figures were nicknamed. For both sides there were five of each shape, twenty in all, to be given proper floor insertion.

As the audience and the *robotics* teams watched mesmerized, the robots began to show their different approaches to addressing the *geobjects*. For both sets of competitors, some of the machines practiced grasping and releasing the little figures. Other robots lifted the *geobjects* from the floor and seemed to acquire skill in spinning around with them. On the LeBlanc side, #7, and in the *Hughe* camp, #2, appeared predisposed toward a sort of tactical nudging of the objects. Others among them just rolled along on their wheels locating the figures and moving them various distances, haphazardly.

After an hour of studying their robots' behaviors, both teams began to draw similar conclusions, independently. Each of the machines, so far, could be placed in one of four activity categories. Later, there may be other divisions or even subdivisions, but that remained to be seen. As they knew, a robot's pattern was significantly shaped by that of its predecessor in the previous generation. For that reason, both the LeBlancs and the *Hughes* kept track of each memory's "placement" in the successive generation.

Also, both teams followed the same practice in robot memory assignment. For each machine of the first generation, its memory would be placed in a robot of a different number throughout the ten trials. Actually, McPeak had requested it. He said he didn't want any robot patterns that developed to be identifiable by "number." It would, he thought, introduce an unwanted predictability factor.

Sitting in a small row of seats designated for the LeBlanc *robotics* professors, Dr. Haxsaw scribbled in his notepad. He turned to his colleague, Dr. Box, and spoke:

"Demorest, I'm seeing four different types of behaviors that I think are going to be significant in the outcome of this match."

"One of them," replied Dr. Box, "must be 'confusion.' So far, most of those *dome-heads* don't really *get it.*"

"Why can't they all be like our two *hotshots, Five* and *Seven,*" added "Lu" Haxsaw. "But then, in that case it wouldn't be much of a contest would it? As it stands, our boys show a lot more get-up-and-go than those *slackers* on the other side."

Dr. Quietly, who was monitoring the conversation of her colleagues, while viewing activities in the arena, cut in. "Have you taken note of what looks like one drawback to our higher energy levels," she asked.

"Yes, that damned *Number 8* is starting to worry us all," answered Dr. Box. "Look at him zipping around like he's got an *evil spirit* stuck in his motherboard."

"I don't know," informed Dr. Quietly, "if Bill and the two students at the computers will be able to influence *Number 8*. I understand they've just started trying to calm it down through adjustments made at the monitoring station. Already, it has spoiled one good *geobject* match and fit.'"

"While they're at it," grumbled Dr. Box, "maybe they can do something to sedate the 'clowns' among the group. You'd think they were programmed for silliness."

So, there it was. The present "generation" of ten LeBlanc robots was developing four distinctive styles. On the *Hughe* side, a like quartet of types had emerged. Without even conferring across teams, they had generated similar appellations for the robot groups. Some became known as "neutrals," appearing unable to get the "hang" of object-fitting. The teams had four each of these. Another division was the "taskers," robots that actually made correct matches of objects and shapes in the floor. LeBlanc evolved two within this second generation; the *Hughe*s, just one.

Ignoring the "dictates" of their programs, a number of the machines were given to seeming antics. In these, they hauled the *geobjects* back and forth along the length of the arena. Going about this pattern, they made quite a spectacle of themselves, spinning around and making all manner of charmingly curious motions. Fittingly, they became known as "clowns." Four of these the *Hughe*s had to their credit—or discredit. The LeBlancs squeaked by with only three.

Finally, the two teams were beset with one each of the fourth category of the robots—at least for now. These were the "disruptors." In contrast to design, they appeared programmed to misuse the *geobjects*. Carrying one and then another of the figures around, they in effect harassed their "fellows" by bumping them with their tow. On other occasions, they vied for use of a geometrically-shaped floor-indent using a hopelessly mismatched *geobject*. In so doing, they stymied the valued efforts of "taskers"

Four hours into the session, *Hughe* student, Vashti Nishadimah, turned to the professor accompanying her. She asked: "Dr. Mtofu, are you seeing what I'm seeing?"

The professor who had just returned from teaching a class at the college answered wearily. "Yes, Vashti, I hate to admit it. But it looks like one of our 'neutrals' has evolved into a 'disruptor.'"

Robotics student, Dae'Quan Capp, spoke next: "I've been trying to keep tabs on the LeBlanc activities. If my count is accurate, we're now even in 'clowns.' But now we've got two *disruptors* to their one, so far."

"Let me take a look at their score," interjected Dr. Mtofu, glancing at the tally board. "Okay, they've still got just two successes to our one. That's not too bad. It'll be great if we can keep it close like this until something happens purely in our favor."

Just like the day before, audiences were constantly shifting in hourly and two-hourly segments. As everyone knew, the robots were attempting a feat which, for machines, was quite challenging. Onlookers were advised to expect little scoring in the early phases. For one, robot-*learning* took place during much haphazard robot *traffic*. In addition they were operating quite literally *blind*, and only with the aid of detection devises.

Nevertheless, watching the machines act, even in long periods between scoring, fascinated observers. As it turned out, events this day actually proved more interesting than that of 24 hours prior. Unlike before, some of the robots actually scored points, as earlier described.

Time in this second session neared the end, announced McPeak to the audience. Indeed, only twenty-seven seconds remained. Against all seeming odds, the *robots of Hughe* managed to tie the score. Now, the teams had two successes each.

Standing by the power switch, Mr. McPeak gave his concluding talk. He noticed that on both sides of the robot *arena*, "tasker" robots had a *geobject* positioned over a corresponding floor-indent. Not wasting an opportunity to bring the crowd to pitched excitement in the final seconds, he began a move-by-move account of the machines.

LeBlanc's Number 7, he declared, had positioned a *prism*, or pyramid, over a *triangular* floor-indent. And it was a single millimeter off perfect insertion. Likewise, the "Four" of *Hughe* deftly angled a *cube* over a *square* indent in the floor.

Brandishing a half-sphere between hand-pads, LeBlanc's *disruptor*, Eight, was rushing toward *tasker*, Seven. The time was fourteen seconds before 3:00. On the *Hughe* side, *tasker* "4" was surrounded by both the "old" and most recent "disruptor" of *its* group.

McPeak was shouting with his hand on the power lever. "Look at the clock, folks! Eight seconds left! My God! Both sides are right on the verge of scoring! …Four seconds…three…two…."

Just before the science center director said "one," LeBlanc's Number 7 motioned its object just slightly. With that adjustment the figure slid securely into its floor indent, with only ½ millimeter clearance on all sides. That event triggered a mechanism in the *indent* to admit the *geobject* all the way through the floor. Upon the figure's disappearance, the floor indent swung back into place.

On the scoreboard a score of "3" showed for the LeBlanc team, with the crowd cheering wildly. The time was exactly three o'clock. Power to the robots was shut off abruptly.

On the *Hughe* side, the valiant *Number 4* stood deathly still, radiating heat waves. Just in front of it, on the floor, sat its cube. The *die-shaped* figure was tilted out of place in the floor indent by a mere fraction of a millimeter. Very near to the *Hughe #4* stood two *Hughe disruptors*. Touching against the smoking *tasker* were the "bar" and "hemisphere" *geobjects* they carried.

Next morning, the *Hughe* team would find the two objects slightly melted at the point of contact with #4, indicating how hot the *tasker* had been.

Robotics Competition
Session III

It was Friday morning, just before ten o'clock. The *robotics* teams had completed all preparations for the day's contest. Standing in a row on each side of the glass-covered arena were ten members of the *third* "robot generation." Although they were exact copies of their predecessors, these 20 seemed to have a resolute look about them. As "show time" inched ever closer, the science center director concluded his introduction:

"Keep your eye on the clock, ladies and gentlemen! The robots are about to begin the third round of their contest! But don't see them merely as mechanical *things*! They are *creatures* of these two wonderful groups of engineering students and professors! You've heard the expression, *brainchild!* Well, these twenty *athletes* are the *brainchildren* of scientific minds!

"Right before our eyes these creatures are learning to become proficient at the task assigned them! They are here to thrill you…to excite you…to inspire you! And now, as the seconds count down…*three, two, one*—let the games begin!"

In the first hour of this new match, the LeBlancs observed the same robot "characters" as evident the day before. Privately they jotted 2 Ts (taskers); 4 Ns (neutrals); 3 Cs (clowns); 1 D (disruptor).

In that same period, the *Hughes* made the following notes to one another confidentially:

Taskers (T): 1	Neutrals (N): 4
Clowns: (C): 3	Disruptors (Ds): 2

It had mildly distressed the *Hughe* team that one of its "neutrals" became a "disruptor" in the last hour of the session. But this generation of the robots was destined to alter the numbers yet again, as the match progressed. It would be true for both sides.

At 11:17, a LeBlanc *tasker* moving along a wall found an *IC* or *information center*. Here, it received wave emissions defining a *hemispheric* shape. The signal, in fact, indicated the presence of a corresponding shape in the floor, nearby. The *T*-robot, then, needed to find a round-bottomed *geobject* to match it. As it turned out, an *N*-robot, trailing the *T*, just happened to be toting around, aimlessly, the same figure signaled by the *IC* wall.

In due course, the *T*-robot nudged the *N* toward the nearest "round" floor-indent. Relieving the *N*-robot of its burden, the *tasker* robot inserted the figure quite handily into the floor insert. The set of events amounted to the "birth" of a third *tasker* for the LeBlancs. It would take a number of explorative trials by the *N*-robot. But within half an hour, a third LeBlanc *T* emerged.

Observing from a place alongside the *arena* glass, students, Jipper and Smitten wore pleased expressions. The scoreboard flashed a tallied score of "four" for their team, and they exchanged mutual smiling nods. It farther delighted them that they could see the morphing of their former "neutral" into a *tasker*. On the *Hughe* side, they noted happily, the score still showed the previous day's tally of "two."

"That's how the contest is won," whispered Lindsey Jipper. "Cooperation…the sharing of good info…the predisposition to learn—our guys have it all."

Jon Smitten nodded his concurrence and then replied: "We're friggin' geniuses! We provide our 'bots' a *program*, *sensors* and a *memory*, and they ratchet it all up to…*collaboration*."

"It's how the game is won, 'Smits'—in both the world of robots *and* people."

The robot spectacle had a similar fascination to that of watching various fishes swimming in a tank. On one occasion, McPeak likened them to sightless pups in a great maze, seeking food sources, using underdeveloped senses of smell. Always, his analogies were designed to make the machines seem animate and endowed with intention. Evidence abounded that he was successful.

Assigning *character values* to the robots by number, within a single session, became a common practice for some audience members. Often could be heard such comments as, *"The real trooper this time around is that Number Two"* and *"Number Nine's a tricky bastard today."*

The *engineering* professors of LeBlanc and *Hughe* were each generating theories to explain robot behaviors. Specifically, they considered how different *kinds* of "memories" being passed along might affect the machines. For example, they wondered to what extent *inability to follow the program* might influence behavior. Indeed, they expanded their inquiries to consider how *generational memories* of those "failures" might impact new generation behaviors.

As both teams noted, actions and motions of *taskers* were deliberate, economical, and void of agitation. None of the other "robot characters" exhibited all three of those qualities combined. The conclusion was that memories of behaviors resulting in *task success* yielded actions qualitatively different from other types of robot "recall." Evidence of it was mounting. Within those "other" *memories* resided "recall" of task failure. Evidently, these led to behaviors marked by agitation, frivolity and purposelessness.

For the robots, task completion brought reward of a voltage boost of sorts. It had not been predicted that a kind of *substitute* reward might generate within the robots for off-task behavior. Nevertheless, that which the professors observed forced consideration of the phenomenon. Robots that developed *non* programmed reward for *non* programmed behaviors—the very idea was unsettling.

Regarding this substitute reward, some of the *Hughe* professors began evoking from their memories a possible association. It involved a dubious phenomenon termed *mechanical proprioception*. Among *robotics* engineers, it carried about the same validity as UFOs. Still, the *Hughe* professors referenced it in their overall conversation of *programmed incentives* within robots:

"That tiny voltage boost is almost standard in robots of this type," Dr. Mtofu offered. "As we all know, it is worked into their programs and acts as an incentive to repeat a task. But I'm telling you, my colleagues—with this batch, there seems to be a different motivator at play. Some of them, I believe, are receiving a...*charge*, if you will, from some *foreign* source."

Professor Nigy responded. "Good *God, Phil*, don't tell us you're reifying the old robot *proprioception* myth. A consensus whipped to death, figuratively, that hypothetical 'player' in robot behavior years ago."

"Everyone knows we humans can derive satisfying sensations, from motions of the body," added Dr. Suggs. "For example, in dancing and the like. But applying the concept to machines, well--."

"Hypotheses don't always expire neatly," advised Professor Deal. "Let's face it. Fact is, Meg Shimmy's *The Proprioceptive Machine* captured the imagination of a multitude in its initial publication. And even while it has since become professional suicide, almost, to advocate it, there still exist underground adherents."

Dr. Mary Fission seemed to blush somewhat at the last comment.

"But most importantly," Dr. Deal continued, "we must examine the facts as they exist. Our 'disruptor' and 'clown' robots are acting like they're *high* on something."

"I couldn't agree more, Sheila," exclaimed Fission. "It is as if they've evolved a *second program*. Clearly, those two types have an inexplicable bent toward behaviors beyond our design. You've all seen them: *clowns* 'play' like they enjoy it, although they don't interfere with other robots. *Disruptors* 'interfere' as if they're under reward for the acts, but don't play. What else are we to make of it, if not the presence of, you know…that *phenomenon* mentioned?"

Dr. Dwight Nigy, reared back in his office chair and puffed a pipe as he spoke. "One thing about those silly-ass *clowns*—they keep the audience amused during slow periods. …There's no question, though, that we'll have to get to the bottom of this…*alternate motivator*. Whatever its nature, we need to discover and try to reform it. And it would be nice to achieve it before the LeBlancs do, if at all possible."

Session III ticked down to the final hour. By three o'clock, the keener competition observers realized something significant. For both teams, the 'neutral' robots were taking on characteristics of either a *disruptor* or a *tasker*. For those carefully keeping tabs, the lineup appeared as follows:

		LeBlanc	*Hughe*
taskers	(T)	4	3
clowns	(C)	3	4
disruptors	(D)	3	3

Taking into account the robots' scores for all three sessions, the scoreboard had the appearance below:

	Team Scores	
	LeBlanc	*Hughe*
Session		
I	0	0
II	3	2
III	6	4
Tally	9	6

Even though the score *ratio* was the same for each of the bottom three comparisons, the *Hughe* team wasn't very happy with the trend. Falling behind by one score in session 2 but by three in the *tally* presented a dismaying aspect.

On the following morning, Saturday, the LeBlanc and *Hughe* teams assembled outside the science center. Earlier in the week the director and teams had decided to alter the contest's weekend hours. For Saturday and

Sunday, it would begin at noon and continue until five in the evening. The final five days of the competition, Monday through Friday would proceed as had the first three.

Robotics Competition
Session IV

It was evident that some percentage of all the visiting audiences came mostly to ogle the C-robots. Apparently, the latter had lost "sight" of their original purpose. Although oblivious to cheers from onlookers, the "clowns" raced from one end of the arena to the other. On the way, if they detected one, they lifted a *geobject* from rest, as called for by their programs. Then, with as much un-stymied motion as detection devises would allow, they made moves that were patently *not* part of their programs.

Employing the extent of their capacity for motion, the *clowns* fancifully skirted other robots. They also steered clear of walls and thus the "information" displayed. Sometimes they stopped a straight-line motion abruptly, sidling off at a ninety-degree angle. On occasion, they did this whether or not another robot was in the way. Usually that "ninety" was followed by another *ninety* in the opposite direction from the first. At this point, the *clown* was headed toward the original destination.

In executing an arcing motion around another robot, especially another *clown*, the C would sometimes do half twirls. Above the robots' tractor-like wheels, the machines could pivot upon an axis within its casing. Therefore robots, if sufficiently practiced, could execute two very different motions at once. On wheels, they could move forward or backward or to either side. Simultaneously, they could turn what anatomically would be their torsos.

Thus, as people watched, mesmerized, and as cameras rolled, two *clowns* might circumnavigate one another, each twisting and turning right and left in a thrilling dance. And just as often as not, the pair swung about a *geobject*, carried in tow. It was, indeed, a sight to behold.

In spite of the amazing show, both *robotics* teams eyed the Cs in something approximating disgust. All the time and effort put into designing the *message boards* at the side walls was lost on *clowns*. That they were oblivious to signal emissions from the site was evident.

Compared to *disruptors*, the *clowns* were just colorful athletes, only mildly a worrisome detriment to the contest outcome. Activities of the D-robots, with this fourth generation, increased dismay in both camps. This group raised *disruptive behavior* to a new height. Only occasionally targeting a *clown*, the *D*s mostly sought out *taskers* for "robbing" them of their *geobjects*.

That was just *one* area of their "misbehavior." In addition, *D*s didn't "appropriate" a *geo-figure* to find a matching floor insert in which to deposit it. That behavior, though robotically rude, would still have been in keeping with the program. Instead, they tended to carry it a distance away and set it down atop a *mismatched* shape.

Most vexing, at least to the teams, was when *D*s used the *geobjects* to impede motion of *tasker* robots. Sometimes they "borrowed" that extravagant, pivoting-torso move perfected by the *clowns*. In this mode, the *disruptors* would wallop one of their "fellows" with a *geo-figure* they held. While the audience in general couldn't get enough of the shenanigans, the teams had had just about enough.

In addition to the "wilding out" of *disruptors* in the fourth generation, another change was in evidence for this batch. Actually, it was happening only among the LeBlanc ten. Right before the startled eyes of team members, a fifth robot-character *identity* emerged. One of the team's four taskers began to change its role just after 3:00 on this Saturday.

Involved in the incident was a *tasker*, Number 8. "Eight" was appropriately fitting a "bar" *geobject* into a rectangular floor indent. One of the three *disruptors* of this LeBlanc generation approached carrying a cube *geobject*. At this point, the *tasker* and the *disruptor* both vied for fitting their respective figures into the indented shape in the floor. Within the audience grew a plethora emotions ranging from nervous anticipation to bloodlust excitement.

In the struggle, the wrangling, the pushing back and forth, the *disruptor* made headway. It managed to fit a corner of its cube into a corner of the rectangular floor indent. Thereupon the *D*-robot braced itself against its *geobject* such that the latter could not be slid out of the way. Whereas just earlier, the *tasker's* persistent shoving was sufficient to turn the cube about, now it didn't budge. Stymied from scoring, the LeBlanc tasker almost seemed flustered.

Monitoring robot behavior on the LeBlanc team were Dr. Trimolke and students, Saul Caristmas and Vander Sanbo. The three sat at their computers doing what they could to maintain, remotely, equilibrium within the robot programs. Needless to say, they weren't happy with the scene on their side of the robot arena. The scoring of every single point by each of the machines was a thing to be hailed, applauded—even cherished. Here, one of their *taskers* was on the verge of bringing in the sixth success of this new contest. And diabolically—seemingly—the score was being thwarted. To the trio, at this moment, the very planet knew no greater injustice.

Suddenly, the keystrokes, swiftly and deftly tapped by Sanbo, took on a vengeful, angry aspect. Glancing to their right, the professor and Saul eyed Vander with quizzical and concerned expressions.

"Vander…are you all right?" Trimolke asked while watching Sanbo fitfully typing commands as if in a rage.

"There must be a way to lock it down, damn-it!" said Sanbo in a raucous whisper.

"I doubt it, but that would be against the contest rules anyway." Trimolke spoke with concern in his voice. "We can't intentionally eliminate a robot—only troubleshoot the programs."

"That son-of-a-bitch '*Ten*' is blocking our sixth score, sir! For this session, we're only one ahead of the *Shit-Heads*—I mean the *Hughes*. …I'm sorry. I'm just--. *God*, if I had a gun right now, I'd shoot that platinum-gilded bastard!" As he spoke, Vander still searched frantically for a command that would "slow" the *disruptor's* "role," so to speak.

"Hey, Van" interjected Caristmas from the professor's left, "get a grip, man. This is…."

"Shut up, you fucking pea brain!" Catching himself, Vander self-moderated his fury. "Hold it, hold, it…I am *so* sorry, Saul…Dr. Trimolke. Please forgive me. But we've got to do something! We can't risk having our *disruptors* cost us the contest. We just can't…*we just can't!*"

Trimolke emitted a forceful sigh, while staring at his screen. "Look, Saul, Vander…I've been turning something around in my mind for the past hour. It's a process. It's a series of commands I discovered that might re-channel one of our more profuse *IC* readers."

Saul Caristmas was intrigued. "Really? But…what--? Why would we want to alter a *tasker?*"

"Well, think of it, guys. Imagine if we can add to the signals coming from an *IC* wall. Then imagine if a *tasker* develops a new mission from it—the mission being that of *countering* the *disruptors*. Look, let me show you something." With that last remark Trimolke tapped away at the keyboard. At the same time, he instructed the students sitting to his left and right in how to follow his activities on their computers.

"The big question, of course," continued Trimolke, "is whether or not I'm altering the *design* in doing this. If so, there's no way we're going through with it. Now, just watch this--." With execution of some startlingly sophisticated programming on-screen, the professor laid out the processes he had in mind. The students were awestruck.

"*Wow*, Dr. Trimolke," Saul exclaimed. "Wow…look at that…gosh… Jees…incredible! The path—it's all right there! I know I wouldn't be able to navigate it, but I can see it!"

"*Hot damn, hot damn, hot damn!*" It was Vander's expression. "*Dr. T,* you're the only one with knowledge of the sequences to pull it off. That shit's beautiful! Look at it! I hope you don't mind my saying so, sir: But I'll be damned if you're not two levels below God Himself!"

Dr. Trimolke intervened. "Okay…whoa, guys. Let's just…sober up. The question right now is: Would this or would this *not* represent an alteration in the *design* of the robots?"

Saul Caristmas fielded the question. "I don't think it would. It's…it's a…it's just a tradeoff, really."

"*Carist, you glorious son-of-a-bitch, you just hit it on the head!* Doc… Doc, did you hear what that veritable fucking genius sitting beside you just said? It's a friggin' *tradeoff*—a splendid, magnificent friggin' *tradeoff!* This wouldn't be design *alteration*. It couldn't be. The design is set. Those little fucking machines are what they are. We're not changing a screw, a gear, a wire, or a unit of energy input. We're just transmitting something a little different from an *IC* wall and adapting the program to it.

"And it's a *gamble*, sir," continued Sanbo. "Oh, hell yes, it's a gamble! We'll be screwing around with a tried and true *tasker*. That tells you right there, we're not off limits. We're gambling with causing a *disadvantage* with one of our own. And maybe we'll get a little reward for it…hopefully…if there's a *God*."

Near the robot arena, students note the time of 4:20. The LeBlanc "8" *tasker* seemed completely thwarted in trying to win the floor indent. Still embracing its bar-shaped *geobject* at floor level, T-8 pushed constantly to get it in place. Continually, however, it came up against the immovable *cube* being wedged in place by the *disruptor*. But *T-8* needn't have despaired, even if capable of it. Help would be arriving soon enough.

Another of LeBlanc's four *taskers*—one embracing a pyramidal-*geobject*—brushed by a wall *IC*. The *tasker* paused, receiving wall-emissions for almost half a minute before setting down its *prism*. On a new "mission" now, the *tasker* moved about tentatively. It rolled forward a ways, stopped, changed directions slightly, stopped, and repeated that pattern. Apparently, it sought detection of something within the arena with which it had prior experience. It searched, in fact, for a *disruptor*.

LeBlanc students observing the robots up close, right at the glass casing, glanced around at one another. To their near disbelief, they were watching the emergence of yet another robot "character." Ivan Api was the first to put to words their collective astonishment:

"Just when you think the game has stabilized and there are no more surprises, this crazy shit happens!"

Tasha Heffergel responded: "I know! We've just lost a *tasker*. He quit his fucking job and walked off!"

Brian Noos commented next: "This is just plain *wrong*. I'm going over to the computers. Somebody back there should know something about what the hell's happening. *God*, I hope it's not an irreparable malfunction in the program.

"Uh-oh, wait. The 'quitter' is making way over to the standoff between *T-8* and that damned *disruptor*. …Whoa, what is this…what's going on?!"

"What's going on," added Mona Novapovka "is the start of a good ass kicking—well, a good ass *pushing*. He's nudging the *disruptor* from the side, turning it around a little. Look, now he's backing the disruptor away from the floor insert!"

Next, Lindsey Jipper happily stated her observation: "There it is! Number 8's free to get its piece in place. It's coming, it's coming. It's about to go down! …Wham-bam, score-time! A new phenomenon among our 'guys' is developing as we speak—the ability to act cooperatively!"

Jon Smitten gave his offering: "That may be so, Lindsey, but I'm sensing that something else is in evidence here. I think we've just seen the birth of the *vigilante* robot."

Just before five p.m. when the robots were stilled for the fourth time, the LeBlancs had scored yet again. This was in addition to the crowd-pleasing point advanced by *Number 8* at 4:44. On the *Hughe* side, the three *disruptors* had wreaked havoc on the ability of *Hughe*'s four *taskers* to score. Even so, the *Hughe* machines had managed five "drops" just in that one session. On the "down" side, it compared to eight successful inserts for the LeBlancs.

At the end of Session IV, the scoreboard flashed:

	LeBlanc	Hughe
Session IV	8	5
Tally	17	11

27

Robotics Competition
Session V

At the session's start, the *Hughe* team was quite unaware that the LeBlancs had lost a "generational" *tasker*. If given that information, it would most certainly have uplifted their spirits. They had, however, taken note that a sort of *renegade* was on the loose among the rival robots. But, unsure as yet how it might impact LeBlanc scoring overall, they tried not to be overly concerned. Rather than focusing on advantages the LeBlancs may have incurred, they examined more closely their own main *dis*advantage. And of course, that was the presence of the three *disruptors* in their population.

For the *Hughes* it was nearly traumatic, watching their *taskers* being, in effect, stalked and harassed. Scoring, in this *robotics* competition took on a "feel" and meaning that was almost *spiritual* for the team members. Therefore, sitting idly and watching prevention of points was quite demoralizing. It was akin to NASA scientists watching obstruction of a grand Mars mission.

Halfway into this fifth session, that is, by 2:30, the LeBlancs had already scored four points. Considering that the achievement occurred even with the loss of a *tasker*, it was a good sign. It especially appeared so to Dr. Trivolke and his two student cohorts. So far, the robots' scores were equal to those in the same time frame of the last session. In relief, they thought the result of their gambit to be, at worst, neutral in effect.

Thinking in terms of optimal outcomes, the three pinned increasing hopes on the new *vigilante* robot. As the *vigilante* improved its "tactics," albeit by trial and error, scoring by *taskers* should increase accordingly. It was the hope of the LeBlanc trio—their desire. When, by the end of the Sunday session, the LeBlanc score reached "9," their wish seemed granted.

For Session V, the robot *character* lineup was as follows:

	LeBlanc	*Hughe*
taskers	3	4
clowns	3	3
disruptors	3	3
vigilantes	1	0

As can be seen, the robots of *Hughe* enlisted a *tasker* from within its *clown* population. Even so, the effectiveness of the fifth "generation" of *Hughe disruptors* topped that of the fourth. So adept was this trio at stymieing *geobject* "drops" that the scored points for Session V were only

28

2 above those of IV. While, obviously, this constituted progress, it was not nearly enough to sustain hopes of winning in the end.

Something, the *Hughes* determined, had to be done. Even with the *loss* of a LeBlanc *tasker* and *gain* of one by the *Hughe* team, their robot-rivals still managed to prevail score-wise.

Finally, now, at Session V's end, the Hughe team became aware of the new *evolution in robot behavior* from which the LeBlancs benefited. Routine observations of goings-on among the rival automatons disclosed the "one-robot police force" that had emerged. As the Hughes' interpreted it, LeBlanc machines were actually forming *associations* to aid in meeting contest objectives.

At about six o'clock on this Sunday evening the *Hughe* team took seats in a reserved area of a local restaurant. It was a sort of *silent synchrony of intention* that flowed among the seven students and five professors. Painfully aware, they all were, that the contest was half over. In five sessions of robot learning and practice, their machines had managed an accumulative score of 18 points. LeBlanc robots had scored that amount *without counting their scores for an entire session*—the fourth! Things looked bad, alright. Something needed to be done.

There was something in the facial expression of Professor Sheila Deal that interested the group. One by one the *Hughe* team members had taken note of it. It was as though she was holding back some delectably controversial, or even lurid, thought or scheme.

Drs. Mtofu, Fission, Nigy, and Suggs eyed one another across and down the long table. Somehow Bertram Suggs silently received the consensus arrived at. His colleagues had put upon him the task of probing pertinent thoughts Dr. Deal might have.

"Let's have it, Sheila. You're on to something and it's showing all over your face. You know you're going to relent eventually. Spare us the unpleasantness of having to 'tweezer' your thoughts out, unit by unit, in front of these kids. You've got...*ideas*, and we all know it."

Professor Deal said simply, "*Sterilization* and *abortion*."

"Huh? What? Excuse me--?"

"A minim, a mere *dot*, of iodine," resumed Dr. Deal wistfully, "will sterilize a robot's memory, so to speak. A proper keystroke-sequence while laying commands to a robot program will *abort* memory access. It's *sterilization* and *abortion*." Everyone knew she was referring to the memories of the *Hughe disruptors*.

"Is that...contest-legal?" inquired Dae'Quan Ezekiel Capp.

"That, indeed, is the question," answered Professor Deal, nodding. "Look, group, I've been wrestling with the ethics of making the alterations for two days. Just on the face of it, without giving any deep consideration—it's breaking the rules, pure and simple. It's a solid, unequivocal 'no-go'. Thus, I put the idea away…shut the door on it…*locked it down*. But I guess the *ghost* of it shows through my eyes."

"It's practically *haunting* the restaurant," declared Professor Fission.

Student Vashti Nishadimah broke the ensuing silence. "I think we need at least to discuss it. Think of what it could mean for us. I mean…we don't want to break the rules. But we should be sure that it's truly *out of bounds* before we reject."

"Professors," spoke student, Saltina Bittergrizle, "Vash is right. Can we take a vote on it? Shouldn't we employ the *democratic method* in this case?"

Dr. Mtofu cut in. "Yes, but only after we give the matter good and full discussion."

As they dined, the *Hughe* team did their best to present a balanced argument on the robot-tampering issue. After a time, they even considered analogies that might be made between their robots and *humans* in society. It was Dae'Quan Capp who mustered the brazen will to set the topic up for analysis. At a point in the dialogue, he made this offering:

"I'm just going to lay it out. My dad says half the problems in the world today lay in what he calls 'inauspicious reproduction.' People with the least means of guiding their offspring toward life-success and/or socially positive behaviors typically have the *most* offspring. You find this to be true in all the worst places in the world to live.

"Societies and communities with the worst standard of living show the freest and most profuse procreation, seemingly without thought. And what is the result? Perpetuation of poverty and a stifling of progress!

"Our *disruptors*," Capp continued, "are the beneficiaries of a *tradition* of *bad* behavior. Only it is *we* who pass on their tendencies from one 'generation' to the next. But unlike in human populations, where you just have to let people keep on reproducing *problems—generation* to *generation* to *generation*—we can *stop* the transfer. And Dr. Deal has the answer. I vote to *sterilize* and *abort*."

Capp's team didn't mean any harm when they smiled and chuckled and stretched their eyes, looking around. Certainly, they meant no disrespect when they let several seconds pass, while mumbling "humph" here and there. Nodding their heads, they appeared very thoughtful.

Collectively, they hoped it didn't hurt his feelings when they simply moved on, introducing new arguments for and against the issue at hand.

These alternate foci for debating their matter, however, lacked anything like the provocative force of Capp's offering. And everyone was uneasily aware of it. Alternate cases made for animating Dr. Deal's brainchild could be likened to the finely cracked canister placed on the group's long dining table: They didn't "hold water" well either.

In the end, though, and with a hint of compunction, they all agreed on the plan to tamper with the robot *memories*. For the most part, however, there was one thing of which they were sure. It was that Dae'Quan's rather sensational discourse hadn't influenced them an iota. *It would have been too politically incorrect to have allowed it.* That was the private thought of *Hughe* student, Jack Eaglefeather, but it mirrored the sentiment of most sitting around the long table.

In their final minutes at the restaurant, the *Hughe* team discussed the display on the robot scoreboard when they left the science center that Sunday afternoon. It had appeared thusly:

	LeBlanc	*Hughe*
Session		
I	0	0
II	3	2
III	6	4
IV	8	5
V	9	7
Tally	26	18

Business as usual was the appearance at the *InnerGalaxy* on the following Monday morning. With the intense efficiency that was their custom, the LeBlanc and *Hughe* teams went about their work. On the *Hughe* side, however, there was a small but important *extra* procedure performed. Here, some unusual items made a debut appearance. A tiny vial of liquid, *element*-strength iodine, and a point-tipped swab—those were the alien articles present. So small and unobtrusive were the items that smuggling them in presented no problem whatsoever.

The "operation," though, was a delicate one. A slightest over-dosage of the chemical could wreak havoc on the robots' program-board housing the *memory*. One cause would be iodine's reacting with energy radiation within the robot arena. There might even be a total and unusual shutdown of the machines indicated. Worse, the consequence might be tiny explosions within the "dosed" robot, sufficient to alert everyone to irregularities.

So, those delivering "sterility" were to apply a mere speck of the iodine. Professor Mary Fission made a quiet utterance, while lightly touching the chemical to a robot *memory*-board. "A little dab'll do ya," she whispered.

Upon completion of that task all remaining preparations were carried out as scheduled.

Robotics Competition
Session VI

In the session's first half hour, the rival camps each scored a point, thrilling the audience. While the teams applauded their respective tasker, most of the robot builders' attention was elsewhere. For the LeBlancs, fascination rested with the machine that cruised the arena scouting for others to tail. For the *Hughe*s, the robots to watch, for this *generation*, were the trio of *sterilized* "bad boys," that is, Numbers 1, 5 and 10.

The *Hughe* team could only envy the LeBlanc development of a *defender*. Painfully, they watched attempt after attempt, to score, by their own *taskers* blocked by their own *disruptors*.

Then, sometime after eleven o'clock on this Monday morning came the awaited change. As the *Hughe*s watched, their Number 10 *disruptor* began to falter in its assault on the *Hughe* "working class." It lurked but could not lunge. It stalked but could not subdue. It hampered but could not hold on with the former tenacity. To the *Hughe*s, it was the proverbial "*evening* of the playing field." In fact what they were witnessing was the gradual *sterilization* of Number 10's *disruptor* "memory."

Wearing secretive smiles, the professors and students present at this time "high fived" one another. However, further observation of their machines revealed something less heartening. It was that *disruptors* "One" and "Five" were just as "criminal" in their behavior as ever, in spite of the *sterilization* attempt. While two grossly menacing *disruptors* were better than three, having none had been the goal.

It was approaching the end of Session VI. For the near five hour period, the *robots of Hughe* had achieved a breakthrough. They had staunched the alarming increase in scoring difference between the two teams. By no means were the accumulated points close to even. They just were not as discouragingly discrepant as in the past scoring pattern.

In a sort of huddle at the program-monitoring computers, the *Hughe*s discussed the matter. Dr. Nigy spoke with suppressed excitement: "We've stopped the *massive blood flow*, crew. I mean, in terms of our performance vis-à-vis the LeBlancs. While half a chance is all we have now, it's better than no chance."

"Yes, sir," responded student, Vashti, "the small turnaround is fantastic."

"What about our other two *disruptors*?" It was "Ezy" inquiring, as Capp was sometimes called, in reference to his middle name. "Those little *fiends* behaved just as wickedly as ever."

Professor Deal answered: "Clearly, the sterilization didn't take effect."

"One of those two," added Dr. Suggs, "I 'dosed'. I guess I was a little too sparing of the iodine."

"You did perfectly well, Bertram" Dr. Deal corrected. "The catastrophe would have been even the slightest *over*-application. I repeat that sentiment for you, too, Mary."

"Well, I appreciate that, Sheila. But it's still too bad Bertram and I couldn't have been the perfect 'swabbie' that Dominic was."

"I'm sure it was all luck," stated Ratroprekocius with playful humility.

Dr. Mtofu stood to Deal's left, peering along with her at her computer screen. He placed a hand on the shoulder of her immaculate white engineer's jacket. "Well, there's still Solution Two. What odds do you give it?"

Everyone knew Mtofu referred to the Deal's earlier proposal of robot *memory* "abortion." It was not at all certain whether or not the two professors and one student assigned the task could achieve it. Debugging a faltering program within the robots was one thing—difficult enough. But rearranging an operating program was quite another—bordering on unfeasible. Dr. Deal answered:

"We've already begun the preliminary steps to finding codes and code sequences to apply. By all appearances we're still a good ways away from the *interlock* process."

Sitting to Deal's right, student Doris Cokespoon added to the professor's comment. "Yes, and *interlock* is just the first step to finding and creating useful commands. We've got a job ahead of us."

Informed Dr. Fission: "And what's more, we can only work on it while the robots are active. So it's not something any of us can discover in the hours leading to the next session." The team members solemnly nodded their comprehension.

Placing his arms about the shoulders of fellow student team members, Capp commented:

"I'm just tickled...*pink*, sort of, about our improvement this last session. That 'sterilized' *Number 10* won't be passing on memories of *disruptive* behaviors. The robots that get *10's* set of bytes throughout the rest of the competition will be starting new. I think that's not only *fair* in this competition—it's the right solution at the right time."

The *Hughe*s glanced over at the rival team a distance to their left. Unlike them, the LeBlancs kept a large "contingent" studying the robots' behaviors up close at the robot arena. It was clear the whole team was excited about something. In fact two of their four *taskers* were in scoring mode. Once the audience became aware of this latest "last minute" hair-raiser situation, it started cheering.

Suddenly, as if to raise elation to a higher level, everyone noticed that nine of the ten *Hughe* robots held *geobjects*. Only once before had it happened—lasting about half a minute. And it had been the LeBlanc team in Session IV. Now, nine robots of *Hughe* motioned about their half of the arena, intent either on work, play or crime, figuratively speaking. The audience was not aware of the character identities. In fact, though, they were comprised of four *Ts*, three *Cs*, and the two remaining *disruptors*.

A successful *Hughe* "drop" of a *geobject* into a floor insert, not matched by the rivals, would actually tie the score for the session. It would be 10 to 10. But then the LeBlanc robot team, as stated, was at this time poised also to score. In the absence of a *Hughe* success in these remaining minutes, two LeBlanc "fits" would put them up 3 points for the session: 12 to 9. For all watching, there seemed a lot at stake as the last minutes ticked down to 3 o'clock. *Hughe* members not monitoring at the computers returned to the main floor to watch and cheer on their machines.

In the seconds before Miteus McPeak turned off power to the robot arena, the teams, kind of, split the success. The LeBlancs didn't get the three-point lead in the session they sought, for two reasons: One, a LeBlanc *disruptor* spoiled one of the two "drops" that were on the verge. Two, literally in the final moment, a "drop" occurred on the *Hughe* side.

For Session VI the scores were as follows:

	LeBlanc	*Hughe*
Session VI	11	10
Tally	37	28

Robotics Competition
Session VII

In the first hour of the session, five "drops" were scored, 3 of them LeBlanc points. By the noon hour a total eleven points were posted and the LeBlanc lead remained at "one," for the session. Within that second hour, then, both teams had scored an equal amount of "drops," that is, three.

That condition got the attention of the LeBlanc team. It was the first time during seven days of contest that the *Hughes* had matched them point for point in an hour's duration. Naturally, they began to discuss the matter seriously:

"You think it's just a lucky fluke?" The question was that of Brian Noos. Sitting at a computer, he directed it to the two professors accompanying him.

Dr. Hortzenstal replied first. "I'd guess so, at least for now. It's true that the skill level of their 'working class' has improved. But on the whole, their machines still operate with less vigor than ours."

Dr. Quietly gave her opinion next. "I think it's more than just happenstance." She glanced over the expanse to her right separating the two computer stations. "They're debugging like crazy over there." As if "feeling" her rival's stare, Dr. Deal returned the glance from the *Hughe* area. To end the awkward moment, both women waved flitting fingers at one another as they smiled. With that, Sheila Deal resumed her feverish pace in the search for programmatic *abortion*.

"Yes, they're making headway, alright," continued Quietly. "Deal's in manic mode over there, although she's trying to hide it with a calm expression. She and the two *ducklings* sitting with her are *on* to something. They may even be finding a way to debug the programs of their *disruptors!* Now, that would be bad news, if it were true."

"Well," answered Dr. Hortzenstal, "there's every reason to believe that the design problem leading to their *D-robots* is the same as ours. As you know, the *disruptor* memory contains a sort of *electronic incentive* that no one foresaw. The *power* driving the behavior simply cannot be overcome during operation. It will require going all the way back to initial design to alter it."

Responded Dr. Quietly: "Solving the *disruptor* mystery will be quite a breakthrough. And you're right—the *D-robot* phenomenon represents a classic case of unpredictability in program design. But let's just hope that reprogramming or deprogramming is no more possible for them at this point than for us."

"Suppose," ventured Noos, "they're discovering the procedure for evolving a *vigilante*."

"Virtually impossible," replied Hortzenstal. "That could only come out of the mind of a 'Trimolke.' And as you should know, there are no *Trimolkes of Hughe.*"

"Then suppose," returned Noos, "they're beating us to debugging another *clown.*"

"Highly unlikely," iterated Hortzenstal. "A *Hughe* can never outdo a LeBlanc, all conditions being equal. While we imagine and create solutions, the *Hughes* stumble up on them. Usually that is not a very effective means for making advances. Which team will find success in converting the next *clown*? Well, let's see how much progress we three can make in that endeavor, to hand to our replacements in the next half hour."

Stooping, crouching, and crawling about the LeBlanc area around the glass arena, the eight *robotics* students couldn't have been prouder of their machines. By now, some had even reserved a tiny "soft spot" for the trio of *disruptors*. To them they were "rascally little bad-asses," to use their term. Doubtless, their decreasing animosity was due to increasing failures of their *disruptors* to foil *taskers*. This was in turn due to the heightening effectiveness of the LeBlanc *vigilante*. As revealed in their talks, the latter was like a *robotic superhero* to the LeBlanc team.

"Look...over in the arena...it's a *toy*...it's an Erector Set *reject*...no, it's *super-vigilante!*" The parody came from Ivan Api. He'd grown up on old cable-t.v. programs.

"I don't concur," added Chichingski. "To me that's no less than *Robert Downy, Jr.,* in *Iron Man* miniature, over there kicking ass."

The LeBlancs had a lot to be proud of in their machines. Twelve minutes into the final hour of the session, the team was within two points of the last session's total of points. So there were still 48 minutes left. One thing, however, kept them from being unattractively "beside themselves" with glee. It was the *Hughe* score for the session. After matching LeBlanc "drops" in the last hour, the *Hughes* continued to "answer" every point made by their rivals.

Then, in a breathtaking turn of events, fifteen minutes into the final hour, the robots of *Hughe* dropped two *geobjects*. Realization by the audience of the *Hughe* achievement steeped them in waves of wonder. Of the 20 total points made so far this session, 11 were to the credit of the *Hughe* team.

Dr. Mtofu sat at the *Hughe* computers with a student at either side. Ten minutes earlier, he had taken over monitoring from Dr. Deal. "She did it," he uttered staring at the computer screen. "She found the *interlock*...she broached it...she devised the next sequences...and the two of you students helped usher it all in!"

"Well, sir," stated Cindy Phizo, "Dr. Deal led us, essentially, to perform a miracle. I'm still kind of trembling from the tension of it. At times, I really doubted it could be done in time."

"I quite understand, Cindy. We're talking about something that might easily have taken two, three more days to work out! And that's given that the procedure was possible at all—which we were not at all certain it was"

"The iodine, helped a lot, Dr. Mtofu," Jack Eaglefeather revealed. "The iodine, or *sterilization* as we like to say, altered nearly all the program configurations. In short, it made finding the required sequences a lot less difficult."

Mtofu spoke in a kind of soliloquy. "So, as we speak, the *disruptor* memories are gradually *aborting*."

"Yes, sir, Dr.," answered Phizo. "But only in the two for whom initial *sterilization* did not 'take.'"

Between 2:15 and 2:40 the audience cheered 3 additional points scored by the Hughe team. Needless to say, the LeBlanc mood was less festive. Something was amiss, and at this point their understanding of it was frustratingly incomplete. However, there was good news for them, also. They took heart in knowing their team had recently achieved a valued identity conversion within *their* ranks.

Application of the "Trimolte treatment" yielded another roaring success. One of their two remaining *clowns* was turned *vigilante*. The fruit borne was two successful "drops" in the 25-minute period indicated.

On the *Hughe* side of the robot observation floor, the student team gathered. Their common interest was in viewing a diagram put together by Dr. Suggs and Dr. Nigy. The two had collaborated and combined results from careful observations made of their own, and the rival 10, robots. It reflected conclusions drawn as of 2:40. One of the robots undergoing memory *abortion* showed periodic resistance to the effect. The other, however, appeared more and more to be losing its "criminal" inclination.

The *Hughe* professors' schematic is shown below:

	LeBlanc	Hughe
Taskers	4	4
Clowns	1	2
Disruptors	3	1
Defenders	2	0
Sterilized	0	1
Memory-aborted	0	1
Semi-Disruptor	0	1

By the end of the session the scoreboard presented the display below:

	LeBlanc	*Hughe*
Session VII	13	16
Tally	50	44

With a total number of twenty *geobjects* present per side, per session, both teams gradually approached a perfect score. But the *Hughe*s now led that progress. As is shown, they were four points from being "20 for 20."

Robotics Competition
Session VIII

"Something's not right, goddamn-it! I'm telling you, something's not right!" Vander Sanbo stood looking across the LeBlanc half of the arena at the *robots of Hughe*. Intense worry and indignation lined his chiseled face. Again he spoke to team members standing with him. "No way those fucking guys—fucking losers!—could have outscored us, *legitimately*. We need to take this shit to McPeak!"

"What do you think they're doing, Van," asked Caristmas. "At worse they're doing what we're doing—trying to de- and re- program. Hell, who knows whether it's contest-legal, but everybody's doing it."

Vander peered directly into Saul's eyes with that penetrating gaze that was his. "I hate you, man," he whispered loudly. "I fucking hate you right now."

"Vander, man, Saul's only saying we can't fault them if they're just doing what we're doing."

"Back off me, Ivan, or I'll uppercut the both of you!"

Mona cut in abruptly. "Just knock off the drama, Van. We don't threaten to punch each other at LeBlanc just because something goes wrong. The *enemy* is over there across the floor. So, they're making some points. We got stuff in the works, too, you know. And we still got a good lead on the scoreboard overall."

"You fucking *jugheads* don't *get* it, do you? Don't you realize that you can't *fucking* alter the programs of *disruptor* robots?! Haven't you... damned 'Sponge-Bobs' been watching what's going on? Their *disruptors* are morphing into *fucking zombies!* What are you…*fucking blind?!* Can't a one of you little *'shits' think* anymore?! *They're shutting them down illegally!"*

"Okay, that's it," informed Tasha. "I'm reporting this *Loony Tunes* to staff. I'm not going to stand here and be insulted by this *maniac*." Tasha Heffergel started to turn away, but was urged back by Jipper. Then the latter spoke:

"Hold on, Tasha. Vander's…well, *high-strung*, but I think he may *have* something. How *are* they losing they're *disruptors*? Maybe something *is* going on that's waay out of bounds."

"Yes, Lindsey…yes, yes, yes! *Ding-ding-ding!* Wake up the rest of you…." Vander thought twice before delivering more name-calling. "*Wake up and smell the goddamn, son-a-bitchin' coffee, for God's sake!*"

"I'm with Lindsey," added Smitten. "We should give this thing a lot of consideration and take it to the professors."

Before the student reporting-committee even announced its concerns, the LeBlanc professors had been having discussions. *Hughes* outscoring LeBlancs, when the latter possessed one *strong* and one *up-and-coming* rookie *vigilante*—it was preposterous. And yet there was not even the slightest indication that something untoward was afoot—except for the scores themselves. As the session progressed, one thing was blatantly clear to everyone. It was that the *Hughe* "working class" robots went about their business almost free of "criminal" targeting.

Some of the LeBlanc professors and students came close to concluding the unimaginable. They nearly ventured to consider that the *Hughe robotics'* design allowed for an exclusive alteration *denied* the LeBlancs. *Could,* they almost wondered, *the Hughe design actually allow thorough debugging of disruptors?* After careful thought, though, they knew it couldn't be so.

Something patently contest-disallowed was going on, implemented by the *Hughe* team. The LeBlancs knew they'd better figure it out and report it before contest-end at 3:00 the coming Friday. That, of course, would mark the end of the final round of the competition.

As McPeak cut the power this Wednesday afternoon, all eyes shifted from the robot arena to the scoreboard. It read:

	LeBlanc	*Hughe*
Session		
VIII	14	17
Tally	64	61

As far as the LeBlanc team was concerned, they had had just about enough. It was very near time to take the matter to the *InnerGalaxy* director. In concise but fully comprehensible terms, they would lay before him their case. While a contingent of the team monitored the upcoming session, that is "IX" on the following day, another would refine the planned presentation. There would be diagrams, *PowerPoint* displays. Ultimately, they would request audience with McPeak.

At that point they would demand that the final ten *Hughe* robots scheduled for performance Friday be inspected. If the overall makeup of these incorporated no aspects of design differing significantly from "the norm," it would be telling. In other words, if all 100 of the *Hughe* robots were identical, as they should be, then something *foreign* must be influencing the *Hughe disruptors*. What else could reasonably account for the dramatic *Hughe* successes so late in the match? Discovery of this foreign influence may reveal its status as quite *unapproved*.

A finding of no special feature in design for the final ten, pristine, *Hughe* robots was expected to sound an alarm, of sorts. The LeBlancs believed presentation of their case to warrant not only a halt to the contest but also a comprehensive inspection. In the latter everything would be a candidate for analysis, from early burned-out robots to present *memory* boards. In addition a history of activities at the computers may even come under scrutiny.

But all that effort would be set to motion—that is, presented to McPeak—on one condition. If, when confronted with the LeBlanc suspicions, the *Hughe*s revealed their "secret," resolution could come without fiery accusations thrown about. All the *Hughe*s had to do was bring their clandestine activities to light. Indeed, it could be a revelation to everyone, possibly adding to knowledge of the *science* as a whole.

Of course adjustments would have to made, to bring matters related to scoring back to their *natural order*. But at least a "good" mystery would be solved. And the *Hughe*s would have the pleasure of knowing they had for a brief period baffled their *betters*.

Wrapping up for the evening in their usual manner, the two teams often glanced back at the robots. When they weren't thinking of the planned confrontation for the next day, the LeBlancs focused on the same topic as did the *Hughe*s. The issue was the ninth and tenth generations of *Hughe* machines operating free of their group's *disruptors*. To the LeBlancs, it gave the *Hughe*s an "unnatural" advantage. To the *Hughe*s, it was an opportunity to show all observers the grand performance of which *robots of Hughe* were capable.

Robotics Competition
Session IX

The LeBlanc plan was to observe performance of *Hughe* robots for an hour before confronting the rival team. Goings on in that period, they determined, would provide enough evidence to justify the route they'd chosen.

Now, at the arrival of eleven o'clock, they were convinced they had been right. Already the *Hughe* "working class" was contributing a score to the *gross robotic product* every fifteen minutes. Just as troubling to the LeBlancs were the conditions under which points had been made.

Hughe machines that appeared to have the proclivities of *disruptors* were obviously disoriented. Employing the same behaviors that formerly had impeded *taskers*, the newest generation applied them randomly now. For example, former generations had used *geobjects* to push *taskers* off their course. In the same apparent attempt, this newest generation often dropped the figure but seemed unaware of the loss. Without its "weapon" the would-be *disruptor* was easily avoided, escaped, or even out-maneuvered.

LeBlancs felt certain they were seeing a generation of *disruptors* that were the "victims" of contest-illegitimate tampering. Squint-eyed and shaking their heads all through the "critical" period, the LeBlanc team stole minute-long stares at the rival machines. The strange behavior of three robots not identifiable as *taskers, clowns,* or *neutrals*—and certainly not as vigilantes—rankled them.

Whoever heard of a "criminal" robot unable to hold on to its "weapon" in the commission of "robot felony"? What kind of robot "miscreant" shows pitiable inability to catch up to its "quarry" in the chase? A mechanical "thug" that can be pushed aside and even chased off by its intended "victim" was a fabricated, *unnatural* thing. These were the sentiments of the fuming LeBlancs as they observed performance in the *Hughe* arena.

Finally, it was time. To keep their program director, Dr. Attababy, apprized of developments, the LeBlanc team had summoned him. When four professors from the rival university tread steadfastly toward them, the *Hughe*s knew what to expect.

The *Hughe*s, too, had been watching carefully the feckless behavior of their memory-sterilized and memory-aborted machines. Of course, while the LeBlancs had been appalled, the *Hughe*s grinned like *Cheshire Cats.* Tellingly, their snickering had sort of an embarrassed flavor. Indeed, they realized the robot anomaly had reached a level that might invite an inquiring confrontation. Now, it was taking form. The LeBlancs were "on the war path," although quite civilly so.

Drs. Box, Haxsaw, Hortenzstal and Attababy stepped across the painted line that separated the teams. Their expressions reflected cool resolve. Hortzenstal led in giving "air" to concerns of the makeshift committee. Appropriately, he addressed the lead professor of the *Hughe* team:

"Sheila…Dr. Deal, I wonder if we could have a word with you and your esteemed colleagues in private."

"Certainly, Glef. You seem at some unease. Is anything wrong?"

"Well, Professor, to be perfectly up front—it's your *robots*. Some of them seem of late to be, how shall I say—breaking the rules of our contest."

"Well, that *is* serious. By all means let's have an open forum. I'm sure Mr. McPeak will be able to provide us a conference area here at the science center."

"That is most gracious of you Sheila—characteristically so, I might add."

"I do appreciate the compliment. And let's be perfectly clear: From our position, nothing less than complete candor is acceptable." Dr. Deal turned to address her *Hughe College* colleagues. "We're all in total agreement on that point--?"

"Oh, absolutely."

"Unquestionably."

"Yes, indubitably."

Two *Hughe* students were present to experience the seeming electric atmosphere accompanying the LeBlanc "approach." Cindy Phizo and Jack Eaglefeather exchanged brief glances during the preliminary talk. Silently, they concurred that they were watching only the tip of the LeBlanc dissatisfaction iceberg. How the resulting controversy would unfold was, they knew, a matter to be awaited with bated breath.

As the professors all stood in a gaggle, planning their convention, Jack summoned two fellow students to join him and Cindy. While one took over a computer monitoring seat, the other was given the "latest" to take back to the other *Hughe* students.

For the entire *Hughe* team, now, the feeling was either tense anticipation or mild anxiety. They were all, however, level enough of temperament not to show it. As for the robots of *Hughe*, they were, of course, unaffected by issues raised by the LeBlancs. The machines merely plodded on within the sort of *new society* they'd formed. Therein, the "descendants" of *disruptors* were reduced to bungling, inept agitators. *Taskers* showed high productivity regarding the contest mission. *Clowns*, back to three in number, entertained the center's audience with the accumulated skill of seven prior generations.

By one-thirty on this Thursday, Mr. McPeak had set a meeting place. He also directed assembly of the *robotics* professors. In half an hour, the *Hughes* laid out the essential processes undertaken over the past sessions—those that had so changed the course of the "game." As did the LeBlancs, McPeak listened intently to the *Hughes'* description. Likewise he gave great consideration to the *Hughe* professors' request for a second disclosure session. In it, they desired the opportunity to argue *merits* of the controversial adjustments made. As Dr. Deal stated, her group had not expected the present meeting and therefore had not prepared for it.

Now, Dr. Attababy gestured to address the group. Given "the floor," he stood to lend his voice to the LeBlancs' concerns.

"Mr. McPeak...esteemed colleagues, I should like first to make clear our appreciation of the foregoing exposé. The *Hughe* team's willingness to reveal their methods is to be applauded. In a brief dialogue among our own professors, we came to two agreements.

"First," Attababy noted, "we have no serious objections to the offer to debate the legitimacy of our rival team's manipulations. Always there are nebulous areas that crop up regarding rules of a contest. I will admit that, on the face of it, the *Hughe* procedures seem...well, quite inappropriate. But that's the purpose of having further analysis and dialogue, that is, to discuss that characterization.

"But, second, we have grave concerns about allowing the contest to continue, while the matter is discussed. We are presently in the fifth and final hour of the *ninth* session. As we speak, the *robots of Hughe* continue to operate according to a *suspect* advantage. We question whether or not the results of the present session should be counted as legitimate, before our debate is completed. While we request that disqualification of session IX be considered, we positively *urge* the *suspension* of session X. The final 'round' should not proceed until all the issues pertaining hereto have been properly explored."

Responding to the concern expressed, McPeak called an adjournment of the meeting. As he stated, the purpose was that of returning to the contest area to observe the scores thus far. There needed to be discernment of just how profoundly the questionable *Hughe manipulation* was affecting the contest. At that point, he would make a decision as to whether the outcome seemed to warrant radical steps taken. When, at precisely 3:00, McPeak cut power to the robot arena, the scores appeared thusly:

Session	LeBlanc	*Hughe*
I	0	0
II	3	2
III	6	4
IV	8	5
V	9	7
VI	11	10
VII	13	16
VIII	14	17
IX	15	19
Tally	79	80

In a huff, the LeBlanc students thronged around their professors. In their faces and gestures were expressed a plethora of questions. These all related to just what the plan was for remedying the outrageous turn of events. In turn, the LeBlanc professors looked to the center director for delivery of justice. After a brief and thoughtful hesitation, McPeak acted.

The director called an impromptu open conference with reporters and made the announcement for all to hear. A matter, he reported, of momentous importance to the contest had arisen. Although the robots had entertained, amazed and enthralled the audience, they had developed a problem internally. It was one that necessitated delay of the next session until resolution was achieved. No less, he said, than accurate interpretation of contest outcome was at stake. Over an indeterminate period, the teams would work collaboratively to settle the crisis. So, given the realities of time involved, Session X, scheduled for the following day, was postponed.

Gasps could be heard in the audience. Reporters gathered around McPeak with microphones.

"Can you tell us what the problem is with the robots?" they asked.

"Well, let's just say some of them may be operating under influences that have to be corrected," answered McPeak.

"What kinds of 'influences' and how?"

"Some of them seem to have 'caught' something extraneous to their original design. It is believed to have occurred during a daily morning preparation."

"So, what's the nature of this extraneous *something*, sir?"

"Well, from what I understand, there may have been an accidental spillage."

"The implication is that this problem has affected the contest. If so, how?"

"The full determination of that will be made during the resolution."

"What about the course of the contest thus far? Can what we've seen up to this point be counted as legitimate?"

A pause ensued, as McPeak raced his thoughts to find the "right" answer for the question. There was much to consider. The publicity and interest generated by the robot competition was having very favorable outcomes for *InnerGalaxy*. As he was keenly aware, his reply had the potential of undoing a good deal of that benefit. He forged ahead:

"Absolutely it can. Fortunately, the potential contamination was discovered before it has a chance to sully the outcome pending. I believe I can say this with a measure of authority: Both teams are generally in agreement that concern is reserved for Session X. In other words, only in the final session would contamination be a serious issue, if it were not properly addressed."

"Do you have an estimate on the amount of time that may be required for resolution?"

"Not really, ma'am. But I can say that every effort will be made to have Session X cleared for early next week."

As good fortune would have it, all the professors were able to carve out time in the following three days for debate. Gathering in advance of the Saturday morning start of the planned talks, the *Hughe* team collectively suspected the same thing: It was that justification for their competition-related tactics might be a hard sell. Nothing in the contest rules sanctioned debilitating one's own robots. Denaturing them, so to speak, with iodine might be considered totally *beyond the pale*.

Upon leaving the science center both teams studied carefully the bylaws of the contest. Diligently they searched for the damning or forgiving stipulation that would make or break their respective cases. As it turned out, rules that came closest to addressing the *Hughes'* actions were these:

Article 4-d: *"None of the robots nor the arena shall be tampered with in a way such as to cause the rival team disadvantage."*

Article 4-g: *"Upon the start of the contest, neither the robots nor their specified environment shall be altered such as to improve performance beyond that related to monitoring and program maintenance, the latter to include program debugging."*

Professor Deal, who principally would state the *Hughe's* case, refocused on the argument advanced previously by student, Capp. It was a *long shot*, she determined. But she would defend the status quo among the *robots of Hughe* from a *sociological* perspective. She set the discussion's title in her mind as *The Case for Abortion and Sterilization in a Robot Population.*

The debate scheduled for Saturday morning came and went. In it the two teams agreed on only one point. It was that the final one for Sunday should be held soon after the usual time of church services. The mood of both camps reflected the desire to get "deliberations" over with. In two hours of back-and-forth among the professors, Saturday, there had been no coming to terms on the main issue.

The *Hughe* professors, by now, were eager to make their final plea and have McPeak decide one way or the other. If the outcome favored them, that would be great. If not, then "Oh, well—we tried," was their sentiment. The LeBlancs, however, were less casual in considering the possible outcome. Indeed, they were still smarting over McPeak's pressured, spur-of-the-moment, allowance of scores for Session IX. They were determined, now, to have a ruling in their favor. For example, they would demand that "Ten" be allowed procession only with drastic changes made.

Sitting around the big oval table in an *InnerGalaxy* conference room, the professors carried out the final discussion. Positioned at a far end of the ellipse, McPeak listened intently and took notes for quick reference. Later, when he was of a mind to replay the whole proceeding, it would be entirely possible. At the table's center, a recorder taped the event second by second.

Dr. Deal reiterated points made the previous day but embellished them, seeking a more compelling presentation. Direct and unyielding, though, was the LeBlanc response. Thusly, the impassioned discussion coursed forward, McPeak the model of an impartial arbitrator.

Dr. Hacksaw: "Bottom line, Sheila—there's no way the competition can continue with the presence of *iodine-tainted robots.* The rules state clearly the allowable influences, and *taint by iodine* is not one of them."

Dr. Deal: "True, *Lu.* And I won't try to make the case that iodine *taint*, as you call it, is not *specifically* forbidden. Essentially, again, I want to make my appeal from the view of the contest as a whole. In essence, we have been pitting two *societies* against one another, in terms of skill level. Yes, I say *societies.* For the throngs of spectators who, over nine sessions, have come to witness the performance, this has not been a mere display of moving *toys*. Not at all. In fact, the arenas have become microcosms of their own *communities*."

Dr. Quietly: "Oh, Sheila, don't you think that analogy's a bit of a stretch?"

Dr. Deal: "I don't, *Bree*. We've all heard the exclamations from the audiences, the references to *human* situations and motives. Even in our own formulations, we use terms that suggest our attributing to them *human intent*...."

Dr. Box: "None of that matters, though, Sheila. The rules are the rules. There can be no non-sanctioned manipulations made in the contest. Case closed...really."

Dr. Deal: "Well, not quite, Demorest—the clock over there says there's still time left."

There were chuckles around the room as everyone gave regard to the big wall-borne timepiece.

Dr. Deal: "As I said, while onlookers have been *watching* complex maneuvering (some more some less) by machines, they've been *seeing* much more. I'll just go on and say it:

"The *robots of Hughe* began as *underdogs* in the contest. Your, the LeBlanc, design was in fact the better one—in certain specific aspects. Perhaps it was your better understanding of reapplied solar energy that allowed you to give your robots higher energy levels.

"Just as important, your LeBlanc machines developed an uncanny organization—yes, a *social organization*—that enhanced their effectiveness. Giving credit were it's due, that last factor has to be attributed to the LeBlanc *better design*.

"Now I ask you: What is the quality of any contest wherein the end is predicted by advantages held from the beginning? What manner of contest do we have if a debilitating condition within the *robots of Hughe* cannot be ameliorated by a literally *miniscule*, um, application? The answer is the same for both questions. Without the intervention, the game is vapid, foretold, uninspiring, its outcome forecast from the start. ...Booorrring!"

Dr. Hortzenst.: "Oooh, no, Sheila! We're not going to allow you to play that *card*. You-all knew what the rules were from the very start. You were to design the best machines for the tasks at hand, under the restraints prescribed. If your design was...*inferior*, then you lose the competition and go back to the drawing board. You don't alter the contest in the middle just to make it more *interesting* to the public. The competition was one of *design*—which school devised the *better* one."

Dr. Quietly: "Glef's right, Sheila. I think you have to admit he's got a point."

Dr. Deal: "I admit that an implied and inferred condition for claiming victory in the contest is quality of design. The actual and *stated* criterion, however, is accumulation of points."

Dr. Box: "I object! It sounds as though you're saying that the *means* by which points are scored are of no consideration. But they are! That's why we have *rules of the game!*"

Dr. Deal: "Hold on, Demorest. I'm certainly not saying that the *means* don't matter. I'm saying we have multiple things to consider. If the contest is specifically construed to be all about *quality of design*, disregarding all other factors, then you win.

"But, we at *Hughe* are making the case that it has also been about the robots' scoring through *learning*. It has indeed been about unpredictable factors that affect scoring. For us, an inappropriate intervention would be a post-design *addition* to enhance robot performance. That's a specific violation of Article 4-g. As you know, our intervention, in contrast, *subtracted* from our robots."

Dr. Hacksaw: "Ooooh, Sheila—now, you're *playing* with *words* and *meanings*...."

Dr. Deal: "Not at all, Lu. Look, in a nutshell, we found that *debilitating* some of our robots improved the learning and function of others. Is the contest not about the robots' scoring through improved *learning* with each successive generation?"

Dr. Attababy: "Yes, Sheila—but *on their own*. It is about them learning *based on the programs installed.*

Dr. Deal: "We simply removed something that was preventing *optimal* learning from the programs installed."

Dr. Quietly: "In your own terminology, Sheila, you *sterilized* and *aborted* robot memories. How can you consider those legitimate practices in a contest of this sort?"

Dr. Deal: "Again, we simply removed something that was preventing the *robots of Hughe* from competing successfully. Is the event not titled *Robot Competition*? We *removed* something in some of our robots that made the event a *true* competition. Without our adjustment, it was just a bland, one-sided show of LeBlanc superiority of design."

Dr. Box: "I wouldn't have had a problem with that."

Dr. Hacksaw: "You're engaging us with pure casuistry, Sheila, and you know it. The LeBlanc team has graciously accepted results from session IX. Or perhaps more accurately, we held our noses and swallowed them, with *nausea*. But I'll be damned—*we'll* be damned—if we'll enter the LeBlanc robots in session X under the *Hughe* conditions of this *sterilization* and *abortion*. I'm sorry, but no. Esteemed professors of *Hughe*, Mr. McPeak, unless any of my LeBlanc colleagues disagree, I don't see how we can acquiesce to Dr. Deal's viewpoints. My *God*, they're robots! This is not *a social experiment* with *human beings*."

Dr. Nigy: "It is as if it were, to us, sir. Over the nine sessions, the *robots of Hughe* have indeed, to us, become as a *society*. As Dr. Deal expressed, this contest may be viewed as two human populations in miniature."

Dr. Attababy: "I dare say, you folks are taking this thing far out of context. These are *machines* we're talking about. And perhaps it would benefit you all to realize this: If it *was* human society in question, any artificial means devised to *prevent human reproduction* would be unconscionable. And it would be so even if the activity was 'proven' somehow to benefit the group in question."

G. Hortzenstal: "I concur, Eazl. It just would not, could not, be done."

Mr. McPeak: "Thoroughly engrossing presentations, professors— thoroughly engrossing! I believe I have enough here to ponder over and soul-search over and, yes, agonize over. Over the past several minutes I was able to draw this conclusion: A decision will be forthcoming by Monday next, some time after noon. I hope, and pray, that it will be one that both teams can abide by and live with.

"Thank you again, professors for granting me the privilege of mediation. I can say without fear of exaggeration: You all have provided thus far a competition the likes of which this great state of ours has never before seen. Your respective institutions have much to be proud of in you, as well as your students. I promise you, regardless of the contest's outcome: I will lend my support to maximum financing of your programs by our state's governor and legislature."

The next day was business as usual for the LeBlanc and *Hughe* institutions. It was just before the noon hour that Professor Attababy and Professor Deal got the call, on three-way conference, from McPeak. In short, he stated what he deemed a fair compromise. Under the circumstances the scores from Session VI *on* were of questionable validity. However, they had already been publicly legitimized for right or for wrong. This being the case, averred McPeak, it was only fair that LeBlanc have its wish regarding Session X. Thus, there would be no *iodine-daubing* of any robot's program board. Likewise, Dr. Deal and her team would engage no activities to deprogram, or abort, robot "memories" in Session X.

As the *Hughes* knew, this meant that the old disruptor memories would "resurface." And there would be no manipulation of this tenth generation's programs to subvert the memories.

As for the LeBlancs, they were glad not to have to make a gut-wrenching decision. It concerned making good on Dr. Hacksaw's threat of boycotting the contest. Nevertheless, Session IX had resulted in the *Hughe's* having edged them out in overall scoring. Now, they were not at all certain whether the final session's adjustments would be enough to set matters "right."

Shortly following the phone chat, a press conference was called by McPeak. In it he announced that the competition was scheduled to resume at 10 a.m. the coming Tuesday. In the reporters to whom he spoke he could sense the excitement. He felt he had reason to believe it would transfer to the public once the news spread.

At exactly 3:00 the next day, McPeak pulled the switch to end power to the robot *arena* amid a roar of applause. Those given permission to do so rushed down from the audience to throng the two teams. With happy, excited faces, they couldn't express enough their admiration for and gratitude toward the team members. What entertainment! What excitement! What a spectacle! What fanfare it had all been! The *robotics* teams drank of the praise lavishly, neither side showing the least disappointment with the final scores. That which showed on the scoreboard is as follows:

Session	LeBlanc	*Hughe*
I	0	0
II	3	2
III	6	4
IV	8	5
V	9	7
VI	11	10
VII	13	16
VIII	14	17
IX	15	19
X	17	14
Tally	96	94

Weeks later, Dr. Trimolke, who had effectively *created* the "vigilante" machine for the LeBlancs made a confession. In a private meeting, he told McPeak of his own programmatic manipulations with the robots. Time and again, he insisted that he attempted to mention it during the two days of debate among the professors. Somehow, though, he never was able to get it out.

Wistfully McPeak uttered, as much to himself as to Trimolke, his "take" on the revelation. He wasn't at all sure it would have made a difference in the final decision he made. The *Hughes*, he concluded, had had a four session advantage accruing from their manipulations. Perhaps, he determined, it all balanced out in the end.

"I don't see," stated McPeak, "any need to take this any farther than right here. Your team and the *Hughes* both benefited well from the contest. *All's well that ends well*, I always say. *Let bygones be bygones* and *let sleeping dogs lie*. Forget about it. You've shown great *character* in eventually bringing it to me for consideration. I tend to think that's enough."

But of course, it wasn't enough—not for Dr. Trimolke. He has come to my associate and me with the whole story. As good journalists we substantiated the professor's accounts as best we could. We, in fact, conducted myriad interviews with all the parties involved. Thereby, we collected details that Trimolke could not have provided.

So, for what it's worth, the true story is now revealed. We suspect that a number of those who observed the famed *robot competition* at the *InnerGalaxy Science Center* will be surprised. Others may be shocked.

Hopefully, these latter will be able to step back, take a consoling breath and appreciate the overall picture presented.

We think it significant to mention that some names were altered slightly, to protect, as they say, the "innocent." In the final analysis, though, it probably makes little difference that we did. The fact is, as we made clear at the start, this story is primarily about the behavior of two sets of robots.

—Lefty Person and DeeDee Day

Saved

On the day that Joycina Rose Lushas was born, both Garvey and Pricilla Lushas were ecstatic. The uncommonly angelic bundle, however, would be the final offspring for the couple. Three within a six-year span, they felt, was perfect, the third arriving a week short of their seventh anniversary.

From the surrounding county of Holy Oak the pair had haled. After high school and the start of steady and reliable employment, they married. Upon that accomplishment, their dream home was found, the domicile within which to start a family, in Feytown.

In every essential way, Pricilla and Garvey had fit right in with their new environment. They were *God* fearing, sociable, church-going. Indeed it could be said of Holy Oak in general, and Feytown in particular, this one thing: Folks almost always looked to *Heaven* for answers to the most perplexing of personal and social problems. They did so also for the most enigmatic of developments in their lifetimes, both local and world-scale.

Unfortunately, life in Feytown wasn't all "angels" and church services and piousness. Two *big* families resided in Feytown Village and were sometimes as troublesome as pestilence. The "big," it should be noted, refers to size rather than affluence. Accordingly, their numbers only increased their negative impact on the community.

Nearly everyone in town had incurred a significant, or at least memorable, interaction with a Begeeber or a Caskett. Indeed, it was a rare individual for whom mention of one didn't evoke a sensation of some sort. It simply was the case that many, from both families seemed destined to evolve antisocial tendencies. Those who gave the matter any depth of thought believed it the result of some sort of bad *family culture* that was promoted and passed on.

But the "bad" bloodline wasn't limited to the two *big* families. Feytown saw a third, smaller, family *blown in* by an apparently "ill wind," just before Joycina was born. Poor, uneducated, unskilled, and unmotivated, this clan was bound to be trouble, many concluded. The family surname, Frisky, became a familiar one to the legal community there. It would read prominently on such documents as eviction notices, court summons, and arrest warrants. Often, one did well to know Casketts, Begeebers and Friskys on sight in travels about Feytown.

But the focus returns now to the more divine "side" of Feytown. By the age of six months, Joycina was the prettiest, "smiley-est" baby the villagers could remember having seen. No one had trouble acknowledging Baby Joycina's purely angelic appearance. Actually the cherubic face made onlookers don a frowned, puzzled expression. This was most often when they thought no one was watching. On such occasions, the viewer would shake her (or his) head just slightly almost as if in disbelief. They really supposed an *actual* resident of heaven couldn't be more beautiful.

Speaking of *heaven*, Feytown had a good many *churches*, for a community its size. In area, it was roughly a square mile-and-a-half. This was a boon for those with a tendency to fall into disillusion related to goings-on discovered in the present place of worship. Within a few blocks distance, there usually was another, minimizing the logistics issue of changing "pray stations."

Sometimes the "alternative" church was grander of scale; at others it was as humble in size as a mere storefront. Either way, pastors and supporting congregations served up the same gospel, designed to make sense of all existence for believers. It was nourishment without which few in Feytown could even imagine trying to forge ahead.

In spite of being *one* in emphasizing religion, the Feytowners were actually *two* industrially dissimilar groups. About a third of the community was dependent upon assistance of one type or another. Generally, these found residence in one of three conditions. Most resided in well maintained public housing, in a sort of offset area of Feytown. A smaller number lived in privately-owned dwellings with rent subsidized. The rest were young adults who benefited from accommodation by parents or grandparents. Often these were raising one or more new offspring of their own.

Then there were those comprising the remaining two-thirds of Feytown. Although not, themselves, a totally homogenous group, they were nevertheless of similar mind in some matters. One was the issue of relying on aid from state and local government. About half were ineligible for it due to income requirements; the rest wanted no parts of it even if they qualified. Each showed a stubborn determination to plod through difficult times by means of sacrifice and what they called "making do."

Two elementary schools and one middle school sat within the acknowledged boundaries of Feytown. Fair or not, it wasn't until Feytown children reached ninth grade that they met really challenging academic environments. By that time they usually found extra academic demands to range from scarily fascinating to just plain overwhelming. The former case was reserved for Feytown students who, for one reason or another, saw the value of education. From kindergarten through eighth grade, this particular set enjoyed learning and worked on given assignments diligently.

For most of the Feytown *high achievers*, the value was instilled early by one or both parents and maintained. With others, it was a combination of above-average *native* intelligence and trust in teachers. As fate would have it, Joycina was gifted, or "blessed" as Feytown folk would prefer, with all the above. Many of her kindergarten classmates were very fond of their teacher. But Joycina loved her like a second mother. That first relationship confirmed all the good things Pricilla had told her younger daughter about school and learning.

Then came middle school. Without question, Joycina was more than prepared for the academic experience awaiting her. From the first day of classes her teachers could tell there was a keen minded *logiaphile* in the midst. Funny, though—it was at just this time that most other kids her age were succumbing to non scholastic impulses.

Fair or not, Feytown began as a segregated enclave of Holy Oak. Not effectively represented within councils making policy for the county, it was often neglected financially. Nevertheless, the proud Feytown citizenry of three quarters of a century past had an ideal. And the ideal was to develop local schools dedicated to providing its children sufficient-to-superior academic skills. They succeeded for a time.

But then something happened in the community that no one foresaw and for which none was prepared. Gradual and insidious, that "something" swept over Feytown morphing successive generations into distorted shadows of their forebears. Outside of Feytown, it was sometimes identified as a destructive *subculture*. They claimed it had even attached itself to church youth, like some kind of weird *virus of attitude* and *demeanor*.

In the year Joycina turned twelve, her brother Garvey, Jr. completed his final year of high school. Sister, Rochelle, turned fifteen and was well ensconced in the emotional rollercoaster ride of adolescence. In terms of non-family social interactions for the trio, it was a year of revelation, trial and transition. Facing new *discoveries* was more the lot of Joycina.

As Joycina recalled years later, something came over her neighborhood friends when she was twelve. Consciously or not, they started setting social guidelines, sort of, for their cadre. "Feeding" jejune conversations about boys was nearly mandatory. But it was all right, given that it titillated the mind and was a natural tendency for them anyway.

Another "must" was mastering intricacies of the latest dance moves. For Joycina, that was a trickier matter, given the inchoate hints of sensuality in some fad dances. Not only was "fashion" dancing not promoted in the Lushas household, it was in fact subtly discouraged. Both Garvey and Pricilla, like a long line of their forebears, felt that dancing of that type was, well, unproductive.

An additional phantom "rule" governing the girls' social interactions might have been called *advisory gossiping*. In short, the mandate urged each to take stock in furtive bad-mouthing of others.

Then there was an unspoken doctrine of "distancing." It too gained quiet entry into their *conceptual* adolescent rulebook. In order to be truly deserving of benefits accruing from girly camaraderie, *distancing* from parents became necessary. But unlike in gossiping there was, in distancing, a sort of artistry to take into account. Few girls within circles of twelve-year-old friends in Feytown similar to Joycina's advocated outright at-home mutiny. Distancing from their parents' solidly-constructed value systems was to be gradual, subtle, skillfully applied.

A host of other *de facto* criteria outlining proper behavior and displays of attitude cropped up around this time. Chief among them involved proper and effective communication with peers. Crafty usage of the latest slang in relating ideas was a real sign of group worthiness. Artistic use of *body language* to express feelings brought admiration and even respect. Important also was mounting the correct response to offenses delivered by a peer, inside or outside of one's cadre.

As Joycina discovered, there was so much to learn about reacting to challenges. Selecting a *good* option yielded "honey." A bad one might invite a whole swarm of stinging situations to ward off in the future. So, thank *Goodness* for religion. It was the one arena allowing everyone old enough to understand the concept of *God* to feel a measure of inner harmony.

The Lushas family of five sat in the second row of long, laterally-stretching church seats that sprawled before the minister's stage. Behind them were more groupings of seats, each slightly elevated in relation to seats in front. Time-wise, it was nearing the end of the preacher's sermon and termination of services altogether.

The whole congregation felt their *spirits* to be lifted, so powerful the pastor's message had been. Actually, it was that, *in addition to* the entire church atmosphere, which gave them a feeling of buoyancy. Also, it was the sense of being surrounded by folks of singular spiritual mind and purpose. Wherever one gazed laterally—front, back, side—believers abounded, *sisters and brothers in Christ*, as it were. Experientially, it was nothing less than intoxicating for all—*spiritually* intoxicating, or course.

The slow, peaceful, almost dreamy, discharge of the members transpired as it did every Sunday at this time. The serene amblers stopped periodically to make tranquil exchanges with one another. Everyone was all smiles and holy feelings and concomitant holy expressions. Gradually, ever so gradually, members of similar ages converged, natural in any gathering of people. At length, but for a period of no more than five or ten minutes, various collections of young adults could be seen. Next, and for an even briefer period appeared loose assemblies of teens who ventured away from their attention-diverted parents.

Among one group of the young adults was Garvey, Jr. Having just recently turned eighteen, he was now more popular with those of similar age than ever before. Minutes earlier, he met up with a few of his male cronies. Ambling together they gravitated toward a group of seventeen to nineteen-year-old distaff members of the church. Now, they stood face to face with the young ladies who flashed coy and piously serene smiles at them.

To Garvey and his entourage, the way the attractive suits and dresses showed off the ladies' curves made them look absolutely *heaven*ly. The word, however, that came closest to their actual sentiment was "delicious." Within minutes, they were circuitously discussing avenues for congregating a second time *after* church. The tones used and expressions displayed gave the talks all the appearance of plans for romantic trysts.

Garvey, Jr.'s two sisters had been slower in drifting off to meet with friends or associates. Each was also away from their parents' side for a briefer period than their older brother. Joycina had seemed almost reluctant to make the brief departure. Not so the case with Rochelle. While her parents mingled with friends, dear to them only at church, she located three girls of her social clique. Within a minute they found the perfect spot from which to cast sneering eyes at a trio of their schoolmates. Soon, glances from each side were mutually disdainful.

Talk that was generated in both "camps" got increasingly harsh as stares intensified. One of the three 10th graders, posturing defiantly several yards in the distance, Rochelle's group claimed actually to hate. Each reported wishing all manner of ill fortune to befall her. Chaniya Frisky's getting run over by the school bus was just one fate happily discussed.

After shaking hands vigorously and joyfully with *Garvey, Sr.*, Sam Greens stood a minute to chat about the recent sermon and other church matters. Smiling and waving he moved on until he met up with Ernest Tater. Once Greens was out of earshot of the Lushases, he commented in angry tones to his fellow church member. The complaint was that Garvey constantly refused to head up any after-church activities with the youth.

"If Garvey don't want to sacrifice his time here," Greens averred, "he ought to find his-self another church. We sure can do without them few little dollars he puts in the plate every week."

By and by, the Lushas family of five was back together and walking toward Pricilla's minivan. For Garvey, Sr., Rochelle and Jr., it was a perfect early afternoon of late-summer. "Sr." derived special pleasure from knowing how his constant rejection of church assignments flustered his friend Sam Greens. Venting intense misgivings in the company of "her girls" minutes earlier gave Rochelle an easy, peaceful feeling. Jr. was still reeling from memories of how fine the young ladies looked in their church-wear. Somehow, the fact that they, and their attire, had relation to *church-going* made them seem all the more seductive.

Moods, however, of the mother and younger daughter were slightly less elated. Lingering in Pricilla's mind was something told her by Janice Hamm of the church choir. It seemed that someone employed in the same office building as Pricilla had been commenting unflatteringly about her. The latest in a string of the reports happened just prior to services that morning.

"Don't go back and tell him I told you," Janice had requested urgently. "But 'Moe' Caskett says you act kind of flirty sometimes over there where y'all work." Although she knew it wasn't true and that Moses was a reputed tale-carrier and pariah, it bothered her. If her husband got wind of this latest episode of Moe's "carrying tales" it could be trouble.

Joycina, riding in a back seat of the minivan, looking sadly out a side window, had her own woes. In the brief social gatherings after church, Angelina Caracha was continuing a blatant snubbing of her former best friend. According to report from other girls, Angelina resented Joycina's excellent rapport with teachers at their middle school. "She's not like us," Angelina often accused. "She needs all that extra attention from those *wrinkle-faces* that make the rules."

For the Lushases, parenting with the firstborn had been essentially trial and error. When Rochelle came, they put into effect knowledge gleaned from early experiences bringing up Garvey, Jr. A little more certain of what to expect in parent-child interactions, the experience went smoother. By the time Joycina made appearance in the household, Pricilla and Garvey felt, finally, that they knew what they were doing.

In the very early years of parenting both fear and determination abounded. Both parents, but especially Garvey, were apprehensive about "Jr." displaying out-of-control behavior. They knew that its occurrence during adolescence would be particularly unwelcome. To avoid that outcome, they took concerted measures to keep his actions and attitude in check. It was Pricilla, however, who often gave in to her son's little schemes to get leniency.

The result, now that Jr. was eighteen, was his having become fairly well-disciplined young man. At the same time, however, both parents had fortified him with two oddly juxtaposed views of himself. One involved his self-perception as possessing uncommon personal strength. In addition, however, he felt himself quite capable, if he so chose, to apply it in the manipulation of others.

With Rochelle, the Lushases reversed positions, kind of. To some extent they also reversed *errors* they had made in bringing up "Jr." From the end portion of Rochelle's toddler phase, Pricilla was the more consistently demanding of good comportment. Garvey, Sr. was now the wishy-washy one—stern in one instance of unapproved behavior, languidly silent the next. Unlike Jr., who tended to be more a leader in his relations with peers, Rochelle blended effortlessly with them. By adolescence, she "bought" totally into the culture she and her peers both constructed and "inherited" from older girls. It was an earlier-model facsimile of the one her younger sister was facing now.

Contrasting the two older siblings' foibles in the teen years might yield this summary: While Jr. tended toward self-centered individualism, Rochelle followed with ease some of the least attractive ways of her peers. They each possessed great "people skills" but employed them differently.

At one and the same time, however, Rochelle had been brought up to respect her parents, and did. The result was two Rochelles. At home, she kept the throes of adolescent turmoil she experienced under wraps, for the most part. Outside, she could gossip, throw slang, attitudinize, parent-bash, and meet insult for insult with the best of them. It only added to her regard among the fifteen- and sixteen-year-olds she now "ran with" that her parents seemed unaware of Rochelle's, sort of, dual life.

Joycina, however, was not inclined to develop the same aptitude for changing with environments as her sister. Both a "mommy's" and "daddy's girl," and, in effect, the preeminent *teachers' pet*, she was inextricably type-cast, so to speak. Still, as dictated by inner, social tendencies, she was compelled toward bonding with at least one circle of her peers.

Starting, then, in early adolescence, Joycina was discovering a new world. "Laws" governing it she was essentially disinclined to learn and perhaps psychologically unable truly to master. Without knowledge and skill in how best to act socially, the road along which she was impelled promised difficulty.

By the time of her own final year of high school, Joycina had weathered many storms in her social life. The circle of her closest friends changed several times. During good times, the *ring* contained ten or more girlfriends. During the bad, it had only two—that is, Joycina and another. But whether composed of two or ten, there seemed always to loom before her a sort of invisible wall.

At first, Joycina had no awareness of the barrier, although she felt its effects. Gradually, over time, though, she sensed its presence. Resignedly, she chalked it up as evidence of her own social inadequacy. It was similar, she thought, to the case that some people, no matter how much they practice, will never play a musical instrument professionally. She believed, likewise, she lacked the talent to win the true and genuine high regard of her friends.

In the final analysis, Joycina concluded, such concerns were all *academic*, as the term goes. God, she had been taught, made everybody the way they are for a reason. Not everyone who can carry a note has a beautiful voice and will become a singer. But she or he can become something else admirable. By all accounts she had no future in a career wherein possessing great interpersonal-skills was a must. Nevertheless, she had been told that she did have *brains*. So, Joycina decided she wanted to become an *electronics* and *computer graphics engineer*. First, though, she had to finish high school.

Nearing eighteen now, Joycina had undergone essential changes from when she entered adolescence. Sometimes subtle, they ran throughout various aspects of her life. In school, staid, keen-minded, studiousness replaced the earlier effervescent interest and curiosity. At home, the view of her parents as flawless models was jaded by discovery of certain examples of their failings. Socially, she learned the fine art of subtle accommodation in order to get along.

From *certain* members in their clique, some girlfriends want guidance mostly. From other friends, the young ladies mainly seek mutual trust and bonding. From still others, they come to expect a perennially nonjudgmental ear, when telling their troubles. Finally, other girlfriends are relied upon to render aid of various sorts without expectation of immediate recompense. It was into the latter two categories that Joycina snugly ensconced herself. As was her desire, it kept "life" simple and conflicts at a minimum.

Also, at the edge of eighteen, Joycina realized she'd always had sort of an odd relationship with Rochelle and Jr. She thought she knew why she had never really seen it before. It was, she suspected, due to her closeness to their parents. Because the pair had loomed so large in her life, her focus at home had been uneven. To her, Rochelle and Jr. had approached the status of dearly loved "boarders" in the household. Much more independent than she, they made their way with minimal requirements of parental nurturing and oversight.

But with Joycina a different agreement, sort of, had been made and kept. In exchange for her nearly perfect obedience, Joycina enjoyed Pricilla's and Garvey's uncommon availability. Until recently, their "sunlight" had shown upon every facet of her experience. It facilitated her growth and warmed her during the frosty times of, say, social rejection.

Now, both Rochelle and Jr. were out on their own. Twenty at this time, Rochelle rented an apartment in Feytown with a roommate. She held down employment as a department store supervisor. As for Garvey, Jr., he had married against everyone's better advice. With a wife and nine-month-old daughter to support, he did oil and tire changes at a local auto repair shop. It was just part-time employment, while he studied professional vehicle repair at a trade- and technical-center.

Joycina noted how strange the sensation was when she visited Rochelle and Garvey. Enjoying the fruits of self reliance, they were more emotionally independent than ever. It was almost like getting to know them for the first time.

The last "bird" in a now increasingly troubled nest, Joycina's home experience had become less than serene. How, in a five year period, both parties in a formerly stable marriage slip into infidelity is sometimes incomprehensible. But it was so for Pricilla and Garvey. Somehow the identities of their paramours seemed to make it worse.

He had fallen for a local Caskett woman, Noelle, ten years younger than he. Pricilla was now enamored of a Begeeber who lived on the outskirts of town. Although Elwood "Woody" Begeeber, was one of the more refined of his clan, he still bore the stigma of relation to the not-so-civil members of his kinfolk.

Fortunately, both of Joycina's parents had the good sense to keep their affairs discreet. Even so, there were whispers carried about Feytown, most of it originating inside or nearby church grounds. For her part, Joycina endured the household's reduction of bliss with some level of denial.

Among all *three* Lushases, it became a game of pretense, actually. The patterns of coming and going regarding her parents certainly suggested something untoward. But Joycina refused to acknowledge consciously that which was increasingly evident. It was that her parents had lost interest in one another romantically. When Pricilla and Garvey had home encounters amid all the "overtime" worked, they were distant but cordial. Preferring not to focus on what the other was about during times away, each contented herself or himself in the bliss of ignorance. Both found satisfaction in their individual doings, so why, each concluded, make waves?

From age fourteen, Joycina had gotten the attention of virtually every adolescent male in Feytown. The cherub of six months who so astounded the villagers underwent over time a gradual and steady blossoming into the perfect rose. In those early teen years she showed the slightest signs of moving to the stunning young woman she would become.

Now, on the verge of 18, she was there. The unwanted focus received from boys all over Feytown for the past two years was escalating. Most disturbing was the near harassment she was receiving from a Frisky boy.

DeVon Frisky was seventeen, innocent of having seriously read from a textbook, and was out of school for nearly a year. A second generation Feytown Frisky, he was one of four sons issuing from Alicia Frisky. With six children, the latter was unmarried to date. Virtually independent of parental control, DeVon looked up to his older brother, Tywaun who had already fathered two in public housing. In turn his two younger brothers, Mishonte and Xavier saw DeVon as a model to be emulated.

So, DeVon had set his sights on Joycina. Selecting from his store of methodologies, he applied a number of schemes to win her attention and favor. Such tactics had brought him success with other girls in Feytown. There was no reason, he thought, to believe they wouldn't work with Joycina. With that agenda, he walked behind her and accompanying friends, talking loud and obnoxiously.

Before he quit school, he used to give her lascivious stares standing outside her classroom door and in the cafeteria. On occasion, in the walk after school, he would show up suddenly requesting to "taste the honey," as he put it. Such were DeVon's ways of being charming to the opposite sex.

As often as not, he was attended by one or more equally wild looking friends in these activities. Once he'd even brandished a wad of bills he obtained through one or another illegal means. He was stunned when Joycina seemed uninterested. It was known that everybody in Feytown could use extra money.

Ironically, DeVon's known affection for Joycina had one positive effect. It kept other "bad boys" in the community from getting too bold with her. For DeVon, the fine line between agitation and harassment was not a "place" he was willing to share with others of his ilk.

But there were dozens in the community of better social quality than DeVon and his crew. And most of these young fellows were also head over heels for Joycina. Many were intimidated by her good looks, though. Others had more or less steady girlfriends of their own. The rest had made their bid in one way or another to befriend her. Among the latter, a few had secondary status in her social network. An even lesser number of them had gotten to attend her in a group gathering or single-pair date.

Most girls nearing eighteen in Feytown found all manner of ways to be alone with their boyfriends in rendezvous unapproved by parents. For Joycina there were a number of *secondary* reasons she didn't follow that pattern.

One, she had never settled into comfortable regard for the popular mannerisms of Feytown teens: posturing, "slanging" and the like. Thus she always felt a bit like an outcast, even with the boys. Two, it seemed that all of the town's youth were in one way or another socially linked. A girl, she concluded, was almost sure to have selected some other girl's old boyfriend once she'd entered into a pair-bond. And that seemed always to lead to pointless conflict. Third, she'd seen too many cases of boys spreading lurid details of an old girlfriend's behavior during their relationship. Whether or not these were rooted in truth, Joycina preferred to avoid being the focus of such gossip.

As stated these were secondary reasons not to engage in *heavy* dating at this time. For her, a preeminently overarching justification loomed, to forego *secluded* romantic encounters. This caution had everything to do with revealing talks she'd had once. The co-communicator was the much older half brother of one of her girlfriends. At the time Joycina was fifteen—the man confiding with her, twenty-four.

It was an afternoon in late March, two years and some months prior. Sherrel, a girl in Joycina's circle of friends, had just completed a period of babysitting. Without monetary pay involved, it was done as a goodwill gesture on behalf of her half brother and his wife. As a return favor for sitting with the one- and three-year-olds, Sherrel, had requested chauffeuring to a distant mall. The passengers were to be Sherrel and four girlfriends.

In the impromptu agreement, Sherrel's half brother "Mac" drove the entourage to their preferred destination. The plan was to give the girls a couple of hours to browse the mall before Mac retrieved them. Meanwhile Mac ran a few errands of his own, all the time listening for the call from his sister to begin the drive back to collect the little group. In terms of each side completing their respective missions, all went well. The girls were even where they said they'd be when Mac arrived to board them in the SUV. Next, one by one Mac deposited the girls to the front of their respective homes. Because of its location, Joycina's residence was the last stop to make.

Neither of the two kids Sherrel sat with on occasion, as a favor to Mac, was a "Petey." That was the last name of the father Sherrel and Mac shared. Mac, then, as one might guess, was not their biological father. Among Feytowners, Mac Petey was characterized as "one of those do-gooder types."

At twenty-two, he had married a woman two years older than he; she, already pregnant and with a one-year-old. Although still quite attractive when they betrothed, his bride, Shayna, had had rather unhappy prior experiences with men. Some of these fellows were Feytowners, others were not. But they all had one thing in common: a bit of a sadistic side. When Mac stepped in, Shayna's life stabilized. He was hardworking, read a lot, and was forever taking a low-cost, study-related course of some type, being offered somewhere.

As described earlier, one by one Mac returned Sherrel's friends to their residences. It didn't occur to Joycina until the third girl was taken home that she might be the last to be dropped off. Now, only Joycina, Sherrel and Mac were left. Traveling in their current direction, the three would arrive at Sherrel's house in minutes.

Joycina's was five blocks beyond that. So, in a logical procession, Mac's vehicle stopped in front of the home resided in by his father and family. When he noticed Melvin Petey's van missing from the driveway, Mac commented to his younger sister:

"Ol' Mel's out with his big gas guzzler tonight. I was gonna' stop in and holler at him after I take Joy home."

"He just took Momma somewhere," Sherrel clarified. "That was Monique and Deidra I was talking on the phone with, a few minutes ago. I don't think they'll be gone long."

"I can swing back by and see if they're back. If not, I'll buzz him later. Oh, and you never did tell me how you're doin' in school? You doin' your schoolwork like you're supposed to?"

Sherrel issued a "tsk"-like sound of mild indignation. "You ain't my daddy. Are *you* doin' *your* schoolwork like you're supposed to?"

"Oh, it's like that? Well, you just blew your four-grand Christmas *bag*."

"Yeah, right. I'll tell Daddy you're coming by if he comes home in a few minutes." Sherrel turned to Joycina: "See ya,' Joy. Call me when you get home, when you can, alright?"

"Okay. See ya," answered Joycina. When Sherrel exited the vehicle, she held the door open for Joycina to move from the back to the front seat. In the transfer, Joycina noted the coldness of the outside temperature. She was eager to shut the front passenger door and block the cool winds that chilled both her and driver.

Having ridden around with Sherrel a number of times with Mac as driver, she felt comfortable with him. They had even talked one-to-one a time or two.

Now, for some reason, Sherrel's words, just earlier, came back to her. She asked Mac about it as they coasted down the dark street:

"You have schoolwork?" She had turned her face slightly toward him.

"Yeah, I got this course in culinary. It's mostly learning how to do preps. But there's also a lot to know about *safety* with different types of foods. But, you know...it's interesting. ...So, how's tenth grade over there at Fountain High?"

"It's all right. They give us a lot of work but it's all right. We got a really tough exam coming Thursday. In fact that's what I'm gonna' do when I get home—study more for it."

"That's awesome. You are on the ball. So, what's the exam?" inquired Mac. Considering the class content, Joycina felt a little discomfort in preparing to answer. It came with some delay and hesitance:

"*Human physiology*...and...." Somehow the final word of topic did not find voice.

"'HP&S' we used to call it," Mac interjected, shaking his head. "It was—how shall I say?—a *wild ride*. One week, you're all 'into' the class, you know. You're really 'feeling' the revelations. Then the next, they start to get too *rangy* with it."

Mac followed with a mock classroom-based inquiry: "'*Hey, why'd you have to go there?*' That's what you feel like sayin' to 'em. '*Alright, alright— enough!*'"

"I know, right!?" Joycina was surprised to hear Mac express so concisely her own sentiment.

"But, I'll tell you, Joy—out of all that stuff they fed us, they left out some'em I wish I'd known when I was fifteen in those classes. And I think it's some'em every teenager from thirteen should know. It could make one hell'uv'a difference in their lives."

Mac was just turning onto the street running alongside Joycina's home. Joycina wasn't even sure she should make the inquiry. The overall topic was, in this situation, one of much sensitivity for her. Nevertheless, she thought it would be impolite to seem obliviously disinterested. At length she decided on a neutral response.

"I don't know how there could be any more," she sighed as though already fatigued with the subject.

"See," added Mac, "they talk about body changes going on by the time you hit middle school. And they follow up with the ol' sexuality thing and reproduction. But when I was comin' up, they left out an explanation of some'em else important. I call it *the body plan*."

On one side of the Lushas home was a half-paved, half gravelly area that extended to the front. It was there that Mac stopped his automobile. Neither of the two family vehicles was present in the respective driveways. Except for light shining dull through living room shades, the house seemed void of inhabitants.

In spite of her hesitance, there was something in the *term* used by her attendant that piqued Joycina's curiosity. She thought she should affect a tone of adolescent annoyance. "What is *the body plan?*" she inquired, with some attitude.

"It's the body's *plan* to reproduce." Mac had turned to look squarely at Joycina. "Now, before you 'wall-up,' think about it. There are times of the month when your body—and I mean the body of any female within age—*wants* to get pregnant. I know it sounds funny...or *crazy*. But here's the other side of the deal: When it comes to males, you might say the body of males *always* wants to *get* a female pregnant. It's *the body plan*, and Joy it's no joke."

The dead-level seriousness of Mac's delivery caught Joycina by surprise. She didn't get the sense that he was intentionally moving along the borders of erotic talk. Unable to conjure a good verbal response she communicated puzzled interest in her expression.

"Now, you're probably thinking '*Why would the body want to get pregnant*,' right?" Mac noted Joycina's grimacing concurrence. "Well, it does," he continued, "and those who don't know it are the ones playin' with fire. But like I said, an *of-age* female's body only wants to get pregnant at a certain time of the month. Dudes' bodies always want to get some female pregnant. And we don't even know what's going on. That's the bad part. If you knew your body was trying to *hook* you into some bad shit, you'd be prepared. And you wouldn't let it happen."

Fairly captivated now, Joycina tried to reflect on her own experience, feelings that came and went with the month. She thought she'd better venture a question to stave off a sudden termination of the talk. "What good does it do the body…to get pregnant? What good does it do boys…?"

"Two ways you can look at it. We can hang it on *'Be fruitful and multiply.'* Or we can open our eyes to what's going on all around us. It's *reproduction*…everywhere, all the time—damned birds, bees, ants, dogs, cats, microscopic shit, everything that's alive. You name it—it's multiplying right now somewhere in the world, all over the world.

"As people," Mac resumed, "we don't like to think of our bodies as following a plan we ain't in control of or that we didn't help make. But, Joy, I'm telling you, our bodies are *dangerous*. If you don't know what's goin' on, you can find yourself in a world of poop—*baby* poop to be exact." Within Mac's pause, he could see that Joycina appeared intrigued. He went on:

"Now, when I was your age, I was all messed up. I knew I didn't want to make no babies. But the girls! I'm telling you, they were all I thought about. I didn't know my body was trying to get my *poor ignorant ass* in trouble. So, I would be alone with a girl and I'm a damned *mess*. I want the girl but I'm more scared of a baby rollin' up in nine months.

"So, usually, I would wind up flunking out with the girl and looking *soft* like 'cotton boy.' But the thing is: if I had known my body was trying to *ball me up*, I wouldn't have felt so much like a *loser*. It woulda' been like a contest, see. I'd a' told my body 'Hell no!' 'Back off!' 'Stop the madness, you damned fool!' And I would have known I was in the *right* and my body was *off the chain* with that damned program it was tryin' to…execute.

"'*Yield, beast, yield!*' I would have stood up and shouted it right in the basement, while I was alone with the girl." Joycina's laughter had spurred Mac to exaggeration.

At just that time, both Mac and Joycina saw her father's pre-owned Lincoln pull up into the driveway. Alighting from the vehicle's front seats were Garvey, Sr. and Rochelle. Before taking groceries from the trunk each glanced curiously at the black SUV stopped at the side of the house. In seconds, however, they realized it was someone returning Joycina to the house. When she moved around to the driver's side of the vehicle, Joycina uttered a few words tothe twenty-four-year-old.

"Thanks, Mac, for the ride home. I'd better go help 'Chelle' with the bags. Daddy's gonna' take *one* in and that's gonna' to be *it* for him. See ya.'"

The idea came to her also to thank Mac for his talk on the "body plan." But somehow part of her preferred to keep the intrigue she felt about it concealed. Although she kept poker-faced with Mac about her inspiration, Joycina nevertheless would act on his formulations. She determined to pinpoint those days when, according to Mac, she was predisposed to sensuous feelings. During those times she made a concerted effort to keep a distance from boys. As stated, that had been three years prior.

When, finally, Joycina turned eighteen, her graduation from high school was three weeks past. Those two "feats" combined brought a new and heightened sense of maturity for her. School counselors, detecting her unusual focus and orientation toward a goal, helped her map the next academic course. Utilizing a select group of student grants and loans, they engineered her entry into a good technical school. As it was located in a neighboring county, access to it while still living at home was feasible. All that was needed was a vehicle at her disposal.

In addition, Joycina felt ready to take a young fellow up on a suggestion he made. They had gone out together on numerous occasions: for meals, movies, meetings with other friends. He wanted now for them to consider stepping up the seriousness of their friendship.

Something else was happening with Joycina around this time. While she still rarely missed a Sunday church service, her feeling about the experience was changing. Indeed, it frightened her. Profoundly fearful that she was losing her faith, she kept the emotional ordeal private. Practically everyone in Feytown had been taught early that belief in "the Word" was essential. There was no afterlife-salvation without it nor expectation in this one of *divine* grace and protection.

Thus, sermon after sermon, she sat in church surrounded by folks immersed in *the spirit*. The memory was fresh in her mind of having earlier felt the exact same way. She watched them swaying in serenity amid what was perceived as *God*'s divine presence. At the very least they had become saturated with religious passion from the minister's preaching. Now, she swayed less, attended with diminished fervor, and "drank" of the atmosphere as one sipping stale wine. As the Sundays rolled on, her decreasing shows of zeal got the attention of some number of the members.

It was early August and hot. In order to pass time in a comfortable social setting, Joycina and her friend planned a visit to Rochelle's. As it turned out, the gathering would be made all the more a family affair by Garvey, Jr.'s presence. Unknown to Joycina, he had scheduled a visit on the same day. Arriving with him would be his wife, Corynthia, and their one-year-old, Asia Mon`e Lushas. The young man, nineteen, who now stood above all those courting Joycina's favor was Rahim Vangrad. He was one of two siblings whose parents had slightly more lucrative careers than the average Feytowner. Indeed, they made a good-looking pair.

As Rochelle informed her guests, her roommate, Angie, was out of town briefly with her boyfriend. Not until midnight or so were they expected to breeze back in. So, Rochelle and her own paramour, Antoine, and their company, had the townhouse apartment to themselves. In addition to the five Lushases (including Corynthia) company included another couple, unmarried, with little ones.

Joycina and Rahim, as promised, arrived at 8:00, following dinner they'd had together. All the other visitors had been there an hour or more by that time. In a small area where they could be watched constantly, the toddlers engaged one another in intermittently raucous play. Every now and again, parents stepped in to mediate little disputes. This was the setting that greeted Joycina when she and Rahim walked in. Now they joined the adults who sat or stood around the bar enjoying the music.

As time passed, members of the social gathering were sated with snacks and buzzed by light drinks. Exceptions were those under 21, which included Rochelle's and Jr.'s younger sister and her friend. By and by, somehow, the group's chitchat took on a, sort of, playfully sly "tone." Its target was the newly-arrived. The mid-twenties couple consisting of Syrita Pounce and Donnel Battey were chief antagonists. Syrita led, so to speak, *the charge*:

Syrita:	"Look at the two of them sittin' there, like they're scared to leave each other's side. This could be it, y'all! Maybe *Miss Perfect Lady* has finally found the one she wants to *give it to*. Oh, check their expressions. Could be a change-of-wardrobe coming soon for Miss Pricilla's little angel!"
Rochelle:	"No, not Joycina. She's holding out 'til marriage. Aren't you, Joy? She's what the old folks call a '*good* girl'. But you're doing right. See how long Rahim can hang around without the 'goods.'"
Corynthia:	"They make a good pair, though. Shit, if you pushed their asses off the church roof, they'd prob'ly both float down like two *spirits*. Garvey can tell you what my nickname is for 'em: she's *Sunday School* and he's *Bible Study*. Like the pastor said last week: 'No two finer young people in the church.' And ain't nothin' wrong with it. Look at 'em. They just as pure as them angels on the church walls. …Ha-ha!"
Joycina:	"How did the conversation turn to us all of a sudden?"
Antoine:	"A lot of people just wondered when you'd ever kind of, you know, get with somebody in a kind of, you know, serious way. They don't mean no harm."

Joycina:	"Well, let's change the subject, please. It's not really...."
Syrita:	"That is a cute outfit you got on, Joy. I don't think I've seen that one. Oomph, girl's startin' to show a little more leg, now, too. I meant to say some'em when you walked in. Them little legs are just as long and pretty. Some men like little thin legs. Not Donnel, though—he's always sayin' he likes meat on his woman's legs.
	"What about y'all two: y'all *little-leg* men or *big-leg* men—or some'em in between? ...Get your minds out of the gutter! Y'all know what I meant!"
Garvey:	"I'll venture to say that the four of us guys prefer the legs that walked in here with us. ...Yes, damn right that's the *safe answer*. Pricilla and 'Sr.' didn't raise a fool here.
	"So, uh, Rahim, how's it going over there at Windermere Business School? I heard you started taking classes there early this year. They be kickin' ass over there, don't they? Dudes I used to run with say they pile on work like they're tryin' to make *sure* you don't have time for anything else."
Rahim:	"F'sho', f'sho'. But it's a good experience. If I make it through, I'd like to do something, you know, *commercial* in Holy Oak and then relate it to some *enterprise*, you-feel-what-I'm-sayin', here in *Fey*."
Garvey:	"There you go. See? Joy's hooked up with a young fella' with brains. Keep that *silver spoon*, girl. Don't accept some joker that's gonna' have you takin' your meals with a bent-up brass fork."
Joycina:	"Why do you keep saying I was born with a *silver spoon*, Jr.? We all came up in the same household. Why am *I* the one?"
Rochelle:	"Come on, Joy. You know you were always Mommy and Daddy's perfect *honey child*. The *Golden Girl* who could do no wrong. And they made sure nothing got in the *golden girl's* way or even rubbed the *golden girl* the wrong way. They fed you with the proverbial *silver*—you know that."
Joycina:	"...We were all treated the same, Chelle. Why...?"
Garvey:	"Hey, let's let it go, y'all. That stuff's in the past. We've grown up, flown the coup and doin' damn well on our own. And Joy's done what Mom and Dad wanted. ...You're going to college next month. And you got yourself a good church-going college guy.

"So, you know what I say about it? *'God's in His Heaven and all's right with the world.'* So let's talk about some'em we can *really* fight over…politics, for example. Raise your hand if you believe that Supreme Court Justice Thomas really used to talk about hardcore *porn* in the office."

It was just a week later that Joycina sat working out a plan with Pricilla and Garvey, Sr. at the kitchen table. She needed either to get possession of a really, really *used* car or arrange something with them involving the two family autos. In two weeks, she would be starting classes in Sparton County. The Lushases determined that they could scrape up, at most, another $1,500 in Joycina's behalf. They had already invested a few thousand in her academic expenses not covered by grants and loans. The issue was that of finding a dependable vehicle for that total amount.

Neither Pricilla nor Garvey wanted Joycina to continue the little summer employment she typically obtained. With a sense of the academic challenges that lay ahead, they preferred she forego work. She should move along that path and use her savings to get by, until she got a "feel" for what would be her academic workload.

Suddenly, Garvey recalled something he'd heard, in private, regarding a member of the Caskett family. It seemed to have potential for addressing the family's issue.

Ephesus, a middle son stemming from one of the eleven "second-generation" Casketts, allegedly shot an associate. As he sat in a local jail awaiting trial, his bond was set at $20,000. According to local mandate, a tenth of the amount needed to be posted in order to set Ephesus free. There were, at the time, forty-three Casketts residing in Feytown, including the old couple constituting the "first generation." No combination of them could muster, in the immediate, more than half the two-grand required to make Ephesus's bail. It was just a bad time for the young man, as bonds for seven cousins locked up before him had taxed family coffers to the limit.

Certain that once out on bail he could persuade the alleged victim to recant, Ephesus was desperate for release. He had one major asset. It was a pre-owned Lexus he'd bought in a rare moment of lucky prosperity and put in his brother's name. Spectacle-riding with his older brother, Isaiah Caskett made all the Feytowners aware of their fine possession.

Thinking back, Garvey, Sr. recalled "Jr.'s" report of having done work on the vehicle. He'd judged it to be in fine condition. Indeed, all technicians in the shop the day it was brought in concurred with their "minor-repair" coworker. Now, as Garvey, Sr. had heard, the brothers were "willing to let it go" for as little as "*a G and a half.*"

When the purchase proposal was made at the kitchen table, all three of the parties had mixed emotions. Garvey was having a very secret affair with one of Ephesus' younger aunts. He would have preferred not to have any further close dealings with the family. Pricilla had uneasy relations with some of the Casketts at church. It had somehow become known that she voted against admission of fifty-eight-year old Zena Caskett to the deaconship. Zena's "arch rival" Minnie Begeeber-Munk had been selected in her stead. For Zena it was church-centered "war." As for Joycina, her feeling of pause concerned the idea of taking possession of a car owned by two notoriously bad Caskett brothers.

In the end, though, the Lushases came to the same conclusion. It was that the transaction planned to begin on the coming Monday was a benefit to both sides. Ephesus, it was *well* known, wanted out of jail in the worst way.

It quite excited Joycina to anticipate having a car to drive. Consequently, she settled into a happy, talkative mood, flitting gingerly about trailing behind her parents. As each moved through the house tending their separate affairs, Joycina prompted conversations from them. These were designed to enhance the joyful image she had of being a new automobile owner. After some time, Garvey recalled a matter he needed to address across town. Now, mother and daughter were alone, tending to the family laundry. Joycina resumed her jaunty and talkative mood.

Joycina:	"Mommy, you ever find yourself, you know, wondering about…things?"
Pricilla:	"What kinds of things, Joy?"
Joycina:	"Well, like why so many teenaged girls in Feytown get pregnant?"
Pricilla:	"They're not following *the Word*. It's not like they haven't been taught. Most all the young people in Feytown are raised in the church. But some just don't follow what's been preached to them."
Joycina:	"It's not just some, Mommy. There're a lot of them. You think that's all it is—not following *the Word*?"
Pricilla:	"Well, obviously, Joy, if they followed *the Word* they wouldn't get pregnant, would they?"
Joycina:	"Yeah, that's true, but…."
Pricilla:	"Take you, for instance—and Rochelle. You both have followed your teachings from the Bible. So, my girls are among the ones who can be proud not to have slipped *down*."

Joycina:	"Mommy, I'm sure you know that Chelle has used forms of birth control."
Pricilla:	"No, I don't know. And I don't *want* to know. Your sister has always made me proud of her. Like you, she never slipped *down* like a lot of the girls around here do."
Joycina:	"You ever feel lost…sometimes?"
Pricilla:	"Lost? Like how?"
Joycina:	"I mean like not sure--."
Pricilla:	"Not sure of what?"
Joycina:	"Well…kind of not sure of your…faith. You ever feel like you're not so…*sure* that everything is like…what is taught?"
Pricilla:	"Oh, Joycina, that's just *the Devil*. Satan tries to make you question your faith. What you do if you feel *that Devil* trying to work on your thoughts is *pray*. Pray hard and go to church. If you have to, you go to church on *weekday evenings*. The pastor and deacons can help you get back strong again. …Are you having any problems, Joy? Has anything come up--?"
Joycina:	"Well, not really…I just wonder about things sometimes."
Pricilla:	"Like?"
Joycina:	"Like, why are we made the way we are? It just seems odd to me sometimes that *God* would create people who want to do things that aren't good. Why not just create people that are good all the time? I mean since *God* can do *anything*, why not create all good people, as His children."
Pricilla:	"Well, Joy, we can't question *God*. That's just not the way to go about things. Now, Reverend Posson can probably answer it for you. So, that's what I would do. I'll bet the Reverend can make it clear just what it is you need to know. You know how good his understanding is of the Bible. He'll probably be able to go right to the Scripture that answers your questions."
Joycina:	"Mommy, the Bible really has all the answers, as far as you're concerned?"
Pricilla:	"Well, sweetie, you know what your father and I have always taught you and Rochelle and Jr. that the Bible is the Word of *God*. So it has all that we need to know about what to do and how to think."

73

Joycina was quiet for several seconds, then she made an abrupt change of topics.

Joycina:	"Are you still happy working over there at the Medical Building, Mommy?"
Pricilla:	"Yes, it's a secure job. The pay is good. A lot of people in the country would like to have our benefits."
Joycina:	"Some of the things you've told me about how they *are* seem kind of…crazy."
Pricilla:	"Well, you know…people are going to be people. You've seen it, a little, on the summer jobs you've had. When you enter the work-world full time, in your career, you'll really see it."
Joycina:	"I hope I don't see the things you described. Your supervisors, Mr. Todey and Ms. Clay-Johns, sound like two idiots to me."
Pricilla:	"Well…I've worked out how to get along with them."
Joycina:	"You all sound like people in the story 'The Emperor's New Clothes.' Everybody pretends that the two big-wigs of the office have sound supervisory manners and skills. When really, to me, from what you've told me, they sound really…stupid, almost sickening."
Pricilla:	[laughing] "Joy! That's a little harsh. They're just people, like everyone else."
Joycina:	"Mommy, they're *full* of themselves. And yet the only knowledge they seem to have is of medical records and policy. They parade through the offices like they're on a higher plane than everyone else and can't talk intelligently on anything other than office stuff.
	"And, Mommy, from what you tell me, sometimes they can't even do that! They have you and your assistant doing all those crazy back-up procedures that never get used. Most of the time Mr. Oracle won't even participate, leaving you to do it."
Pricilla:	"Well, sweetie, that's why Mr. Oracle is the office *reject*. I learned early that it's a whole lot better just to do things the way the supervisors say. Why question it? They're the supervisors. If it turns out to be wrong, then it's laid on their doorstep—no skin off my nose."
Joycina:	"You've been there twenty-seven years this year. Thinking back, it seems like each of the three departments you've

worked in had real bozos as supervisors. *God*, I hope that's not what I have to look forward to."

Pricilla: "Twenty-seven years, Joy. It's helped keep a nice roof over our heads, clothes, a fridge always full of groceries, a fairly comfortable home environment in general. Your father and I have done what we had to do to make a living and take care of our family."

Joycina: "But working everyday under people you have to pretend aren't rotten and don't do rotten things, routinely, on the job--. *God*, I hope that's not my future."

Pricilla: "Joy, sweetie, don't you think 'rotten' is a little strong? I mean people are...people. You'll see when you're making your career."

Joycina: "Oh, Mommy, that *Todey* and that *Clay-Johns*—they play *favorites*, they cut some office workers down behind their backs, they form...*collusions* to disadvantage some people. They're nasty, rude and vindictive; they're arrogant, unreasonably hostile and petty. And I'm coming from what I'm sure are sugar-coated accounts *you* give me. I think 'rotten' fits those two perfectly."

Pricilla: [after laughing] "Judge not lest ye be judged, angel. You know what *Scripture* says. They're just...*people*, Joy. We, none of us, are perfect. We all have things we need to work on correcting. It's just part of being human. Mr. Todey and Greta—they're just people. No more, no less. Always remember this: Everyone's the way they are for a reason."

Suddenly an impulse betook Joycina. She felt on the verge of inquiring about something that agitated for entry into her consciousness from time to time. There was every indication that her mother and father were subtly distant from one another. And it wasn't just a recent phenomenon but one appearing to date back a couple of years. A number of their absences from home, it seemed to Joycina, weren't attributable to regular or overtime work. Nor, she determined, did they result from usual outings of one sort or another. Even the faintest idea of them conducting secret affairs gave her chills.

In due course she abandoned intent to pry into the status of her parents' marriage. Instead she resumed their discussions of other matters.

The Vangrad home was one of the nicer ones, in terms of exterior cosmetics, in Feytown. Resurfaced with siding, outfitted with new windows, and showing a fresh coat of paint here and there, the property looked rejuvenated. Inside, however, sixty years of bearing up under ownership by one family and another took the usual toll. The interior, then, was no grander in appearance than that of other homes decorated fashionably by residents. It could, however, boast a fairly large, finished, basement. It was to that destination that a party of eight young adults repaired, having just left an after-service gathering at Christ Redemption Baptist Church.

With ages differing by no more than two years, they were, generation-wise, a fairly homogeneous group. Accordingly, they had all reached comparable levels of maturity. Gone were the lively, unbridled expressions of emotion and attitude within and between peer groups. In their place were skillful concealments of misgivings, with only an occasional and lighthearted "gotcha'!"

The focus was also on refining years of clumsy, adolescent approaches for attracting the opposite sex. Without knowing it, this group, like countless others, had for years been honing skills to be used to vie for and win a life-mate. Now, coolness, cleverness and control replaced the earlier non refinement.

At first the four pairs of eighteen-to-twenty year olds had sat about the Vangrad living room. They played modern gospel music low, from CDs. They chatted gaily and politely among themselves as they sipped chilled sodas. All the while the television quietly showed images of late Sunday sermons in session. Patiently and reverently they awaited the arrival of Rahim's parents and his younger brother from the post-sermon assemblies. They knew it wouldn't be long in coming and what it would mean for them.

When Horace, Shirley and Markee Vangrad finally entered the front door, Rahim knew just what to expect. Accompanying his parents were a paternal uncle and his wife and a couple that were friends of the latter. With a total of fifteen good church people in the moderate sized home, Shirley Vangrad wasted little time. After giving friendly re-greetings to the young people, she and the other women moved quickly to the kitchen. Although most of the *big*-time food preparation had been done prior, there were still items to be warmed over.

There was nothing for the young people to do *but* go to the basement. That was if they chose to show proper deference to their elders. Also, there was no guarantee the adults would opt for the same gospel entertainment being enjoyed by youth in the living room. So what, then, were the reasonable possibilities? With humble respect, the young people headed "south."

By and by, the gospel music emanating lightly from below gave way to the faint sounds of secular music videos. It had not the least effect on the "upstairs" crowd, however. The older adults were busy enjoying their own brand of entertainments. Their only reminder of activity below came from occasional sightings of Markee appearing and disappearing at the cellar doorway. Eventually, the sixteen-year-old found the group of eight young adults too stodgy for his taste. With no other refuge than his own upstairs room, Markee went to visit the home of a nearby friend.

The Vangrad's basement had a small, dark enclosed area at the back, near a little bathroom. When a couple among the four needed to talk privately for whatever reason, it was a convenient place to carry out that activity. Making the area all the more attractive for having such a tête-à-tête was its *de facto* designation as Rahim's alternate sleeping quarters. Indeed, the entire basement had gradually come to be regarded as his "study hall." Contentedly, everyone in the home observed the arrangement with a good amount of consistency.

Those heady afternoon hours this Sunday in the Vangrad home seemed by 5:45 to have flown by. The eight basement occupants had all gotten plates of dinner from upstairs, dining contentedly among themselves. In accord with the music videos, they had sung and danced and imitated the moves of recording artists displaying on screen.

A few had run errands and returned, and various couples had visited the back area to "talk." During the earlier planning phase at church, they had each expected the social gathering to be thrilling. As it turned out neither was disappointed.

Now, Shirley and Horace and company were headed for a six-o'clock attendance of a church function. Markee would be dropped off for a couple of hours at a cousin's who lived near the church. Once again, the Vangrad couple had before them all the fine young church-goers who'd so enjoyed fellowship-time in their basement. Soon came the obligatory hugs and expressions of appreciation for good times had. Everyone felt truly blessed.

The group was filtering through the front door, now, to go to their various destinations. Just before departing to catch the 6:30 start of a movie at a mall-cinema, Rahim got an idea. He and Joycina had just enough time to tidy up the basement a mite. Ten minutes or so and they'd be done.

After a hurried marathon of running empty containers and discarded paper items upstairs, the pair paused. The next function to undertake was putting the basement furniture in pre-festivities arrangement. Except for music playing low on the CD player, the house was totally quiet. In the midst of quiet serenity, Rahim took Joycina's hand, urging her to sit with him on the couch. For the past minutes, she thought she detected something undercurrent in Rahim's intentions. She actually anticipated their subsequent dialogue:

Rahim: "Joycina, I think you feel what I feel right now."
Joycina: "Your parents think we're going to the movies, Rahim."
Rahim: "All the better. We got a good hour and a half, two hours, before anyone will be returning. It's perfect. You feel it, don't you?"
Joycina: "Well, yes, it is a good time, if we were going to do it. But, what about the overall…kind of…situation? We were just in *church* this morning. That doesn't …bother you, in a way?"
Rahim: "Hmm. Uh, look at it this way: I love you, Joy. And I think that's more important than the fact that it's Sunday. We have a real relationship now. It's just you and me and the future."
Joycina: "What was the point of going to church this morning? What were we doing? What were we supposed to be… learning?"
Rahim: "How to treat one another? It's all about *love*, Joy. And you know I love you."
Joycina: "And sinning in the eyes of *God*? Isn't that part of what we were supposed to learn about? Don't we go to church to learn how to behave?"
Rahim: "We're human. We commit sins everyday, all day. Sometimes it's just in what we're thinking. What we learned from the pastor is that *God* forgives our sins. We just have to believe and be faithful."
Joycina: "So, we learn what to do and what *not* to do, and then we 'fall off' and *do* what we're *not* supposed to do, and then pray for forgiveness."
Rahim: "Pretty much. But, what's the problem? You didn't take it all apart and analyze those other …what, three times."
Joycina: "Maybe I should have. I mean, are we being *real*, Rahim, or are we just doing whatever is good and convenient at the time?"
Rahim: "I don't get it. Did some'em happen today that I didn't catch? You're my girl, now, Joy. And I love you. You love me. You've told me. We've talked about our future and everything. We both have strong faith in *God*. Love is the

	most important thing for human beings. I love you and I want to express it in the special way that we did those times before. Joy, I know you were just as much *into* it as I was. You told me how great it was—then and afterward. So, what's the problem, now? It can't just be that it's Sunday."
Joycina:	"I do love you, Rahim. And it was…fantastic. See, I've been having doubts in church. I'm trying to decide what's real and what's not. I want to know what's real about *me* and what's not. I don't really know how to explain it. I just don't want to feel like a *flip-flop*."
Rahim:	"I'll tell you what. Let's go in the back, and you just relax and try to clear your mind of all these thoughts. Sometimes, baby, thinking too much ain't good. Wha-d-ya' say, sweetie? Let's just go in the back and let me handle everything. In a few minutes you'll be in that special place you were those other times."
Joycina:	"I don't think so, Rahim. Sweetheart…sweetheart…if you love me…really, *really* love me, let's stop now and keep our original plan. We can still make it in time."
Rahim:	[taking a deep breath for composure] "Fine, Joy, fine. …I guess you enjoy exercising this kind of control over the situation. But it's all right…I'm good, I'm good. Let's just go and get the hell on to the movies."
Joycina:	"I'm sorry, Rahim. I don't mean to…."
Rahim:	"I know you're sorry. To the movies—let's be out."

Joycina had noted that on those three prior "occasions," it was during *ovulation* that she was with Rahim. As she recalled it, she had been in, sort of, a trance of consent and excited anticipation. When faced with the prospect this evening, she suddenly resolved to test her ability to resist the very powerful, primal urge. Since her talk with Mac, her old friend Sherrel's half brother, that night three years earlier, she had followed his advice.

But during virtually all that time she had not had a "real" and steady boyfriend whom she thought she loved. That fact made avoidance of the dangerous mixture of *ovulation and boys* a lot easier. Then came the relationship with Rahim, and with him she had seen the awesome power of it. On each of those three occasions Rahim referenced, the "O" factor had been present.

This evening she had set out to compare her present will with that of former times with Rahim alone. Her conclusions: Had she not been consciously testing her resolve, she would probably have been willing to participate. On the other hand, had she been tonight in that special *receptive* state of which Mac enlightened her, there simply would have been *no* saying "no."

In addition to preliminary *engineering technical math*, Joycina's classes contained the usual array of *lib arts* courses. The *Sparton Technological Institute* where she was enrolled operated in four *quarters* per year. With a schedule featuring 18 "quarter hours" for the period of late September to late mid December, she had her hands full. Along with *engineering math* she was required to have a course which reviewed advanced high school mathematics. Those two comprised ten of the 18. The other "8" were general courses in college-level English/Writing and history. For the following quarter, her schedule called for basic electronics and an "Intro Psych."

Spared the need to have employment, Joycina was able to immerse herself in long periods of uninterrupted study. As an additional boon, her grasp of the material was quick and lasting. She had two factors to thank for the latter. In high school she had worked hard and was in command of essential formulations taught there. Second, as stated earlier, she was just plain gifted, or "blessed," with a keen mind for academics.

Much to her family's relief, the Lexus purchased from the Caskett brothers lived up to earlier reports. It ran well with its only fault being oil leakage when revved in high gear on the highway. Proper repair at the source of the problem was estimated to cost about fifteen hundred dollars. The immediate "remedy" however, was simply to add a quart of oil every week.

To school, to church, and occasionally to Rahim's made up the balance of her trips from home in the vehicle. Beyond that, it sat discretely on a side of the house that made it inconspicuous to passersby.

Ephesus Caskett was bonded out of jail a week after the title change. Knowing the brothers as she did, Joycina wondered if the gratitude Ephesus felt at his tentative release would last. Or would they cast covetous eyes once again on the prize they had so willing traded for Ephesus' freedom. So far, she managed to avoid sightings of either brother while she drove. She wanted to keep it that way for as long as possible.

December, now, was a mere week in the offing. A handful of notable issues were in development. Ephesus' case had gone to court and all charges had been dropped. That bit of news Joycina learned in church. Regarding school, the "quarter" was slightly more than three weeks to its end. Everything looked good. In spite of the demanding schedule of courses,

Joycina had stayed on top of all assignments. It seemed just a matter of maintaining her pace and focus another twenty-some days.

Her relationship with church, though, was another matter. While, still, she never missed a Sunday service, her manner there was generating increasing interest.

On this particular Sabbath, as usual, a concluding song was sung by the congregation. As usual also, it signaled the end of the church session. All seemed normal right up to that time. Then Pastor/Reverend Posson did something unusual. Instead of awaiting the usual throng seeking his attention, he began making his way forward hurriedly. In his sights, as he passed graciously through the rising flock, was the Lushas family. Specifically, he sought out Joycina.

Some number of the young ladies who grew up in the church he prefaced address of them with "Miss." Joycina was among that group. After the handshakes and smiles and pleasant conversational tones, the reverend got to the point. With a gentle hand placed on Joycina's shoulder he began his dialogue:

"Miss Joy, I've noticed over some weeks that you wear a troubled look at times. Also, your mom, here, says you have some, I guess, *questions* about life that maybe I can help with. Do you think we all could—Garvey, Pricilla, you and me—have a talk in my office? That is, if you don't have something important you need to get to right now."

Surprised by the reverend's straightforward statement of his concerns, Joycina recovered quickly and acquiesced. She read in her mother's facial expression: *I hope you don't mind, sweetie.* At length Priscilla took Joycina's hand. "I think this will be good for you, Joy," she advised. Relieving everyone's concerns with a smiling nod, Joycina then walked with the entourage to the reverend's counseling room. The four sat in an arrangement that facilitated open conversation.

Rev. Posson:	"First, I'd like to assure you-all that it is not unusual in the least for us to have questions about matters of the *spirit*. And I for one think it is especially true for our young people. Now, Miss Joy, as I said before, I've noticed that you appear, how shall I say, distracted and thoughtful, during the services sometimes. Is there anything that perhaps you'd like to talk about, with your parents and me sitting in audience?"
Joycina:	"Well, Pastor…it's kind of hard for me to say it, like, to *you*."

Rev. Posson: "Now, keep in mind, Miss Joy, I wasn't always a sixty-four year old reverend. I been around the block a few times, as they say. I doubt that there's anything you could say that I haven't heard before or felt, myself, before, in one way or another. Just feel free to say your thoughts and feelings. As Pricilla and Garvey, here, know: I can pretty much talk on any topic."

Joycina: "Well, Pastor...sometimes it's the view of *God* that we get from the *Bible* and from church teachings--."

Rev. Posson: "Go, on, Miss Joy. Just let it come out."

Joycina: "It just seems strange to me that *God* would create us the way we are. We're always wanting things, for example. But only *God* knows what's best for us. Why did *God* create us to want so much without us knowing what's really good for us?"

Rev. Posson: "Ooo-weee. That is such a wonderful and mature-minded question! Most your age, I don't think, would have the clear thinking required to form it. Alright! Now the answer goes to the core subject of sermons I often preach.

"You see, *God* made us in a way that we have *choices* to be one way or another and to think one way or another. It's our fault when we find ourselves wanting that which is not good. And, of course, there's that 'little' matter of *the Serpent* always standing by--."

Joycina: "Well, that's kind of exactly what I mean. *God* gave us the... capacity to want what is bad. That seems odd to me, when *He* could just as well have made us *incapable* of wanting the bad. We have hundreds of incapacities: we can't fly like birds, for instance. One *extra* incapacity—like not wanting the 'bad'—wouldn't have hurt, it seems."

Rev. Posson: "I understand what you're saying...I understand. But you see, we aren't capable of understanding *God*'s reasons. God had a *reason* for making us the way we are. *He* wants us to learn and grow to do and think what is good instead of bad."

Joycina: "But why not just make us good from the start? Look at all the misery it would have spared us."

Rev. Posson: "The thing you have to understand, Miss Joy, is that misery and pain are essential for man's spiritual *growth*. Oh, *God* is wise beyond what we can really determine and appreciate.

We look at misery and pain as a curse. But *God* put those conditions here to make us better.

"Misery and pain are both a teaching guide and the test we pass to be worthy of *Heaven*. Without misery and pain present on earth we couldn't enter the Kingdom of *Heaven*. And I think you would agree that that would be a real tragedy."

Joycina:	"May I be honest with you Pastor?"
Rev. Posson:	"Oh, indeed, I insist upon it!"
Joycina:	"To me, the real tragedy is that *God* didn't make us perfect from the start. *God* is all-powerful. That's what you teach us. Therefore, *God* can do anything. Why not make us perfect from the start and have us worthy of *Heaven* from the start?"
Rev. Posson:	"Actually, that is a question that has been asked many times, over the ages. Theologians have wrestled with it, and philosophers. The answer, though, is simple: *God* preferred it the way *He* did it. He knows what's best for man. He simply chose to have man earn his place in *Heaven* through overcoming temptation, which is the same as the 'bad wants' we've been talking about."
Joycina:	"And so the bottom line is that we don't question *God*. We just accept that He *could* have created us without sin had He wanted to. But for *His* own reasons, *He* chose, instead, to fill our lives with suffering."
Rev. Posson:	"…Miss Joy…are you in any…personal pain that you're dealing with…privately?"
Joycina:	"Oh, no, Pastor. I think my life is good. I just look around me and I see pain and suffering and misery in the world. And it comes, in large part it seems to me, from human beings wanting bad things…and doing bad to others to get those things. Something just doesn't seem right about it, when *God* could have made it different."
Rev. Posson:	"How do you question your *Creator*, Miss Joy? How? *God's* understanding is so much more powerful and immense than ours. How can we, His *creatures*, question *Him* who's responsible for our…*being*? It's ungrateful…when you really think about it."
Joycina:	"If I may continue to be honest with you, Pastor, I think you just made it clear exactly what the…problem is, for me at

least anyway. I *do* question it, whether it seems ungrateful or not. I question it and don't like what I see."

Rev. Posson: "Oh, Miss Joy...now you don't want to say that. I mean, as I said before, I think we all have questions, even doubts sometimes. That's *Satan* working on us. But please don't allow yourself to say you don't like *God*'s, uh...arrangement. Miss Joy, that is worse than if you were to tell Garvey and Pricilla, here, that you don't like the fact that you were born. I don't think you want to say that. I'm certain you could never *mean* such a thing."

Joycina: "Pastor, Mommy, Daddy...I *do* question *God*. And I *do* question what I see of *His*...set-up. It just doesn't seem logical and it doesn't make sense to me. I'm sorry but I just can't make myself accept what doesn't make sense."

Rev. Posson: "Miss Joy...are you *rejecting* God? You know that is exactly what *Satan* wants--."

Joycina: "I just have questions, Pastor. They won't go away just from everyone saying...'*just accept.*'"

Rev. Posson: "Prayer! That's what's required here, Miss Joy. Would you pray with us, Joy? Would you pray with Pricilla, Garvey and me?"

Joycina: "I'm...I'm sorry Pastor. But maybe prayers among the three of you will have to be... what gets done what you want done. *God* gave me the capacity to question, to decide to pray or not pray. I'm going to choose to stop praying for answers, for now. At this time, *God*'s ways are just too mysterious for me to pretend to accept."

Rev. Posson: "Garvey...Pricilla, don't be disheartened. I see the worry in your faces. In fact, you have a lot to be proud of. Miss Joy is a *diamond* on the *shore*, standing ground against waves and tide and sand. I see the broad picture here. Miss Joy dazzles within the 'sand' that's all around her, folks—a real jewel. *God* won't let her get swept out to sea.

"As a very smart and honest young lady, she's the kind that, in time, makes some of the *Maker's* most faithful. And Joy, you're right. We are going to pray for you. And we're going to pray for *God* to give you the *will* to join us. Of this I feel certain: *God* will not give up on one of *His* best and brightest, as you are. We'll get pass this. *Satan* will not win over this one!"

It was the week before Christmas, a Friday. Joycina was driving homeward from the campus of *Sparton Tech*. Having completed two exhausting final exams this day, she felt ready to "chill" the rest of the day with friends. Tossing an earlier plan to take a long nap in the refuge of her room, she decided to call Tamia Neely. Tamia worked at a fast food restaurant outlying Feytown and would be getting off in about half an hour.

As was well known, Tamia at nineteen was a restless spirit who thrived on a variety of lively associations and intrigue. Time spent with her was anything but preparation for tranquility and sleep. Upon hearing that Joycina was arriving to patronize her shop and provide the commute back home from the county, Tamia was delighted.

In the ride to Feytown in Joycina's freshly washed and cleaned Lexus, Tamia was verbose:

Tamia:	"Girl, you got it *going on* in this ride! This ship is 'bum.' I bet you could streak it up to *80* without even feelin' it. Girl, you ought to let me drive. On the *real*—I'd be shookin' all these road *snails!*"
Joycina:	"You don't have a license, yet, Tami."
Tamia:	"So?! I drive Vondray's car all the time."
Joycina:	"Nah, I don't think I should take that chance."
Tamia:	"Girl, you too scared. You got to take chances in life. …Oh, did you hear about Shareese? She had to dump two 'bags' last night—*good* weed, too!
	"*Five-O* was right up on her, girl. She *flashed off* around the corner from Pitt Street and ducked into Lennox. And right there near the corner she fed the whole stash into the gutter. You know that shit hurt!"
Joycina:	"*God*! What was she doing with two hundred dollars worth of marijuana?"
Tamia:	"Ha-ha-ha-ha! You funny, girl! She was takin' it to donate to charity. What do think she was doin'?"
Joycina:	"She sells it?"
Tamia:	"Damn right, she sells it—almost six months now. She's just startin' to get up a reliable clientele. But now she knows that *Five O* is watchin'. She's got to be careful now. Once the 'jake-squad' get on to you, they *stay* in your shit. You can't sneeze without 'em runnin' up on you harassin' you with a whole bunch of questions and wantin' to do a search.

R.M. Ahmose

"Shit, girl, I was gonna' get into it myself, but I seen how people will turn you in—sometimes your own customers, if they start hatin'."

Joycina: "You think somebody went to the police on Shareese?"

Tamia: "Girrrl, who knows? But, even without that, 'jakes' is always watchin'. They hate to see poor people tryin' to make a little extra money."

Joycina: "I hope she stops. It doesn't seem worth going to jail for, to me—you know, losing your freedom and all?"

Tamia: "It's some good money in it though, if you can hang out there awhile and don't get caught. Damn, girl, we're back in the hood already. I meant to ask you to stop over at--.

"Oh, turn down here, Joy! I thought I saw Princess turn the corner. ...Princess! ...Princess! ...PRIN-CESS! Damn, that girl is deaf! Go down the alley here. It's clean. There she go! PRIN-CESS! ...Damn, she finally heard.

"Girl we been callin' you for two blocks. You must be runnin' to meet your *man* or some'em. Look who I'm ridin' with."

Princess: "Hey, Joy. No, I was hurryin' over to my auntie's to borrow some money before she leaves out."

Joycina: "Hop in. I can run you over there. She's still on Gallipoli, right?"

Princess: "Um-hm. Oh, this is nice, Joy. This is the first time I've been in the *Lex* since you bought it. I had some wild times cruisin' with Phese and Bae-Bae, though. ...I ain't seen you in a good while."

Joycina: "Yeah, my classes at *Sparton* have had me tied up. I really haven't had time to get out much."

Tamia: "School, home, and church—that's what everybody says. Girl, you got to make time to *do* shit. If it was me, I'd put this *winch* on the interstate and floor it all the way to Indiana. ...What damned red lights! What damned stop signs! All speed-limit suckers—begone!"

Princess: "Hey, look at the squad doin' their huddle down there. Joy...can you stop a minute so I can holler at 'Q-Boy'?"

Tamia: "Is that Phese with 'em? Yep. I heard he's supposed to be mad 'cause he had to sell you the Lexus, Joy. Let's see what he got to say. This is gon' be good. Don't let him 'shook' you, Joy. Him and Bae-Bae sold his *whip* to you. Ain't nobody put a *nine* to their heads either.

86

                    "You should'a seen 'em the day Phese got bonded—big *Kool-Aid* grins on both their faces. Happy as white people at a yard sale, then—both of 'em.

                    "Watch this. …Hey, y'all, what's happenin'? Hey, Waun. Hey, Q. Hey, Lo. Hey, Murkey. Hey, DeCent. Hey, Phese, what's up, gangsta'?"

Ephesus:	"Chillin', chillin'. What you been up to, sweetheart? …Oh, I know it. …Hey, Princess. Girl still flashin' them cat eyes. …And look what the *wizard* done brought us. Damn if *Sunday School* ain't stepped down off her cloud to pay the *homies* a visit. Bum-ass ride you sportin' there, *Sunday School*. Who you gon' thank?"
Joycina:	"I was lucky you kept it in such good shape, Phese. It's still a *peach*."
Ephesus:	"Well, I'm glad to hear it, *Sunday*. Umph. Y'all got the *whip* smellin' like honey suckle. Mmm-umm. But it's good. It's all good. …Maybe one day soon, Sista' Joy, we can talk about a price? How much to let me buy *shortie* back from you? Think we can work out some'em, Sista' Sunday School?"
Joycina:	"Well, Phese, my dad actually bought it. You'd have to ask him."
Ephesus:	"I'm sure pops'll do whatever his baby-girl asks. Let's at least just keep it open for discussion. How, about that? I know we can work some'em out. Don't you think we can, if we really put our minds to it?"
Joycina:	"I don't really know…."
Ephesus:	"Leave it to Phese, sweetheart. You know what they call me: Phese-the-Beast, slicker than a priest. There ain't nuttin' to do *but* leave it to Phese. You *feel* me what I'm sayin'? I know you feel the vibe. …Hey, what up Tamia?! Girl still got that smile. It take a homie a *while* to get over that *smile*! …Oh you liked that one didn't you? Boy got more rhymes than a little dealer got 'dimes.'"

    Through that set of events, Joycina incurred that which she had been avoiding for months. Here and there she'd been hearing it from this or that associate in Feytown. Ephesus, it was said, had expressed, on several occasions, his intention to get the Lexus back. Although he had been fairly cordial in his talk with her, especially for him, Joycina was apprehensive. Always, she had given trouble a wide berth. She certainly didn't want any now.

Something else gave her unease as she thought on it. Her father, she knew, would not tolerate even a hint of intimidation designed to urge recasting of a done deal. She hoped it never got to a point where he would be involved again. At length, in the course of the day, she put the matter aside and enjoyed time spent with friends she'd known since childhood. When the day was through Joycina re-trained her focus on remaining final exams at *Sparton*.

By two p.m. on Christmas day, the Lushas home saw a reuniting of the nuclear family. Present also, of course, were Garvey, Jr.'s wife, Corynthia, and young daughter, Asia Mon`e. Keeping the family tradition, gifts tagged with the intended recipients' names were placed about the decorated tree. One by one, each was retrieved and opened. Amid "ooohs" and "ahhhs" the gift-receiver tried to guess the identity of the giver. It was a ritual reliable in its ability to bring the family joy and excitement.

In all the gift-centered commentary that followed, Corynthia digressed to the issue of employment. Though typically a stay-at-home mom, she had bagged a few weeks of seasonal employment. Actually, it was courtesy of her sister-in-law's industry. Rochelle had urged both Corynthia and Joycina to apply for work in the department store where she supervised a segment of its overall activities. As it turned out, only for one of the two did "strings" have to be pulled, to have special consideration given. Suddenly, after Pricilla and Garvey, Sr. had left the room, Corynthia felt that she'd like to know why that was:

Corynthia: "Did you ever fill out the application, Joy?"
Joycina: "No. I had my classes at *Sparton*."
Corynthia: "And? Everybody I ever knew who went to college worked at least part time."
Joycina: "Right now, Mom and Daddy prefer that I don't work. They want me to wait until I got a year complete. It's a really tough program. Doing well the first year is essential."
Corynthia: "So, girl, how did you buy these gifts?"
Joycina: "Well, I saved money from when I did work, before I started Sparton. And…Mom and Daddy…give…."
Corynthia: "Girl, you know you're too old to be gettin' an allowance. I see it now. Y'all are right. Joy is spoiled."
Joycina: "Spoiled? …Jr., is that what you say about me? …Chelle?"
Rochelle: "Well, you know Dad and Mom always go out of their way to hook you up."

Joycina:	"I don't know if they go out of their way. You make it sound like I'm…an inconvenience. But even if they do go out of their way for me sometimes—what's wrong with that? They've always made sacrifices for the three of us."
Garvey, Jr.:	"But, lil' sis, that was when we were kids. We're all grown up now. You'll be nineteen next year. And they're still…."
Corynthia:	"—Feeding the *baby* with the *silver spoon*. Girl, you ought to be ashamed, still living at home and not working."
Joycina:	"Weren't you listening? I'm trying to become a computer-programming and electronics *engineer*. That's not just a *programming specialist* or something. Mom and Daddy know that the first year is crucial. They just want me to have a good chance to make it."
Rochelle:	"Joy, I'll bet you're the only one in any of your classes who doesn't work…somewhere."
Joycina:	"I can't believe that none of you understands!"
Garvey, Jr.:	"That's because all you know, right now, is the way it's always been. I mean…look, I'm not trying to be overly harsh, Joy. But right now all you know is taking Mom's and Dad's last dime to meet your needs. And they give it willingly because they've always done it."
Corynthia:	"Ha-ha-ha-ha! Man, that's puttin' it out there! Girl, you know you're too old to be living at home for free and then acceptin' an allowance on top of it."
Joycina:	[with moist eyes] "I'm going to ask them if they feel the way you say. But I know what they've told me. We've talked about the whole situation, many times."
Rochelle:	"Joy, don't you dare mention any of this to Mom and Dad, when they come back in here. We're just telling you the *reality* of the thing. Mom and Dad don't want to hear the reality. I know they'll defend what the three of you are doing. If you bring this up with them, they're gonna' get defensive and it's going to ruin the whole Christmas mood. Just think about what we're saying, Joy. I know you don't *mean* to be…selfish."
Joycina:	"I'm going to become an *engineer*, Chelle. Eventually it's going to be a high-powered *four*-year degree in engineering, *Jr.* …Mom and Daddy support me, and I'm not going to let anything stop me, *Corynthia*. …So, y'all can say what you want."

89

Corynthia: "Aw, don't you like to see her when she gets mad? She still got that pretty baby face. Skin just as smooth--! We're just tryin' to help you, sweetie. ...Uh-oh, here come your Mom and Dad. We'd better pick this up later."

Planned for seven that evening, the Lushas's church was holding a special function. There would be festivity, fellowship and good, home-cooked food. As it was the week's end, few had concerns about early rising the next day. Actually, about a third of Feytown residents were attending similar church events.

It was a time to meet as a congregation, to solemnly and joyously celebrate *the birth of the Savior*. Indeed the event was christened "Christmas Savior," a term that caught on for all the church-goers. Amidst collective feelings of grateful exhilaration, there would be opportunities to give testimonials. Certain members took turns spilling out accounts of the working of *Christ* in their lives.

For this particular *Christmas Savior* event, Pastor Posson also planned a special convention of deacons. If all the Lushas family were in agreement with it, the reverend would like for them to sit in second session with him. In that last gathering in his chambers, things had gone awry. This time, however, he would be flanked on either side by two of his wisest church elders.

The pastor was convinced that the combined effects of *Christmas Savior* and the Savior-inspired elucidations of his staff would bring upheaval. A grand show of *God's* power would ensue, dissolving that which he determined was Joycina's *Satin*-reinforced will. In his current great enthusiasm, the term he used for the hoped-for talk was "*God's* Thunder."

Try as she might to absorb the full spiritual force of *Christmas Savior* in all its ceremonial sublimity, she couldn't. To be sure, Joycina's mood was elevated and she was happy and excited to be in fellowship with those whom she knew so well. However, it somehow wasn't as intoxicating as in previous years. And she knew exactly what the cause was of this more *sober* experience. Festering in a fragment of her mind was a peevish attitude. She had "caught" it from the talks with her siblings and sister-in-law earlier. More likely than not, it was that, sort of, pent-up anger that spurred her to consent to "round-2" with the pastor. She was in something of a *fightin' mood*, as Feytowners might frame it.

As everyone took proper seats in the reverend's office-like chambers, Joycina contemplated her options. Nestled among her family on one side of the floor, she posited that she could make life easy for herself. She could accomplish it simply by pretending after so many minutes to be reformed.

On the other hand, continuing to voice her true feelings would actually give *power of the spirit* a chance to work its supposed magic.

But lurking in a dark place in her consciousness was a third sentiment. She thought she'd like again to pit the strength of her doubts against the "ammo" to be utilized by the clerics. To her, that with which they would charge forth was the force of *blind conviction*. It was bound, she thought, to crash into a wall, figuratively, at some point.

The preliminary talks were laid out. Therein were described Joycina's, sort of, *spiritual crisis* of reconciling two contrasting givens: One was *God's aims*; the other, Joycina's *reason*. *God* had the ability to have made man without sin, and the world without pain and suffering, but chose not to. To Joycina, that was incomprehensible.

Joycina:	"I guess the first thing I'd like to say about the problem I'm having is that I'm coming to view the religion I grew up in as just that: a religion. The religion you have is largely determined by where in the world you are born. So, what makes the beliefs of one religion truer than that of another?"
Dn. Horzshint:	"I'd like to give an answer to the young lady on that one, if I may. First, I want to say, that is a great question, Joy. It shows that you are a thinker. Now, I will never put down another religion. That's…you know…I just don't do that. But Christianity has that special thing called the *Word of God*? And it is provided us in the Holy Bible. So, you see, our religion, our faith, is based on *God's* own message to us. Now, you can't really argue with that. How do you doubt the *Word* of *Him* that created you?"
Joycina:	"How do we know for sure that the Bible really contains *God's* 'word'? That's still just *belief* just like in any other religion. Not only that but it seems to me that if *God* wants to give us guidance, it could be written across the sky, daily, for everyone to see.
	"Or his message to us could actually be delivered in zillions of…*handbooks*…that come right out of the air. *God*, being *God*, could do that. He could make everyone on earth aware of his guidelines all at the same time. And *He* could do it in a way that everybody would understand."
D. Pyrewood:	"You have to remember, Joy. We are very special to *God*. He doesn't want to just provide us one miracle after another. We could never learn to appreciate, like that. *God* makes us

earn our place in *Heaven* through *faith*. You were brought up to know our definition of faith: belief and confidence in that which is written but not yet seen."

Joycina: "Excuse me if I sound brash, but it sounds like you are *making up reasons* for *God*. Can you state anywhere in the *Bible* where it says specifically that *God* has a problem with being direct with man? It sounds like you're saying something that seems a viable explanation, to you.

"But is there anything *in the Bible* that says *God* doesn't like to be direct, frank, clear…precise? Does it say anywhere that *God* prefers to deal with man through second-hand sources and second-hand word of mouth? Does it state anywhere why *God* won't just come out of the sky…and talk, like in the 'old' days of the Old Testament?"

Dn. Supperes: [chuckling] "Well, now, that's being a bit facetious, don't you think?"

Joycina: "No, I don't think so. With all due respect, Deacon Supperes, I don't think you *know* why *God* doesn't just come out of the sky and talk."

Dn, Supperes: "No man can comprehend all of the ways of *God*. What we have is *His Word* written in the *Bible*—which actually is quite enough. It contains everything we need to know to find salvation. You see, this world was created by *God* but it is a temporary place. *God* simply does not make appearances of the kind you refer to, on this earth. His kingdom is *Heaven*. We have to wait to actually lay eyes on the Master in *Heaven*. Here, Joy, I'm coming *straight* from the *Bible*."

Joycina: "—Which brings us back to where we started. The Bible is the word of *God only* in terms of faith and belief. So, suppose some other group has a book—and some of them do. Why is that not the Word of *God*? Religions, like Christianity, ask us to accept things on blind faith, no questions asked. That seems dangerous to me."

Nymbolson: "The purity of one's faith leads him or her to the truth… the real truth. *God* guides him of good faith to the right teachings and away from those that are *not* His. Now, it sounds like that ol' sly *Satan* has been leading you to doubt the *value* of faith. I'll bet you can think of many cases in your daily life where you rely on faith to get you from one task, or place, to another. And yet you try to devalue faith."

Joycina: "That's true. But it's not *blind* faith, Deacon Nymbolson. When I was a child—yes. But…."

Nymbolson: "Why, we're *all* children in the eyes of *God*. Now, you say, when you were a child you accepted things on blind faith. But you're still a child—just like me—a child of *God*. There's no difference."

Joycina: "With all due respect, there is a difference Deacon. 'Child of *God*' means *creation* of *God*. A *creature* can be a fetus, a baby, a child, an adult, or an old, old woman. I don't think you mean to say there's no difference among any of those.

"But I started to say: when I was a child, I went on blind faith in many cases because that's how my brain was predisposed to function. But as an adult we work from *calculated faith* and *odds*. There's a big difference between *calculated* faith and *blind* faith.

Pastor Posson: "Miss Joy, I'm not sure we know what you mean by 'working from odds.'" [Adding in soliloquy:] "Sounds almost like a *gambler's* analogy."

Joycina: "See, it's like this: Take my drive to church. I have *calculated faith* that if I obey the rules of the road in my drive, the *odds* are I will arrive here safe and on time. But because of factors out of my control I can only speak of *odds* or the *likelihood* of my safe arrival. But it's the *calculated faith* part that I'm really focusing on. *Calculated faith* and blind faith are two totally different things. Religions ask or demand *blind faith*. I think that's dangerous."

D. Pyrewood: "So, if your mother asked you to walk blindfolded with her across a busy street, would you have *faith* enough to do it? And if so, would that be an example of blind faith?"

Joycina: "I would do it if I understood her reason. And then it would be based on *calculated faith* because I *know* my mother. My faith in her is based on real and actual firsthand experience—not something someone wrote in a book or some *word of mouth* that's been passed down over years."

Dn. Horzshint: "Joy, have you lost *faith* in *God*?"

Joycina: [after a pause] "I wouldn't say I *don't* have faith in *God*--."

Dn. Horzshint: "Oh? Well, if you have it, it must be a *calculated faith*—with a regard for *odds*, as you put it. You actually believe you can make *calculations*…on the ways of *the Almighty?*"

93

Joycina: "I guess you can say I sort of separate my faith in *God* from my faith in the Bible. I suppose I've lost my faith in the Bible."

Dn. Horzshint: "I'm afraid that doesn't make sense to me, since the principal way we know *God* is *through* the *Bible*. And, miss, you still didn't make clear what the nature is of your faith in *God*. You say you have faith in *God*, but what kind—*calculated?*"

Joycina: [after a pause] "I'm not sure. I haven't worked it out in my mind yet."

Pastor Posson: "I see--. Well, let me ask this: If the kind of faith Christians have in *the Word* is somehow 'dangerous' or unwise, in your view, then do you have anything to offer in its place?"

Joycina: [after a pause] "Actually...no. But, I'll never convince myself that I have faith in something based on writings in a manmade book."

Pastor Posson's "*God's Thunder*" talks, when they finally grinded to a halt, ended in pretty much a stalemate. It was rather disappointing to the pastor, for he had imagined a different outcome. Not only had he "foreseen" reinstatement of Joycina's prior faith. In addition he had devised a mental plan to perform a soul-saving, adult-level, baptism, as she was no longer a child. He'd dreamed of executing it right in the open among all the *Christmas Savior* celebrants. And while most would be unaware of the wondrous rectification that had occurred prior, it still would have been a magnificent event, he thought.

As it was, however, he could only rise from his seat among his entourage, his heart heavy with knowledge of an unfulfilled mission. *Satan*, he thought to himself, *has the audacity to work his art right in the center of a house of God.* With a stony expression he resumed: *He will not win! He must not win!*

But Pastor Posson wasn't alone in his dismay. Joycina's candid articulation of her doubts startled her family. Although her parents were more prepared than Garvey, Jr. and Rochelle for the discourse, it still pained them to hear it. Joycina's siblings sat in stunned and speechless amazement at her elucidations.

The following week, a religious tenth of Feytown planned for a much grander event. Every other year one among a cluster of high powered evangelical organizations held a New Year's Eve extravaganza. The venue: a sprawling, top rated hotel on a far edge of Holy Oak County. The gala featured three famous and highly esteemed wife-and-husband ministerial couples. Each was noted for an ability to rouse large assemblies of the *faithful* to fever pitched religious excitement. In three separate arenas within the hotel complex the pairs were commissioned to work their magic.

For those able to muster the admission, the $400 fee paid in advance or remitted at the door was well worth it. The benefit accrued went beyond participants having a safe place to *ring in* the New Year. An additional amenity would involve elegant serving of an extravagant banquet with exotic virgin elixirs. Indeed, that marked just the beginning of enjoyment to anticipate. Throughout the event there would abound the heady experience of spiritual fellowship such as to dwarf even that felt at the local churches. Next, in the scheduled events, would come the delivery of earth-moving sermons. But even these would not mark the termination of pleasurable times be had by all. There existed yet another facet to their festivity and feelings of residing in a realm holy and sanctified. This last was privately regarded as the symbolic capstone atop a colossal edificial shrine.

That band of evangelicals booking functions across the nation tended to tailor their message to young adults. Generally, their target group was individuals eighteen to thirty. Specifically, though, they attracted an eighteen to twenty-four set. Of course individuals not within that general span also found the pop-culture deliveries appealing. But upwards to ninety percent of those who most enjoyed the brand of pageantry presented were in the overall cohort mentioned.

To the credit of function organizers, certain specific arrangements were well thought out. These concerned not only believers' *attendance* of the venue but also *occupancy* within it. Regardless of how the participants arrived, they were assigned rooms to stay overnight in a select format. Males were typically assigned single-bed suites as were married couples. But always the young ladies were designated to occupy, in groups of three, spacious units with as many beds. While these galas featured very adequate security from start to finish, no one monitored friendly visitations *among* the guests.

The big clocks on each of the ballroom walls all read 2:13 a.m. With the New Year a full two hours old, the sated guests were filled, too, with the memory of grand times shared. By and by, though, another state overtook the great majority of them. Looking across tables large and small at one another the sisters and brothers were all atwitter at the thought of retirement for the night. Among that group were Joycina and Rahim. Indeed, all evening she had been as excited about the turning-in-for-the-night phase of the affair as she was about the gala itself. But suddenly, right at the "hour" of this next stage of developments, she began to feel, well, incongruent.

The erstwhile spiritual revelers slowly began rising from their seats and milling about tentatively. As they did, Joycina spoke privately to Rahim who sat in a leather-padded seat beside her:

Joycina: "Rahim, I'm not sure now about our plan for tonight."

Rahim: "Joy, please…you don't mean…."

Joycina: "I'm feeling it again, Rahim. It's…it's actually…*sinning*—isn't it?"

Rahim: "Joy, not when…not when two people love each other. We've talked about this before."

Joycina: "I forced myself to accept that…reasoning, before. But it's not…valid. It's a sin to fornicate whether two people love one another or not. You know that, as well as I do."

Rahim: "Joy, please. Don't over-think this thing. You're allowing your mind…these, sort of, wayward thoughts to run wild. You're going to analyze to death something special we can share. Joy, think back on the evening we *just* had. We've been *in the spirit* all through. We rejoiced in those great, *kick-ass* sermons along with all these people sharing the same experience.

             "Joy, I'm telling you: This atmosphere, the atmosphere that's been with us for the whole festivity, is going to make it even better than the other times. Trust me on this, Joy. I can feel it. I can feel it!"

Joycina: "What are we, Rahim—hypocrites? We say we believe something, then we turn around and violate *rules* of the belief. Is that how we want to be? If that's the case, it's all a joke. It's a big fake and a lie. *God*, I don't want to be a fake, Rahim. I sooo don't want to be a *fake*." [Tears falling]

Rahim: "Joy, I swear you're over-analyzing. You know what? Think back on some of the points Minister Caziztri touched on tonight. 'Sin is the *plight* of Man.' We're never free from it, no matter what. *Christ* died to atone for our sins. Remember what the minister said: We shouldn't get overwhelmed and bogged down with thoughts of our sins. We should keep *love* in the forefront of our minds. It's our love for one another that keeps the spirit of the *Lord* alive in us and with us."

Joycina: "So, fornication is a sin, but sinning in this case—in the name of love—is okay."

Rahim: "Uhhh…yeah, basically."

Joycina:	"So, I guess any sin—as long as it's in the name of love—is okay."
Rahim:	"Wellll. I don't…I wouldn't--. You know, Joy, you're over-analyzing again. Let's keep it simple: I love you more than anything in the world. I want to express it tonight. You love me and you love my expressions of love for you. It's *love*, okay? It's all about love. Love-love-love."
Joycina:	[looking out blankly into the distance] "Rahim, you remember Tandra Inkly—stabbed to death near Starkey Hospital. And it turned out to be Tywaan Begeeber that did it"
Rahim:	"Joy, please. Don't bring that up."
Joycina:	"And he said he did it 'cause he loved her and couldn't bear to lose her?"
Rahim:	"Joy…."
Joycina:	"Murder is a sin."
Rahim:	"I know where you're going with this, Joy. Come on, don't go there with it. Why do you analyze so much? We got a beautiful night ahead of us. Do you know how much I *want* you at this…moment? Can't you just think about what you know is awaiting us when we go to the rooms?
	"What do you want me to say? Do you want me to start telling you right now everything I want to do—how *off the chain* it's all gonna' be? Joy, baby, I am totally *on fire* for you right now! Let's just go to our rooms and make the plans."
Joycina:	"You don't get it, Rahim. I'm sorry. I am *so* sorry. I'm going to my room with Quamilla and Desiraye. I won't be coming back out until check-out time. Please don't come by to try to make me change my mind. I know you may still do it, but if you do, I won't answer the door."
Rahim:	"Desiraye and Millie won't be with you long. They'll be waiting for O-Z and Cane. Chances are…you'll be alone in the room all night."
Joycina:	"It doesn't matter. …I just hope you can forgive me, Rahim. I pray that you can forgive me. I really do love you—probably more than you can imagine."

Through the subsequent semester Joycina's avoidance of places frequented by Ephesus and Isaiah Caskett paid off. She had seen Isaiah only twice, within fleeting seconds, and the younger brother not at all since that last meeting. Eventually, the period in question extended through the present quarter beginning in January and ending in late March. With spring just around the corner, she knew the chances of an encounter with Ephesus increased.

Situated time-wise between the second and third quarters of the school year, she was facing a ten-day break. She planned to spend much it in hours of just winding down. For the rest, she intended a revival of social activity.

In spite of the needling they gave her on Christmas day, "Jr." and Rochelle were delighted to hear Joycina's report of her grades. The straight series of As and glaring 4.0 GPA, given the course-load carried, was sufficient to impress just about anyone. As for Pricilla and Garvey, Sr., they were totally ecstatic, overjoyed at their daughter's success. They took much pleasure in singing Joycina's praises, in chorus with Jr. and Rochelle, to anyone within listening range.

Still, the latter did not alter their earlier position regarding their sister's employment status. To them Joycina's having a job and sacrificing A grades for Cs and Bs, would have been warranted. From their perspective, receiving an engineer's degree was spectacular whether or not attained with all "As". During this break-time for Joycina, however, they all refrained from rehashing the topic.

Because he attended an institution that employed *semesters* instead of *quarters*, Rahim was in "spring break." It would span a full two weeks. In this period, his parents had helped arrange full time employment for him. He was thus far from being idle and whiling the time away. Like Joycina, he hoped to make the most of her ten days between quarters. They had been able to make only scant and all too fleeting time for one another over the past three months. From his perspective, the "fire works" they'd make during this period should occur as often as possible. He would just have to avoid planning for intimacy after church functions. As he noted to himself: lesson learned.

It was sort of odd, given the efficiency of the Feytown *grape vine*, that Rahim hadn't heard the talk about Joycina. Some of the deacons "interviewing" her on Christmas Savior had mentioned the talks privately to confidantes. These latter, it turned out, passed the info to other trusted comrades with a similar understanding of confidentiality. On and on it spread, everyone promising to keep the shared material under lock and key, so to speak.

At length, upwards to a fifth of Feytown heard that Joycina had participated in an *inquisition*, of sorts, at the church. In it she had shocked prelates and given her family pause over admissions that she sometimes doubted the existence of *God*. It had been a delectable *feast* for the ears.

Not once since Christmas Savior had Joycina missed a Sunday church service. In all that time, she took no notice of anything out of the ordinary among the congregation. At least not consciously, she didn't. But then given her single-minded focus on school and squeezing in time for Rahim, perhaps she "slept" the signs.

Also, church members weren't apt to express misgivings directly when they were born of hearsay. So, it was only when their gazes weren't being reciprocated by Joycina that "the concerned" gave her the odd looks. Their expressions were a mixture of confusion and reproach.

With regard to Ephesus Caskett, finally it came—the dreaded confrontation. On the first Sunday of her school break, Joycina drove with a friend to the latter's public housing unit. Angelina Caracha and her four-month-old had only been issued the residence for a month. She was dying to show Joycina how comfortable she'd made it. When they were parked in the lot facing the unit, Joycina glanced to her left. Approaching was not one but three of the Caskett brothers, Ephesus, Isaiah and Antwan. Two years Ephesus' junior, Antwan had just been released from a juvenile detention facility.

Following the greetings, the now group of five strolled together to Angelina's apartment. As Joycina noted, the large living room was fully and attractively furnished. She was also impressed with arrangements in the kitchen and bedroom. With her baby enjoying time with his grandmother, Angelina felt free to accept the Caskett's generous offer. It was made as the group sat about the living room. She thus participated in the rolling and smoking of "weed" the brothers provided. After a time, the topic of the Lexus surfaced in the conversations.

Isaiah:	"*Goddamn*, I miss blazing through streets in the *whip*, sho'tie! We had some *times* spinnin' in that cruiser."
Antwan:	"I heard you was supposed to be thinkin' about selling it back, Joy. What's up? They tell me it's been over six months and you ain't tryin' to reconnect wit' niggas."
Joycina:	"My dad made the purchase. Remember I told you, Phese, that my dad would have to make the decision about it?"
Isaiah:	"Shit, just tell him you want to sell it. It's in your name."
Joycina:	"How would I get to school if I sell it back to you?"
Antwan:	"Damn if I know. I just think you should let us get it back. …Shit, take the money we give you and buy another ride."
Ephesus:	[looking reflective] "You know what, I sold it to get out of a jam. On the *real*, though, I was thinkin' about findin' a way to get it back. But you know what? A deal is a deal.

99

You and *big* Garvey made a sweet-ass bargain in this thing. And after I got out'a my...situation I figured, you know, 'why should I let her keep my shit?'

"But, *God*damn it, you know...a deal is a deal. Y'all actually helped me out. I'm just gonna' go ahead and get me another *whip*. Ain't no need in me gettin' gangsta' over the shit—not wit' you. Hell, you ain't never done nothin' against me, or any 'a us. Ain't that right, Bae-Bae? Ain't that right, Ant?"

Antwan: "I guess you know what you doin'. If it was my shit, though, I don't know--."

Ephesus: "I'm'a tell you what: I'm puttin' it to rest. I ain't botherin' you 'bout it no mo'e. How's that? We *twins* on it?"

Joycina: "Yeah, we're *twins* on it. ...I'm *down*. And I appreciate it, Phese."

Ephesus: "Good. That 'gnat' is dead. Now, you think you could do me a favor? I need to do a little *business* cross town that won't take but two minutes to complete. And, see, I ain't got but about fifteen minutes. I was tryin' to call cabs when you pulled up. Damn lines busy on all of 'em. Or they put you *on hold* and shit forever.

"We can be there in ten minutes or less. Plus, there's some'em I'd like to talk to you about in private, too. Is it good? Can we roll out?"

Joycina: "Um...okay. But I got to call my mom while we're on the way. She had something she wants me to do after taking Angie home."

Angelina: "We can make chitchat when you get back, Joy. Ant and Bae-Bae say they got to be out, too. At least by the time you finish the run, the air in here should be all cleared. I know you don't like breathin' *blunts*. And you're still gonna' take me to pick up *Dae-Dae* later, right? ...Okay, good."

When twenty minutes later Joycina returned, she tried her best to appear as if nothing was wrong. She chatted freely with Angelina listening to her friend's myriad complaints about little Daquan's father. In the forefront of her mind, though, was the memory of what was told her by Ephesus during their quick trip. He claimed he had first-hand knowledge of something she might want to know about Rahim. He had, under "suspicious circumstances" been seen in the company of one of her female associates. It was in the past few months and occurred, allegedly, on more than one occasion.

Relevantly, Joycina had long noted something odd about Ephesus. While he had evolved into something of a thug and dealer in illicit substances, he also had a frank, ingenuous streak. That fact made his report all the more disconcerting.

In church the following Sunday, Joycina subtly scoured around for Jonetta Merry's location. Once she'd spotted the nineteen-year-old, she found herself staring on occasion. Fortunately Merry was postured such that she had no knowledge of it. Try as she might she could not dissolve the vision in her mind of Rahim and Jonetta together.

Not once since she received the "dirt" on Rahim did Joycina consider telling him what she'd heard. First, she had to consider the source of the info. She wasn't about to reveal that Ephesus had made the report. Such an act had the potential for causing a whole community of trouble. She determined, too, that making Rahim aware of the accusation but not the accuser would be unfair.

Gradually, she started feeling sick inside, and weak. She could barely remain standing during gospel singing by the congregation. When, mercifully, the service was over, she decided to follow her usual pattern. In it, she tended to drift temporarily away from her parents, to meet with Rahim and his parents. In this period, Pricilla and "Sr." mingled with their church friends. That was if Rahim didn't initiate the process in the other direction.

Moving through the crowd, she had an objective in mind once she made contact with Rahim. She was hoping somehow to maneuver him toward Jonetta without his realizing the course. Once the parties were in proximity, she would study postures, expressions, demeanors. The motive: search for telltale signs of secret collusion between the two.

Unfortunately, that wasn't going to happen under the present circumstances. When Joycina approached, Rahim and his parents were thoroughly engaged in conversation with other church members. Among the participants were the family and extended family of Joycina's friend, Sherrel.

Joycina wondered if she was imagining it. Accept for Sherrel, her half brother Mac, and Rahim, the conversing party seemed just slightly to ignore her. Few in the church were more friendly and personable than Joycina. Usually, when members saw her approach she was likewise extended warm and sincere greetings. Her conversation and melodic voice they'd always seemed to regard as that of an angel. The difference she noted in this instance was stark. Actually, members' regard for her had been cooling very, very gradually for weeks. Joycina just had not picked up on it.

She stood there with the group, not able to get an opinion fully expressed concerning the topic discussed. Finally she turned back to the trio whose attitude towards her was more in line with what she was used to. She engaged them in pleasant conversation, even while a tinge of hurt at being snubbed merged with unease she felt, related to Rahim. It was her last day of the late winter break, and she wanted to feel rejuvenated. Instead, her emotional well-being was steadily "going south."

Suddenly, the scenes she conjured of Rahim and Jonetta, alone together, became overwhelming. In a haze of distressed emotion, Joycina felt as though she could run from the church crying. In fact she did excuse herself as graciously as she could manage and walked away. Before she departed, she told Rahim that she needed to join her parents. The purpose of it was something she made up on the spot. Luckily, she didn't see the glances cast at her as she retreated.

Joycina did, however, hear a voice calling behind her. "Oh, I forgot to say *congratulations*, Joy!" called out Mac. "Congratulations on that four point '0' at *Sparton!*"

Separating briefly from his wife, his unofficially adopted children, and rest of the group, Mac walked quickly the few yards toward Joycina. He spoke loudly so that anyone interested could hear his commentary. "You're representin' us *maximum* over there. It's not many of us in *Fey* who can *hang* with the *shots* at that school."

Before Joycina could give her heart-felt appreciation of Mac's kudos, he spoke again, but more quietly. "Don't let these jokers around here get you down, alright? *You do you.*" With that admonition Mac smiled and quickly returned to his entourage.

At *Sparton Technological Institute* the following Monday, Joycina was back thoroughly focused on her studies. The brief pre-spring break was over and the third quarter was on. Every now and then, however, she allowed her mind to reflect on Mac's somewhat cryptic advice. The implication was that he knew something. But was it just that he had picked up on her distressful state? If so, why would he assume it was due to those "jokers," as he put it, the church congregation.

Or was he stating a warning of sorts based on knowledge of something at the church of which she as yet unaware? Maybe, she thought, she'd have to ask him about it in a future encounter. She couldn't count on that occurring at church, though. It was known that Mac visited church only *once in a blue moon*, as they say. As it turned out, though, Joycina would not have very long to wait to get an inkling of that to which Mac referred.

By the end of *Sparton's* third quarter in the school year, the "chill" emanating from some church members was more evident. It had irritated a portion of the congregation the way Joycina *zipped in* to church just seconds before the start of the morning service. In similar fashion, they noted, she breezed away briskly at its end. Thereupon she'd fly home to engage her "precious" academic interests, many cited. Just as often, they knew, she'd burn the miles to the college library and resource center, in erudite pursuits. Church members felt certain of where her priorities lay.

Pre- and post service congregations were one thing. Actual church proceedings were quite another. Joycina, it was charged, showed little more regard for the latter as for the former. She could be seen wandering off in her thoughts during sermons. Often, it was said, she demonstrated a rude impatience for the slowness of church activity. In these incidents she actually glanced repeatedly at her watch, as though she couldn't believe how extensive, time-wise, a performance was.

Now, those taking issue with Joycina's church etiquette had a two-tiered grievance. One, as was seen, involved her church manners. The other concerned her audacious arguments with church leaders. It was gossiped in dramatic terms: Joycina had questioned the status of *the Word* as being indisputable. She had challenged the very justification of the church's faith in *God* Himself.

Questions circulated: What, now, was her purpose for even attending church? What might she be driven to say if asked her thoughts by the more easily influenced youth of the church? More and more the members began to believe that Joycina's high regard for education had compromised her immortal spirit.

Joycina's teachers and counselor at *Sparton* marveled at her academic achievement. They were astounded by her intellectual prowess as demonstrated in classrooms and school labs. Aware of a students' typical need to earn money, they probed for a solution, on Joycina's behalf. Thus, part time employment, meticulously and conveniently scheduled around her classes, was not just made available. Indeed, it was handed to her, as if on the proverbial *silver platter*.

As word spread through the institution of the novelty in their midst, Joycina started to achieve quiet celebrity status. Often students and faculty alike recognized her and accorded her a sort of friendly deference. It was hard to believe that a student from Feytown could perform academically as she had. In cumulative mastery of course objectives, she was rated in the top five percent of all freshman enrollees at the institution.

Paradoxically, her next year at *Sparton* was likely to be more relaxed in terms of course difficulty. While there was still much to learn, the facility with which new knowledge was added depended on mastery of fundamentals taught in the first year. The *general* academic courses would still require a good deal of reading and study. But those of her *major* were designed to involve *application* almost exclusively. The procession was similar to first demonstrating mastery of the rules of operating a motor vehicle then actually driving.

Like the academic quarter before it, the *summer* quarter at *Sparton* was preceded by a ten-day break. Joycina, having recently turned nineteen, was in the middle of that respite. On the sofa of the Lushas living room she sat with Rahim, watching a cable-featured movie. The time was a little pass six in the afternoon so there was still plenty light outside. Both her parents were out on their own separate missions. As neither had given any word of intentions, there was no telling when they might return. The ring of the telephone prompted Joycina's response and she found on the other end the pastor of Christ Redemption Baptist Church.

Clearly pleased to have caught her in, the cleric hoped she had a minute to talk. In his most gracious tone, he asked if she might be free the following evening, Thursday, at about seven. *Christ Redemption* was having a special function. Attendance of its most long-standing members was sought. As he stated, he'd been informed she was on break and that this might be the only time, for a long time, she'd be available. Joycina conceded and then inquired as to the nature of the event planned.

"We have a group of the members," Posson replied, "who are ready to become *saved*. We want to plan the baptisms for this coming Sunday. One of the folks who want to give themselves over unconditionally to *the Lord* is about your age. I thought it would be good to have you as one of the young ladies considered for participation in the ceremonies. You were practically born in *Christ Redemption*. And you're among those who never miss Sunday services.

"What we want," the pastor clarified, "is just to get all the potential key players together and see what's possible. Of course, we encourage you to bring with you anyone whose presence you think will be helpful."

Joycina was a little surprised by the invitation. After a half minute's more exchange, the two ended the call. While the t.v. movie played on, she discussed it with Rahim. As was true in both their experiences at the church, only *saved* members performed ceremonies in formal baptisms. Anyone within the church could witness them. But typically only those who had vowed to live a life of strict worship and religious service took part in rituals. At the end of their talk, Rahim announced that he would drive her to the gathering next evening himself. He would observe processes as her guest.

As scheduled, Joycina arrived at the church and, with Rahim, took a seat among the score of event planners. It wasn't long before Rahim's secretly held suspicions were confirmed. He had caught a few mutterings, here and there, of criticisms church members had of Joycina some weeks back. Taking them as non malevolent congregational scuttlebutt, he figured it would blow over in time. Upon his most recent awareness that the chatter was intensifying, he chose the option of ignoring it. But when informed, last evening, of this invitation he connected the dots, so to speak.

The real reason the pastor and his ecclesiastical cronies wanted Joycina present was to discuss prospects for *her formal salvation.* In addition to the otherworldly benefit, there were a number of here-and-now issues it would address. Becoming *saved,* everyone knew, or made themselves believe, was a transformational process. The combination of *ritual* and a *professing of total sincerity* by the "volunteer" was supposed to effect fundamental change in a person's *being.*

In the view of *Christ Redemption,* baptism was one thing; undergoing formal *salvation,* quite another. If Joycina would consent to getting *saved,* formally, facilitated by church ritual, it would surely cure her. That is, it would rid her of those pesky and spiritually dangerous doubts she harbored. The *healing* would accordingly mute her blasphemous expressions of uncertainty. And that in turn would calm the growing concerns of the current *true* believers in the church.

With Joycina sitting in bewilderment among the other prospective event organizers, the pastor laid out to her his position. In carefully modulated words he intimated that Joycina's decline to get *saved,* in formal ritual, along with the others, could have repercussions. Certain members of the church, he informed her and Rahim, had grave concerns about her possible influence on their youth. Perhaps nothing short of a total and open recanting of her doubts and questions would mollify them. He would, he implied, hate to lose her to a neighboring house of *God* whose members were more tolerant of her views. But that would be totally her decision to make.

To Joycina's thinking in this moment in time, the pastor wanted a showdown. He had, it seemed evident to her, invited her to this evening gathering on false pretenses. He seemed to her to be hell-bent on invoking a perverted and patently non spiritual doctrine of *might makes right.* He intended, symbolically, a surgical removal her doubt with a "sword." In addition to himself, there were present a score of *formally saved* church members and officers. These were to be his army of *holy warriors*, she thought, waging battle against a lone, lost but recalcitrant lamb.

Among his *soldiers* was Deacon Horshint, who was in his fifth marriage. Next to him stood Bernie Wall a house painter and reformed arsonist. Perched nearby was Gloria Woodpate who occasionally bought "hot" goods from known thieves. At a far end of *the saved* conveners sat Lonnie Shike, who tendered shady certificates purported to assure free legal services when the need arose.

Opposite Shike stood Doris Fryes. Doris once tried to sue a fast food restaurant and barely escaped conviction, herself, for making fraudulent claims. Calvin Skippy, occupying a back row of seats, had to date sired six illegitimate children. Two of them were with the equally "saved" Camille Warmer, not present in the meeting.

Essentially, it seemed to Joycina, the pastor had thrown down a gauntlet. He challenged her to give an answer. He wanted to know where she stood, what her intentions were. He wanted her to lay her cards on the table, so to speak, so as to reveal to everyone who—she or they—held the better "hand." She felt in just the right mood and intellectual *frame* to play the "accused" in the pastor's twenty-first century version of an Inquisition.

Joycina: "I guess the *God* overseeing this church just doesn't tolerate a free thinking mind."

Pastor Posson: "Just the contrary, Miss Joy, *God* created Man *by design* to have a free thinking mind."

Joycina: "So, *He* gives us a free-thinking mind, but doesn't tolerate our using it to search and question."

Pastor Posson: "Just the opposite, really—it is through searching and questioning that we come to find and understand the spirit of *God*. The problem arises when we allow *the Devil* to guide our search."

Joycina: "It just seems too convenient, Pastor, to say that any line of thinking different from church teachings is a devil's product."

Pastor Posson: "Not *a* devil—*thee* Devil, Miss Joy. Don't you even acknowledge the existence of *Satan* anymore?"

Joycina: "The idea seems absurd to me now. It's just part of the whole organized scheme to keep believers locked in. The whole idea of *the Devil* seems to me just a *primitive* answer to an age old question. The question being: why it is that people often behave badly?"

Pastor Posson: [pondering] "I have to ask you: have you been considering embracing a different faith lately?"

Joycina: "No. But even if I did, I'm sure I'd have questions about the various aspects of any other system of beliefs. That's what religion is, you know, a system of beliefs—beliefs put in place to address the needs of people long ago."

Pastor Posson: "Our religion consists of doctrines based on *the Word of God*. We have faith that the *Word* directs us along the path of righteousness. We have *faith* that the *Word* leads us to want salvation. We have *faith* that we can *achieve* salvation through *God*-ordained processes. And we have *faith* that with salvation we resurrect after earthly death and spend a blissful eternity, with *God*."

Joycina: [giving an imagined dialogue] "'*So, you human beings, here's a nice, shiny, new, free-mind for each of you. But don't use it in questioning and doubt and exploration for new truth. Use it only for faith in what this group here says is right.*

"Don't listen to those other people over there who're trying to get you to have faith in their thing. Just use this nice shiny new mind for having faith in what this group says.'"

Pastor Posson: "Miss Joy, you're wading into deep waters. I would caution you...."

Joycina: [continuing the mock discourse] "'*—Oh and by the way, here's an apple I don't want you to eat. I know you like apples. I know you're going to want this apple. And I know you're going to eat this apple. But if and when you do, I'm going to punish you to where you'll wish you'd never seen this apple. You'll wish I had never put it before you in the first place. But I am putting it before you. And I dare you to eat it.*

"'Oh, and see that snake over there? I put him here as part of my plan for you. Try to ignore him if he starts talking. I already know he will, and I already know you can't. But try it anyhow. You don't see the sense in it? Well, that's just too bad. ...See ya'.'"

Pastor Posson: "I have to say, Joy, I'm glad Garvey and Pricilla aren't here to witness this... performance of yours. And I have to ask you: If you feel that the Bible, particularly the *Book of Genesis*, is such a joke, to the point where you poke fun at *God* Himself, why do you attend church at all?"

Joycina: [at a loss for words] "Maybe...I...."

Pastor Posson: "It's obvious that you've veered off course. I really think you should think about whether or not you really want to continue at all with us. Given the views you have, what benefit is the church to you at this point? With the attitude you present, what benefit are you to *our* mission? …I hope you find your way again, Joy, whatever course you decide on. I will continue to pray for you.

"But I give you this warning: Christ offers the only real path to peace. Without Him you are at the mercy of a bleak and cold world. This world is full of *Satan's* temptations for us to put things—things that glitter and look good on the surface—before *God*.

"Faith in Christ is a protection against the world's evil. Once you stray from it, you're a *lamb lost in a land of vicious wolves*. So, Miss Joy, whatever you replace your faith with—and you're going to replace it with something—I pray that it doesn't destroy you…and *damn* your immortal soul."

Rahim: "Joy, tell the pastor you…didn't really mean it…the way it sounded. …Joy's just having a bad day, Pastor. She didn't mean it. …Tell him you didn't mean it, Joy."

Joycina: [expressionless] "I can't--."

The pastor had suggested that Joy think about whether or not she should continue with the church. Actually, though, after that jaw-dropping exchange with him, before the *saved* onlookers, the bridge was burned. There could be no returning to the Church of Christ Redemption short of accompaniment by a grand and spectacular recantation.

So, why, Joycina asked herself repeatedly afterward, *had* she attended Sunday services so…faithfully the past months? She absolutely was consciously aware of her doubts about the wisdom of having what she called *blind* faith. She knew that more and more she had come to view *belief in fantastic accounts from a remote time*, as ludicrous.

The whole Christian viewpoint was based on, depended on, and sprang from belief in past occurrences of the extraordinary. The more Joycina had focused on that point the more disenchanted she had become. Increasingly, one particular fact reverberated in her consciousness, shaking the foundation of her prior thinking. It was that the church taught acceptance of goings-on in the past which, if reported today, only a handful of kooks would accept on hearsay.

Why, she asked herself, had she been so willing to suspend reason and embrace what were essentially nonsensical lines of thought? For example she had accepted that some characteristic of the past made what is impossible today quite possible back then. Then there was the idea of "God's Begotten Son." Why had it seemed reasonable that the *Spiritual Master of the Universe* had need for, of all things, a human *son*? And why hadn't it seemed bizarre that he planted this *co-Master-Spirit* inside a poor, clueless Israeli "virgin" who was part of the, very primitive, *ancient world*?

In addition to these issues, there was the matter of God's showing seeming favoritism to males over females in Biblical accounts. What was the deal with *that* and why hadn't she ever questioned it? Why, for instance, hadn't the story involved God's endowing Mary with son-and-daughter *twins*, to make things equal? Of course, it would have been a lot more straightforward simply to have "created" *from the earth* an altogether extraordinary *messiah* right before everyone's eyes, and do it every fifty years or so. In that way, virtually everyone would have more direct knowledge of *divine* designs.

Joycina now wondered why even in the midst of all her doubts she had continued with the church. Why did she go on attending and doubting right up to the time of her and the pastor's last exchange? In the past year she had become aware of so many odd facets of Christian thought. There was, for instance, the *human-like* portrayal of the *Master Spirit*, God, in the Bible. Indeed, the church's view of *God*-the-all-*wise*, all-*knowing*, all-*powerful*—and apparently *unbalanced*, she dared to muse—seemed quite medieval.

The whole roundabout way, taught by the church, that *God* recruited inductees into *Heaven* was in fact insane. Put into place was a scenario wherein hundreds of billions, perceivably, will burn for eternity in fire while a relative few luxuriate in *Paradise*. This was the handiwork of an all-wise-all-merciful *Spiritual Master of the Universe* who could just as easily have made mankind perfect and *Heaven*-bound, from the jump.

So, again, Joycina asked herself why she continued in the church after bombardment by these realizations. It was a combination of things, she concluded. Maintaining her parents' approval, force of habit, the sense of belonging, and—yes, no doubt—*fear*, all played a role. Now, she was going to have to find out how she'd manage, upon forsaking that collection of influences. To her thinking, the pastor had employed the old tried-and-true, *religion*-typical *scare* tactic, involving specious reasoning:

"Since you don't know what lies beyond, lost lamb, you're better off with us."

"The world is flat and you'll fall off the edge venturing out!"

"*Blasphemer*, you'll say the sun revolves around the earth, or else!"

Up to now, the looming of such warnings had been among the incentives that kept her attached to the church. Now, she was adrift in an untried "sea." She was Galileo Galilee in the twenty-first century, whispering rebuke of traditions that were time-honored but also frayed and fragile.

While Joycina struggled through the summer session at "Tech," Rahim was enjoying his school's summer break. Full time employment kept him nearly as busy as his studies had. Therefore, as usual, he and Joycina scheduled time for each other around their respective obligations. But, Joycina made good academic use of the sparseness of times they spent together. As a consequence, her immersion in work and study made that fourth quarter seem to fly by. The next thing she knew she was, again, in the middle of final exams and after that, the start of a brief break.

The end of the short scholastic rest period brought the start of a new academic *year* at *Sparton*. Most weekdays, Joycina arrived at the college just before 8:00 a.m., making a final exit of the campus at 9:00 p.m. Sometime in between she may whisk home, to a outlying library, or to a store for one thing or another. But nearly all her activity had some relation to her campus job and schoolwork. The exception, of course, concerned Rahim.

Joycina was in fact grateful to have the social pattern she and Rahim settled into during the school year. Given her uncompromising work ethic, she knew a love bond could only work with someone of similar involvement. To her, they were like birds of flight, crisscrossing a region on separate objectives, meeting occasionally. But their respective goals were designed to benefit them both in the end.

Often it surfaced in her thoughts how Rahim had stood, or sat, with her on that last day at *Christ Redemption*. With warm feelings she recalled how he had consoled her afterward, and it would be a lasting impression. Secondary to education, he was an essential player in dreams she had of the future. She was going to become a computer and electronics design engineer, in high demand, maybe the world over. She was going to have Rahim to share with her in the wonder of it all.

When she did encounter a Feytowner other than Rahim, usually on weekends, she could "feel" the displeasure. Often it was subtle, and what she perceived didn't include every community resident who knew her. But she experienced it from enough of them to guess as to what was going on. Many of her friends and associates had, she supposed, taken sides in her clash with Pastor Posson.

It seemed so strange to her: Folks who had known her all her life felt *that* strongly about the matter. And it was so much so that they were actually showing signs of forsaking her. Joycina discovered an "up" side, though, to her break with the church. It freed up precious hours on Sunday for academic engagements.

Sparton's first quarter of the present school year "coursed" forward without a hint of trouble. In this time, Joycina remained essentially unaffected by the occasional brushes with old friends. If they preferred to be lukewarm in their social approach, that was, she felt, their problem. But, inevitably Christmas rolled around again, with another New Year following fast. It would be during this break that her awareness increased of having lost all or most of the closest friends of earlier times. Here was the premier season for family gathering and also of cherished celebration with friends. As it stood, on the social "front" Joycina would have to accept change from what she'd been used to.

Now, unlike during the school session, the state of being a social pariah in Feytown weighed on Joycina. No longer, even, could she include Rahim's parents among those who welcomed her presence. When they started showing ambivalence regarding her association with Rahim, she cut off visits to their home. Given her own parents' busy *separate* schedules she'd see them at home when she could. In solitude, she wondered: Would Rahim be willing to sacrifice his still rich social affiliations to spend every possible moment with her? She knew she couldn't blame him if he wasn't, although she hoped he would.

Rochelle and "Jr.," of course, had their own lives and, in addition, big plans for celebrating the season. Joycina resolved, then, to connect with them when possible beyond the family's usual Christmas get together.

Although with only a minimum of good cheer, Joycina got through the holidays. Now, yet again, she was staring down the road of another *Sparton* quarter. In fact, though, it was completely welcome. Joycina had made a few associations at school and now she found the prospect of reconnection exciting. Relieved to have the holidays behind her, she entered the second, and after that the third, quarter with renewed zeal.

She had become aware of a sort of *communication culture* prevalent at *Tech*. It seemed that, not only were *open minded* discussions with students and professors tolerated, they were essential. When there was disagreement, it was just taken as a fact of life. When there was accord it was regarded almost as *incidental*, as opposed to a requirement of future engagement. But then it was also true that relations she had at the school were almost completely intellectual, rather than close and embracing. They lacked the warm, emotional component she had known in friendships and associations in Feytown.

It was early June, near the end of *Sparton's* spring quarter. Joycina sat alone in a neighborhood "sub-shop," having a quick meal. Peering through the storefront window, engrossed in thought, she watched a shiny sedan park in the outside lot. She saw that the man who emerged from the vehicle was Ephesus Caskett. By the direction of his gait, he seemed headed toward the place where she dined. Joycina noted his usual "air" of insouciance.

If the car driven was Ephesus' new pre-owned "ride," that was a good thing, Joycina thought. Still, she wondered what would be his attitude towards her this time around. In their last encounter he had surprised her by a sort of unrefined gallantry he showed. As he approached she saw that he recognized her through the store glass. He opened the door and walked in.

Ephesus:	"Hey, what up, sweetheart?
Joycina:	"Hi, Phese. How're ya' doin'?"
Ephesus:	"Chillin', chillin'. I saw *sho'tie* parked a little ways down. I didn't know you'd be in *SubHub*."
Joycina:	"Yeah, I was shopping and decided to walk up for the special."
Ephesus:	"If I had got here a little earlier I coulda' bought that for you. Hell, we almost cousins, now. ...I rolled up on *twenty-twos*, girly-girl. Did you see?"
Joycina:	"Yeah, is that your new *whip*? ...Oh, it's nice—looks like an *Acura?*"
Ephesus:	"Yeah, it'll do for now—'til I find a way to get 'Lexy' back. Oooh, just makin' a *clown*, sweetheart. You know I got jokes. Look, let me place my order and I'll come back to be with you."
Joycina:	"Sure."
Ephesus:	[returning] "So look here, *'Sunday,'* there's been some talk on the *vine*. *Niggas* is sayin' you got *buck* on Pastor Posson some months back! And you done dropped out the church and shit! They buzzin' that you in your *own orbit* now. *'Screw the church, damn the congregation!'*
	"What is up with that wild shit, girly-girl?!"
Joycina:	[chuckling] "It's not as dramatic as all that. My thinking just doesn't fit very comfortably with church doctrine at this point in my life. But that's just, you know, for now. After I kind of have time to sort a lot of things out, who knows--?"
Ephesus:	"That education is motha'fucka', ain't it? You always was smart, but *niggas* be sayin' now when they buzz wit' you, your talk is all up in the *attic* sometimes. ...So, you got a new way of lookin' at this mess, huh? You know what? I

think it would be good for you to *break off* some of these new scenes in your head to feed some locals."

Joycina: "Uh, what do you mean?"

Ephesus: "Share the vision, *'Sunday.'* Let *niggas* in on some'a what you know. Oh, it just hit me: I don't guess I can call you *Sunday School* no more—not after you done *smoked* the pastor and *shot off rounds* at the members, like I heard.

"But, look, a lot'a *chillers* around here ain't *into* that church shit. Some'a us would like to hear some'em *different*...and from somebody who's been there, done that, and broke. And a *sho'ty* with the brains enough to talk about *the new.*"

Joycina: "You actually think I should put together a...a speech of some kind? And on what—how to offend and get kicked out of the church? I don't think anyone needs a lecture on that."

Ephesus: "Joy, girl, a *blind man* can see that you *on* to some'em. Look, you know this community. There's a lot'a us just ain't *down* with that church bullshit. But a lot 'em don't really know why. They just feel left out. And they figure some'em ain't *right* about that whole thing.

"People been talkin', Joy. You don't know it, but some of the *homies* is curious about what they heard. They say, 'How the hell did a *church flower* get...goddamn *uprooted* and...goddamn thrown out the church window?' That's what niggas be wantin' to know. You feel what I'm sayin'?

"Everybody 'round here know you smart, J-Rose. Ain't nobody in this town don't know how you been settin' off brain-*grenades* at *Tech*. Some of us want to hear your side. Now, we done heard the other side, over and over. Some of them fools be crackin' that your head was spinnin' 'round that night at church like *the Exorcist*—and you was speakin' *in tongues* and shit. It *was* funny as hell, though."

Joycina: "I didn't know you know my middle name—Rose."

Ephesus: [shaking his head for effect] "Phese knows some shit, J-Ro. This homie ain't too much on book-knowledge. But ain't much go on in Feytown that the *vine* don't catch and run by me. ...Hold up. I gots to visit the counter, to specify my condiments. ...Oh, yeah. I got big words in the store, too."

Joycina: "That's pretty good."

Ephesus:	[having returned] "Look, Ro, I don't like to put shit off. Put shit off, it never happens. This evening, I can touch with eight to ten *church-skippers* who you know and who, *I* know, want the real *breakdown*. Take a minute—if you ain't got nothin' pressin'—to do a *nigga* a turn, girly-girl. You know putin' it off 'til later's a *dead cat*: It's just gon' lay there...and stink."
Joycina:	"Well, uh--. Oh, looks like your order is ready. I'll think about it while you get your food."
Ephesus:	[returning] "Better not be onions on this shit this time. Make a *nigga* roll up and do a *drive by* on this jai'nt.
	"Now, you go'n do this for me, J? You ain't go'n kick a *nigga* to the curb, is you? *God*damn...we practically *cousins*, now. You drivin' my *sho'ty* all over the state.
	"...Yeah, you can see I'm totally in *the zone* over this thing, girly-girl—hyped! *Niggas'll* be talkin' 'bout it for weeks! '*Phesey blazed up in the crib with the Feytown celebrity. Girl's harder to interview than Jada Pinkett Smith!*'"

A number of factors accounted for why Joycina agreed to meet with the *inquiring minds* of Feytown referenced by Ephesus. First, she had no plans for the evening and was caught up on all her studies. Second, she knew the names and faces of those in the prospective audience. "Miss Pauline," fifty, within whose home the gathering was to occur, had been a daycare provider for all the Lushas children. Third, Ephesus had succeeded in overwhelming her with his attitude of urgent insistence. Indeed, she still felt beholding to him for not having made an issue of repossessing "his" Lexus.

Finally, Joycina had grown weary of being an outcast with regard to the faithful in Feytown. As mentioned earlier, these made up the vast majority of its citizens. Her differences with them, and her intense focus on school, had severely limited her community socialization. During periods of lull in her activities revolving around *Sparton Tech*, social isolation took an emotional toll. Even when not consciously aware of it, she missed the old community embrace. She missed the town's congratulations of her academic successes. Now there seemed an opportunity to recoup some of the regard of old. It promised to await her at "Miss Pauline's," according to Ephesus.

As always when she was out in the evening, Joycina informed her parents, by cell when necessary, of her plans. Typically, also, if the outing was not run-of-the-mill, she promised to maintain periodic contact. So, with precautions in place, three hours after the *SubHub* encounter, Joycina was parking in front of Pauline Piper's home. What memories it brought back to her walking up the outside steps. On the side of the house could still be seen all the play items for little children. To this day, little ones in Pauline's care romped around the fenced-in area during operating hours.

With just a hint of apprehension, Joycina rang the doorbell. Pauline's arrival to admit her brought happy greetings Joycina hadn't experienced from non family members in months.

Inside the Piper house already were some of Feytown's *residents-of-little-faith* whom Joycina expected. Others, both expected and unexpected, would be arriving one by one. Perhaps not surprisingly, a majority of the nineteen who wound up attending were Begeebers and Casketts. Two Friskys, one twice Joycina's age, were also in attendance. To accommodate the guests, Ms. Piper mixed *adult* chairs and larger-sized *children's* chairs together. The arrangement had almost the look of a storefront-church gathering. Soon, the entire audience was in place. Facing 19 occupied chairs scattered about her, Joycina brought the session to formal commencement.

Joycina: "I've already expressed how honored I am that you are interested in hearing my thoughts on whatever matters you have to present. Phese explained that some of you are interested in my views on religion these days. I intend to be as straightforward as I can. At the same time I don't want to go on and on talking without your input—*questions, comments, criticisms*, as they say at *Sparton*.

"So...this being a radical change from the cold shoulder-treatment I've gotten used to, I'm eager to talk on any point that comes up. All we need is a lead-off question. I'll be happy to take it from anyone who'd like to start."

M. Caskett: "I heard you told 'em at the church you don't believe in *God* no more. Did you say that?"

Joycina: "No, Makeba, I never said that. My point was that I question whether we should believe things on *blind faith*. The pastor and I disagreed on the *wisdom* of having *blind* faith."

Makeba: "But do you believe or have faith in *God*?"

Joycina: "I believe there is *God*. And we had discussions about this in a *history* class at *Sparton*. This is the position I take: I believe *God* exists, but I haven't figured out how to *understand* God. I can't have faith when I don't understand. Now, that's just me. Maybe it comes easy for other people."

Prettia Sloan:	"Damn, girl! I think that's my problem. I don't think I ever felt like I understand all that stuff. The Bible, man, I tried to read it a few times when I used to go to church. I just put it down. Our preacher used to say the *spirit* will help you understand the Bible. I got some of the stuff, but then I got lost. I guess the *spirit* lost patience with me."
Joycina:	"See? That's what I mean. They tell you to have *faith* in *magic*. Then when the *magic* doesn't happen, they tell you it's *your* fault, because you didn't have enough *faith*. I think most people in the church just *pretend* it all makes sense and go through the motions—like I did. They take the *safe, easy* route, which is just to attend church and go along with the program."
Danzl Plester:	"You say you believe, but you don't *understand* God. So, what makes you believe at all? Why ain't you done just throwed the whole shit out the window?"
Joycina:	"Let me clarify: I don't understand the *God* the *big three religions* present. Their *God* sounds made-up by the human mind. It seems suggestive of a *God* created by man. Each one of them gives *God* human attributes, in terms of emotion, intention and motivation. Some speak of a *jealous God*. That sounds just plain *crazy* and too human to me. One or two of them have it that *God* wants people to be good but created them bad. Here, believers seem to be likening *God* to an all-too-*human* parent. The term 'Our Father' emphasizes it.

"So, I repeat: To some religions, that which *drives God* is...well, anthropomorphic. A 'vengeful' *God*—that, to me, is plain *wild*. Imagine creating a computer program with faults and then being 'vengeful' when the program produces errors. This, from the highest intellect in the universe! My reasoning rejects that kind of belief.

"But also, you ask why I believe in *God* at all? I think there are two basic reasons. One, human beings are predisposed, naturally inclined, to believe in a *God* of some sort. Adults are oversized children with heightened experience with the world. Just like children have a need for a protector and provider, so do adults. So it's naturally *in* us to believe in something that's bigger than ourselves.

"But I think the *main* reason I acknowledge existence of something *Godlike* in the universe is this: Simply put, I *sense* a program. I *sense* a *design* that's in place. I just haven't figured out all the details. As yet, I don't understand the program or the Designer."

D. Begeeber: "Girl, you not afraid to be talkin' 'bout *God* like that? I mean I have trouble with a lot of that stuff, too. But I ain't go'n call *God* crazy and wild and *anthromor-some-shit* you said."

Joycina: "Well…Dawn, I'm not calling *God* crazy. I'm calling that *view* of *God* crazy. But, I don't believe you can offend *God*, anyway. *God* created us, knows us through and through, knows all of the past, knows the present, and knows all the future. How can a speck of dust on earth offend a 'star' a billion times the size of the sun? I think—and this is just my opinion—we should rethink the whole religious presentation of *God*."

Ephesus: "So, what do y'all believe over there at *Tech*—that people come down from monkeys?"

Joycina: [after the group laughter] "The fact is, Phese, that there are a number of beliefs. And many are very similar to beliefs here. Students at *Tech* are from all over, and they believe what they were taught, where they come from. Of course, the ones who are Christians believe the same as most people believe right here.

"But you raise an interesting point. Scientists—anthropologist, genealogist—say they know that all humans come from one race. And the *one race of man* has common ancestors with other primates—which, by the way, include the greater, and smaller, *apes*.

"Now, here again, we're back to faith and belief. Let's say that *evidence*—like findings of *definitive ancestral remains*—allows us to conclude we are akin to apes, in addition to being one hundred percent primates. But, of course, the Bible says *God* created Man, not evolved him along with apes. Now, if you're tied to your religion, you are forced to deny the *facts* in favor of *blind faith*. Or you're forced to get *creative*, yourself, and make loose interpretations that fit things together. But, I'll tell you, my mind just doesn't work that way."

Treka Ballard: "Yeah, you gotta' do some serious jugglin' to make that Bible stuff fit the facts today."

R. Frisky:	"What is the Bible, anyway? I mean, where'd it come from? What, *God* is supposed to have wrote the Bible? People always talkin' 'bout the Bible—'*read the Bible.*' What it's supposed to do for a poor ass nigga like me tryin' to make it from one day to the next?"
Joycina:	"I'll tell you what the church would tell you, and then...."
Royleigh:	"Naw, I don't want to hear them! I want to know what you got to say. They be poppin' off with a whole buncha' *smoke.*"
Joycina:	"I have to tell you both views, so you can compare and decide what's right for you. According to the church, the Bible is the *word of God* written by man. Christians, and regarding the Old Testament, Jews, believe that *God* guided the writing of its Books. There's no proof of it. It's a matter of faith. People feel comforted having something to believe in.
	"All the big and mysterious questions of life are answered, if you have faith in the Bible. And you shouldn't question anything beyond the answers that are given in those Books of the Bible that *God* helped men write. Now, that's the church's side."

Joycina paused to get a sense of whether or not the facial expressions before her reflected comprehension. Then she continued.

Joycina:	"To me, the Bible is just a book of old, old writings by people of ancient times. And some of it has some accuracy but most of it is just wild and outdated and unclear. In it, people wrote that *this- and-that* happened and that they saw *this-and-that*. There's no proof of most of it—how could there be? We're talking about time from almost two thousand years ago, back *another* two thousand.
	"The only way it could have special value to anyone is: One, you have *blind faith* that God guided the writers' hands. Two, it has value if you're a *historian* and want to read the accounts of an ancient people. And, three, it has value if you're a *sociologist* and you want to use it to study human cultures."
K. Spackle:	"Suppose *God* did move them people's hands in writin' it? Then all us who ain't read it and don't read and don't *believe* in it is up *shit creek*. Now, ain't that right?"

118

Joycina: "Kemon, it's the decision you make with your own mind. If you're guided by fear, then *make* yourself belief. Christianity makes it simple. Have faith and you go to *Heaven* when you die. That sounds like a sweet deal—on the surface. The Muslim Bible, if I'm not mistaken, says, fight—kill if you must—and die defending Islam and that's a way to reside eternally in *Paradise*. Other books that people believe in say other things.

"Everybody's got to decide what they want to do with their mind. I guess it depends on how you're made up. Most people are going to *give in* to fear, tradition, and habit. Others won't—or maybe can't."

Jazmin Worty: "I don't know *what* to believe no more. So I just *do me* and try to get along. What you got to say to us who don't know what to believe in?"

Joycina: "I can only tell you what I'm doing. I don't believe the real *God* is jealous, vengeful, of male gender or *any* gender. I don't believe *God* is angry, wrathful, rewarding of those who use their minds for *blind faith*. I don't believe *God* would create imperfect beings and cast the vast majority of them into a *hot* lake to writhe in agony for eternity, because they didn't choose *blind faith*.

"Neither do I believe *God* is particularly merciful, when I look around and see all the misery in the world. And that's even if man is responsible for most of it. *God* is immeasurably bigger and wiser than man. So much so, that anyone who tells you she or he has a *clear picture* of *God* is, to me, either a fraud or a fool.

"I think we can only get the tiniest glimpse of *God* through studying life. But at the same time I think, always, we have to be studying how to treat one another. Imagine believing you're going to be allowed to spend eternity in *Heaven*. And you haven't demonstrated an understanding of how to treat your own kind—*man*kind."

Rico Caskett: "I get it: One nigga standin' outside the *Heaven Gate* and anotha' floatin' around inside. The one say, *'Hey, I see you chillin' and ballin' there in Heaven. How did you get in, after all them you 'carried' and jerked around and screwed over, on earth?'* Say the other: *'Faith, baby—I had faith in this wild shit. That's why I'm in here and you're out there.'"*

The talks carried for another half hour, rather much in the same vein. When she left, Joycina felt happy and exhilarated. While she didn't know what, if any, impact she'd had on the group, she had enjoyed the feeling of camaraderie. As she walked to her car, a number of the participants ambled with her, chatting lightly. Ephesus Caskett led the escort. Now, she was seated behind the wheel with the engine running. This was when the "session arranger" sprinkled a little cool water on Joycina's elation.

"You got brains, sweetheart," he remarked leaning at her window. "Ain't no exaggeration what the *talkers* be spreadin' 'bout your smarts. But, I said it before and I'm sayin' it again: You gettin' played, *sho'ty*. Any one of these sistas standin' 'round can back me.

"Now, it's on you how you want to carry it. But Rahim's got Jonetta Merry *wide open*, from what I can tell. And it may be both ways. Hey, look, we just tryin' to let you know what *time* it is. How you roll wit' it is on you—know what I'm sayin'?

"Look here. Take a look at this. Jaz wrote this out. It's just a little scribble-scrabble, but we put it together to put you in the *light*. Check it when you can. ...Alright, now. Peace out, Ro."

So it was back. The accusation against Rahim had resurfaced and this time Ephesus showed more conviction than before. He and cohorts had even concocted a sketchy list of Rahim's alleged rendezvous. Suddenly Joycina was aware of being faced with a consistency issue. It was one that concerned choices she'd just spoken of to her grassroots audience. Now, given this situation with Rahim, would she embrace "blind faith," choosing not to question his fidelity? Or would she opt to explore, investigate, at least make essential inquiries? Which road to choose now, she wondered, confronting this very down-to-earth, very secular and all too human dilemma? She felt like a leaf amid winds blowing in contrasting directions

In the practical workings of her mind, though, she recognized that opposing emotions can bring balance. Return of the *fidelity* issue served to calm exhilaration she felt from renewed social interaction. Put another way, reanimated charges against Rahim tempered the "high" experienced from group-embrace. On the other hand, her audience had seemed to attend her talk with awe. Thereby she had been rescued from the effects of months of social rejection. With final exams upcoming, she didn't need distraction by extreme emotional highs or lows. Joycina kept herself on an even keel by consciously setting elation and apprehension in counterbalance.

At a future time she'd worry about settling the matter of being consistent in applying a personal philosophy.

In the next two weeks, Joycina handled her work and academic obligations in the usual fashion. She was disciplined, on point, "on top" of everything. Like a swan wading unencumbered through pond water, she sailed to the next school break. Upcoming was the fourth quarter of her second, and last, year at *Sparton*. The time up to this point had involved a lot of work. And yet looking back, it had also seemed to go by quickly. Now, of course, she had more time to spend with Rahim. She determined to find a graceful way to bring up the topic of Jonetta Merry. As it turned out, the issue would practically introduce itself.

Joycina and Rahim were sitting in the basement of his home on an evening when his parents were out. The host's mood had been a little odd the whole time they were there. Finally, Rahim aired his concern.

Rahim:	"What's this I'm hearing about you and Phese Caskett?"
Joycina:	"What? What are you talking about?"
Rahim:	"You met with him over at Miss Pauline's a week or so back. That's what I'm hearing. Is it true?"
Joycina:	"Oh…yes. But it wasn't just Phese. He asked me to come over and talk to some people he brought together."
Rahim:	"Why didn't you tell me about it?"
Joycina:	"Oh…it was near the end of my quarter and your semester. We were both wrapping things up. You know we don't talk that much during the hectic times of the school year."
Rahim:	"But you had time to meet with Phese Caskett somewhere, with a group of the thugs he hangs with."
Joycina:	"It wasn't…. Are you upset over this? It wasn't anything but what I said."
Rahim:	"Yeah, he asked you to meet him somewhere to talk to a bunch a' drug dealers. Sorry, but the whole thing sounds …*unnatural* to me. He has your number—your home, your cell maybe?"
Joycina:	"No. I saw him at the *SubHub*. He came in and…asked--."
Rahim:	"So when did the two of you get to be so *cool* with one another. I didn't even know you *carried it* with him like that."
Joycina:	"I don't 'carry' anything with him. He came in and started talking to me. I was eating. What was I supposed to do, go running out the place screaming and hollering?"
Rahim:	"You're tryin' to be funny, but this shit doesn't sound right to me. You never…."
Joycina:	"Don't curse when you're talking to me, Rahim. That's not how we talk."

Rahim:	"You never once mentioned that you were with him, Joy— not once. First you leave the church, then you start taking up secretly with the *dirt* in town. You know, now that I think about it, I heard that somebody saw him riding with you. That was like last year or something. I took it as a fuckin' joke. You always told me you weren't tryin' to see him, not even just drivin' by. Now, how do I know that that *other* wasn't true?"
Joycina:	[just staring] "What is wrong with you tonight? Are you accusing me of being interested in Phese?"
Rahim:	"Umm-um--. Look how you *say jail boy's* name. A lot of y'all like that *bad guy* type. But I never thought you had that in *you*. And you never answered me. Was he, like I hear, riding with you a while back or not?"
Joycina:	[after a pause] "Rahim, I ran him to Windham and back. That was the whole...."
Rahim:	"What--? So, you *were* with that *hood hustler?!* You're out with him just cruisin' through the fuckin' community like it wasn't shit! ...Oh, *snap!* And you're sailin' with him in his old *'love whip,'* as that idiot used to put it?! Aw, no, no, no, no! This is too fuckin' wild!"
Joycina:	"I would have told you, Rahim, if I had thought it was that important. That first time I just did it to get rid of him."
Rahim:	"You did what to get rid of him?"
Joycina:	"Don't look at me like that. You know what I mean. I rode him to Windham and then back near Angie Caracas's apartment. He didn't even come back in. And his brothers were all gone when I got back to Angie's."
Rahim:	"You're sayin' all this like I'm supposed to take it as smooth as you're puttin' it out there. It sounds like you're tryin' to get *greasy* on me. All of a sudden, when I bring it up, you pop-off with all these motherfuckin' revelations. I have never, ever felt like smacking you before, but right now--.
	"And of all the dirty, *hood hustlers* you could pick, why him, Joy? Why him?! You're all up in these *goddamned* cribs with that *pot head*. Nigga can't even put together a decent sentence, and I'm gettin' all these reports of you spendin' *secret times*, all up *on* him.
	" ...Hell, you may as well bring it all out, now! I'm sure that's not the end of it. I got to pull all this bullshit out of you one incident at a time. Just *front up* and lay out the

whole damned mess. How many other times have been with him, Joy?"

Joycina: "You can take me home, Rahim. You're just talking crazy."

Rahim: "You don't want to tell me all the times you been with that son-of-a--?"

Joycina: "Do you want to tell me all the times you've been with Jonetta Merry?"

Rahim: [stunned] "...Ww...Wha...What are you tryin' to do? You tryin' to shift the shit off--?"

Joycina: "You want to play the *accusing* game? Is it true you've taken her to the cinemas twice in the past year? Did you spend a night with her at the Water Fall Hotel in Braxton?

"Did you and your good buddy, Juan, double date with Jonetta as one of the women, at Lunden Beach a few times? Do I need to say more? Rahim, I can tell by your expression that the rumors about you have some truth."

Rahim: "You're *crazy in your head*, Joy. You know what? I am takin' you home, 'cause you *crazy in your head*. You're listening to that bullshit people around here say. I haven't done... anything. But you *admitted* your dirt. I don't know how I'm gonna' be able to deal with you...runnin' with that damned Phese.

"One thing, even if I *was* with Jonetta—and I wasn't— but if I had been, at least she's not a member of the Feytown *dirt*, like your *thug boy*. You up here in my face making me think he's not even worth speaking to, to you. And then, come to find out you're crusin' wit' the nigga all out in the open and kickin' it with him secretly all up in people's cribs and shit!"

At home, over and over, Joycina revisited the earlier scene of Rahim and her in his basement. Gazing at but not seeing, through her tears, the television images, her mind was in perpetual replay. Alone in the house, she felt cut off from the world as though she were on another planet. Ultimately she reviewed the entire course of their relationship, examining detail after detail. How could a romance that had sailed so easily through placid waters come to such an abrupt halt? This is what she asked herself as she ran through a full box of napkins wiping her eyes.

For two years, she reflected, he had been a mainstay in her life. They had seemed to her inseparable even through periods when schoolwork stood as a glass wall between them. Joycina had actually felt that Rahim was with her when they were apart. Always he was in her heart. And she believed it was the same with him. So heavily had she counted on his presence in her life that now she actually wondered how she would go on.

But she did go on. Her grief swallowed up the remaining break time. Before she knew it, almost, the last quarter began. For the summer session, the weeks would span from July to the mid September. It was time, as she starkly realized, to pull herself together. Here, in the *final stretch* at *Sparton*, was no time to disintegrate psychologically. The dream she had for her future, she reasoned, depended on maintaining success there. Yet, she remained so devastatingly crushed she knew it was not going to be easy.

As the hours, days, and weeks progressed, Joycina regained a good part of her former momentum. Clearly, though, she was not at the fabled "one hundred percent." It showed some in her zest for learning at school and demonstrating competence in employing concepts learned. At work, at the school's resource center, she performed no less adequately than anyone else. However, the infectious smile and jauntiness that students and coworkers had so admired were diminished.

It was a particularly hot summer. While most other students were planning and carrying out vacations, "*Spartons*" were awash in assignments to complete. At length, Joycina, and the others, struggled to near mid August. The classrooms and labs at *Sparton* were cool. But the view outside the windows showing intensely sun-radiated scenes was, ironically, sometimes a distracting force. Some, like Joycina, both dreaded end-of-class return to the unforgiving heat and simultaneously craved it.

A habit of Pauline Piper was that of keeping address and phone contact books of her clients forever. For that reason she was able to phone the Lushas home this Sunday morning in August. Hoping to catch Joycina at home and able to talk freely, she found lucky success in that mission. An exceedingly pleasant woman, the daycare lady was as chatty and folksy of tone as anyone in Feytown. Eventually, Ms. Piper got to the point of her call.

One attendee of the gathering at the Piper home when Joycina gave her talk was Countess Caskett. Visiting with Mrs. Piper, she was standing nearby when the call was made. After a minute or so Joycina found that it was Countess who really wanted to speak with her, if she didn't mind. Mrs. Piper had a sense of propriety. Thus, she had chosen not to hand over the Lushases number without permission, even though the parties were all associates. Joycina consented to taking the call, hoping it would not cut deep into her study time.

Joycina:	"Hi, Countess, how are you?"
Countess:	"I'm fine. Uh, I know you might be busy, Joy. Um, something's been on my mind since we were all here at Miss Pauline's that day. I've been goin' around and around, decidin' whether to tell you or not. Then yesterday, I said to myself, 'Girl, you should just go on and get it over with.' That way I would stop thinkin' about it all the time."
Joycina:	"Well, what is it, Countess?"
Countess:	"I don't want to tell you over the phone. It just don't seem right. Maybe if I can meet you somewhere—here, at Miss Pauline's again or at my house, or anywhere."
Joycina:	"Yeah, I guess so. But is it really that important? I can't imagine why you wouldn't be able to tell me over the phone."
Countess:	"It's just not the kind of thing you should say on the phone. Actually—on the *real*—I haven't told anybody about it. Not even Miss Pauline…she's in another room right now. I found it out early in the year. And I been holdin' it since then."
Joycina:	[after a pause] "Is it about…Rahim?"
Countess:	"Uh-uh, no, it ain't him. It's…I'm going to feel real funny bringin' this to you. But maybe you should know. I don't know what good it'll do. But it just seems like maybe you should know."
Joycina:	*God*, it sounds heavy, Countess. Is it something we can hold off on, maybe for a couple of weeks? I got final exams coming up. I'm already going through some things. Can it be put off a little?"
Countess:	"Sure. It's not some'em that's gettin' ready to *blow up* or anything—I don't think. I just want to get this off me. So, what's good for you, time-wise?"

Joycina and Countess settled on the last day of exams at *Sparton*. She'd drive over to where Countess stayed with her two children. In the intervening period Joycina fought hard to overcome her mixture of doldrums and curiosity. Breaking up with Rahim had been like removing a foundation-piece in an uncompleted building. She continued to feel unsettled, languid, almost lost. Now, something else was coming *down the pike*, as they say. She had at least been able to push that "unknown" to the back of her mind while preparing for the quarter's end.

When it was over she knew she hadn't done as well as in the previous seven sessions. Nevertheless, she believed her performance had been good enough. Only in courses that were nonessential to her major had she sort of dropped off. She, therefore, didn't feel that the hoped-for scholarship, to extend studies at a four year college, was jeopardized.

In the anticipated scenario she would take a year's break. By then, processes for securing the desired scholastic grant would be finalized. There would also be ample time to apply for an "exchange" transfer of quarter credits to the appropriate institution. Of course she'd find full time work, most likely computer-related. But she would also have twelve months to get her emotional state in order.

With *Sparton's* "finals" behind her, Joycina was ready to pay Countess Caskett a visit. Hesitantly, nervously, gradually, Countess finally got out her report to Joycina's anxiously curious ears. The "serving" had come at Countess' kitchen table, a *dish* that, as expected, was not easy to consume. All the while that Countess relayed her information, her little ones scampered wildly about, in the next room.

The report substantiated that which Joycina only suspected in far reaches of her mind. While her heart sank to an even lower depth than in prior weeks, an out-of-place sentiment emerged, somehow. This new feeling brushed coarsely against the state of sad disappointment brought on by Countess's revelation. In the adjoining room, she could hear the children romping about. The sounds contributed to Joycina diverting her own focus from Countess' news. Out of nowhere she thought about how depressing it must be to live out one's entire life in a *public housing project,* as many did.

As it turned out, a subgroup of Casketts had held the monumental secret among them for an amazing three years. Now, obviously, it was starting to leak farther. Sitting there in Countess' little kitchen, it was difficult for Joycina to know how to respond. Should she be casually grateful for the sharing of *infidelity "dirt"* on her father? Maybe grateful with angry overtones would be appropriate. Or maybe the combination of grateful and sad was in order. Rising from the table, Joycina opted to relieve Countess of her anguished uncertainty about being a harbinger of unwanted news.

"I want to thank you again," announced Joycina, "for the way you handled this, Countess." Someone else in your place may have chosen to put it all over Feytown. But you brought it to me in hopes that maybe I can do something. And I am *going* to do something, although I don' know, yet, just *how* to do it. I'm sorry that my father and your aunt Noelle chose to do this. I guess it was just…I don't know--."

Driving home, Joycina thought, *Thank God, I waited until final exams were over to do this.* Her brain felt numb, her mind incapable of intricate and complex processes. In her chest was a hollow feeling, as if her heart had bled away into her other organs. All she could do was cry.

The task of confirming Countess' report would have to come sometime later, after she'd gained more composure. At this point, Joycina wasn't sure how long that might be. But she had Noelle's county residence address. She could drive out there any time. Thereupon, she could match her father's non-work absences from home with the sight of his car parked at Noelle's.

As bad as she felt at this time, Joycina was in for an added blow. It would come as her queries brought her to intimate conference with Rochelle and Garvey, Jr. After days of semi-confinement to her room she devised a course of action. With relief she realized that the weight of this new burden was to be shared by her siblings. Scheduling wouldn't be an issue either, not on her end. No longer was she compelled to ration every half hour of her time. No longer was she faced with school-related deadlines to meet. Suddenly now, she had, it seemed, all the time in the world. So, whenever Rochelle and Jr. were ready for her requested assembly, so too was she.

Joycina did have one obligation, though. It was to plan for graduation on stage at *Sparton*, later in September. From here to the day of talks with her siblings, she would have to pretend that all was normal.

It wasn't until early October that "Jr." and Rochelle were able to synchronize their time to comply with Joycina's plan. By then the younger sister was eager to present her findings and collectively map a course of action. Along with Garvey Sr. and Pricilla, Joycina's sister and brother had attended the graduation. But that was the last time the three siblings had been together.

Now, Rochelle was preparing for the arrival of her guests. As Joycina had asked, Rochelle chose a time when her boyfriend-roommate was at work. Similarly, Jr. would be arriving without his wife and daughter.

When the trio had settled in, they made the usual light familial exchanges, preparatory to having the "big" talk. In it the older siblings offered more congratulations to their sister for her academic accomplishment. They were genuinely proud of how Joycina had so monumentally represented their town at *Sparton Tech*. Also, they wondered what apparently troubling issues she could have amid all her success. The answer came soon enough. At length they got down to business.

Jr.: [joking] "Alright, as that old movie title went: *What's eating Gilbert Grape?*"

Joycina:	"You're not going to believe this, but I think I have proof that Daddy is…cheating."
Jr.:	"—Cheating who, the local grocer?"
Joycina:	"No! It looks like he's cheating on *Mom*."
Rochelle:	"Oh, dear…it looks like she's opened the closet—and behold: a *skeleton*."
Joycina:	"How can you joke about something like this? Daddy is… cheating!"
Jr.:	"Are you going to tell us you never, kind of, you know, *suspected* it before? I mean, come on—you've been living there right under it all the time."
Joycina:	"You're saying that you *know*, you've *known* all the time? …Rochelle?"
Rochelle:	"Well, sweetie, let's just say the handwriting was on the wall…and the ceiling…and the floor…and…."
Joycina:	"What are you talking about? You're saying there were *distinct* signs, that it was *obvious*?
Jr.:	"Uh…*yeah*. I mean, where do you think he's spending all those times away from home—at the gym?"
Joycina:	"Yes…and at work…with friends…visiting *Grammy* and *Grandpop*…playing golf. With no *minors* in the house, he, just like mom, is free…both are free to do all kinds of things they like to do…separately."
Rochelle:	"Yes, all *sorts* of things—and *separately*."
Joycina:	"So, both of you have known all the time? And you obviously decided not to tell Mommy."
Jr.:	"Well, sis, look at it like this: Maybe you had a good reason for missing the signs. It's like, all three of you are in your own separate worlds—and that's for, what, at least two years now. You know how you are when you're studying: blinders, one-track-mind and all."
Rochelle:	"Like you said, Joy, we're all grown up now. Let them do what they want."
Joycina:	"Neither of you, *especially you*, Jr., never considered talking to him, maybe in order to…?"
Jr.:	"Nope—not to him or to Mom. At least *I* never did."
Rochelle:	"They're *grown folks*, Joy—'growner' folks than we are. This isn't *the movies*, sweetie, where the grown children get together and set up a plan to set their parents on the road to reconciliation. This is reality. …It's their lives. I think the

best thing we can do is just continue to be their adoring children and let them work out their own thing."

Joycina: "It almost sounds like you think Mom knows about it."

Jr. and Rochelle exchanged amused glances.

Jr.: "Sis, now don't go getting yourself all in a state of *world catastrophe* over it. It's life. Things like this happen. It's just like you leaving *Christ Redemption* after all those years of faithful attendance. As a family, we just *rolled* with it. Nobody tried to talk you out of your position.

"Now, I'll say we were shocked. You dealt some heavy arguments to Pastor Posson that time with the family. And that *last* time—they say the *last* time he went up against you was worse. According to the faithful, you hit him with three *right 'crosses'* and two *unholy* uppercuts. ...Left him hemorrhaging the blood of Christ.

"But did we hassle you over it? Noooo. The family just said, *'Hey...Joy just likes to fight.'* ...We were shocked. We didn't *know* you like to fight. But, hey--."

Rochelle: [laughing] "Man...that's funny!"

Joycina: "I think I need to know if Mommy knows about it."

Jr.: "Leave it alone, lil' sis. I'm telling you. This is not something you want to get too deep into. You ever watch that old movie *Planet of the Apes*? You're gonna' keep digging until you find something you don't want to know."

Joycina: [pondering] "Something I don't want to know? Are you saying that Mom knows, already?"

Jr.: "Oh, *God*, I think she's seeing one of the 'head spokes' on the *Statue of Liberty*. I warned you."

Joycina: "You've got too many jokes, today, Jr. This is serious... terribly serious! Rochelle, please tell me what Jr. is hinting at."

Rochelle: "Joy, you take some things too hard. Sweetie, let it go. You've done the near impossible: outshining most of those upper middle class preppies at *Sparton*. You've got a whole year's break to wind down from that mad pace you've been keeping. You live in a comfortable home, no bills to speak of, no worries. Chill out. Give Mom and Dad their space, just like they give you your space."

Jr.:	"Did you notice she said 'give *them their* space'? It's not a *one*-sided situation, Joy."
Joycina:	[speaking in a low monotone] "Mommy is also having some sort of…affair?"
Rochelle:	"Let it go, Joy. …Let it go."

Back at home Joycina entered into a new phase of an already unsettled state. In rapid succession, her thoughts covered a wide range, often positing extremes. At one time, she absolutely *must* talk with her parents about their infidelities. At another, the idea seemed grossly meddlesome and absurd.

Maybe finding a job and moving out on her own was the way to go, she considered. Thereupon, she would take the position held by Rochelle and Jr. The next minute, though, she realized that living independently before the start of her next school enrollment was unwise. It would disallow the savings she planned to have while attending class and living, later, on her own.

She thought, as she had many times over the past weeks, of calling Rahim. Maybe he was sorry about everything. Maybe he would drop everything, dash over, and convince her that he wanted her back on any terms. Or maybe he would refuse to accept her call, or, if available, be mean and unapologetic. Either one of those last conditions, she deemed, would be more than she could bear. The alternative was to do what she'd been doing now for weeks: wait for his call.

It even crossed her mind that she'd like to be back in the embrace of her old friends. That would be all those who treated her differently when they heard she'd denounced *Christian* faith. With much discomfort she envisioned a scene of her "back peddling" in order to propitiate. She thought about what it would be like to "blaze up," at one of Feytown's many churches one Sunday, *on fire* to be back in good graces with a church.

Feytowners did it all the time: leave one church and start anew with another. Of course, Joycina's situation had a slightly different twist. Those others hadn't left their old pastor "hemorrhaging the blood of Christ," as Jr. had put it. In the end, she knew she couldn't revert to pretending faith where there was none.

It was one of those rare occasions wherein schedules for the household of three converged on a point. In this case, it allowed Pricilla, Garvey, Sr. and Joycina to be present, altogether, at the dinner table. To Joycina, the atmosphere seemed charged with piteous and intolerable pretense. At twenty, and still not in full-time employment, she felt she masqueraded as a self-contained adult. At the same time, she role-played a child in a stable, two-parent household, as in earlier days. In farther fantasy, each of her parents pretended, for Joycina's benefit, to be a happily betrothed pair.

It was, perhaps, Joycina's frazzled emotional state that accounted for her boundary *overstep* during the meal.

Joycina: "Mommy, Daddy, I know you still love one another--."
Pricilla: "Yes…and I hear a pause as though there's more to come."
Joycina: "Can't…things…go back to the way they were in the beginning?"
Pricilla: "What are you talking about, sweetie?"
Joycina: "You and Daddy…you're not--. I know about…it."
Pricilla: "You know about what, Joy?"
Joycina: "Mommy, I just want to see both of you back together, like it should be."
Garvey: "It would probably be best if you come out and say exactly what you mean, Joy."
Joycina: "Daddy, both of you know—you have to know what I'm talking about. You're living… separate…lives."
Pricilla: [quite taken aback] "Joy, why would you…how could you…what are you trying to do?"
Garvey: "Let her go, *Cil*. She wants to drag it out. Let her go, for what it's worth."
Pricilla: "Joy, what are you trying to do?! I can't believe you've brought something like this up!"
Garvey: "She wants it out, *Cil*. Let's have it out."
Pricilla: "Why would you encourage this, Garvey? We had a silent agreement. We were managing to move along smoothly enough. Maybe it's been a fragile balance, but we managed to…keep things steady just the same."
Garvey: "Well, I've held it in, and it hasn't been easy. The vision of you with that self righteous maggot has been turning my stomach for too long. …Damn, I'd better settle down. I'm starting to get worked up. I don't like to feel like this."
Joycina: "Daddy, Mommy—this isn't what I…."
Pricilla: "Self righteous…you need to be looking in the mirror when you say that, the way you sound right now. I can't believe we've taken this turn. There's only four years left on our mortgage. We always talk about that. We had a silent agreement to keep everything together, to try to keep things smooth, at least until then. I never once brought up your little thing with…you-know-who."

Garvey:	"Who went off the tracks first, *Cil*? Who went off the tracks first?"
Pricilla:	"You want to scatter the *dirty laundry* all over the dining room table, *Gar*? That's just as sick as anything I've seen! You're willing to risk my exposing you and the *real* cause of all this, in front of Joy?!
	"I've tried, *Gar*, I've tried to keep my respect for you. I've tried to forget and just live in the present. But you don't know how many nights I cried knowing you didn't love me anymore. You don't know how it destroyed me knowing that all your affection was transferred—to another woman!"
Joycina:	[crying] "Mommy, Daddy...please!"
Garvey:	"Sure, *Cil*, go on, shift the blame for Joy's sake, to make yourself look like the *victim*. Before I even looked at Noelle sideways, it was all over the church. You think that crap didn't kill *me* inside? I had to put up with all those nasty whispers, the occasional tip-offs. While I'm at work, my wife is 'fishing' for better than what she's getting at home."

That was it. Joycina had heard enough. From the dining table, in a stream of tears, she ran up to her room, burying her head under a pillow. Compounding her abysmal sadness, she started developing an excruciating headache. There was nowhere to turn, nowhere to go, nothing to do but lie there in a sort of agony.

It is commonly said: Time heals all wounds. Well, at least enough of it passed to allow Joycina to get out of her room and to the job interviews she managed to secure. It would, however, be a rash overstatement to say that the emotional lacerations she bore were repaired. Over and over, she had apologized to her parents for the reckless intrusion. Her pitiful appearance, crying almost hysterically, sometimes on her knees, moved them to great sympathy. Accordingly, they tried their best to console her, but she, in fact, remained an emotional wreck.

Traveling to her interviews, she looked a lot less haggard and distraught. But she was by no means the Joycina she was before the dinner table fiasco.

Just as she and counselors at her old high school had calculated, one thing was true: Two years at the *Sparton Technological Institute*, alone, translated to an *employment genie*, or sorts. It would take no more than a handful of job interviews before she struck "gold." That was only where the "magic" began. Two additional years in her major would make of Joycina the proverbial *genie*, herself. But that status was as yet a ways down the road. Two weeks after her third job interview, she started work, entry level, at *Johnston Computer Programming Corporation* or "JCP Corp."

At home, conditions had become, well, raw. The previous pretense of goodwill and moderate affection between Pricilla and Garvey was all but gone now. Thank *God*, so to speak, they were still graciously civil with one another on occasions when their paths crossed. But in the absence of the show of amity for Joycina's sake, the Lushas home was a paradox. It was still decorative and comfortable but had a dismal aspect, lacking *emotional* warmth.

Ultimately, talks were put forth of selling the house before the scheduled mortgage payoff date. As Joycina construed it, clearly it was time for her to go out on her own. Plans of accumulating ten months of savings before making that move would have to be revised.

In short order, Joycina found a second-level, one bedroom apartment. It rested over that of an elderly churchgoer who looked more suited for a senior citizens' complex. Nevertheless, Mrs. Haint had been fortunate to have good neighbors above and around her since she moved in. With the advent of Joycina, of course, her luck, or *blessing* as some might prefer, had remained true. Although she was no longer an ardent Christian, Joycina was very disciplined and reserved.

As, perhaps, it is for most, for Joycina having her own *first* apartment was totally gratifying. Of course, the other four members of her *first* family, with the "extensions," all made great fanfare of her move. Although Pricilla cried a little it was all-in-all a happy occasion.

Joycina settled immediately into good habits. She arose early for work, locked the apartment conscientiously when she was away. The little furniture she bought on credit she kept neatly arranged. She played her music and t.v. at a volume that did not disturb the neighbors. She never missed a day of work. Still, with all this, in due course she slipped back into a sort of hollowed-out apathy, and then sadness.

A young coworker, Gene Cornblas, almost from the start, took an interest in Joycina. Inclined toward a professional demeanor, he didn't show it at first. He was perhaps not very consciously aware of it himself, not at first. But in time, and in the course of work-related communication, he found her rather intriguing.

To Gene, there was something about her—well, a number of things. She was very pretty. Over the past weeks she had gotten a little thin but was still shapely. Positively she was smart, job-knowledgeable, and displayed an admirable work ethic. But it was the sadness in her eyes, it seemed, that most fascinated him. Why would someone with such superb qualities appear to be so sad?

Before long, Joycina ran into a younger sister of her old friend, Sherrel. It was Sherrel that had the two younger sisters, Deidra and Monique, and the half brother, "Mac." Standing at a street corner with Deidra was one of Mac's cousins on his mother's side. The two chatted genially while awaiting appearance of their bus. As a longtime member of *Christ Redemption Baptist Church*, herself, Lynette Jekall was well acquainted with Joycina. Indeed she had been among those in Feytown who abandoned her after the "fall from grace."

Normally, she would merely have cruised by and waved, choosing not to *put upon* those inclined toward snubbing her. But Joycina was still not fully "herself" these days, and without calculation she slowed to a stop near the pair.

Would they like a lift to where they were going, she asked, after the greeting. Following a moment of hesitation, Lynette Jekall, with a sort of glint in her eye, cautiously accepted. Deidra just sort of followed the lead of her unofficial older cousin. They were actually headed to the home Mac Petey shared with is adopted family. As usual, at his wife's request, Mac prevailed upon family to baby-sit while he attended an evening class. Shayna Petey, still unemployed, seemed curiously to have other affairs to attend to during these times.

In the ride to the Petey's rented townhouse, Lynette who, like Sherrel, was Joycina's age warmed up gradually. Surprised and ingratiated, Joycina took it as a welcome sign. Maybe, she dared posit, people were learning to forgive the position she had taken on Christian faith. Maybe this was the sign that she was turning the corner, so to speak, emerging from *de facto* excommunication. In a gesture of conciliation, she wrote her phone number for her passengers. One was for Lynette the other for Deidra to give to Sherrel.

At first, Joycina felt her mood lightening. Days later, she felt her *spirits* implode as she waited and no call came from a former friend. Still, she plodded on, with at least the old discipline, day after empty day.

Then at lunchtime on this particular Wednesday, Gene Cornblas asked if he could accompany her in the break. Usually, Joycina just walked across the street to a café for her forty lunch minutes. There was no reason not to follow that pattern just because she'd have a tagalong today. For his part, Cornblas was determined to try to get to the bottom of his coworker's unhappiness.

Gene just assumed that Joycina was a Christian. Everyone of her race whom he'd ever known had given one indication or another that they were. He, himself, was an unrelenting *holder-* and *keeper-of-the-faith.* Indeed, he believed there existed no earthly problem or predicament unsolvable through Christian faith. At twenty-four, he'd been helping deliver that message for a few years now. He would bet—had he been a bettor—that *the faith* could be utilized here, too, to address whatever was Joycina Lushas' issue.

Sitting with her at the diner, Cornblas began his mission:

Gene:	"Once, as a teenager, I was riding a bus, going happily along, and a man sits beside me. Just out of nowhere he asks, 'Are you *saved*?' Well, I felt kind'a *knocked* by that question. So, I answered, 'How the hell do I know?' At that time I wasn't exactly the friendly, approachable type. It actually happened a second time some years later.
	"Of course, now I know what those two gentlemen were getting at. And when I did become *saved*, it just changed everything in my life for the better.
	"You'd be surprised to know the conditions I grew up in, in Buster County—yeah, *the sticks*. But like I said, when I got *saved*, all my past washed away like a clump of street mud in a rainstorm. So, every now and then I ask someone I know that same question. Do you mind if I ask you?"
Joycina:	[with a bland expression] "No, I don't mind at all. The answer is 'no'—not in the sense that you mean it."
Gene:	"I don't understand."
Joycina:	"You're referencing the belief that *God* has a pre-selected horde of human hypocrites on whom he plans to lavish eternally happy times. This, while untold billions upon billions get escorted to the 'the lake.' So, you're asking if I'm one of the former. The answer is: *I think not.*"
Gene:	[stunned, to say the least] "Uh…uh, wh…where did you get that…perspective?"
Joycina:	[sighing] "Does it matter? And can you dispute my description?"
Gene:	"You described the *saved* as…*hypocrites*?"
Joycina:	"A 'horde' of them to be exact—and can you dispute it?"
Gene:	"Why *hypocrites*? Why would you describe the *saved*, as hypocrites?"

Joycina:	"Why would you say otherwise? The only one you can legitimately vouch for is yourself. Why would you try to argue that anyone else is *not* a hypocrite? I think you'd be a fool to exhaust precious energy arguing the point on someone else's behalf.
	"I could see you trying to make the case—provided it was important enough—*for yourself*. But you don't know what's in other people's hearts or in their private practices."
Gene:	"It's all given by the *spirit*. When the *spirit* is in a person, it cleanses them of...*hypocrisy*."
Joycina:	[chuckling dryly] "You could barely get that crazy statement out. Tell me of anyone you know, *saved* or not, who is incapable of hypocrisy—besides yourself, that is. I exclude *you* because you may know something about yourself that I don't know. Like, maybe you're the *Second Coming of Christ*. That's the only way you could be incapable of hypocrisy. But everyone who is *not* the 'SCC' is a hypocrite.
	"And Gene, if you are *not* the SCC, *you* are a hypocrite. So, it follows that all of you who are *saved* are a bunch, or horde, as I like to say, of *hypocrites*. And please, if you are going to try to argue the point further, please have indisputable proof of existence of someone *incapable* of hypocrisy. If not, let's change the subject. ...Oh look, our trays are arriving."
Gene:	"I see your point, Joycina. But I'd like to say one last thing. Everybody's *capable* of lying but that doesn't make everyone liars."
Joycina:	"It does in my book. Now, let's not allow religious-talk to *eat away* the lunch break—pun intended."

Even as he participated in segueing to alternate topics, Cornblas felt he was in the company of a rare *find*. Never had he met anyone before who mocked *salvation*. And, he thought, she did it without the least hesitation or show of concern of having committed a *spiritual* offense. She was a *rare bird*, this one, alright—a beautiful and perplexing *rare bird*, in his view.

In her years of growing up, Joycina became accustomed to her parents' huge store of grocery and beverages. Her sister, Rochelle, too, followed that pattern. Her apartment was stocked with wines and other drinks for the frequent entertaining she and her boyfriend did. In the first month of her new residency, Joycina prevailed upon her sister to make similar purchases on her behalf. Joycina provided the money and Rochelle did the transaction, as Joycina was not yet twenty-one.

During lonely evenings at her apartment, Joycina took to opening a bottle of wine and salving her mood with a few drinks. As the process goes, at first it elevated her *spirits* only to bring them crashing "down" later.

It was soon after the Christmas and New Year's holidays that Garvey and Pricilla put the house up for sale. When Joycina got word of it, the news erased whatever gains she was making in her bout with depression. That the residence she'd known all her life would no longer be home-base for her and her siblings seemed incomprehensible. Justifiably or not, she took the blame, emotionally, for early-scheduled dissolution of her parents' marriage. Afterward, she willed herself to stop crying enough to get to work, perform adequately, and return home. There the cycle picked up again.

Sometimes she didn't make it upstairs to her apartment before emotion overtook her. On these occasions she would fight to keep the tears back. Over the months Mrs. Haint had developed the habit of watching the parking lot for Joycina's afternoon return. Often, the elderly lady would greet her at the building entrance. Occasionally she even invited her in for tea and a snack and some religious talk.

The last thing she wanted was for the old lady to see her crying. The few times she was "caught," Joycina told her neighbor she'd just gotten some bad news. While graciously making a stair-ascending getaway, she had promised to explain later.

Appearing as a thing *heaven* sent, Joycina's "cell" rang one evening and it was Lynette on the other end. To Joycina's delight, they talked like the old friends they had once been. The chief source of her updates on gossipy tidbits circulating about Feytown had, to this time, been Rochelle and Jr. The siblings had dutifully filled Joycina in on secretive goings on blocked from her awareness. But, as it turned out, there remained much of which even *they* were unaware. In this exchange, Lynette's demonstrated *knowledge of details* reduced her brother's and sister's stories to mere sketches.

Around breaks to tend to one matter or another, the two talked long into the evening. Lynette seemed interested to hear Joycina's stories and accounts and even seemed to lament her misfortunes. Listening to the voice of her old friend since childhood relating news that underlay the larger, more publicized, Feytown news was almost intoxicating. The chatty exchanges were sips of mellow wine.

The two followed up that *first-time-in-a-long-time* phone conversation with a visitation plan. Lynette was eager enough. For one, she was just dying, so to speak, to see Joycina's apartment. Two, she was anxious to witness Joycina's appearance after having reportedly loss so much weight to emotional depression. Third, Joycina had revealed that she now partook of "the fermented grape" at night as a mood modifier. Divulging that she too imbibed lightly on occasion, Lynette announced a corollary: A little wine might make a great facilitator for the plethora of *girl talk* in store for them.

Caught up in exhilaration, Joycina stated, perhaps too generously, an exaggeration. She said happily that Lynette's reappearance as a friend may have moved her from the brink of a nervous breakdown.

In vain, she waited next for Sherrel's call. To Joycina, renewed contact from a second girlfriend of old would add to her rejuvenated hopes for a new start. But as days passed, Joycina's vision of a world-wind return of past conditions gradually faded. She considered initiating the call to Sherrel, but reconsidered as she recalled the last rebuff received from her.

Employing all her will, Joycina had refrained from asking Lynette the big question. It was why she thought Sherrel had not responded, as Lynette had, to provision of her phone number. Instead, Joycina chose to make just a general inquiry as to how Sherrel was doing. Lynette's reply: "Oh, she's been busy doing a lot of volunteer work, hoping it'll lead to employment. You know it's hard to find a job around here with or without a college education, unless it's fast food."

Two, three, up to four times a week, Lynette either visited Joycina's apartment or joined her for lunch. In the latter case she would have her boyfriend drive her to the county in which Joycina worked. One thing got Joycina's attention about LeVonte. When it was just she and Lynette dining, he never sat with them. He chose instead to pick Lynette up after lunch. However, when Gene attended Joycina in the break, LeVonte made it his business to join in.

Whatever—the more the merrier, Joycina figured. And yet, gradually, she began to get a troubling feeling about Lynette's and LeVonte's motives. She would have done just as well to have suspected Lynette's motives from the beginning.

Here, at May's end, Joycina's parents got a buyer for the house. As planned, the equity was split equally between them. Now, they seemed almost in a race to use the proceeds as a down payment on the new home each selected for purchase. Whether by design or chance, their new residences were located on opposite sides of Feytown's outskirts. The house she grew up in was now formally in the possession of strangers which further depressed Joycina. It made Lynette's visits all the more valuable.

Regarding Joycina, Gene Cornblas was unsure about something. Was he more interested in her as a friend or as a candidate for receiving *new life* via Christian faith? While he had kept his silence on the subject after that first talk, he hadn't dropped it from his thoughts. He had grown to like Joycina quite a lot, still captivated by the apparent shifting of her moods. At one time, she seemed constantly on the verge of tears. At another, like of late, she appeared to enjoy a lighter state.

If she stayed true to pattern she'd be "down" again sooner or later, he lamented. What she needed, determined Cornblas once again, was a stabilizing force in her life. Anyone as friendly and likeable as she, he thought, deserved that much. He wondered if she'd let him visit her, his *Bible* in hand, for a second—hopefully more tolerant—discussion.

On occasion, when Lynette phoned Joycina, she was visiting her cousin, Mac. It was how Mac first found out the two of them were talking again. Through his wife and others, he later discovered what his cousin was really up to. As he had always had a *much-older-brother's* fondness and admiration for Joycina, he wasn't too happy about it. He wasn't, however, sure as to what his response should be, or if, in fact, he should respond at all.

When his three much younger half-sisters and his cousin Lynette were teenagers, he figured "girls will be girls." That was his attitude when he got wind of half-pint intrigues into which they had enmeshed themselves. Back and forth little "character assassinations," he knew, were common at that age. Unfortunately, among a faction of much older Feytowners, it continued to be a favorite sport. It disappointed Mac that his cousin had set her old friend up for a similar "execution."

A number of distortions being spread among the *faithful* in the community *were* veritable stabs in Joycina's back. She abused alcohol and was emaciated from malnutrition and misfortune. She was at the heart of her parents' marital problems. She was evolving into a paranoid recluse on the edge of emotional collapse. So starved for *company* was she that she practically begged Lynette for visitation. So starved for *affection* was she that she shamelessly pursued a white coworker who was probably an atheist. That part, of course, was deduced based on Joycina's known religious position.

Even if true, thought Mac, talk of her ill-fate should not contemptuously be carried about town like that. All this *figurative* violence, he concluded sadly, was being done to Joycina's reputation at his cousin's hand. And, unknowingly, Joycina was providing the ammunition. But circumstances were brewing that would allow Mac to take, at least *some*, action.

On her own, and although she could not explain it, Joycina was becoming a little wary of Lynette. It was just a feeling, and at times she actually attributed it to the steadily declining equilibrium she'd undergone before the bus stop encounter. In short, sometimes she thought her mind was playing tricks, so to speak. Then she noticed a waning in Lynette's calls and visits. Naturally, she wondered if her new hesitant feelings were driving her friend away again. As self blame increased she began to feel panicky, fearful of a return to social alienation.

It was in this state that Joycina assented to Gene Cornblas' request to pay her a friendly coworker's visit. Even when he stated his *religious* co-motive, Joycina was tolerantly accepting of the proposal. Somehow, she felt she could not afford to be turning away a friendly face and offers of a comrade's discourse. She did, however, issue a caveat: He would be allowed to give his best shot at making his ecclesiastical case. After that, religion was a topic off limits for them. For the chance to sit with her in a social visit, Gene happily agreed.

Five workdays later, Joycina sat primly cross-legged on her inexpensive couch behind a coffee table. Across from her Gene occupied a seat pulled from the kitchen. With him he had brought not one but *two* Bibles. The extra holy book was provided so that Joycina could read along with him when he thought it beneficial. Both had been placed on the coffee table and opened to the Book of *Matthew*. What he didn't know yet was that she was about as familiar with the Bible's texts as was he.

When Joycina's clock read 7:12 the telephone rang. It was Lynette on the other end, calling again from her cousin Mac's house.

Lynette:	"Hey, whatcha' doin' girlfriend? Do you know we haven't talked in two weeks? You won't call a sista'. Everything's all right isn't it?"
Joycina:	"Oh, sure, everything's fine. I guess I've been a little busy. Right now, I'm just entertaining."
Lynette:	"Oh, Rochelle or Jr. came by?"
Joycina:	"No, it's actually Gene, from work."
Lynette:	[with jaw dropped] "Huh? Did you say Gene…from work? He's with you…in your apartment…right now?"
Joycina:	"Um-hm. You want to speak to him?"
Lynette:	"…No—uh, yeah. Let me just say 'hi.'"
Gene:	"Hi, Lynette, how are you? …I haven't seen you and LeVonte at the café lately. We miss you."
Lynette:	"Oh, we'll be dropping back by there soon. LeVonte, um, had to get something fixed on his car. Uh, Gene, do you

	mind if I run by there real quick? I won't be long. I just absolutely have to…um, show Joy something."
Gene:	"Mind? No…I mean, that's totally up to Joycina. Here she is--."
Joycina:	"What's up?"
Lynette:	"Gene said he wouldn't mind if I drop by for a second. Can I, please? I just have something, girl, that I *have* to tell you *in person*."
Joycina:	"Sure, Lyn. Gene is just, uh, reading Bible passages to me."

Joycina wasn't sure herself why she added that last revelation. Maybe it was that she wanted to show the innocence of Gene's visit. Or maybe she thought it conveyed evidence that she wasn't the "devil's spawn" everyone thought she was. Whichever of those it was, it didn't work. When they'd hung up, Lynette was practically bursting with malicious excitement.

Lynette:	"Oh, my *God!* Oh, my *God!* She got him up in her apartment—*just the two of 'em!* Oh, my *God!* I knew she'd be sluttin' sooner or later, in her *own place*, with nobody checkin' her out!
	"…Oh, no…Oh, my *God!* …I can't get LeVonte on the phone! How am I gonna' get over there?! I got to get over to Joy's, and *now!*
	"…Mac! Mac, you got to run me over there! …Shayna, let him run me over to Joy's! Please, you just *got* to! I'll baby-sit *for free* next time—*for free!* …Shayna? …Oh, yes, yes, yes! Thank you, baby doll! You know I'm gonna' give you the whole *dirt*, girlfriend—every ounce of it that I see! You're gonna' get it first, before everybody!
	"Oh, *snap*…and guess what! She tried to *front-off* about some *Bible study!*" [laughing loudly]
Shayna:	"Bible study?! What--?
Lynette:	"Yes! She said ol' Gene was up in there reading her the *Bible! Ha-ha-ha-ha-ha!* And Shayna—they probably got a *Bible* with 'em up there to *smoke screen* the *dirt* for any visitors! I'll bet you! I'll bet you! You watch! …Ooooh, this is gonna' be soooo good! …Let's roll out, Mac! …Come on, *cuz*…let's roll!"

In the apartment complex parking lot, Lynette positively insisted that Mac come up with her. "I need you to be my witness to what's going on up there," she advised. "With both of us reportin' the same thing, there ain't no way people will doubt what we're about to be witness to."

Without wasting a second, Lynette was standing outside Joycina's apartment door, knocking. Just as she predicted, Joycina and Gene appeared *to her* to be "fronting-off," or faking, *Bible study*, when she and Mac entered. She couldn't stop smiling at what she thought was the weakest, the shallowest of ruses. When, eventually, Joycina asked what it was she had to tell to her, Lynette had to come with some impromptu gossip. It was so apparently off-the-cuff that Joycina guessed immediately its status as a stand-in reason for her visit.

Nevertheless, Joycina was really glad to see Mac again, just as he was to see her. Mac and Gene were properly introduced, and it was all quite cordial. As was Mac's nature, he couldn't resist making a quip in Joycina's favor: "Which one of you is the *teacher* in this class," he inquired jokingly. He was well aware of Joycina's history of *Bible study* at the church in which she had grown up.

"You'd better come *right* with your presentation, Gene ol' buddy," added Mac playfully. "Joy ain't no stranger to what's in them pages."

While Mac commandeered the *single* seat of the living room suit, Lynette made excuses to re-browse the apartment. She wanted to see "this" again and "that" again, especially in the bedroom.

Finally, Lynette reached her boyfriend, LeVonte on his cell. He'd be by in ten minutes to pick her up. At this point, Lynette did something which she considered an undeniable *tour de force*. Certain that Joycina's Bible-centered visitation was bogus, she set out to subvert what she thought was the real agenda. Execution of her simple plan got underway without delay.

"My cousin, Mac, is smart, too," Lynette informed Joycina and her guest. "He knows all kinds of stuff—don't you, Mac? I'll bet he can tell both y'all some things, even about the Bible, you don't know—can't you Mac?"

"You weren't doing anything at home," she continued. "Shayna's all right 'til you get back. Plus, Mac, you know you don't always find people you can *get your knowledge off* with. I'll bet you and Joy and Gene, together, can talk the *spirit* of *God* right down into the living room."

The sincerity of Joycina's additional urging of Mac to stay and talk surprised Lynette. *Oh, she's a clever one,* Lynette thought to herself. *She'll find a way to get rid of Mac as soon as I leave.*

Then again, that little skinny winch might just scheme to set up something in the future with Mac! God, what a slut!

But it's all right, she resumed in her silence musing. *Mac is my and Shayna's 'mole in the hole.' We'll twist and pull out of Cuz every grain of the mess that goes down this evening, while he's here with that whore and her monger.*

It astounded Mac how conveniently his cousin had arranged for him to inform—against her. Not that he had intentions of telling Joycina all he knew about his cousin's treachery. But at least he was elegantly in position, courtesy of his cousin, to give her some kind of warning or clue. For now, though, he would honor Joycina's request to participate in these apparent Bible talks. Actually, he was honored that she seemed so genuinely eager to have his input.

But, why *the Bible*, he wondered. Practically everyone in Feytown knew of her faithless view of religion. Was this Gene fellow there to be religiously *de*programmed? Or had Joycina somehow become predisposed to backtracking? Although he had kept it to himself, Mac admired all he'd heard about Joycina's "rage" against convention. A few pointed questions, he determined, would disclose just what was "the deal" here tonight.

Mac:	"You got to take what *Nettie* said about me with a grain of salt, y'all. I know a few things but I'm definitely no Bible scholar. So, what is this all about? I mean, are the two of you, like, searchin' for some'em?"
Joycina:	"No, not really. Gene wanted a final chance to convince me that Christian faith can, I guess, make my life richer, or something."
Gene:	"Well, see, a few years ago, I found *peace* with myself, and with the world. And it came through having the faith that Christianity teaches. Finding Christ was the best thing that ever happened to me. Now, every opportunity I get I try to lead people to find what I found. I try to lead them to realize that only in *Christ* can true peace be found. Even more important, belief in *Christ* is the only road to *salvation*. Are you a Christian, Mac?"
Mac:	"Well, let's put it this way.... No. So, unless I'm missing something here, you might want to consider yourself a *polar bear* in the *tropics*. You're with *brown bears*, now—totally out of your element."
	[Turning now to Joycina] "He must not know a whole lot about your situation with the church you used to go to."
Joycina:	[chuckling] "No, we haven't even gotten into that, yet. But, Gene here, is your typical, *fired-up Christian*, just like I used to be."

R.M. Ahmose

[Turning to Gene] "You believe it's your Christian duty to try to bring as many people 'to Christ' as possible. You're that *Good Samaritan* trying to help all *those that you can* be among the *saved*. And you do it while believing what your Bible says: that the number of these is already set, and the identities of the people already established. Like the former *me*, you refuse to see the nonsensical picture before you."

Gene: "Have you…turned away from *Christ*? Obviously, you were once a believer."

Joycina: "I *used* to have *blind* faith. But now I don't. And it's really as simple as that. The three of us sitting here don't really have to do readings from the Bible or get really, really deep into its promises and warnings. A whole lot of energy can be saved in a simple realization: I no longer have blind faith in the Christian Bible or in Christian teachings."

Gene: "I'm sorry, but I just don't understand how anyone could not want *salvation*."

Joycina: "You got to *believe* in it to want it, first and foremost."

Gene: "So, you don't believe *God* has a plan of *salvation* for us."

Joycina: "Here's another thing that is crucial to *get*, if you're going to understand my position. I no longer hold to the Christian interpretation of *God*. There's no *salvation* of the type described in Matthew and Revelations, no 'beast,' or *dragon*, or *devil*, no *sea of fire*. It's all *myth*. … Correction: To *me* it's all myth."

Gene: "Joycina, if you say those things and believe those things, you can't be…*saved*."

Mac: "He doesn't get it. He just…. Man, you're in a *brainwashed* state. You can't see anything other than your *faith*. And you can't see why anyone else *can't* see it. You're just…you're just *programmed*, man. Your mind is *locked down*.

"Listen! Just listen! If someone doesn't believe in that stuff, to them it's all fairy tales and shit. You have to *believe* in it, for it to make sense. You have to *buy into* it, in order to *take stock* in it. Joy is saying, she doesn't *believe* in it anymore, and she owns *no stock* in it! … Gene, my man, stocks are only important to you if you *own* some! Now, you *know* that's right."

Joycina: [chuckling] "I'm sorry, Gene. But, you know—Mac's right. So, just…let it go. Hey, you know what? If I were a Hindu

144

or a Muslim or something, I doubt you'd be so concerned. Yet it would still mean I'm not *into* Christian faith."

Gene: "Maybe—but I'd still believe that *Christ* is the *true* way, the *only* way. In that case, I guess I'd just have to leave it to the *Holy Spirit* to reach out to you, in time."

Mac: "It always kind of amazes me to come across people who're not only convinced that *there's only one way.* More than that, they want *you* to believe what *they* believe. Why ain't it enough that *you* have total faith in *your thing*? Why do you feel that other people need *what you need*?"

Gene: "*Jesus* advises all of us *who believe* to spread the *gospel.*"

Joycina: "He also warned not to feed a *dog* that which is holy or to cast *pearls* in front of *swine.*"

Mac: "Awesome reference, Joy! Gene, my man, you know how you should take that, don't you? Where your gospel is not wanted, you should keep it to yourself."

Joycina: "Christians just pick and choose those Bible passages that suit them, to do their teaching. I know. 'Cause I used to be part of it. But the fact is, for those who believe the Bible, there are a number of *Christ's* quotes that warn against religious arrogance. And I mean the kind that Christians display when they act as if they have a *monopoly on the truth.* Case in point:" [Turning Bible pages]

"Matthew 5:36: '*Don't be so certain of something that you swear on this or that, as you have not created this or that.*'

"Matthew 6:1-4: '*Be mindful of how you do your good deeds, as man is given to hypocrisy.*'

"Matthew 6: 4-8: '*Avoid making a show of your faith— it's between you and God.*'

[Laying the open Bible on the coffee table] "And that's just a few examples. But the main thing, Gene, for you to take away from this is that Christianity is *your* thing. It's *the thing* for those *who have faith in it.* You have no more legitimacy in trying to put it on me than I would have to try to convert you to, say, Buddhism."

Gene: "Well, I guess if you two are just dead set against *salvation--*. So, you have faith in nothing? You don't believe in the *Creator* even?"

Joycina: "Let's just keep it real short and simple. For me, *God* is not the *God* of the Christian faith. Simple as that. I acknowledge existence of *God*. But *that Spirit* has little in common with the *God* of Christians, Muslims and Jews. That's it! End of story! I don't want to get into it any further. Even though I'm not clear in my mind just exactly what *God* is about, I feel certain the agenda or program is radically different from what 'the big three' religions teach."

"Mac: "—And different from what the advocates *claim* they believe, out of fear. Now, I'll tell you something else that amazes me. It's how those of us with roots in slavery in America can still be holding on to the slave-master's faith. I mean...think about that thing. Why would anybody keep the faith of someone who made a slave out of him?"

Gene: "History tells us that not everyone who holds to the faith acts in accordance with its principles."

Mac: "I would say that's the proof that there's nothing *magical* about the faith. It's all about the *people who claim it*. If the *people* holding it are rotten, then in their case, the faith is rotten. If the person is *jive all right*, then the faith is *jive all right*.

" And that leads me to another thing that I've given thought to: I would bet that in most cases where Christianity has done good, it was really the quality of the *people*—regardless of Christianity. And *ditto* that for any other religion."

Gene: "What do you mean?"

Mac: "If you look all around, you'll see *rotten* Christians, *not so rotten* Christians, and *jive all right* Christians. I'll bet you that what makes the difference is the *upbringing*.

"See, look. Suppose Christians of each group had a mark identifying which group he or she was in. I'll bet you the ones that were brought up to respect other people's rights would wind up as the *jive all right* Christians. Those whose upbringing was...a little shaky: the *not-so-rottens*. Spoiled, no decent oversight as children, no guidance, bad guidance, hurt early to the point of becoming mean and mean-spirited—your *rotten Christians* are overflowing with these.

"I'll say it's the *upbringing* that makes the difference among people, regardless of the faith they attach to or whether they even have faith. If I was a world-respected researcher in social science with big-time resources, I'd prove it."

Gene: "Well, here's something: I was, let's say, *wayward* coming up. But I found my calling with the Christian faith. My case would seem to go against your theory of upbringing being more influential than faith. In other words—bad background but 'all right Christian.'"

Mac: "Always, good buddy, as you know, there are exceptions. I'm laying out a kind of *blueprint*, a general *guide* for thought. Now…who knows whether it can actually *be proved*? I think my *upbringing theory* is right on the mark, regardless of the exceptions.

"But then, *let's look* at your case. Who knows? If we could really analyze your upbringing, highlightin' things you ain't even totally aware of, you might fall into the better one of the categories, after all, that I put out there. Your case may fit more neatly in my…*scenario* than you think it does right now."

Gene: "Well, you know, the time has kind of gotten along. I hadn't planned to take up a lot of the evening. I think I've pretty much said what I wanted to say. So, Joycina, I really appreciate you giving me this last opportunity *to present*. You are a most fascinating conversationalist.

"And Mac, I have enjoyed our dialogue also. Your ideas are, at the very least, food for thought."

Mac: "Well I think you're a pretty good guy, Gene. You're a fair-minded listener and a man of your faith. Whoa, look at the time. I'd better be heading home, too. I would like to take a few minutes to run something by Joy, before I go, though."

Joycina: "Gene, thank you for coming by. I enjoyed our talk, too. I hope you have a better understanding of my…way of looking at things. Drive safely, now. I'll see you tomorrow morning."

Mac: [with Gene gone] "I really do have to get home, but I'm glad to get this chance to *buzz* you on something. Now, Nettie, I love her to Mars and back, but--. …*Man*, I don't know how to say this!

"Look, from what I've gathered, this town ain't been very friendly to you, for some time. At *times*, in some *ways*,

	with some *people*, you gotta'...*play your hand*, as they say, 'close to the vest.' You've heard that saying."
Joycina:	[looking thoughtful] "Yeah, I know what it means, Mac. But--. Well, you know what? I won't press you farther on it. It's a *'word to the wise'* thing, right?"
Mac:	"You're right *on* it, Joy. You're right *on* it. One thing about people like you—with *brains*, that is—you *get it* quick. You don't need a long speech and diagrams. Thanks for the snacks and the...what did you call it—ale? ...Alright. I'm out of here. And you take care, too. See ya."

When Mac left, Joycina opened a bottle of wine. She began pondering his sketchy, darkly significant, it seemed, advice. Lynette's company over the last two months had been so welcome, so needed. Even though she had light-heartedly exaggerated the case to Lynette that time, she really *had* feared the advent of some sort of dysfunctional state. But being able to communicate her problems and feelings to Lynette had pushed that dread in the background.

Now, she wondered if, perhaps, she had said too much. Maybe she was overloading Lynette with her issues. Maybe, she thought, that's why Lynette seemed to be backing away a little. Finally, Joycina concluded that she'd just have to lighten up in their talks, be a little less effusive.

It was the following weekend that Joycina decided to give Lynette a call. In her mother's voice upon answering the house phone, Joycina could hear the profound sadness. The news crashed into her consciousness like a wrecking ball. Screaming, "Nooooo!" she could barely keep her hold on the telephone receiver. Lynette had been killed the night before in automobile accident, as a passenger with LeVonte. He was in serious but stable condition.

By now, Joycina's mother and father were residing in their respective residences, with their respective love interests. But upon hearing the trauma in Joycina's voice that weekend in a phone call, Pricilla came right over. Indeed, over the following two weeks, Pricilla and Rochelle took turns staying a night here and there with her. As an additional measure to keep her occupied, Joycina spent several hours visiting with her father. She even stayed over a night with Garvey, Jr.'s family.

The end result of all the time spent with family was that it kept her in a state of some balance. Actually, though, it only *postponed* her failing emotional and spiritual condition. In reality, when it seemed she was "out of the woods," it only reflected surface remediation.

Unfailingly, though, she went to work. She showed up even when it was clear to her supervisor that she needed to return home to rest. While such benevolent dismissals happened only twice, there was, in addition, a trio of close calls. In these Joycina was allowed to work but was treated with deliberate delicacy.

At home, she continued to rely on her favorite alcoholic drink to get her through the evening. Unfortunately, she didn't accompany it with sufficient nourishment. Gradually she began to look sick

"Joy, you need to see a doctor or somebody," remarked Rochelle during a visit. "You don't look good." In reply, Joycina would usually give assurance that she was getting better. "I'm starting to eat more," she would fabricate.

Then there was the downstairs neighbor and the inevitable encounters with her. Try as she might to find a way to avoid Mrs. Haint upon arriving home from work, nothing was reliable.

"Joy, *baby*," Mrs. Haint would say in alarm, meeting Joycina at the building door, "you ain't lookin' yourself. Are you eating enough? My *Lord*, you look as weak as a newborn. Come on in here, *chile*. I just cooked a pot of stew. You come right on in here and eat a bowl. I got juice in the refrigerator and everything.

"Oooh, no—now don't say you ain't hungry, *sugar*. You look like you can hardly stand. I'm go'n call your momma and sister again, if you don't straighten up and start eatin' right. …There you go, *sugar*! Sit right down here and *Momma Jean* go'n fix you a nice big bowl of stew and crackers."

One could say 'the saints,' or something, was with Mrs. Haint the day a burglar broke into her apartment. He had hoisted himself up a few feet and crawled into a side window she usually kept cracked open. As it occurred right around her typical naptime, his access could easily have happened without her detection. That was if she had been at home.

Fortunately, or by *God*'s grace, Mrs. Haint was visiting a relative when the break-in happened. Unfortunately, even though the criminal found a little money to take, he felt compelled toward more evil. Before exiting the apartment and running off, he set it afire.

In due time Garvey, Jr.'s wife, Corynthia, planned to find work. For now, the couple deemed it best that she continue as a stay-at-home mom for another few months. At that time their daughter would be almost three. While she piddled around the house straightening up, a local news update reported a fire at a familiar address. She rushed to call Garvey and he rushed to call his younger sister's cell at work.

"Please let Joycina be at work," Jr. prayed silently. *Thank God*, he thought, when she answered. But his relief was sorely dampened by the report he had to relay.

When Joycina finally arrived at the scene, firemen had thoroughly dowsed the blaze in her building. Mrs. Haint's unit and hers above were completely destroyed. Other, adjoining, apartments had also sustained damage but not to the same extent. So, as Joycina looked on, incredulous, she realized that much of what she owned was gone. Furniture still being paid for, all clothing except the garments she wore, all other belongings beside the Lexus—all was lost. She had put off purchasing renter's insurance one week too late. Still, that same day, she returned to work.

Her boss had allowed her to go home to investigate, to see if it really was her apartment involved. Mrs. Blanche Goodley actually cried with Joycina upon hearing her confirming report. There was no way she was going to *require* that Joycina finish the workday or even *allow* her to, if she had tried to insist. Mrs. Goodley couldn't remember feeling so sad for anyone her entire life. It was a sentiment shared by everyone in her office, especially Gene Cornblas, who took it the hardest.

As she walked out of the office and out of the building altogether, Joycina appeared broken. She thought about her plan for starting school in a few months. That seemed a faint and distant dream now.

She started up her car—but where to go? Joycina decided on a drive to "Jr.'s." In a sort of torpid state she sat with Corynthia, who, feigning grief, tried to get the details of all that was lost. While there, she phoned Rochelle. Quickly, her older sister got permission to leave work early. Her rush was in part to spare Joycina undo time spent—not counting little Asia Mon`e—alone with their sister-in-law.

Compounding Joycina's grief was the idea of having to stay with Rochelle and her live-in boyfriend, Antoine Kayser. He was now a young deacon within a church some nine blocks from *Christ Redemption*. Given to airs of religious pomposity, he always seemed to Joycina to be sort of standoffish. It was as though he felt besmirched by the presence of anyone not tightly associated with a church.

Joycina didn't return to work the rest of the week. She was told by Mrs. Goodley she didn't have to. But in fact it was because she had become too sick to get out of bed in Rochelle's guest bedroom. As was clear, now, Joycina was in pretty bad shape, for her malady was double-edged. Malnourishment was affecting the functioning of her internal organs. Depression had robbed her of the will to eat, even to thrive.

She steadfastly refused to go to a hospital. "I just need rest," she kept saying over and over when pressed. Then she started to make odd demands for family members—those visiting her frequently at Rochelle's—to "find Mrs. Haint."

"She can be found if you try," Joycina would advise. "Go to the apartment rental office. Go to the police! Go to the fire department! Somebody knows how to reach her. You've got to tell her I'm sorry I wasn't home to do something." Of course, the family members tried to tell her she was not at fault. But Joycina kept insisting:

"I would have smelled the smoke if I had been home! And the fire department would have gotten there sooner, put it out before all her things were lost. She tried so hard to help me. I let her down! None of this would probably have happened if I had let her help me. But I tried to duck her. I wonder why I didn't like her. She was the nicest person in the world."

It was that kind of talk and rambling that intensified the family's resolve to have Joycina hospitalized. And it was as if she sensed the collective sentiments. Afterward, Joycina quieted down just enough to ward off forced commitment. She remained, however, in a pitiful state.

Next, came the shift in the family's focus from medical care to *spiritual* care. Indeed it had come naturally given their belief systems. One after the other, the various individuals tried to get Joycina to re-accept *Christ* and *faith* in her life. They tried as a group. At times it almost seemed that a séance was in session, given the *Bibles* and *candles and all* that were present. Mostly, Joycina just stared blankly ahead or turned away.

Something happened, though, that would change Joycina's living arrangement. By now she had lost her job and was a bedroom-to-bathroom recluse. While driving on the highway, Rochelle's boyfriend, Antoine, was violently run off the road by a tractor trailer. Its driver had fallen asleep briefly and lost control of the enormous vehicle.

Even though everyone involved was left, generally, unscathed in the incident, Antoine departed the scene really shaken. He just couldn't help considering that Joycina's presence in his and Rochelle's home might be a cause. In short, their toleration of a *nonbeliever* might, he thought, be stirring wrath from *Heaven* itself. Accordingly, he issued to Rochelle a number of weighty talks.

With no job, no money, no apparent will to do better, Joycina had become quite a burden. On top of that, family members were becoming increasingly convinced that *God* was punishing her. She was relocated to Garvey, Jr.'s home for three days and then sent to a local hospital. The diagnosis *there*: As young as she was, she would die if she didn't somehow increase her will to live.

Now, the issue of medical coverage complicated the matter. Information to the hospital had been *finagled about* to have the expenses carried by her father's insurance. However, she turned twenty-one while in the hospital.

At this point, all the intravenous feeding and other medical amenities would have to come to a screeching halt.

Other matters were brewing in *the hood*, too. Some were clearly related to Joycina's situation, while others were only nebulously pertinent to it. Courtesy of Antoine Kayser, the news of Joycina's precipitous decline spread like wildfire through Feytown. All the ardent churchgoers who had predicted that "it would come to this" gained prestige in their respective churches. Moderate goers prayed a little harder for Joycina and then stepped up their own attendance, as a safeguard. Those whose visits were few or none were numb but also saddened that Joycina could not represent them better as a "fellow" dissident.

Then one hot Sunday morn, there played out a remarkable set of events—right in church. One of Mac's non legal stepchildren made an innocent but damning comment. It was issued quite audibly amid the assemblage of Mac, his wife, Shayna, and four others. Naively recounting events from her memory, the child implicated his wife, Shayna, in acts of infidelity. Pointing toward a man standing alone at a distance, the child remarked: "That's mommy's *other* husband." Suddenly, the beautiful day became symbolically overcast as if by dark, ominous clouds.

In like fashion, the following Sunday morning was warm and sunny, seemly awash in the *spirit* of the Lord. At Christ Redemption Church much of the congregation waited serenely for the end of services. When that time arrived, Sherrel, like others throughout the church, stood listening to some particularly gossipy talk among members.

Much of it started with suppositions of Joycina's impending death. Later, the murmurings speculated that the cost of Joycina's prospective burial would throw her family into financial turmoil. That was assuming they planned to send her off "right." For five minutes Sherrel took in the morbid and unsettling discussions.

Suddenly, another member approached, averting Sherrel's attention. As a matter of pure happenstance, or so it seemed, the talks between the pair turned to employment. From this church member, Sherrel got a "lead" to job opportunity involving a volunteer-to-work arrangement. Stymieing her, however, was a serious transportation issue, as the site was some sixty miles away. If only she could afford a vehicle, she pondered.

Finally, in this cauldron of bubbling exigencies and swirling, intertwining concatenations, Ephesus Caskett toppled into "the mix." At a location centrally fixed, just incidentally, between Joycina's old church and the hospital where she lay, he lurked. Mentally weighing matters keenly, he saw an opportunity to make a deal to get back "his" Lexus.

After days of intravenous and semi forced-feeding in the hospital, Joycina was able to walk out. She did, however, require occasional bracing up by family members as she stepped slowly along. Again, at Rochelle's insistence, it was to her townhome that Joycina was headed. In terms of her mental functioning, she was in a fog. To some extent she actually felt she deserved death. In her hazy state, she considered it a thing both justified and desirable as a release from anguish.

Everything she cherished had seemed one by one to fail—from her affiliation with the church to her relationship with Rahim to, now, her will to live. But even in her fragile, fragmented state of mind she remained defiant, with regard to *blind faith*. In effect, she was choosing death over pretence. Even in her condition, she knew she could never have faith in that which *reason* screamed to her was myth.

Problems continued to mount for Joycina and those around her. First came a significant increase in Rochelle's and Antoine's rent. He surmised it was because the rental office found out they boarded an extra person not on the lease. Next, Rochelle had a reduction in her work hours at the department store. Then, semi-annual automobile insurance premiums came due. For the previous times Joycina had stayed with Rochelle and Antoine, it had cost money to maintain her. These were funds Rochelle pulled from her own savings. By now, those monies were quite diminished as bills lined up impatiently for payment.

It was for these reasons that, when Ephesus came calling with a proposition, the family welcomed his deal. He had heard through "the vine" that Joycina was destitute, and he knew she could use a "g." He was thus prepared to buy back the Lexus for a thousand dollars cash. Indeed, he deemed it a generous offer, all things considered. It was only $500 less than what her father paid him for it.

So, in effect, she had ridden in style for three years on a mere half a "g"—and the cost of several quarts of oil. That was, of course, if she accepted his deal. From his viewpoint, she needed a grand, now, about as much as he needed the fifteen hundred, before. He surmised finally that, in her state, she wouldn't be able to keep up insurance on it, in any case.

With Rochelle's and Antoine's blessing, and Joycina's weak signature, Ephesus had the title changed over. There was not the slightest hint of emotion shown, nor was there a second's hesitation. The younger sister quietly handed over the fifty twenty-dollar-bills to the elder one. Actually, beneath her languid mental functioning, she was glad to be able to give something back.

The very evening after the car-money transfer, Rochelle frantically called all the family to her rented townhouse. She feared Joycina was dying.

Upon arriving they all saw the vacant look in her eyes. They witnessed the resignation in her expression. Regardless of the absence of healthcare coverage, it was decided that she must be rushed to a hospital emergency room.

Some of the family had taken note of a little group of four standing around outside Rochelle's unit among the townhouses. It was as if some sort of *intuition* had compelled them to *stand watch* in front of the residence. Although no one there was aware of it, they were four of the folks Joycina had conversed with at the home of Pauline Piper. Silently they watched as Joycina was being walked to a family member's car for re-transport to the hospital.

As Ephesus had indicated, "the vine" in Feytown, at its best, was an astounding information-transfer phenomenon. Shortly after the Lushas family's arrival at the medical center, a crowd began to form near its front. It was just pass dark in the evening, warm and humid.

In his nine-year-old SUV Mac pulled slowly around the corner where the gathering of people was very slowly increasing in size. The turn put him en route to a destination sixty miles beyond Feytown. Beside him in the front seat, his half sister Sherrel gazed out her window in some astonishment at the spectacle. They glanced at one another a few seconds as if to get agreement on what to do next. Though unspoken, the mutual decision was to park rather than continue on to Skylar County as planned.

Once inside the hospital, Mac and Sherrel took in the pitiful sight. Joycina lay partly in her mother's lap on the small sofa-like chair in the emergency waiting room. Garvey Sr. and Jr. were wiping their eyes occasionally with hands. From reddened eyes, Pricilla cried tears into numerous tissues pulled from a box. The two new arrivals walked to where Joycina lay. In a kneeling posture, with Sherrel standing beside him, Mac called out softly to Joycina. As he and Sherrel identified themselves verbally to her closed eyes, Joycina actually responded.

The space and seats of the emergency room wound around, forming three connected open areas. At Mac's request and the cooperation of other sitting visitors scattered about the room, the family took a new location. They now occupied seats in an end section surrounded by three walls. It was here, in the presence of all the Lushases and their partners and extended family, that Mac and Sherrel engaged dialogue with her old friend. It astonished the family to see the new, faint, spark of life in Joycina's eyes. They had not seen it for weeks.

Mac: "So, you've given up, Joy? That's what I'm hearing."
Joycina: "I'm so tired, Mac. I'm just so tired."

Mac:	"I know you are, Joy. But that's not a reason to give up. It's a reason to take a rest, but it's not a reason to give up."
Joycina:	"I've *been* resting, Mac. But I can't come out of this feeling of being soooo tired—sooo, sooo tired."
Mac:	"You want to know what you're really tired of? …It's the same thing that I'm tired of…and that Sherrel here *has just gotten* tired of. We're all tired of the same thing, Joy."
Joycina:	"Sherrel…Sherrel…you're *tired*…too?"
Sherrel:	[eyes welling with tears] "Yeah, Joy, I…I'm tired of a lot of things--."
Joycina:	"Mac, you're…*tired*…too?"
Mac:	"Yep. I didn't realize *how* tired, until kinda' recently. But I been around a lot longer than you and Sherrel. So, I guess I was able to figure some important things out, before you. I kinda', sorta', a little, let Sherrel *in on* some of it. Sherrel didn't know how tired she was until I explained some things. Tell her, Sherrel."
Sherrel:	"Joy, you can be *sick* and tired and you can be *angry* and tired. I had got *angry* and tired. I turned *mean*, Joy. I was gettin' mean and hateful, and it was startin' to make *me* sick. Angry…tired—and that leads to *sick*."
Joycina:	"What are we tired of, Sherrel? …What are we *tired* of Mac? Are we *tired* of the same thing?"
Mac:	"I think, in our case, yes. We—all three of us—are *tired*, Joy, of trying to *shine* in a community that only burns *five watts*. We're tired of the fact that people *we come to care about* are satisfied to *shine* with just a damned *half watt*.
	"We're tired of people *we care about in the community* walking around with their eyes half closed pretendin' to see things that aren't there. We're tired of presentin' questions to a community that's *distrustful* of questions. We're tired of the *community*, Joy. …We're tired of the damned *community*."
Joycina:	[pausing several seconds] "You mean *Feytown*?"
Sherrel:	"We mean Feytown. I know it's time for me to move on, Joy. I know it is. It's that so many people are locked into one way…."
Mac:	"But what makes it so bad, Joy, is that we have let these people into our hearts, our minds, our beliefs. When you *care* about people—I mean really *care* about people—and find out that they're *zombies* inside, do you know what that

does to you? …Of course, you know. Maybe you know it better than me or Sherrell."

Joycina: "—*Zombies.*"

Sherrel: "Zombies, Joy. As Mac says, there are people who are afraid to think above what they've been taught to think. See… Mac says *cultures* guide us in our growing up. *Culture* makes us fit to live in a society. But some parts of a culture can put a *lock* on your thinking. And guess what, Joy. That's what you were fighting, at church before. You wouldn't let 'em put a *lock* on your thinking."

[Continuing while fighting back tears] "I thought you were wrong, too. I admit it, Joy. I thought you were wrong, too, for fightin' against that *lock*. Like everybody else—well, most everybody—I thought you were going to *hell* when you died. And I *turned against* you and didn't want to be around you.

"But then *my* time came. But, Joy, instead of facing my doubts like you did, I started *acting out*. Sometimes I felt like I hated everybody. That's a bad feeling, too. It eats at you until you do some'em …destructive."

Joycina: "—*Zombies.*"

Mac: "That's a good name for people whose minds are *locked down*, ain't it? It fits people who are afraid to say, even to themselves, 'I'm sorry, but this sounds like bullshit.' *Zombies* are locked-down, scared, can be guided to act like pure fools, and will turn against you in a *humming bird instant*, if you're not another *zombie*."

Joycina: "*Humph.* …You don't hate me anymore, Sherrel?"

Sherrel: [in tears again] "No, Joy. I love you…you are my best friend. You always were my best friend."

Joycina: "We're…*tired*, Sherrel. We—all three of us—are soooo *tired*. …It's *Feytown*, you say? You think that's why we're tired? It's Feytown?"

Mac: "It's Feytown…but only because we cared about the people too much. If we hadn't cared about the people too much, Feytown is like any other town. There are *zombies* everywhere. But you don't want to *love* a *zombie* unless you're another *zombie*. You know what I'm sayin', sista'?"

Joycina: [in almost a whisper] "*Humph…zombies, God!* …'You don't want to *love* a *zombie* unless you're *another zombie.*' I

	could say that over, and over, and over, and over. I sounds so…so simple. And yet--."
Mac:	"Many truths are simple—or *elegant* as they say in *science*—and yet so powerful."
Joycina:	"So…why are there *zombies*, Mac…Sherrel? …Why?"
Mac:	"Really, Joy, I think you already know. People are afraid and they need to belong. Put the two together. Take a mind that's afraid to question and then give it a need *to fit in* or to belong, and you got a 'Z.' You got a Z-man or a Z-woman. Excuse my language but Feytown is *full of Zs.*"
Joycina:	[chuckling] *"Full of Zs. …Full of Zs.* Humph, that is *so* funny. …*God*, how did I get so *bad off?* …I loved a *zombie?*"
Mac:	"You and Sherrel and me—we all loved *too many* zombies in this town. That's why all three of us are *sick and tired* and angry."
Joycina:	"…*God*, I haven't felt hungry for food in sooo long. My stomach--."
Pricilla:	"Joy! Oh, sweetheart! You're hungry? You want something to eat?! Quick, someone get something from the vending machine for her!"
Joycina:	"No, Mommy! Not right now. I need to hear more. … Where is *God*, Mac? Where is *God?*"
Mac:	"I actually think I can answer that. You know I read just about anything I get my hands on that looks good. I will tell you there's proof—kind of—that *God* is…*everywhere.*"
Joycina:	"Right here in this room, Mac?"
Mac:	"Right here in this room. Watch this: I'm lifting this pen and letting it go. …It fell because of *the law of gravity*, as you know. The *law of gravity* is part of *God*. You can name more laws of science than I can. And guess what. They are all expressions of *God*.

"Let me put it like this: *Laws* of the world and the universe are ways that you can 'see' *God*. You don't have to accept *gravity* on *faith*. It's there, and when you get out in space where there's no *gravity*, there's a thousand more laws that are *proof* of *God*." |
| Joycina: | "*God*, I feel *hungry*, Mac! I feel *hungry*, Sherrel. …No, no, no, no, no, no! I don't want anything yet. I want to hear more about *God*! Tell me more about *God*, Mac!" |

Mac:	"Well, *little-sis-number-four*, how about you tell me what you'd like to *know* about *God*, and I'll tell you what I've come up with so far. And remember this: I will never give you an answer that requires you to have *blind faith*. It'll always be something that you can test it for yourself and see it, or feel it or know it—like that ol' *gravity*."
Joycina:	"What do you think *God* wants from people?"
Mac:	"That's an *easy* one. This is what I think and it's simple. *God* would have us learn how to treat one another and to use our minds for critical thinking.
	"...Now, if you want more detail: *God* would have us *practice being honest* and *practice being sincere* and *practice being decent* toward others. We should study and learn whenever it's possible. And *dadgum-it*, we should always struggle against some of the *crap* in our *human nature*, like *going to extremes* and like *having babies carelessly*. How's zat?"
Joycina:	"I want a bag of potato chips! ...And a juice!" [Joycina watched family, and one stranger present, race to the vending machines.]
Sherrel:	"Joy, all those things that were going around—things they said *you said* in church?—I thought about them a lot. I believe, now, that you were...a lot of what you said was *right*. I talked about it with Mac. Mac doesn't believe either that *God* punishes people and *saves* some other people. The Bible is...I don't know...I don't know how to put it--."
Mac:	"It's a book full of old, out-dated ideas and myths, and a few useful ones. It's *old, old* writings that tell of an ancient people's fears and wants and hopes and needs. But its use is timeless, apparently. And I guess that's because people have, basically, the same fears and wants and hopes and needs today as when that stuff was written centuries ago.
	"Now, let me be clear: For those it serves—*more power to 'em*. But *one's religion and belief* should really be a *private* thing, I think.
	"Joy, you *pointed that out* when you referenced a *scripture* the last time I saw you. It's like, for those that believe in the Bible, why don't they pay attention to *Matthew 6:5-8?* Well, I know why church folk don't like to keep it private. It's because they feel more secure in their *belief in the absurd* when they're backed up by a crowd."

Joycina:	[pausing a second from crunching chips and drinking juice] "Why did *God* make us, Mac?"
Mac:	"*He, God,* or *She,* however we want to call it, didn't make us *to burn a portion of us in the center of the earth for an eternity.* I'm as certain of that as I am about those damned... *zombies.* At least the *God* I know didn't make us for that purpose."
Joycina:	"So, why--? Who or *whatever God* is—what was the point of man's creation? Do you know?"
Mac:	"I will say, Joy, that we're here as *part of the universe*—no more no less. We're here for the same reason that *trees* are here. We're here for the same reason the *stars* are out there. We're here as only *part* of *God's* overall work. And, I'll tell you with a hundred percent conviction, none of *God's* creation is singled out for *punishment.*
	"We would never think of *God* as punishing a *tree*—for *acting* like a tree...or the *moon*—for *acting* like the moon. Now church folk will say the difference is that people have a choice in our behavior. I will say that *psychologists* can give us a whole lot to think about, when it comes to that. The more you understand *psychology,* the more you realize this thing of *will* is greatly overestimated.
	"When the pastors say you have *freewill,* they really mean you have the ability to say *what they want to hear you say.* Think about it. Preachers and reverends and pastors don't know what's really in your mind. They don't know what you *do* in private. They just want to *hear you say what they want you to say.* As far as they're concerned, you have the *obligation* to *say* you believe whether you do or not. That's the pastor's definition of *free will.*
Sherrel:	"Yeah, as long as you do that, you're fine...you're *in...* you're in that *saved* 'number,' as far as they're concerned."
Joycina:	"*God,* Sherrel! Aren't you afraid? You're not *afraid* anymore?!"
Sherrel:	"I'm not *brave,* Joy. I'm just *angry and tired*...tired of just *goin' along.* I want to believe in a *God* that don't punish me for wondering and questioning. I want to believe in a *God* that only wants to guide me to be a good person."
Joycina:	"*God,* Sherrel! I could cry! ...I could scream and cry and turn summersaults to hear you sound so...free!"
Sherrel:	"I'm *gettin'* there, Joy. I think I'm *gettin'* there."

Mac:	"Speaking of *free*, Joy—me and Sherrel, we're *leaving* Feytown. We've got clothes and stuff packed in the truck, and we're headin' for Skylar."
Joycina:	"—No, please…*not now!*"
Mac:	"We're all set, Joy. It's all planned. Sherrel's got some'em set up that's gonna' lead to a job there. I got a little money saved. I'm gonna' rent a cheap room until I find a job. Oh, and I did the research. I know the kind of work that's available."
Joycina:	"But…."
Mac:	"I've—how do say—*amassed* a number of skills over the years—*training* in this, *training* in that. You remember how people used to tease me about all those classes I've taken. Well, guess what. I got *certifications*, lil' sis…'mad' certifications. I know I'll be all right."
Sherrel:	"That's right. And we're gonna' look out for each other."
Joycina:	"Where will you live, Sherrel—in a room?"
Sherrel:	"Well, sort of. I'm doing volunteer work at a woman's facility. I already worked it out with them. They'll let me stay in a unit while I work for free at first. I don't have much saved, but like I said: Mac and me—we're gonna' look out for each other."
Joycina:	[speechless and withdrawing]
Sherrel:	[idea-struck] "Oh, my *God*, Joy! Why don't you…*come with us?!* …Mac, can she? I can get Joy put up in the same boarding house where I'll be staying and working! Can she, Mac?! …Joy? You want to come with us?!"
Joycina:	[glancing around at her family] "I…I…."
Mac:	"Joy, this is one of those cases where you'll have to make a quick decision. Me and Sherrel—we're set. We've made up our minds. It's *on*. …Now, when you do a thing like this, you think *fast*, you make the decision, and you *do* it. Who knows how it's *really* gonna' turn out. It's a gamble.
	"Now, we *feel* certain that it's gonna' work out. We got a reasonable plan. But ain't no guarantees. What each of us *does* know is that it's time to get out of Feytown. Now, what you need to decide right now, on your own, is: Is it time for *you* to get out of Feytown?"
Sherrel:	"Joy, you're twenty-one, like me. If you want to come with us, nobody can tell you 'no.' Think about it, Joy. Think about it hard."

Joycina:	"Mommy and Rochelle are crying--."
Mac:	"I feel their pain. It's hard. Life is hard. Making decisions is hard. But we've stayed as long as we can. It's time to go, Joy. We got to be movin' on. ...You know, I believe this is one of those occasions where *it's now or never*. You know what I mean? It's a crossroads."
Sherrel:	"Listen to him, Joy."
Mac:	"You know, Sherrel, this is reminding me of something I read once. The author, I think, was Peter Goldman. See, *Malcolm X* was in Africa and this African leader was giving him advice on what to do next: *'Brother, it is now or never,'* he warned, *'the hour of the knife—the final operation, the break with the past.'* Joy, you got to make a decision. Stay with the past—or cut it loose."
Sherrel:	"Joy, we're leaving. Please, make a decision!"
Joycina:	"...I...I have no money. ...I don't have *anything* anymore!"
Mac:	"Sherrel said it: We'll look out for each other. Joy, with your smarts and education—in no time at all you'll be soaring. You just need a change ...and a new adjustment."
Joycina:	"Mommy, Daddy...Jr.--? Oh, my *dear, dear* Rochelle--. ...I *have* to...I *have* to--. It's *time*! It *must* be time! This has to be where it's always been leading! ...It's *time*! ...I *have* to!"
Mac:	"It looks like you've made up your mind, lil' sis! That's it, walk with us straight forward. Don't turn--."
Pricilla:	[weeping] "Joy--? Joy--?"
Garvey:	[wiping tears] "Oh, my God. I don't know what I should do. I feel like I'm lost. I don't have a clue as to what I, or any of us, should do!"
Rochelle:	[weeping] "I can't look. My God...I'm so torn between emotions--!"
Mac:	"This is not the time to turn, lil' sis. This ain't the time to stop and turn, to look back. Your family understands. They want what's best for you too. But you must keep forward."
Sherrel:	"Mac's right, Joy. Keep forward...don't look back. It's time to *leave* Feytown. It's time for you, just like it's time for us. And don't look back. Walk with us. And don't look back. If you look back, you may not be able to continue. Just walk with us...walk with us...that's it...walk with us. And don't look back."

Outside the hospital, the streets showed scattered clusters of Feytown's typically "silent agnostics." Drawn to the locale by word of mouth reports of Joycina's impeding demise, they waited to get the official word. Without prior planning, without prior intention, without organization—just spontaneously—they followed an *inner* call. Each had collected whatever monies were available to them, to start up, and add to, a burial fund. Amazingly every member of the sedately mournful, milling crowd had been driven by the same idea.

So certain they were, that the Lushases would emerge from the hospital having left Joycina at death's door. They actually gasped when they saw her exit the hospital's electronic doors, one weak step at a time. At her sides, right and left, were Mac and Sherrel, each firmly holding a hand.

The trio looked upon the erratically-spaced sprinklings of Feytown's religiously cynical, skeptical, and unsure. They were those of least stature in the community. But they appeared somehow as a small sea of strangely, enigmatically, *enlightened* cohorts. Gazing upon the image of, figuratively speaking, *the walking dead*, they became quietly infused with the energy of an ocean wave.

A number of them lost what little inhibitions of expression they had and cheered loudly. Many others chimed in with slightly more reservation. Someone walking innocently upon the scene might have thought the excitement was being driven by sightings of a celebrity, or a miracle.

When she was finally able to acknowledge that all the hoopla was for her, Joycina nearly lost her footing. Fortunately her escorts kept her impelling forward. Collectively, though, the three felt as though they were in the middle of scenes being played out on a movie set. It was at once surreal, enchanting, bordering on *unbelievable*. From the hospital entrance, the Lushases eyed the same spectacle with a mixture of heavily mournful amazement.

Engaging the crowd with welcome discourse, Mac revealed that Joycina was joining Sherrel and him in leaving Feytown. He spoke of how relocation was going to facilitate, indeed make possible, her recovery. She would transform in the manner of the legendary *phoenix*, while in a new environment.

In her state of deep gratitude—and continued shock—Joycina could only acknowledge the throng with frail utterances. Weakly, she called out names she knew belonged to the smiling faces vying for her attention. Almost mesmerized, the gathering of "witnesses" watched as Joycina was gently helped into the SUV front seat. Taking their places at either side of her, Mac and Sherrel pressed buttons that lowered the windows of the vehicle. This way, as many as possible could stand around and voice their well wishes.

But members of the crowd saw another usefulness of the opened windows. Throughout the vehicles' back areas were stacks of luggage and boxes of other belongings. But also there were spaces in which to toss paper currency. It was money individuals had gathered to offset Joycina's funereal expenses. These they deposited into the SUV windows as nobly as they might, if paying tithes at church.

The sight of Joycina's and Sherrel's eyes, all full of tears, spoke much to the witnesses. From it they perceived this evening all that might have been *stated*, in another situation, *with words*. When the final witness had rendered the final alms, the crowd stood back, as if it had been arranged *a priori*. Amid waves and cheers, Mac pulled off slowly, disappearing from view down the long street.

In preparing for the present adventure, Sherrel managed to secure an importance alliance. It concerned a sort of telephone-rapport established between her and the woman to supervise her *volunteer-to-work* activities in Skylar. Mrs. Swann had seemed delighted at the prospect of finally meeting and training her new volunteer. In talks with Joycina earlier at the hospital Sherrel felt certain of her friend's future welcome status at the facility.

For official confirmation of the latter, Sherrel gently dialed her cell, as she and her companions traveled toward Skylar County. Sherrel had been given the supervisor's home number to call. It was in the event that anything out of the ordinary cropped up before, or during, travel to the women's shelter. In the brief talk, Mrs. Swann provided hoped-for assurance to her soon-to-be protégé. Regarding Joycina's impending arrival, she offered this heartening confirmation: "That's what the facility is for. We'll have her strong again before you know it."

Bracing sidewise against Sherrel, Joycina was close to entering a sleep of exhaustion. It came both from her physical state and the excitement of the recent events.

Slowly and carefully, Mac had driven about half the distance to his troupe's destination. The ride was smooth, the road clear, and the night scenery tranquil. At length, Sherrel reached to turn down the music playing. It was in response to Joycina entering suddenly into a drowsy and winsome dialogue.

Joycina: "I never looked back, Sherrel. I did just like you and Mac said."

Sherrel:	"You did good. Looking back would have made it so much harder."
Joycina:	"I didn't tell Mommy and Daddy and Rochelle and Jr. I'd be back to see them when I'm strong again. ...Do you think they know?"
Sherrel:	"Oh, absolutely. I'm sure they know you left to save your *life*—to get your life back. Once you're strong again, they know you'll come back to see them. And before that, they know you'll keep in touch—just like I will with my family.
	"They took it hard, but they had to figure they weren't in position to try to stop you. They saw you slipping away, Joy, before Mac and I arrived. Which do you think was harder for them—watching you slip away or watching you *walk* away? I felt terrible for them. But I think they realized that you were saving your life in walking away."

Joycina could feel her eyes misting as she reflected on the voices of her family, calling to her. At length, she deemed it too painful to dwell on. Accordingly, she searched her mind for an alternate topic upon which to focus.

Joycina:	"That vending machine sandwich you brought with us from the hospital was the *best I ever had*. One of the finest things in life is to have something good to eat when you're starving."
Sherrel:	"Your appetite is coming back big. That is just so *awesome*, Joy. You'll be your old self in no time, as you keep with it."
Joycina:	"All those beautiful, wonderful people: Countess...Phese... Isaiah...Felicia...Jazmin...Darryl Frisky...Daryl Smoots... Danzel ... Makeba...Dyemond...Quantae...Prettia... Treka ...Dawn-Rae...*Miss Pauline!*... Samantha...Sonja... *Mr. Trodden!*...Swareena...Markees... Malaysia...*Mr. Discart and Ms. Losley!*... Teneia...Kemon...Royleigh... Toni...Twakya...B-Boy...Tywaan... Corey... more who I only know by face--."
Mac:	"That really was *something* back there! *Wild*—I never saw anything like it. No tellin' how much money they all threw in the back. You thanked as many of 'em by name as you could, too. They appreciated that."
Joycina:	"What's your real name, Mac? I've never known you by anything but Mac. Is that it?"

Mac:	"You don't want to know. It's crazy. I don't know *what* my mother was thinkin'."
Sherrel:	"It's *Macintosh*, Joy."
Joycina:	"Macintosh?"
Mac:	"Yeah, bad as it gets, ain't it? That coulda' had people callin' me 'apple-head' or some'em. Of course, most of 'em in the hood don't know nothin' 'bout *Macintosh apples*. That's what probably saved me."
Joycina:	[reflecting] "Something Pastor Posson said to me just came back all of a sudden."
Sherrel:	"Oh, yeah? What is it?"
Joycina:	"We were talking about blind faith. He said if we *lose* faith in *one* thing, we have to, and will, *replace* it with something *else*. I know he was saying that the thing we replace it with will likely be bad. …Do you think that's true?"
Mac:	"I wouldn't say the pastor was *off in the woods* somewhere on it. But I don't see him as the *end-all* of wisdom, either. Here's how I see it, and here's how I explained it to Sherrel when we talked about it: "First off, I think Posson was referrin' to the, uh, how should I say, *principles* we take up with. See, we live by *principles* of some sort or another. You can live by a principle of *greed*. You can live by a principle of being an *opportunist*. There's a principle of *ruthlessness* to live by. "People can *conform* to this or that as a *matter* of *principle*. We can *submit to power* as a *principle* of survival or gettin' ahead. There are all kinds of *principles* to live by—constantly or just *periodically,* when it's convenient or beneficial."
Sherrel:	"Mac and me—we talked about a set of *principles* to test where *God* is comin' from. Like to help us figure out what *God* is about—we came up with our principles *to test*, sort of."
Joycina:	"I want to hear them."
Mac:	"Well, there are seven principles that I put together—and with Sherrel's input. The goal, you see, is to shed light on us as *humans*, to clarify, sort of, what we're about. We think that when you clarify what us humans are about, you kinda' clarify what *God* is about, sort of."
Joycina:	"Okay…."

Mac: "Look, this is the thing, Joy: Other than in our brains, there's no real difference between us and animals."

Joycina: "I remember you saying that before."

Mac: "Right. So, we need to figure out what's in our brains or minds that point to what we are, *in the real*. The seven I live by, and test by looking back over results, have the power to make a more settled person. They have the power to make us behave more humanely and *less* animalistic.

                "Now, let's say we test these principles and find that they are effective. Guess what. I say in that case we then have *insight* into *God*. Why?—because *God* made all the principles and laws of the universe. I think you can tell a lot about the *designer* by looking at the *design*."

Sherrel: "We believe God has set *principles* for us to live by that are not written in any book. They are to be discovered through a sincere search by each person. And it's no different than when people search to discover *other* laws of the universe. Remember Mac's *gravity* reference at the hospital, Joy?"

Joycina: "Oh…yes…. So, you say you have *seven* of them…those *principles*…."

Mac: "Sure do. One, *God* **is** the universe and makes all the *laws* and *principles* that rule it. Now, for us *humans*, *God* sets up an *ideal* or *design-model* for us to live by. When we've been raised right, we act in accord with that design. And, Joy, the design *model* is a simple one. It's the same one that the Bible calls the Golden Rule. Those of us who were lucky enough to be *raised right* know it and do."

Joycina remembered Mac's talk at her apartment on the influence of child rearing on the quality of one's Christian *spirit*.

Mac: [continuing] "Two, because of limits in our intelligence and foresight, we have to be careful about overly accepting our own *interpretations of events*. You might call it the *principle of avoiding arrogance*. I can talk more on it later when we have time to get deeper into it. For now, I'm moving to the next *principle*.

                "Three, even though our *interpretations* of what events *mean* in the *long run* are usually off, that's not true about our *general impressions*. We can have very accurate *impressions*, in the *immediate*, without having *dead-on* accurate, long term interpretations.

"Four, we *can not* always trust our *wants*. Believing we can't *trust* our *wants*, though, don't do a damned thing, unfortunately, to *stop* our wants. We're always going to *want* this and that and the other. But we should learn to be *distrustful* of our wants. Guess what: I'd say, more often than not, gettin' what we *want* turns out, some *how* some *way*, to be not so good for some *other* person. And I know from experience it often turns out to be not so good for the 'wanter,' him or her self. Now, the *up-side* of being a continual 'wanter' is that our wants sometimes guide us to what is right.

"Five, *discipline* is essential to living a life that's good for everybody concerned. I'll just leave it at that for now since that one's kind of obvious and easy to see.

"Six, in this life, each person has a guidance system in place. Some might call it a *guiding spirit*. Others might say a *guardian angel*. But whatever or whoever it is, it only activates when we settle into a 'right' disposition and attitude. In short, we practice treating people the way we want to be treated and we will be *guided* in a way that we will actually *see* and *feel*.

"Now, a word of *warning* about always treating people the way we want to be treated--. That's to be done only until the 'other' person proves *undeniably unworthy* of that treatment. For example, if somebody is deliberately and evilly trying to hurt you in some way, the 'deal' is 'off.' And I mean *big time*."

Sherrel: "Let me do the last one, Mac. ...Okay, *Seven* is realizing that practicing the previous *six* brings us more in line with the *spiritual law* that *God* set for us—that is, God's *design* for us humans that we talked about

" In general, though, Joy, we want to keep in mind that *God* sets the laws of the universe. *God* has a set of *laws* for planets and stars *in space* and we think a set of *laws* also for humans. We have to learn how to treat one another, though, to be *in line* with God's *design* for us."

Mac: "*A-men, sista'*. And I'd like to add to that that we don't believe that God *personally* punishes man for his *out-of-*

line behavior. No—each person's breaking of God's *design-law for man* is what gets him his *just desserts.*

"God's laws are set. Bend 'em, break 'em, step on 'em, or try to disregard 'em and it'll be like steppin' off a cliff. It'll take a little while to hit land. But when we do, we'll know that we've had a '*hard*' encounter.

"Now, you say Pastor Posson warned that if you give up one thing, you'll replace it with another, good or bad. I say replacing *blind faith* with *principles* you can *see* and *hear* and *touch* and *feel* and *taste* in your everyday experience is a good thing—a *real* good thing. *God's* law is there for everybody to experience and know. And that's whether they can read or not."

As so described, the three companions rode along the highway burning the miles and passing the evening. In their hearts was some feeling of uncertainty about their futures. But it was somehow an *exhilarating* uncertainty. The feeling might be compared to emotions that came with a common entertainment feature in amusement parks of old. In cautiously ambling through a dark and spooky "Fun House," one is aware of scary surprises likely to "pop up." But all the while, adventurers know they will be safely returning to the light of day outside, in due time.

It is now six years pass Mac's and Sherrel's and Joycina's move out of Feytown. By and by within that period, the remaining members of the Lushas family moved outside of the community, too. Pricilla and Garvey each found a new-*er* love-interest. Subsequently each settled comfortably with her and his new mate in their respective new digs. Rochelle and Antoine eventually married and had two children. Included in the happy arrangement was a comfortable mortgage in Holy Oak County. Adding to their image of middleclass bliss was "Rusty." That's the family's lovable pet golden retriever, "adopted" as a puppy from an animal shelter.

Little Asia Monet was provided two other siblings, courtesy of Garvey, Jr. and Corynthia. Always the two had had a sort of comfortable understanding of one another. They grew even closer as the years increased. Also in that period, Jr. was able to secure the position of car repair *shop manager*. During good times, he's charged with overseeing operations in four repair franchises.

Near the end of those same six years, and with some college courses, Sherrel became an assistant executive within a *family-aid* agency. The building of her employment is an impressive twelve-story edifice, boasting fifty offices. In addition to charitable organizations, it encloses myriad family-counseling and family-advocacy help sites. By all accounts Sherrel loves the busy workday and the salary that comes with the job. Not far from her office building is the youth group home where she provides consultation services.

Mac, in those half dozen years eventually partnered with an employer who initially brought him in at ground level. The venture developed from Mac sharing his ideas on how the business could be expanded. Risking his own savings, in addition to acquiring a government sponsored *small businessman's loan,* he bought into the company. He has become quite successful as an office-furniture design consultant. Due largely to his initiatives, the company's office-furniture *supply* branch of operations has also flourished.

And finally—Joycina. Yes, she completed the additional two years of study in *computer/ electronics programming and engineering* for which she had earlier planned. Later, another year's training became available, this time in a more highly specialized area of the field. Weeks before her twenty-seventh birthday, Joycina was offered a job—in India. Starting with a six-figure annual salary, she joined a select group who explores new areas in creating computer-generated movie special effects. This, in turn, has led to lucrative contracts with film production companies around the world.

Every now and again she flies her family to India to vacation and spend valued times with her. Mac and Sherrel, however, get that same invitation *every* year.

Joycina has a second practice she engages in…well, religiously. In it, she keeps track of locations for a certain group of thirty-seven. *Once* every three years, at varying times of the year, they each receive a check in the mail. Her plan is to do this for a total of nine years. The remittance for each: *one thousand, four hundred eighty-four dollars.* That was the amount Mac and Sherrel counted in the back of his SUV that special night that Joycina was *saved.*

Psychotherapy and Desserts

From the side of her eyes the young woman surveyed the corridor's length to her left. The assessment was quite indistinct, though, for two reasons. First, the man standing near with a gun at her side partly blocked her view. Second, she dared not turn her head for a better line of sight. That would have violated her promise to follow the man's instructions to the letter. Still, she hoped desperately to catch a faint image of someone in the distance appearing suddenly to witness to the scene.

Nervously placing the key in the bathroom lock, she knew that in seconds its door would be open. Once, as agreed, she began walking slowly inside, she could not be certain the man would keep his end of their bargain.

There. The door was unlocked and set ajar, and she felt the gun barrel press harder against her ribs. According to plan she handed over the key set, over her shoulder. It was then that the man pushed her inside the large restroom.

Just a few blocks away, a far less distressing situation was evolving. The scene: a small deli and café; within, the store owner became suddenly immersed in baseless unease. Yet, the feeling was so real it was hard to dismiss as fantasy. Thoughts running concurrent with his anxiety concerned a woman with whom he felt himself to be in love, at a distance. It was of two outcomes that his odd sentiments "spoke." Mutually exclusive, only one of them could be realized, so he reasoned.

His feeling on the one hand was that he'd be given the opportunity to gamble with romance. In the venture he would defy his natural tendency toward reservation in social situations with American women. Here, he would go *all out* to win the heart of his secret love. But, then, there was the opposite possibility wherein he accepted, totally, the status of his secret love as an unattainable dream. In this scenario, she would remain a heaven-sent delicacy only to be admired from afar. As common logic suggested, a *coming to pass* of either one of those possibilities negated occurrence of the other.

But perhaps the story should rewind a little before proceeding. Following that course, it starts anew an arbitrarily-chosen few hours prior. This change underscores the significance of time and may compel a pondering of its somewhat elusive yet all-influential nature.

Consider that, for any set of events, how it is interpreted depends upon the *start-point* of examination. Of course, *interpretation* of events and the *emotions* evoked are often two very different phenomena. So, here, it is perhaps wise to be reminded that only in fairy tales are *happy* endings more or less guaranteed. That which follows is patently not in keeping with the typical storyline of children's books.

On this day, the Blyne Institute for Cementing Healthy Minds (BICHM) steered toward noon in its usual manner. The center was the proverbial "tight ship," its staff performing duties with the harmony and precision of navigation-clock parts. Within the structure toiled a distinguished group of professionals: six psychologists including the center's director, a psychiatrist, and two psychiatric nurses. Also rendering services important to operations were clerical staff and two practicum students.

While some thought the clinic's *title* a bit overstated with regard to its small size, the facility did provide a valuable service to the community. So far, this particular Wednesday was no exception. Within those cool concrete walls, the clinical *atmosphere* was of the same "*air*" to be sensed within a mental health facility *four times* Blyne's size. It practically reeked of therapy, rehabilitation and cure.

Serving residents within a two-mile radius, the center had been in quiet operation for 57 years. In a little blacktop lot it sat, sedate, unassuming, and unadvertised, seeming to shy away from attention by passersby. Builders, and particularly renovators, had more in mind for the building's *interior*, however. Thus, even while blandness characterized the building's façade, its *inside* was sedately pleasing to the eye. From the quiet maze of corridors to the serene hues and patterns adorning the walls, its inner areas reflected intent to induce calm. In addition, it possessed ample roominess that would not be estimated from an outside inspection.

Spaciousness, attractiveness and tactile comfort were conditions the staff had become accustomed to. Year-round, the center maintained a temperature of about seventy-five degrees. Walls were kept freshly painted or papered. Commodious counseling offices were carpeted throughout, even within walk-in sized closets. Each was provided a localized thermostat to indulge individual preferences. These, however, were rarely used. Although only half the rooms had windows, they all could boast an effective and efficient air circulation system.

Dr. Mae-Ellen West, the center's director, always saw fewer client/patients than the other staff. This morning, she had listened empathically to the troubles of only two—an approximate fifty minutes each. That was the standard duration, session-wise, for all the counseling staff. For the rest of her time, Dr. West attended a plethora of administrative matters.

At least one day a week, though, when she wasn't engaging either task described, she slipped away to be with one or another paramour. At thirty-three, she had already been married eleven years, her twelfth anniversary just a few months away. The union somehow hit a bland spot about midway and left her feeling unfulfilled. Still, a largely unhappy marriage and three resultant children—ages six, eight and ten—did little to undo her physical attractiveness. Dr. West had a sultriness about her that was matched only by her highly professional demeanor.

Without taking a formal break, by 11:30 each of the staff psychologists was seeing the fourth client for the day. Even the practicum student, Kaye Spritey, who came in around nine was attending her third so far. She was thus, herself, *one up*, so to speak, on the director. As for Spritey's student cohort, he had been assigned non-counseling duties for the morning hours.

The time was now 11:46 and six members of the counseling staff were all privately navigating their respective sessions toward termination. For her part, Dr. West was preparing the conference room for "noonish" occupancy by her staff—minus the two students. There were important matters to discuss. That lunch would be delayed an hour was just a fact of life sometimes at Blyne.

An unusual condition was set, however, with regard to the meeting. It was that one of the regulars, psychologist Nathan Fletcher, would not be present. Only three or four times in a year was a counselor saddled with a noon-time "assignment." Usually, it corresponded with the clinic's aim to accommodate difficult and uncommon circumstances of those they served. This was one of those times for Fletcher. The client in question needed a "lunch hour" session to avoid missing time on a job with low tolerance for absences.

Now, typically, when one of the counseling staff was unavailable for a staff meeting, it was rescheduled. Yet, Fletcher's 12:00 appointment wasn't sufficient in this case to warrant putting off the gathering. But then, due to the topic to be discussed in this particular case, his absence was quite appropriate.

The newer of the two practicum students was assigned to help with *in-takes* this day. Arriving at just before ten, Mickey Duncino had the task of interviewing walk-ins. From these he took, and logged, pertinent demographic information. He also summarized the main issues reported by each, for review by the director. In between these duties, he steered "appointments" to their office destinations within the complex.

It was the latter that he fulfilled when Nathan Fletcher's 12:00 appointment walked in at 11:55. The client was twenty-five year old, Mark Cuzdorf. Mandated by the courts to attend substance abuse and anger-management counseling, Cuzdorf arrived in a solemn and somewhat testy mood.

"Alright, Mr. Cuzdorf," stated the young practicum student pleasantly, "everything's all set. We've got you logged in and Mr. Fletcher is expecting you. I'll just need to make sure he's completed his last session before taking you to him. So, if you'll just have a seat right over there while I check a few things, we'll have you in session in no time."

Duncino glanced down at the appointments roster just as he heard footsteps in the corridor to his left. Looking upward he noted the graceful strides of his fellow practicum student. The auxiliary office used on Wednesdays by Kaye Spritey was next to Mr. Fletcher's. Duncino's inquiry was based on that fact.

"Kaye, do you know if Mr. Fletcher has discharged his eleven o'clock?" Duncino's eyes scanned again Fletcher's morning appointment sign-ins: *Lester Faltline, Lorna N. Shipping, Andy Jay Pratt, Fleety Lee Waco.*

"I think," responded Spritey, "I heard him leave at about a quarter of. It's almost twelve now." She stopped in front of the desk behind which Duncino worked. In an automatic gesture she shifted her gaze briefly at Cuzdorf. With her, his appearance registered a favorable assessment. Spritey then resumed her discourse. "Mr. Fletcher's always diligent about having at least ten minutes in between sessions."

"How was his door set when you walked pass just now?" Duncino's question reflected his knowledge of Nathan Fletcher's patterns. A closed door meant he was in session. If half open, it suggested that Fletcher awaited his next client as he read or scribbled notes.

"It was open a ways," Spritey answered. "And I didn't hear any voices." The twenty-two-year- old master's level student leaned discretely forward to speak more intimately to Duncino:

"Knowing the mood he's likely to be in," she whispered, "I wouldn't send his noon appointment in late."

With that caveat, Duncino beseeched the newly arrived Cuzdorf to follow him. When he could see that Fletcher's office door was wide open, Duncino knew it could be a gesture of the therapist's intolerance of a late client arrival. To make coworkers aware of his dislikes, Fletcher paired certain manipulations of objects in his environment with a stern facial expression. In that way, he could communicate misgivings—at a distance— by the way he left items situated.

"Mr. Fletcher has all your paperwork," stated Duncino standing beside the doorway. "And, look, it's exactly 12:00." He had uttered the latter loudly to apprize the psychologist inside. "You are *perfectly on time.*"

When Cuzdorf entered the office, Fletcher was standing at one side of the big desk with arms folded. He almost seemed prepared for confrontation. A little put off by what he perceived as faint traces of a scowl by his therapist, Cuzdorf reacted:

"Your *lunch date* is here," he reported sarcastically. "Mark Cuzdorf… the man Judge Gish wants you to turn into a freakin' *choir boy.* Maybe you'd like to run and make a plea to your boss to have me transferred to somebody else."

"Well, Mr. …Cuzdorf, if you'll be so kind as to push the door to, and take a seat, we'll see what can be done." Fletcher seemed to think it was in his best interest to soften his approach.

Standing once again at the check-in desk for arriving appointments, Duncino addressed his "student colleague." Spritey had been standing nearby awaiting his return. "Now I just need to let Dr. West know I'm leaving for lunch," he said, "so she can get one of the *clerical* ladies to stand in."

"They're all still milling about in the conference room," informed Spritey. "You'd better hurry before they get started. I'll be waiting for you in the foyer."

This was Kaye Spritey's second and final semester of putting in two days a week at the Blyne "institute." By now, she moved about with ease and confidence. Not only did she know the center's operation fairly well but also the at-work personalities of the staff.

This being Duncino's first practicum experience there, Kaye sort of took him under her wing. A year her junior, Mickey was like a younger brother. In fact he actually did remind her of the eldest of her three male siblings, all of whom were younger than she.

When Duncino returned, the two headed lithely for the entrance door and into the March chill. Walking the two long, serene rural blocks to Commerce Street, the students talked about matters at the center. It was their custom to do so whenever they had ample time. Trekking to have lunch at a favorite eatery on Commerce provided that juncture.

"I notice we didn't get invited to *this* meeting," announced Duncino. "I guess it's because of the *noon* timing?"

"Well—*that* and the fact that they're having the meeting for the sole purpose of *discussing Mr. Fletcher.*" As she spoke, the natural sway in Spritey's walk was lessened by her sort of bracing against the cold in her tan, virgin-wool overcoat.

"They're having a meeting *about* him at a time he can't attend? Damn, that seems a little foul."

Spritey cast a pretty smile forward. "Wait until you've been there awhile. You'll see a lot of crazy shit that goes on."

"I know. You always tell me that. So far, though, they just seem like regular people. Of course, that Mr. Fletcher--."

"Well," resumed Spritey, "you're just scratching the surface now. But you'll start to see things, in time. Mr. Fletcher's just a more *outward* case."

"So, what's the big deal with him today? What's he done that justifies this kind of...*behind-Caesar's-back*, secret meeting of the *Roman senate?*"

"Well," uttered Spritey in a dramatic sigh, "from what I understand, Dr. West has been getting complaints about him from some of his clients."

"Whoa! That's not good," Duncino remarked, hurrying across a street with Spritey, several yards ahead of a slow moving vehicle.

"You're damned right that's not good. People you're there to help complaining that you're being *mean* to them? Imagine a *mean counselor.* What a paradox. I mean how *sub prime* can you be?"

"Yeah, that's some bad shit, alright. But why do you think Dr. West doesn't just talk to Mr. Fletcher in private about it? I mean, that would be the standard--."

"They *say*...she *has*," answered Spritey with a mischievous grin, looking sidewise at Duncino. "But—and I don't know if you've noticed or not—but Mr. Fletcher can be sort of a...*snippy snot-head*, when he wants to be."

"He comes off a little vain. I noticed that much," reflected Duncino. "The office you use on Wednesdays is right next to his. You ever hear anything sort of...*wild* from him?"

Spritey thought on it. "No. The walls are I guess acoustically designed to keep the sessions private. But if what they're saying is right about him, I'd give a couple of *twenties* to hear him at his worst." The pair was now walking the half block down Commerce to "their" restaurant.

"Can you imagine talking even slightly abusively to clients?" Spritey asked. Her expression was one of incredulity.

Duncino snickered, shaking his head. Spontaneously, he went into a mock dialogue, simulating an *imaginary* exchange with a BICHM client. *"'But sir, I have the same bad dream every night.' ...'Oh, yeah? Try this: Lay off the raw-fucking-pepperonis before bed, you moron.'"*

The pair laughed fully. Thinking up other fictional and bizarre counseling exchanges, each seemed to them funnier than the last. A final one conjured by Spritey was equally irreverent: *"'Sir, my boyfriend is terribly abusive.' 'Probably fucking justified, too—based my impression. ...Ya' bird-face, ya'!'"*

Leona Fletcher wept on the phone as she talked to her sixty-seven year old mother. Married to psychologist, Nathan Fletcher, for twenty-five years, she saw divorce looming before her. Regrettably, its advent would mean a total restructuring of her life, the prospect of which she found dreadful. Nathan had made clear his intention not to be generous, nor even gracious, in dividing their assets, consequent to the legal split.

With sympathy, the elder woman listened to her offspring, the "middle child" among Matti Pepper's three. *What had gone wrong*, she wondered, feeling the depth of her daughter's pain. The question didn't concern Leona's marriage. Instead, it referenced the younger woman's history of emotional fragility.

Even as a child, Leona *Pepper* found difficulty in representing herself before others with resolve and vigor. In short she was a diffident youngster who moved through life avoiding confrontations at all costs. Once married, Leona exhausted her conciliatory skills, trying to please her husband.

To her credit, sort of, her appeasements sufficed for a score-and-some years, exceeding the duration of many, less one-sided, matrimonial unions. In the end, though, Nathan finally found justification for wanting to divorce the woman who put him above all matters except their children. He was in love with another woman.

Leona tried to relate her great dismay to *Mother Matti*: "Why, Mother, *why?!* I've done everything I could possibly, *humanly*, do! It's almost as if he waited until Lisa's college graduation to start this all up. Now he's saying it's over! It's not fair. I can't go through divorce—I've told Nate this time and time and time again, over and over. He knows I can't...I don't want to live...divorced."

"Leona, honey, I guess...it just seems like...I would say...."

"What is *wrong* with me, Mother? Why am I unable to keep my marriage together? I tried so hard—you know I did. I always gave in when

Nate and I disagreed. It kept us together, and I didn't mind. Nate's a smart man. His decisions were never really, *really* bad, so I didn't mind letting him have his way most of the time. And it kept us together.

"Twenty-five years, Mother. Twenty-five years of raising Nate, Jr., and Kimmy, and Lisa and sending them all to college—and now he wants to end it.

"*Twenty-five*, Mother! We have all those years of establishing a good life, good patterns, good routines—a comfortable life together! I know we were happy. I did everything I could think of to make sure Nate had a tranquil, comfortable life with me. And now--. It's just not fair, Mother. It's just not fair!"

Behind the heavy mahogany desk Fletcher had taken his seat, facing the smirking face before him. His grayish peppered suit had clearly seen a lot of wear. Showing beneath, his shirt also suffered fabric fatigue and was a dulled version of its former white. There appeared a bit of strain in Fletcher's eyes and cast-of-face. But his smile was one of someone determined to meet a task. It required his best version of the all-important *initial session* with an obviously "resistant" client.

Periodically, he glanced down to peruse the report describing Mark Cuzdorf's profile and circumstance. It was during one of these instances that Cuzdorf broke the brief silence with his own commentary:

"It looks like that suit you're wearing has seen better days. What's up? The *psychoanalyst* business is in a recession like the economy?"

"It says here, Mark, that you have some substance abuse issues. Do you want to tell me a little about that?" Fletcher resumed eye-contact with the client trying to maintain a serene expression.

"Hell no. But, I guess to get through this *court-ordered* bullshit I have to be cooperative. Look, I smoke a little *weed* and drink a little beer. What the hell's the big deal?"

"Well…that …*weed* is illegal maybe?" responded Fletcher.

"Yeah? Well, beer's not illegal. The damned judge has got a problem with that, too."

"How much of it do you consume and how do you act, kind of, afterward?"

"Look, you got the paperwork right there. You know what's up. I do a little *ass-kicking* when I'm 'hopped' up. Get it—*hops*, beer…."

"I get it. That's pretty funny," Fletcher allowed. "But, fighting as a result of intoxication isn't. My son was injured badly in a violent attack by a drunk."

Cuzdorf, sneering, seemed to be weighing his planned remark for degree of inappropriateness. Then he spoke: "Maybe your son brought it on. Did you ever think of that?"

Pausing to peer briefly down at the profile, Fletcher inquired, "How long would you say you've had this anger management issue?"

"What does it say in the report, *Mr. Therapist*?"

"The name is—never mind. I'd like to know your sense of first awareness of it. I mean did it come *before* your drinking and smoking?"

"Well, let's get one thing straight: Smoking mellows me out. *Weed*, you understand, calms my nerves. I get in a—what do call it?—almost a.... What do you call it when you're just in your own world of thought?"

"A meditative state?"

"I was thinking something more down-to-earth, like a *zone*. But, yeah. Damn right—damn near a *meditation* state. Now, beer puts me in a happy, *good times* mood. It allows me to socialize with bastards I wouldn't *speak to* sober. But then, bastards being bastards, they just have to push my good mood too far. And that's when *shit happens*."

"You mean, you pick fights at that point."

"No, I turn into a fucking bird and fly off into the sunset. ...I never said I '*pick fights*,' Mr *Therapist*."

"I'd really prefer that you not address me that way, uh, Mark...Mark Cuzdorf." At Fletcher's admonishment, the patient looked directly at the wood-engraved desk-plaque that clearly read, "Nathan Q. Fletcher."

"I guess we're going to sit in here and call each other by our full names, for an hour: '*How do you feel about that, Mark Cuzdorf*?' '*It sucks, Nathan Q. Fletcher. It really, really sucks*.'" Cuzdorf performed the latter in dramatically mocking tones. He then continued.

"They got psychological names for *overly formal* people, you know. *Tight-asses*, I think it is."

Fletcher's response was calm: "'Mr. Fletcher' would be appropriate, I think," advised the older man. "But if it would make you more comfortable, just *Fletcher* will be fine."

"Just plain old *Fletcher*, huh? I think I might be able to *roll* with that. Goddamn-it, now you're starting to sound like a regular, *down-to-earth* head-shrinker, as opposed to a *stuffy-head* one."

Fletcher was pleased with the sudden shift from mocking to seeming admiration. "Actually, folks who know me well," he offered, "call me F--."

"*Son-of-a-bitch!*" exclaimed Cuzdorf. I left my watch at work rushing to get here. What the hell time is it? I can't afford to get back to work late."

"You've only been here ten minutes," answered Fletcher looking at his watch. He summoned his most professional affectation. "You should be mindful, Mark, that the courts expect you to attend the entire session. So, I hope you've planned the timing in a way that won't jeopardize your employment. Of course, if--."

"Don't sweat it. And save me the lecture. I'm here to be counseled, not preached to."

The four counseling psychologists at the big conference table sat in unbroken sequence. They were Reginald Fairfax, MSCP/LP; Britany Burrows-Duck, MSCP/LFT; Pamela Ricochet, Psy.D.; and Aaron Johenisen, MSCP/LCP/ABC/LSD. At either end of the quartet were the two psychiatric nurses, Violet Hardening and Ilsa Popovfski. The BICHM director had situated herself centrally at the oval table. To her left was the facility's one psychiatrist, Dr. Zhental Sovtee.

In the first fifteen minutes of this staff gathering, Dr. West carefully presented the issues for consideration. For purposes of corroboration, she read reports she'd taken the time to document, of complaints issued against their colleague, Nathan Fletcher. That these were not only from clients but also *family of clients* was particularly damning. She cited concerns brought to her by members of staff regarding the man in question. For all these she fastidiously included times, dates, and contexts.

In addition, she brought up a non personal relationship topic concerning Fletcher, one important at the center. It focused on expectations for staff to take part in professional development activities. Each of the non-doctoral therapists was *encouraged* to take full advantage of opportunities of the sort offered by the state. The doctoral staff was *invited* to do so. Fletcher, it seemed, had not taken a course toward that aim in over a year. Now Mae-Ellen West invited input from her staff.

"Group," began Johenisen with a sigh, "Fletch is going through a tough time right now. I mean, his marriage is on the rocks—. Shouldn't we give him a little more time, cut him just a little more slack?"

"He purposely *steered* it onto the rocks, Aaron," interjected Dr. West. "He gets no sympathy points in that area."

"Well, true...true—but he's our Blyne 'brother.' We're talking five years here with us. Maybe if we all have another talk with him--."

"And after that, *another* talk and then *another* and *another*, and in the meantime the patients—you know, the folks who pay the bills here?—they suffer."

"God, he can be an arrogant bastard sometimes," offered Burrows-Duck looking thoughtfully into the distance. "He comes in some days acting like *he's* the director. I mean, he's asking about the progress of our cases--. And it's not just courteous *professional concern*. His manner has sort of a *critiquing* edge to it. Nobody wants to be exposed to that crap—not from a …*peer.*"

Dr. Sovtee wore an intensely commiserating expression as he nodded at Burrows-Duck and her report. He then spoke to the group in a lightly accented, almost melodic tone:

"You know, I've often wondered what is the model upon which Nathan bases his approach to therapy. During the conference-reporting of our cases, his description of how he applies counseling sounds like a hodgepodge delivery. I, myself, don't see where his style reflects any paradigm of the major psychotherapies."

"Yes, he's an odd one," responded Fairfax. "I confess I've sometimes wondered about the institution that presented his credentials. He always cited a school in Wyoming. You ever look in his file, Mae, to see whatever verification was done of his academic history? I know you arrived as director a year after Nate was already working here."

"Actually," began Dr. West, "I never really explored around in any of the staff's background files. Everybody was dedicated, disciplined and professional, from what I could tell when I assumed the office. I felt, and still feel today, that I walked into a fine organization. It's just that by and by these little issues began popping up about Nathan—some actually 'catching fire.' These, of course, I *put out* through various means, but now, you know…enough is enough.

"After," continued the director, "we get all the major issues with Nathan on the table and discuss them adequately, it will be time for consensus. As you know, I could dismiss Nathan on my own with what I have at present. But I'd like us all to be on one accord—well, more or less."

As usual at this time of day, *Jollet's Deli-Café* was brimming with patrons. These were of both the take-out and eat-in variety. One thing about Louee Jollet, the owner: he was a good businessman with an instinct for people and food-order efficiency. For example, he saw the folks who entered his shop not simply as *dollar signs*. Instead they were "relatives" of various "distances" who at first wandered in but then found a sort of kinship with the proprietor.

So, in Louee's deepest sentiment, he prepared each day to feed "family" who graciously paid him for his efforts. Among his store of refrigerated and perishable goods, he sought to stock no more and no less than what they desired. Efficiency, of course, meant meticulously noting his customers' preferences.

Savings Louee accrued from stocking foods wisely often translated to extra amenity for his "patron-relatives." It allowed him to keep attractive prices for his wares. When there was the occasional oversupply, some of his customers were in for a free treat. Among these just happened to be Kaye Spritey. Indeed, he felt lucky to have her walk into his shop even if she didn't make a purchase. To anyone taking careful note, he had cast a romantic eye on her.

Mickey Duncino had taken note. As he and Kaye Spritey sat at a table within *Jollet's*, he made reference to it:

"Louee sometimes sets a little *snacky-snack* on the table for you when you're almost finished lunch. But I never hear you mention it in your order."

"My, what an observant creature you're evolving into," remarked Spritey sipping her drink. "That's good in *psychology*. It pays to take note of every little thing."

"Well, it didn't take Sherlock Holmes. I mean, he just zips over out of nowhere and slides a 'saucered' goodie beside your last bite of burger. So, what's that about?"

"First things first. Now, you see, you apparently *listen to my order* at the counter, amid the other chatter. Let's say, you do this although, often, you're *placing* with a different worker than I am. Then, we should consider that you didn't just *inquire* about your observation, the first time you took note of it. No. You waited—consciously or unconsciously—for further evidence, so to speak.

"Finally," Spritey continued, "you stated your awareness of an interesting pattern. You're demonstrating either *natural* or *learned* sequences of the psychologists' mental functioning."

"You're pulling my leg, right?" Duncino bit into his Reuben sandwich.

"Well, yes, but only partly," answered Spritey with a sort of dreamy, confident, reflective expression. "Now, secondly, and because I know *you know* how to keep your mouth shut, *Louee's got the love bug*."

"For you?"

"None other, my insightful friend. It actually happened last semester when I was doing my first field-work at the center."

"What's he about, twenty-eight, twenty-nine?"

"Thereabouts. He doesn't seem to be married from what I can tell. Not at all a bad looking chap, either—hard working, mature." Spritey's thoughts suddenly turned to the young fellow arriving newly at the Blyne center just at the lunch hour. "Now, if Louee had the same sort of coarse good looks as that guy you took to Mr. Fletcher's office before we left--. Then I might start giving Louee a few enigmatic *green-light* glances."

"Oh, so you thought ol' Mark, uh...*Cuzdorf*, I believe it was—you thought he had *the look*, huh?"

"No, I didn't *think* he had the look—he *had* the look."

"Horsepoop," joked Duncino. "He was just a dark-haired, chisel-faced, smirky-expressioned, tough-guy type. Few words and probably less character--. Don't tell me someone as sophisticated as you finds that kind of package attractive."

"You hit it on the head, Mickey-Mick. The *package* is attractive, not necessarily the contents."

"Yeah, God only knows what's in his profile." As he spoke Duncino looked around at all the cheerful and animated customers who regularly flock to *Jollet's*. "I'll let you in on something: He was checking you out rather intently when you walked up."

"I'm not surprised. I mean, I'm *honey*. Men are *bees*. Bees will be bees."

"Oh, that's funny. So…any of those *older bees* at the center ever *buzz* overly friendly with you?"

"Let's just say, Mickey dear, that a couple of them have shown that special delight in their eyes when I stroll up in my usual mesmerizing fashion."

"Your lack of positive self-image is so distressing. Now, names and descriptions—even though I'm sure one of them is probably Mr. Fletcher."

"*Lecher-eyed Fletcher*, I call him," returned the flawlessly attractive student.

Resigning himself to make the most of the minutes he was required to endure, Cuzdorf found a relaxed posture within his chair. Unfortunately, that didn't mean he had chosen to relent to propriety in this initial phase of therapy. Instead it meant he would try to derive pleasure in toying with the man he knew was charged with his reform. To that end, Cuzdorf reared back with legs outstretched sidewise instead of in front of the desk. He crossed them in a relaxed fashion at his ankles, gazing lazily about the room. To him, it was more irritation than rehabilitation, to hear Fletcher talk.

"So, what would you like to see come out of these sessions, Mark? I mean, so far, I'm not getting the impression that you even *desire* change."

"What I *desire* right now, Doc, is a 'hit,' a long *drag* on a stuffed *blunt*. You've probably got a *bag* stored somewhere in here your damned self. Now, tell me you don't. You're looking kinda' glassy-eyed there, Doc. You knock down a strong one in *the little boys' room* before I got here?"

"Okay, Mark, I'm going to ask you once again not to refer to me as 'Doc.' You can see there's no such title on the nameplate there. It sounds like you're being sarcastic."

"Alright, alright, *Mr. Fletcher*. Don't start getting teary-eyed on me. Look, Fletcher-old-buddy—I need you and you need me. Why don't you tell me what I need to *say* for you to report my *progress* in your notes. That way, you look like the great *Houdini-therapist* or somebody, and I get a good report-card to Judge Gish. Sound like a plan?"

"So, you don't really want anything out of these sessions," concluded Fletcher. "All you want is the freedom to go back to your old ways. That's right, isn't it?"

"What can I say? You see through me like a goddamned glass window. So, wha-da-ya' say? Is it a deal or what?" Cuzdorf noted Fletcher's silent and thoughtful study of him. He continued. "Look, let's be real, Nate. You can't change me in a month or two of this bullshit therapy. At best, I'm going to figure out what I need to say to get by. The result *then* would be the same as *now* if we just drop this pretence and talk, say, half a session about the chicks we've *nailed*. The other half, you let me get the hell out of here early.

"What are you, near *fifty*," inquired Cuzdorf scrutinizing Fletcher's face. "I'm sure you've *twirled* enough between the sheets in your time to have something to say about babes in bed. ...Ah, no wedding ring! Hell, you must *do* one every few weeks or so, even at your age, if you're single."

Even before it happened, Fletcher knew Cuzdorf's eyes would shift to the pictures facing sidewise on the big desk. "Who's that there? Hmm, nice looking *honeys* in them photos. Aw, don't tell me--. You're *divorced*. Still carrying that family torch, though, huh? Now, you see what I'm saying? You see how much shit we got to talk about instead of you trying to talk me out of *blunts* and beer and bar fightin'?"

"You're headed for a lot of trouble in your life, Mark. You realize that don't you?" Fletcher, as he spoke, leaned forward resting his elbows on the desk.

"Screw it." Cuzdorf gave a quick shrug of his shoulders.

"You must be able to come up with reasons why you should act more responsibly, Mark. As you think on it, can't you name even a few? You have a job—that's something. What about a family? You don't feel you have a single reason to care about the direction you're going in?"

"News-flash, *Fletcherino*: I'm happy as a *son-of-a-bitch* with my life the way it is. Just like you read in the goddamn report there, I got a girl and a child. I work and take care of my responsibilities. And goddamn-it, I like to have some fun every once in a while. Good *weed* makes me mellow. Beer makes me sociable. Kickin' the *dogshit* out of an idiot every now and then makes me feel like a king. What the hell's wrong with that?" Cuzdorf retracted his legs and sat up tense in his chair. He continued.

"You see what you did? You slid back into that damned *therapy* talk. Now, how about let's just calm down and talk about *chicks*. So, how long were you married to that good-looker in the photo? I hope you don't mind my saying so, *Fletchy*, but she looks like she might have been 'good-times' back in the day. Now those two daughters of yours--." At that moment Fletcher reached over and laid the framed pictures face down on the desk. His eyes showed the same strain but now with diminished friendliness. He spoke:

"Do you know what happens if I report a lack of sufficient progress with you to the judge at the end of these sessions?" Fletcher himself had not read enough of the paperwork on Cuzdorf to know the answer himself. He hoped his "patient" would offer it up.

"A freakin' jail sentence. You think I don't know my own shit? So, now you're threatening me. I get it. You want to do this the hard way. You want me to sit here like some little *piss-faced angel* and listen to your bullshit. Okay. If that's how you plan to run it--.

"But I'll tell you some'em," Cuzdor resumed. "I thought you might have been smarter than this. Sure, I'll clam up and play ball. But before I get into *character* for you, I'd like to say this one thing: That son of yours in the picture—if he's like you I see why somebody like me opened a tall can of *whip ass* on him."

In similar fashion to her colleagues sitting around the oval table, Dr. Ricochet pondered the prospect of Fletcher's dismissal from BICHM. "Well, it's not like he'd be *on the street*," she assured herself. "As you said, Harshberry Hospital would sweep him up in a heartbeat with a good recommendation."

"Oh, absolutely," confirmed the center director. "And right at this time, the two *military centers* on the edge of town have an opening for a therapist. A commending note from here would catapult him to the top of their list of candidates." Around the table everyone nodded her or his agreement. Popovfski spoke next:

"If for whatever reason all of those failed, the *prisons* in the outlying areas always need CPs."

"Great point," exclaimed Johenisen. As did the others, he found comfort in the mounting evidence of Fletcher's prospects for *life after* BICHM.

"Well, there you have it," reasoned the center director. "We don't have to have sympathy cloud our judgment about how to vote. And you can all be confident that Nathan would be given ample time to secure transition, if the final decision goes that way." West then took a deep breath as she glanced around briefly at the staff.

Donning an expression of renewed animation, the director continued deliberations. "Now, let's alter our course a bit. Rather than air grievances, let's do a little *devil's advocate*. But, people, I assure you I use the term only figuratively." The concluding disclaimer lightened the heavy mood and even brought chuckles. "In all fairness, I think we should generate a list of Nate's positive points. I can start by citing his punctuality and reliability at the center."

The group sat in reflection a few moments. Then Violet Hardening spoke: "I'll say this: Although he can be something of a prig about it, Mr. Fletcher does demand precision in how his people are medicated—when they need to be."

"Yes, I guess you could say," added Fairfax, "he fancies himself the center's *de facto whip* or overseer. I mean you don't want him to know about any detail you've *slept on* in some matter. Now, while it sounds at first-glance like more criticism, what I'm saying is that his sometimes overbearing style kept us on our toes. I know it did me."

"I think I have to agree," reported Burrows-Duck. "God, it's annoying. But at the same time, you tend to double-check your procedures just to avoid his little snide remarks."

"Okay," the director said with satisfaction, "we've got a couple of pluses. Nate's a dependable employee and a sort of *beneficial gadfly*. Anyone else have something to put into his 'good' column?"

Ilsa Popovfski, answered the request. "I think that on the whole, Nathan is a fairly personable guy. Yes, he has that annoying side, but I'll bet we all can say we've enjoyed conversations with him. Goodness knows he can talk on just about any topic. It seems he knows a little something about almost everything."

"That," added Fairfax, "is another one of those Fletcher-positives that's a double-edged sword. It's true he can talk with you on any subject. But if he just wouldn't, at the same time, be such a know-it-all about it, it would be nice."

"I can tell by the expressions around the table that you all agree with Reginald's assessment. But, maybe we can overlook the *addendum* for now and grant Nate a third positive attribute."

It was Dr. Sovtee who next pitched in something to help Fletcher's cause:

"You know, like me, some of you may have had this experience with him: If Mr. Fletcher is ever in a position where he needs some kind of small favor, and he receives it, he seems deeply touched. And his *grateful appearance* is all the more, I guess, pronounced, given how unpleasant he can be.

"So, what it suggests to me," the psychiatrist resumed, "is that he probably has an idea of the effect he has on people and is moved by a *gratuitous* kindness."

"I think I know where you're headed, Zhental," offered Dr. Ricochet. "You're seeing something positive in what may lie at Nate's *core*. He's, maybe, the *wounded wolf* that growls and snaps but really needs succor?"

"I'd say yes, essentially. We all know that anyone who has an inappropriate side is struggling with something deep within." Dr. Sovtee was often very "clinical" in his speech.

"Well, you know, Dr.s," interjected Fairfax, "I'm with you in commiserating with what may lie at the heart of Nate's intermittent spells of obnoxiousness. But it's not the case that our therapist-colleague is himself a candidate for therapy. He'd bridle intensely at even the implication."

Fairfax concluded: "So, I don't think we should give special consideration to possible *contributors* to his personal style. I mean, each of us likely has inner compulsions toward bad behavior, but we inhibit them. If he can't do likewise, we shouldn't feel obligated to suffer his abuses."

"Okay, then. I guess instead of four positives we're at perhaps three and a half." On a notepad in front of her, Dr. West jotted a brief note. Observing time on the wall clock, she continued dialogue:

"It's almost 12:35. I say let's wrap up the discussion and make the final determinations by vote as planned. I've prepared these little cards with five choices to circle." To each of her seven staff members she passed an index card.

"These," she continued, "correspond to five discrete sentiments referencing your feeling about Nate's future with Blyne. Choosing '1' signals a definite 'no' and '5' a definite 'yes.' Here are the possible voting outcomes that give Nate another chance to improve at this center:

"Three or more votes of '5' will do it. Sparing his place here also will be five votes of '4' or better. Notice—that's over half our group.

"In addition to those conditions, I've added this: At least three votes of '4' *along with* five '3s or better.'

"I just don't believe," concluded Dr. West, "I can be any fairer than that. Any and all other combinations of voting choices among us send Nate packing. So, let's take these next ten minutes," Dr. West continued, "and make a determination. That should put us at five minutes before the end of Nate's present session. As we've pointed out, among his good qualities are structured-ness and reliability."

Riiiiiinnnggg! In the Fletcher home, the telephones sounded off for the sixth time. It was as though the house were empty, rendering each rapid succession of bells a loud, impatient cacophony. Through the first five, Mrs. Leona Fletcher occupied her bedroom, sitting on a small, cushioned, wicker chair. With each raucous ringing, she stared down at the.32 caliber pistol. It rested in her hand which in turn was positioned limp in her lap. She was "seeing" the specter of death in her immediate, or near-immediate, future.

Somehow, Leona found the will to interrupt the seventh ring with a lift of the receiver. "Hello," she addressed languidly.

"Leona! What took you so long to answer? Why didn't you call me right back like you said you would after speaking to the mailman?" Leona's mother had become very apprehensive about her daughter's present emotional state.

"Mother, I don't feel like going on. I barely had the strength to pick up the phone. I'm just so tired now."

"Leona, you have to start putting a plan of action in place. Don't let this *rock* just…roll over you. You have to start planning. That's how you make it through these next hours and days."

"I'm so tired, Mother. All I can think about is how he can *hate* me so. After all the years, all the trying and doing and being, and not only is he leaving, but he'd prefer, if he can, to leave me with *nothing*."

"I know. You told me all about it. It is terrible, what he's doing. But now, you've got to start thinking about *you*. Nate's--."

"He's asking me to sign a *no-fault* divorce, did I tell you that? That way he can get married again as soon as possible." There was a pause and had Leona listened very carefully she would have heard her mother's quiet sobs.

"Nathan's…girlfriend has no health insurance. She can't afford it. So he wants as soon as possible to get her set up. Mother, he didn't seem to know *or care* how it made me feel to hear him saying it. He was telling me about his concern for the welfare and well-being of *another woman*! But not just *another* woman—the *other* woman he plans to marry!"

"Leona, please--."

"I'm *out* and she's *in*, Mother. It's like he already regards me as…gone… irrevocably gone. He says I need to go back and live with you and Dad. '*They're rich*,' he kept saying to me. '*They're rich. Matti and Leonard will take care of you until they die*.' He actually said that."

Leona continued relating from memory her husband's words. "'*You don't need my health insurance and death benefit. When Leo and Mattie die, you'll be very well-off, along with Dory and Lee. We know for sure it'll be an even, three-way split*.' Mother, he talked about it as though he were talking about…about characters in a movie.

"I hear him over and over in my mind. …It's like I'm in a deep well and I hear the echo of Nate's voice over and over and over and over and…. He keeps telling me how much he cares for…*her*. …I'm just…in the way. He says I must not continue to stand in the way--."

"Leona, I'm going to catch a flight there. I'm sure your father will want to come too. Don't you *sign* anything, Leona—today, tomorrow or anytime. *Sign nothing*. And that's however long it takes us to get there, which shouldn't be more than a few days. We have to get a plan of action and carry it through according to what an attorney advises."

"I already told Nathan I wouldn't stand in his way. There's nothing left."

"The kids, Leona! Jr., Kimmy, and Lisa! They--."

"Oh, Mother, please, let's stop pretending. I've taught them that they and Nate always come first, before me—*before* me?—no, even *in spite of* me. I know now I actually participated in teaching them…teaching them that I exist for *their benefit*. What's wrong with me Mother? What's wrong with me?"

"Leona, I want you to call one of your friends there. Call Julie, or Karen, or Theresa. Call them and have one of them come over. I don't want you alone at this time. I'm reserving a flight as soon as possible."

"Did I tell you he cancelled his life insurance?"

"Yes, dear, but let's not talk about it right now. Will you promise to call a friend to come over—maybe stay with you until I get there?"

"He called to cancel it this morning, at work. He phoned me right after to let me know it's done. He said…*Lois* could not tolerate the idea of me being his beneficiary if something happened *before* the divorce…and their marriage…together."

On the other end of the line, Mother Matti had her own idea about the matter Leona described. *Probably,* she thought, *that rat feels that he's given Leona more than good reason to want him dead. Canceling his policy may be a sort of insurance itself against Leona deciding to have him…expunged. He's too stupid to realize that she'd actually rather die, herself, than see him dead.*

"Leona, I need for you to do me a favor more important than anything I've ever asked of you before. Will you do it?"

"A favor, Mother?"

"Yes—an extremely important favor. And I need your promise that you'll do it, after I tell you what it is. It can be done right while you sit or stand there. It's very simple but the absolute most important favor you could ever do for me. One thing I know for sure is that if you give a promise you will keep it. So, I'm going to tell you what it is and hopefully get your promise to do it."

"Well…what is it, Mother? You sound so…nervous. Is Father ill? Please don't tell me Father's ill? …Mother…Mother, what will we do?!"

"No, no, it's not your father, dear. He's fine. I'm fine. I simply want you to give me the telephone numbers to your girlfriends there. After that, I want to put you 'on hold' until I reach one of them. In a very short time, just a few seconds, we'll be talking again and one of your friends will join us. I need the three of us to talk together for just a minute or so. That's not much, is it Leona? Can you promise that you'll do that one set of acts for me? You know I don't ask much, Leona. But I need this from you. I really, really do."

"Well…alright…I--."

"Promise, Leona. Give me your promise."

"Well, yes…I can promise--. …You say you want a phone number, Mother?"

"Yes, dear—I need the first number that comes to mind belonging to one of your friends there."

The *Jolette Deli-Café*, at this time of 12:38, was a site practically buzzing with the light and upbeat dispositions of its customers. Within, students Spritey and Duncino, finished off their sandwiches and conversed with a breezy enthusiasm. In the distance, from behind the counter, the restaurant owner engaged customers with his usual affable style. Every now and then, though, he stole a tiny glance at the young woman who melted his heart at the thought of her. To his credit, he was smart enough to be very subtle about it. The last thing he wanted was to *creep out* the practicum student with what might appear as staring or leering.

As he had with almost every patron, Louee made occasion to elicit little exchanges with the lady of his dreams. That's how he knew the circumstances that led to her patronizing his eatery. Often he found himself in reverie about how he'd like to be friends with her such as, maybe, to aid in her professional goals. For example, suppose she ran into sudden difficulty with her final year's tuition. Then, what if he were in position, he continued in his imaginings, to offer his help? He saw the scenario as having great potential for his becoming someone special to her. For many, he surmised, love had sprung from less nobler interactions than that about which he fantasized.

Sometimes Kaye cut admiring eyes toward Louee, also. At this particular time, however, she was engrossed in the edification of her student-colleague.

"So, how are you feeling overall about it?" Spritey asked. "...I mean, the prospect, you know, of entering the field?"

"For the most part, I guess, I'm good with it. It's just that there are those times--."

"Oh, I think every *psych major* has uncertainties along the way. And that's especially true when you start applying the *book* and *classroom* stuff in the *real world.*"

Responding to the counsel, Duncino elaborated his concerns. "Yeah, I had just started to feel a good grasp of the *interventions.* Then I get this assignment at Blyne and...sometimes it's like I don't know what the hell I'm doing in the sessions."

"Well, this is your first semester at it. You're bound to feel a bit clumsy in the beginning."

"Sure—a *bit* clumsy is okay. How about *totally fucking lost?*" Duncino smiled and shook his head in reflection. "But Kaye, already you're like *regular staff.* By all, what do they say, *'accounts and appearances,'* you got it nailed."

"This is my second semester there. I think I was as unsure of myself as you in that first level of the practicum."

"Well, it doesn't show now. Like I said—you are practically *staff.* Even in my second go around I doubt I'll have it down like you."

"Sure you will. Give it time."

"Even the regulars there—they treat you like *one of them.* Me, they treat like a...a *cactus seedling* that everybody feels obligated to throw a little water at, every now and then."

"Oh, Mick-Mick, they like you just fine. But there is one thing you're missing—and it's the art of *tailored giving.*"

"Tailored giving? What do they want from me, dress-suits," joked Duncino.

"Not at all, Mick-Mick. They don't *want* anything from you—it's what they *need.*"

"Uh-oh, did I miss something in the *psych* classes? 'Topic: *Needs* of Practicing Therapists. Subtopic: Expensive Attire. To be supplied by broke, destitute, practicum students.'"

"Real funny material you got there, Mickey. But, actually it goes to the *psychology* of being *human.* Everyone enjoys an *unexpected* gift. While at times it might be a windfall tax refund, at others, it's as inexpensive as a smile. I call it a *need* rather than a *want* because of the *unexpected* aspect. We *consciously* want expected things but not unexpected things. The reason, obviously, is that unexpected things are not in our conscious minds. Therefore we can't *consciously* want them."

"Oh, yeah—you're in the right field, alright. You sound like Dr. Borgen in *Fundamentals* and *Social*. So…I guess you're saying I should smile more."

"Oh, heavens no, don't do that. You don't want to appear *unbalanced* or anything. Remember, it's *tailored* giving. You have to have a sense of what little things have a good effect with people."

"So, you have to be *selective*," Duncino self-clarified.

"Absolutely. You go around smiling at people who don't appreciate smiles and they're liable to think you're making private fun of them or something. Some people, on occasion, like a little *Dollar Store* gift. Others never want one. Some like a little *high energy* meaningless chatter. Others regard it as wasteful and stupid.

"You have workers," resumed Spritey, "that *feed off* gossipy tidbits; others wince and nearly scowl at them. A professional address of *work-related* topics without ever showing interest in *non-work* concerns ingratiates one person; to the next it's unforgivably *banal*. You have to learn the workers' styles, Mick-Mick. You have to discover the kind of *gift* they would appreciate."

"Actually, as I think on it, Kaye, the only one who sometimes eyes me like *road kill* when I pass by is that Mr. Fletcher. I think it would take the *formal wear* I joked about earlier to soften that *meanie*."

Duncino noticed that Kaye's smiling eyes left his and shifted gently upward. In their subtle movement he saw that Kaye was watching someone's approach. When Duncino glanced to his right, he saw the sketchy image of Louee placing items he carried onto a nearby table.

In seconds, the café owner leaned to set two delicacy-bearing saucers in front of the two students. Without uttering a word, Louee's expression "spoke" for him. He was delivering a gratuity in appreciation of patronage—no more, no less. In the next second he was moving quickly to take his place again behind the counter.

Spritey and Duncino looked down at their pie slices and then at one another. "My *God*, Kaye," Duncino said low, "you're such a great *people-person* that now even your *sidekicks* get lavished."

"Louee's stepping things up a notch, it would seem. But, you know, incidentally he may have addressed your issue." Kaye eyed her recent gift with thoughtfulness.

"Out of the corner of my eye," reflected Duncino, "it seemed that Louee was dropping off goods at the table back there also. Maybe he's giving free goods to everybody? He won't be in business long like that."

"Smokescreen, Mickey-Mick. I've heard him tell the waitresses sometimes that he'd deliver certain items to tables for them while they did something else. It has the appearance of *employer generosity* on his part. But I think he also does it to circulate in that brisk and easy style of his. Also, it allows him to make a *gift*-delivery without anyone noticing. Louee's a smart man."

"I'll tell you one thing, Kaye: When I go crazy I'm coming to you. You are good." Suddenly, something in Duncino's recall surfaced. "Oh, what was that you said about addressing my 'issue'? You said Louee may have addressed it—something like that?"

"Look at the table, Mick-Mick. You've got a tiny, though delicious looking, slice of apple pie. I have a hefty slice of cheesecake. On a hunch a few weeks ago I took one of Louee's free slices back to the center and presented it to Mr. Fletcher. I told him I'd over-ordered lunch—eyes bigger than my stomach syndrome—and wondered if he liked this kind. Now, Mickey, I had to be careful. It had to look genuine and not the offering of a *flirtation device*."

"Ha! A *flirtation device*—oh, that's funny."

"Funny, fanciful and clever—I'm guilty. But, look, it wouldn't have been funny if he had taken it the wrong way. Remember I told you he'd, on occasion, given me faintly lascivious glances. But I'm going to tell you: my instinct was right on-target that day. There was something about that slice of cheesecake—and my innocent delivery, of course—that moved that paunchy *middle-ager*. He looked real surprised and at first confused. You'd have thought nobody ever offered him something he really liked with no strings attached.

"You see, it's just like I told you: Everybody has a *need* for an unexpected good. Now, as we wrap up another great lunch doing, consider my suggestion."

Duncino checked his watch which read 12:41. He was about to stuff the last third of apple pie slice in his mouth. "As much as I've come to worship you as a *psychology* goddess," he joked, "please don't suggest I bring that guy a half-eaten pie sliver."

"No, silly. In a *misquote* of Shakespeare: 'The cake's the thing'— cheesecake, that is."

"You think I should reuse your tactic: namely, the eyes-bigger-than-the-stomach routine? That old ruse is dying under several layers of dust."

"Mick-Mick, never underestimate the creative mind. You'll tell him you're giving all the staff gifts in appreciation for their accommodation, guidance and tolerance. Keep it simple. You're in the process of finding out what little things the folks there like. You heard from me that he accepted a cheesecake slice once. Look dead serious as you *act it out*.

"So," added Spritey in a wrap-up, "say it…hand over the cake. Pause a few seconds to get whatever ol' Fletcher has to respond with. Then, be gone."

"Then, *be gone?*" echoed Duncino.

"Be gone. But be an *actor*. Believe in the *act*. Believe in its justification. It's a simple plan with a simple premise and it's partly true.

"Look, *Frere Jacques*, you want to be a *psychologist*? You got to learn how various interactions affect people—which means you got to interact, try stuff out. Look at it like this: he's just another human being whose reactions you're studying. The experiment is exceedingly simple, unobtrusive, completely noninvasive.

"They have in fact *all* agreed, though tacitly in some cases, to aid in your professional development. So there you have it. Put the *psychotherapist* to the test, Mickey-Mick. It's…it's *'mission butter up'*."

"Butter up."

"Sure. 'Butter up'…*'cake up'*—however we want to phrase it. It's a small mission but an important first one for your survival at Blyne. Mickey, I've known kids who *bit* the proverbial *dust* in their *first* practicum experience—never recovered from the trauma. Sadly, they had to back up a whole mile or more, course-wise, and take a different route."

Spritey dramatized her discourse but with some joviality. "We're not letting that kind of crap happen to you, Mick-Mick."

The two practicum students collected their dishes and disposables onto their trays. In the short walk to place items in proper place, Kaye Spritey nudged her companion. "Watch this," she whispered. Navigating in a slow, deliberate pace and a circuitous route, she caught the café owner's eye. Smiling sweetly, she waved pretty, slender fingers at Louee. In response he waved back and commented in a manner both perfunctory and polite. It was the address he reserved for outwardly friendly customers exiting his shop.

"The queen *and king*…of *cool*," uttered Duncino. As he spoke he held open the café door for Spritey. "No one at a distance would ever imagine that a sort of *prospects-scouting* event just happened back there. Hey, wait—how do you know Louee's not playing the same *charm*-game with other ladies who come in?"

"I don't," Spritey answered nonchalantly. "But right now, who cares? I get a free item here and there—not every time I come in, but here and there. And it doesn't hurt anything. I'm fairly certain that Louee likes me, along with whomever else he might find to be worth a freebie. For now, though, it's all plutonic. He'd have to have more to present than clever, café-owner cordiality and cake to get my further interest."

"Clever, café-owner cordiality and cake," repeated Duncino. "That's it, I'm carrying a notepad and pen the next time we go to lunch."

Fletcher had planned to have Mark Cuzdorf out, at right around 12:50. But that was a whole nine minutes away. By now, he had lost nearly all his former patience for dealing with the surly and peevish individual on the other side of the desk. Though he had been tempted several times to dismiss Cuzdorf early, he guessed correctly it would arouse suspicions. Premature session terminations, he knew, required explanation by the therapist. He definitely was not prepared for undo encounters with an inquisitive staff, as would occur with an early "out."

For Cuzdorf it was all a game. His objectives were two-fold: First, he would see just how outwardly resistant to therapy he could be in this initial session. Second, he designed to carry out the *first* objective without causing Fletcher to abandon all hope of successful treatment. As far as he was concerned *psychotherapy* was a contest of minds. The weaker would bend to the will of the stronger.

I am going to mess his head up, if I can, mused Cuzdorf to himself. *At the very least I'll ruin Fletcher's fucking day by making him feel like a total, piss-poor failure.*

"Okay, *Fletch*, you got me to open up a little about my childhood. So, yes, my mother was, and still is, a lush. My dad was never home—always on his cross country tractor-trailer hauls. I was neglected and damn-near raised myself. Wahh-wahh-wahh." With the latter, Cuzdorf gave his mocking impression of a crying child.

"Now," he continued, "how about a little reward. Turn those pictures back upright. I want to see those babes of your *used-to-be* family again." Cuzdorf took note that Fletcher just looked back at him silently. In the older man's face he thought he saw the emergence of defeat. Emboldened by Fletcher's apparent exhaustion, Cuzdorf reached over somewhat tentatively to right the pictures himself. He was pleased at clearly having fatigued his adversary. He had taken delight in challenging Fletcher to keep coming up with just the right response to his crass utterances.

Often, during Cuzdorf's verbal antics the older man diverted his thoughts to other, more pleasant, matters. One was a trip to Canada he'd planned. Suddenly, though, as he met the younger man's smirking gaze, his semi-reverie crashed back to here and now. It was Cuzdorf's gall at slowly stretching over to handle personal items not belonging to him that jogged Fletcher.

"You know, Mark, when you made that comment about my son earlier you almost brought something *out* of me."

"I thought I *indicated* to you a little earlier that I prefer to be called *Mr. Cuzdorf*. If you don't want to have fun in this bullshit, then let's keep it strictly *formal*. Now, what do you mean I almost brought something *out* in you?" Cuzdorf turned his mouth down into a scowl as he spoke the latter. Then suddenly, a mischievous glint showed in his eyes. He voiced his current thought:

"Oh, I get it. This shit is like therapy for *you*! Okay, *Fletch*, let's talk about it. What did I make you see? Was it, maybe, that you were as *piss-poor* a father within your family, as my dad was?"

"No. I thought about reaching over and knocking you out of that chair." The words were liberating to Fletcher. But he remained calm and collected. Cuzdorf, on the other hand, was stunned as his smirk dropped off and became a sneer.

"Why, you gray-haired, tired-suit-wearing piece of dog crap--!" Now, Cuzdorf, too, felt liberated. Intuitively, he knew what it was that kept matters from going *buck wild* in a psychological counseling session. It was the therapist's calm. In its absence the counselor had broken the implied therapeutic contract that obligated the client to be civil.

Nevertheless, Fletcher resumed dialogue with the ultimate composure. "Now, you see, calling me names doesn't accomplish what clearly is your objective: namely, rattling me. But about my son, you said--. Do you remember what you said about my son, Mr. Cuzdorf?"

Cuzdorf was sitting breathing heavily in his chair. Only gradually, very gradually, did the extreme levels of his anger roll back. His stare at Fletcher was menacing, though. Now, his mind raced to decide the intensity of anger and resultant outbursts he was entitled to. In a flash of clear recall he answered Fletcher's question in a malicious paraphrase of his earlier remark:

"I said, like you, he deserved gettin' his ass kicked. And let me tell you something. Anytime you feel *man enough* to lift your *half-a-century-or-so* out of that chair to take a swing at me—be my guest. I'll--."

"Oh, come on, come on. Let's not go back to that. Our time is short now. I just want to tell you about my son."

"Look you brought this on," demanded Cuzdorf. "You're the one that took it to that *level*. Now, I was willing to work with you to get this shit over and done with. But if you can't act like a *real* fucking counselor, goddamn-it, then *you get what you get*."

"Time's running out, Mr. Cuzdorf. Now, let's both be, as *you* say, *real* here. I think I know it's, kind of, against the rules for *you* to request a different *therapist*. It just makes it look bad for *you*—further evidence of your being out of control. Of course it makes the therapist look bad if his techniques aren't sufficient to get the job done. So, it's actually like you said before: We're bound together, sort of."

"Oh, so you're finally coming around," Cuzdorf concluded triumphantly. "I shook you off your *high horse*, didn't I? *Now*, who's *superior*?"

"My son never recovered after being hospitalized, Mr. Cuzdorf."

"And what the hell do you want me to do about it, *Mr. Fletcher*? You want sympathy from the *patient*? You want *me* to start counseling *you*? They call that shit 'role reversal'. That's fucking pathetic! What the hell kind of therapist *are you*?"

"You know, that's really a good question, Cuz. You may be brighter than you look." Fletcher's abrupt change to cavalier flippancy confused Cuzdorf momentarily. He bridled:

"Look, didn't I fucking warn you not to push me?!"

"And didn't I tell you my son died in the hospital after being victimized and brutalized by a drunken bully like you?"

Cuzdorf wanted to feel mounting anger. It would free him from psychological restraints, as it did when he was under influence of alcohol. But somehow, something in the "atmosphere" Fletcher was creating inhibited his going happily berserk.

Rerouting his ill will, Cuzdorf decided to engage Fletcher in this "new" unprofessional mode he had adopted. If Fletcher wanted to exchange nasty insults in the minutes that remained in the session, he was "on."

"So, your son died, huh?" Cuzdorf looked at the eighteen year old male in the photograph. "Good. Serves him right. I just wish it had been me that did it." Cuzdorf watched Fletcher simply rear back relaxed in the big leather chair.

"Must have really got to you, too" added the younger man. "You went off when I mentioned 'Jr.' But you didn't have shit to say when I talked about *having at the panties* of those three babes in the pictures."

"Well, the fact that they're not really my wife and daughters might have a little to do with that."

Cuzdorf donned an exaggeratedly puzzled look. "Damn, I can see you disowning your 'ex'—but the *daughters*, too? It's starting to look like you're becoming unglued, Doc. You got any sedatives in that big closet behind you? You're sounding more and more like a fucking wacko, old man."

"It's amazing, Cuz, how you keep dancing like a drunken fool around the truth without knowing it. You referenced a 'fucking wacko,' but it's *Waco*, you moron."

"What the hell are you talking about?" Now, Cuzdorf was starting to believe he had driven Fletcher over the edge. "Look, man, before I report your nutty ass to the *head-hauncho* in this joint, let's get back to the deal we were making. You admitted that we need each other in this crazy shit. I want to know if you're going to be able to keep your end of the bargain."

"I'm sure I will, Cuz, but I need reminding. Just what were the terms, exactly, of the agreement we made?"

"Goddamn-it, I need a report from you after five or six weeks, saying you feel I'm benefiting from this bullshit!"

"Hey, calm down, Cuz. I remember now. You and I will sit in here and either exchange insults the whole time or talk about our private experiences with women, right? I remember. You got your way on this one, bud."

Taking a deep nasal breath, Cuzdorf paused, trying to determine if Fletcher could really come through. This crazy situation, he mused, might not be so bad twice a week for the duration, if Fletcher could hold up. On the other hand, there intruded a contrasting thought: Suppose Fletcher was putting on a crazy "front." Suppose he was stalling to get rid of him at the end of the session only to report his behavior to the center's "chief." Cuzdorf conceived a remedial idea.

"I'm going to be honest with you, *Fletch*. I don't trust you. Let's you and I walk out of here and march straight to *the chief's* office. I want to hear you tell 'im that this first session was, goddamn, *off the fucking charts* successful. In fact, let's do that every week, so I know you're not planning some kind of a *shaft*.

"Now how about it Fletch? Are you competent enough to carry that through? Guess what. If not, I have a few things to tell your boss about you. You know, this thing might cost you your job, if I'm convincing enough." Cuzdorf paused a moment. "And where the hell do you get off calling me 'Cuz'? You lookin' for some *real* trouble, *Fletch*?"

"Would you please stop calling me *Fletch*, Cuz? You cut me off before, when I was about to tell you how my closest associates address me."

As Cuzdorf stared with squint-eyed intensity at Fletcher, he *really* began to question the older man's sanity. Still, in all his search of Fletcher's eyes across the distance for evidence of lucidity, a memory protruded. Fletcher had started earlier to state the name by which his closest friends call him. It began with the "f" sound, so Cuzdorf had assumed it was "Fletch."

"Okay, I'll bite. What, if not 'Fletch,' do the idiots in your life call you? And after that, we need to get to, and agree on, the business I spoke of."

"I can tell you, you already have my agreement to what you proposed. You have my *solemn* agreement. Now, indulge me one last request as the minutes tick down to the end." Fletcher outstretched his left arm to show Cuzdorf his watch's time of 12:47.

"Like everyone else," reported the older man, "you had to sign the log-in roster when you came in. Did you take note of the, let me see, *four* names that preceded yours, as Fletcher's 'guests'?" Cuzdorf just stared reflectively in Fletcher's direction, from the other side of the desk. Fletcher continued: "The one just before yours would have read '*Fleety Lee Waco.*' I often sign informally, when I can."

With that revelation, Fletcher Waco pulled the Lugar, complete with silencer, from his jacket pocket. "Don't worry, Mr. Cuzdorf," he advised coolly, "I have no intention of using this unless I have to."

Startled and speechless, Cuzdorf nearly overturned backward in his chair. In Fletcher's eyes was the look of a man not to be trifled with. His tone conveyed the same meaning when he spoke next:

"I have a few very simple directives for you, Mr. Cuzdorf. I won't repeat them, so listen carefully.

"First, stand with your hands raised where I can see them clearly. Second, if you must talk, use the same volume as we've carried over the last, almost, fifty minutes. Third, walk to the closet behind me, open it, step inside *facing me*, then close it and wait an approximate *fifteen minutes* before leaving.

"I won't repeat. Do those things and you'll live. Renege an iota and you'll be as lifeless as this table in a matter of seconds."

At 12:47 the BICHM staff were unexpectedly still in convention. Talks went slightly pass the intended deadline and voting was just getting underway. Although the director had outlined an exceedingly simple procedure, Fletcher's colleagues waffled. They seemed to agonize over just the right number to circle on the "fate" cards.

When the center's clocks read 12:50 the decision was made to open the conference room doors. If their colleague Nathan Fletcher were to appear from his session, the secretiveness of their activity would not be so evident. The team might then appear simply to be awaiting the arrival of a lunch order.

By now Kaye and Mickey had just returned to the center. Together they paused to have work-related small talk with the two non-counseling employees. The clerical and *client-intake* workers informed the students that the staff meeting seemed to be over. So when the pair was passing by the conference room doorway, they gave friendly waves to those inside. In his "free" hand, Duncino carried Spritey's napkin-wrapped slice of cheesecake.

Having *visually* reported their return from lunch, the students continued on their walk toward the center's south corridor. Their destination was the counseling room Spritey used earlier. She had now just a little tidying up to do before turning the space over to Mickey. As prescheduled, his 1:05

session would commence at that time. The two spoke in private tones as they walked casually along the isle.

"Oh, look—Mr. Fletcher must be finished with his 'twelve-o'clock.' His door is open." Spritey made reference to illumination of the hall outside Nathan Fletcher's office. "This is perfect," she continued. "Just go in, give the spiel, hand over the cake, and leave. You got it down?"

"We'll see," Duncino replied in a whisper. When he was standing in the open doorway, however, Duncino and Spritey saw that the room was empty.

"Damn, what do I do now? He's already left."

"We must have just missed him, Mick. Well, you could ask around, hunt him down, or put the cake in the staff's fridge and make the offering later."

Duncino continued walking with Spritey to the adjacent office. "Or I could just eat the damned thing myself," he mused. "I think I could make room for it."

"That's an option, Mick-Mick. Louee serves an awesome cheesecake. I predict you would not be sorry if you put off the *appeasement plan* for now, and have *at* it." Spritey stood in the open doorway of the auxiliary counseling room.

"Speaking of Louee, you think he'll ever, maybe, ask to call you or something? I mean dropping off an occasional delicacy is fine. But, as you indicated earlier, it's not thawing all the *ice*. The way I sum it up, Louee's going to have to get more *personal* in his approach. That's if he's really one of the 'bees' you spoke of."

"Very perceptive of you. Actually I'm not sure if Louee has it in him to take the kind of brazen initiative a girl sometimes appreciates. It's clear that he's very nice and polite and all. But Mickey, it's hard to explain, but sometimes that's just not enough."

"Man, I tell you. A guy's got, pretty much, to be *psychic* to know exactly what to do with you women."

"Pretty much, Mick-Mick. But we don't *write* the rules, we just *live* them."

"Well, I'm going to the lounge and knock this cake off before my upcoming *performance*. Maybe it'll calm my sudden stomach gitters" An instant before Duncino turned toward his next destination, he decided to request a small briefing:

"Oh, Kaye, can you brace *a beginner* up one more time? You know how to give this textbook-perfect *nutshell* of how to approach therapy. I swear I'm getting it gradually. First you have the person rehash the issue. And you listen carefully. And then you--. That's where I start to stumble. I got all those *treatment modalities* crashing into one another in my head.... How do you pull the right one out?"

"Well, keeping note of the time, Mick-Mick, this has got to be brief. But, look, as I've always said, you have to become two people at the same time. You ask, you listen, and you *become* the patient, feeling and understanding what *their* feeling. Then, you try, subtly, gradually, to get them to see things that they're *missing* but which *you* see because you're also *outside* the person. You're the client and the therapist at once, so you have both *in*-sight and *out*-sight.

"Your advantage," resumed Spritey, "is that you're not totally swallowed up in the pain or the anguish. Remember, it's all about how a person *perceives* the thing that's bumming them out. As far as the intervention *paradigm* is concerned: they all have pretty much the same goal. If you do what I've described, you will find yourself naturally following one or another model. You don't force an approach out of yourself; you slide into one that matches your predisposition.

"So, are you getting it...again?" inquired Spritey in a playfully chastising expression. "You seemed to be right *on* it before."

"I think I'm back on track. Thanks, Kaye. You're two *Sigmund Freuds* and a *Carl Rogers* wrapped up in one gorgeous package."

"Oh, you're much too generous, Mickey-Mick—I mean about the *Freuds* and *Rogers*." With that retort, Spritey walked into the counseling room and took her seat behind the big desk. She could hear Duncino's retreating footsteps down the corridor. Suddenly, within the room, a voice spoke very clearly but non-threateningly:

"Excuse me. I'm lost."

At the same time that Kaye Spritey looked up abruptly, she saw the office door swinging closed. The man formerly standing behind it was now in full view—along with the gun and silencer. The latter was pointed directly at Spritey.

Fletcher, a.k.a. "Fleety" Lee Waco, wasted not a second in cautioning the young woman with words and symbolic gestures. It would, he warned convincingly, be in her best interest not to scream or attempt any foolish action to alter the present circumstances. But also, he sounded quite sincere in relating his next advisory. It was that "absolutely, positively no harm" would befall her if she followed a set of very simple instructions.

"You're much prettier, my dear," uttered Fletcher as he walked closer to Spritey, "without the look of fear and shock. There also appears a bit of recognition in those youthfully enchanting eyes. Yes, you've seen me before *in passing* through the center. Unless you can, on your own, attach a name to me, I'd just as soon keep that to myself for now.

"And as I think on it," he added, "that's further proof that I have no intention of a fatal end for you. For, if I did, I wouldn't care whether you know my name or not. Isn't that so? Or as the *French* say, *N'est pas qu'ain si?*" Fletcher smiled just slightly. He'd suddenly thought about the French café owner that Spritey spoke of, some minutes earlier. He had, of course, overheard her and Mickey's talk from his place behind the office door.

Frozen with mouth just barely open, Spritey could find no words to say. Fletcher's gun, just feet way, pointing downward toward her heart appeared fantastically menacing. Somehow, the silencer attachment enhanced its sinister aspect. Behind Fletcher, the closed door lent an added dimension of terror to the environment.

"I'll just take a seat here in front of you, Miss," Fletcher informed. "I think it rude to stand over a lady with a Lugar. Sitting, I believe, will make us both much more relaxed." Fletcher still, however, kept the weapon trained at Spritey's chest. His aim was to maintain his look of "meaning business."

"I hope you recognize this little apparatus," spoke Fletcher pointing to his weapon's auxiliary feature, "as a 'silencer.' Basically it means I could kill you and no one would know for…well, who knows how long?"

Fletcher could see that, as he'd planned, the words put Kaye in a semi-petrified state. He continued. "It's clear you're not in much of a talkative mood at just this time. So, I'll do the talking and you may just listen carefully. Oh, and don't take what I'm about to say as a *'mean-ish'* variety of sarcasm. But as you *put yourself in my place* while *taking in* my plan for us over the next few minutes, you'll do well to realize that I'm *dead-serious.*" Kaye was able to register in her mind that the man referred to her counsel to Duncino earlier.

"Keep matters as simple as possible, I always say." Fletcher donned an expression that was at once staid and non-threatening. "Here it is: My problem is that I need a way out of here that doesn't cause alarm. That means I have to find a course that puts you *out of commission* for *ratting me out*—without doing you harm. If only you and the other kid hadn't walked up at just the time you did--. But, what's done is done. Now I…."

"I won't say anything!" Kaye assured. "If you leave I promise to keep quiet for…as long as you want!"

"Of course, you do. But, I need something with a little more substance than *your word*. Now, as I was about to say, I know this building fairly well. There are two corridors with a bathroom near the end of each. But, as you know, they are kept locked and visitors have to get a key from the staff. Right now, Miss, your life depends on you having a key to the bathroom in the outside corridor. If I had to guess, I'd say you're probably always issued one before a session."

Spritey's eyes widened as she glanced around in a nervous, jerky fashion at her desk top. "Can I look in the drawers? I-I *do* have one. ...Oh, oh God, yes, here it is! What do you want me to--? You want them?"

"That does look like the set," Fletcher conceded. "You are a very lucky young woman. Just think—a little thing like that set of keys stood between *life*, for you, and sudden—and very *silent*, I might add—*death*. The good and bad intertwining fortunes of our existence always amaze me. I'll bet it does you, too.

"Now, hand over your purse and listen to my plan for us, while I fill my pockets with all your belongings. This is going to require a little *luck* with regard to timing. It's going to require that you be quick, obedient, and completely accurate in your movements."

In seconds, Fletcher and Spritey were standing at the center's bathroom door. When it was unlocked and quickly set ajar, Kaye was pushed inside and the door locked behind her. With a deep sigh of relief followed by tears she thanked her "lucky stars" that *Fleety* Waco kept his end of the bargain. He allowed her to occupy the bathroom alone.

Now it was just a matter of following the concluding part of his directives to the letter. She would, as he put it, if she valued her life. The demand was that she find a comfortable place to wait out the passing of exactly twenty minutes. Allowing Spritey to keep her watch for perfect assessment of time, Fletcher gave this warning:

"Alerting sounds from you before the allotted time will bring undo death and mayhem on many—*you* possibly included."

As Kaye noted, at present, the time was 12:58.

Just as Fletcher turned and began a hasty walk toward the open end of the corridor, he noticed the change from seconds earlier. Down the aisle, a staff member came into view, then another and another. Fletcher marveled at his good fortune. The appearance of people had been held off just long enough, within the tiny interval of time he required. Now, in upcoming seconds, he would need to put forth his best "face" of *dull-minded indignation*. Approaching staff at the open end of thirty feet of corridor, he spoke as if peeved and befuddled.

"People leave things all the time and come back to get them! I don't know why he had to make such a big deal of it. *Gosh-darn-it*, I need my glasses just like anyone else." Fletcher then cast eyes abruptly on those of Dr. Burrows-Duck.

"I'm not an idiot" he proclaimed in a pretense of anger. "I understand that *Mr. Importance* has paperwork to finish up. But I simply returned to get my eyeglasses."

Next, Fletcher Waco performed a false and mocking quote he implicitly attributed to Nathan Fletcher. He did so while glancing around at the staff who ogled him. "*You don't come back here without an escort!*" He had scowled and shook his head, mimicking pomposity.

"I don't need people shouting at me like I'm some child," he continued with feigned indignation. "I got a good mind to request another therapist!" Following the outburst, Fletcher recalled with satisfaction the precaution he took of closing the doors to both offices he'd visited. Perhaps that simple gesture would delay the inevitable investigations down the corridor. In the absence of illumination by lighting from offices, the staff down at this end might make the hoped-for assumption. It would be that the closed office doors were a sign of busy workers inside.

As Fletcher walked pass the psychologists for whom he'd spoken his soliloquy, he paused a second. His brain synapses fairly "sparked" in acuity and *presence of mind*. "So *what* if I didn't *sign-in* again, just to be in here a damned *half minute*?!"

He sidled over to the sign-in/out desk, feeling all eyes on him—*amused* eyes he could tell. "*Well, better damned late than never. It'll give 'the king'* one less thing to be fussy about." With those words, Fletcher grasped the tethered pen of the ledger. In the row of the page bearing his signed-in name "Fleety Lee Waco" he found the "time out" column. Across from the accurate "in" time of 10:53, he jotted within the empty space the time: "11:52."

That last act, he hoped, would suggest his having completed the 11:00 to 11:50 session with Nathan Fletcher. Now, he needed to scribble-in "angrily" his brief *sign-back-in* and *sign-back-out* times beside the others. The new "out" time matched what *Fleety* read on the nearby clock: 12:59.

But he didn't stop there. For the row bearing the signed-in name, *Mark Cuzdorf*, he scribbled an "out" time within the blank space, that is, 12:50. It was right in line with Cuzdorf's own signed-in time of 11:56. Owing to Waco's colorful and distractive commentary as he jotted, no one noticed his ruse of falsely entering times. He just seemed to be a man so flustered he could barely see "straight."

Throughout the whole activity which lasted only seconds, the BICHM staff was at a loss as to how or whether to respond. The psychologists and nurses decided in the end to leave it for Dr. West to handle if she were so inclined. The center's director, for her part, concluded that the episode was just further proof that the staff had made the correct final decision at their meeting.

Now, the somewhat seedily dressed client of Nathan Fletcher paced to the center's lobby and out the front door. To him the greeting of a bright day of biting chill was as entirely pleasing as vanilla ice cream atop warm apple pie. It was an analogy, which, when he made it, inspired his next destination.

Inside BICHM, the staff milled around the clients' sign-in ledger. Some wanted to see if Mr. Waco had actually entered a "sign-in" and "sign-out" only minutes apart in time. They knew he was eccentric, "but sheesh," some of them uttered. Others became interested in the logout time of Nathan Fletcher's last appointment. No one remembered seeing him pass through and had assumed he could still be in session. Of course, it would have been very unusual as it was well pass 12:50, they all knew.

But it was the sudden reports of the two clerical and *intake* workers that most fascinated the clinicians. From the time the one saw Waco at the ledger desk and the other noticed him breezing through the lobby, each wore a perplexed expression.

"How did--? I didn't see Mr. Waco come back in. God, he just slipped in without my notice apparently. Did you see him come in, Jeana?"

"Nope. In fact I don't recall seeing him when he left the first time. That's it. Now, it's clear: I need to take *vacation*. I've been holding it off too long. …Look, there it is right there: he signed out at 11:52—at least the *first* time. But you know what? Mickey was at the sign-in desk then."

"Well that still doesn't explain everything. I would have sworn that Mr. Fletcher's noon appointment was still with him. But there's his sign-out time. …This is ridiculous. I get so wrapped up in those medical reimbursement forms, I must tune everything else out."

Glancing at the wall clock Dr. West spoke her thoughts: "Well, we all know Nate wouldn't be in session this long. I guess, like Mr. Waco said, he's writing his reports. Or he could be tied up with a phone call."

The staff had been in the middle of making plans for the late lunch. Now, as they piddled about, each entertained basically the same question: Would the director opt to interrupt Fletcher's *solitude* in writing his after-session reports? She did, after all, have the outcome of staff voting on his continued employment at Blyne. The answer came in her next report:

"I guess it'll be best to let Nate finish what he's doing. In fact, I think I'll postpone my talk with him until after the upcoming lunch hour. He was agreeable enough to take a noon assignment. No need to put off his lunch further—and possibly ruin it."

"Yes," agreed Mr. Johenisen, "there's nothing worse than heavy talks on an empty stomach. What do you say we join Mickey in the lounge as we settle our lunch preferences? Last time I checked he was polishing off a wickedly delicious-looking slice of cheesecake."

"Well," Dr. West began, "he's got a 1:05 appointment. He'd better be getting…. Oh, here he comes now. …Mickey, I'm sure your Mrs. Upswich, as usual, won't be more than a few minutes late. It's just pass the hour…so make sure you're ready for her."

Making his way hurriedly to Commerce Street, Fletcher Lee Waco reviewed the incredible sequence of his morning activities. He began these thoughts seconds after using Kaye Spritey's cell phone to call for a taxi. On his watch the time read 1:04. He recalled his state of nervous uncertainty upon walking into Nathan Fletcher's counseling room.

That had been exactly two hours, five minutes earlier. Through most of the session, he wasn't sure whether or not he'd actually draw the gun and shoot. What he *did* know was that the anger had been building up for weeks. To him, Nathan Fletcher was "an arrogant son-of-a-bitch" who invited a bad end with his ever-ready snide remarks. It particularly was so, *Fleety* determined, given the emotional instability of those he counseled.

Actually, it was an earlier decision, one made three months prior, that spilled over and sparked off a murderous co-plan. Waco's contemplating a *new* life in Canada was the thing that initially laid the dominoes, so to speak. It was more a *second* "new" life, in actuality. Under a different name, Waco had resided in the *nation-to-the-north* many years prior. The prospect of bringing back to life his old identity ushered in thoughts of exacting a deadly revenge on his abusive therapist.

Of one thing, though, Fletcher was quite sure: Killing his partial namesake and paying for it with a long prison sentence wasn't worth it. However, doing it in conjunction with, in effect, *fleeing the country* was another thing altogether. It was all in fact a matter of having good *timing*— and, of course, the *audacity* to set the murder in motion. As Fletcher reflected, *Nathan* Fletcher himself provided impetus for the latter.

All Waco had done that morning was lapse into a bad pattern he sometimes followed. Occasionally his focus detoured from the topic at hand. Only this particular time, Fleety's *annoying digression* happened at a time when Fletcher believed his counseling to border on *brilliant*. In short, he thought he was on a therapeutic "roll" with his client—breaking through "resistances," fostering stunning "insights." So exaltedly pleased he had been with himself regarding his performance.

As Fletcher recalled it, his errant comment had been simple and sincere. He'd merely expressed his view of how lovely the family was, pictured on Fletcher's desk. The comment came suddenly, unsolicited, and out of the blue. Unfortunately, though, it brought out the worst in Nathan Fletcher. He began *rattling-on* sarcastically about Waco's refusal to "attend" properly. He added that the patient diverted his attention to the family in the photos to avoid certain "realizations" about his own former family. In a reckless extension of the negative commentary, he managed to work in Waco's son:

"When he was slipping away on his hospital bed, I hope you showed more interest than you're showing here," he dared utter. Well, that was the last straw for Waco. Almost reflexively, he drew his weapon.

Once he'd ordered the incredulous counselor into the big, walk-in closet and shot him, he had wavered on what to do next. One "silenced" bullet to the heart at close range did the trick, just like he imagined it would. After carefully dragging Nathan to a far side within the closet and closing the door, he had paused. What to do next, he wondered.

Waco had always prided himself on his composure. Yet, now, he had to admit nervous indecision. The office door he opened a ways, and listened. Hearing Spritey preparing exit from the adjacent office, he moved out of view. Sometime after she had passed, he opened wide the door, intending to exit, himself. But then he returned to the desk inside, scouring it for telltale signs he may have overlooked.

Now, in his reflections, Fletcher determined this: Had provocation and deadly reaction not come so late in the session, the initial plan may have been followed. That scenario called for him to walk casually out of the office, down the corridor, and then sign out. With luck, he might have had twenty minutes before Nathan Fletcher was discovered. But, instead, Mark Cuzdorf popped up, disconcerting him.

In the early seconds of Cuzdorf's arrival, Fletcher Waco knew he could still excuse himself and vamoose. Yet something in his immediate impression of Cuzdorf had set off an alarm of sorts. It suggested that the young man might just be brash and curious enough to open the closet while sitting alone in the big, windowless room. If Cuzdorf did this sooner than later, a description of him to police would have seriously crippled chances of escape on foot.

Fleety didn't own a car or a cell phone. So early summoning of police stemming from a Cuzdorf "discovery" and "tattling" would have been a real plan killer. He imagined himself being spotted at a public phone trying to call a cab or in ambulatory flight to his empty apartment.

So, in the seconds of uncertainty, a decision was made to play the role of *therapist, Nathan Fletcher*. Had "the young fool" he "counseled" been a *normal* client, reflected *Fleety* Lee, the original plan may have been continued. Cuzdorf could have been dismissed a little early and he, *Fleety*, would have found a believable pretext for leaving behind him, later. Of course, as it turned out, the plan was complicated by the necessity of a second dead body in the closet.

It had been *then* that Fletcher Waco remembered that the office next door had a *window*. Peeping around the corner in the vacant corridor, he saw that the door was open and the room vacated. To *Fleety's* dismay, however, he discovered the window was set to open only slightly, for air. And that's when he heard Kaye Spritey and Mickey Duncino walking up the outside corridor.

Fletcher had done his best to sound convincing. Inside, though, he hadn't really felt *up to* a third murder. Looking into the eyes of the beautiful young practicum student, he knew it wouldn't be easy. Still, and luckily, his stated intention to kill, if not obeyed, had been sufficient to compel her to follow his directives.

Finally, now, Fletcher was pushing open the door at *Jollet's Deli-Café*. His breathing was heavy from the pace he'd maintained. Standing behind the counter arranging his pastries, Louee took note of the incoming customer. As was usually the case with those who patronized his shop, he recognized the face of the middle aged fellow making entry. Quickly, he made an assessment of the worn, pepper-flecked gray suit under the dark overcoat. Louee gave greeting in his distinctive French accent:

"Hello—*bonjour, mon ami.* Thank you for stopping in. How can I serve you, today?"

"Actually, my friend, I am here to be of service to *you*." Fletcher took a seat near a window. He noted that Louee's wall clock and his watch carried the same time: 1:09 p.m. From where he sat he had a good view of a corner service station a little ways down the block. Typically, Louee's customers went first to the counter to place their orders, whether eat-in or take-out. But Louee, an even tempered and cordial businessman, simply adjusted himself to this unusual format.

Averting his gaze from the window, Fletcher spoke: "If you'd be so kind, *jeune homme*, to sit with me—just a few seconds—I believe you will see much benefit in my mission. …Please…*merci, mon ami.*" While Louee decided his reaction, Fletcher started taking articles out of his pockets. He began laying them on the table in front of him. Somewhat warily, Louee made his way over to investigate.

"These belong to someone you know, *monsieur*—and someone I have reason to believe *likes* you. Now you must listen to me carefully, as I do not have a lot of time. Someone running like crazy dropped these items near me just a minute ago, all of it spewing out of a paper bag. Obviously they were stolen. But it was the person from whom they obviously were lifted that is the most important matter here.

"Le nom de la jeune dame--" Fletcher continued in rusty French, "well, just as it says here—'Kaye Leigh Spritey.' Take a look at the picture in the driver's license. You know her, don't you?"

"Why, yes--. She…works, part-time, near here…the center. You say these things were *stolen* from her?"

"Oui, monsieur," replied Fletcher. *"Cela doit être ainsi.* I'm trying to say: it *must* be so. It is the only reasonable explanation. But there is a far more important thing for you to understand. You are at a *precipice*, my friend. You are poised to carry out a mission that could *win her heart*. Now, let's just say I have reason to believe you and she are presently at an *impasse*, romantically. *Comprenez?* I think I can see it in your eyes as I speak of her that you have a special interest in my report."

Although the latter was true, puzzled cautiousness showed through the Frenchman's expression.

Fletcher expanded his inquiry: "You have *admired* her from, uh, *a distance?*"

"Yes, yes, I think she is…very beautiful—*une très belle femme*." Louee delighted in the fact that his customer possessed some knowledge of French.

"Then, don't miss this chance. I know people *who know people*, Louee. This young lady, *mademoiselle Spritey*, I hear that, in fact, she has *warm feelings* for you, too. But maybe she thinks you're a tad too… reserved."

"What is this…*reserved?*"

In Canadian idiom and accent, Fletcher restated the case with two mild imperatives: *"Prenez l'initiative, mon ami. Soyez plus d'enterprising.* Uh, maybe you're sort of holding back your feelings, there, Louee. Take the *gear* out of *neutral*, m' boy."

Glancing out the café window, Fletcher saw a cab bearing the name of the company to which he had made the call earlier. He could see that it turned tentatively into the service station down the street. Immediately he stood to his feet.

Louee regarded Fletcher with a measure of wonder. Taking precedence over the many questions he had, was his inclination to express approval of Fletcher's linguistic ability: *"Votre français est très bon, monsieur,"* he uttered low.

"Merci," replied Fletcher, looking at his watch. "Well, son, I've got an appointment at a law office down the street. I just saw an opportunity to put you *on to* something that seemed to me kind of special." Pressed for time, Fletcher didn't trust further his command of French to convey adequately his current dialogue. Thus, he continued with a spate of instructions in his native:

"Take my advice, Louee—if you have enough *heart* to do so. Put the café temporarily in the hands of your staff here. Run, don't walk, to the Blyne Institute where this girl works. Trying to telephone them *will not do.* To get the greatest and best effect, you must do this *in person.* By all means, take these little belongings with you. Show the folks there this key—they'll know what to do. Do these things, Louee, quickly—as you have not a second to waste.

"You know," Waco continued, "in this country, the *French* have a reputation of being great *romantics.* I think *mademoiselle Spritey* will be quite pleased at your deed."

With those final words, Fletcher rushed out of the café, walking fast across Commerce. Down at the corner he hurried around to the back of the service station. There he disappeared from view of anyone who might be visually tracking his course.

Entering the station from a back area, he found the cab driver asking around about a fare that was called in. Continuing in this cautious vein, Fletcher asked the driver to pull around and meet him at the rear side of the establishment. There he entered the vehicle, out of view from Commerce. He had his reasons, he explained to the driver. Referencing a Paul Simon classic, *Fleety* stated: "It's true: *There must be fifty ways to leave your lover.* And in every one of them the key is to be quiet, cautious and low-profile." The driver, laughing, nodded his concurrence.

From the backseat Fletcher informed the amused driver of his excursion plan. The first destination was his apartment—just five or six minutes away. There, he would retrieve a small amount of luggage. Following that brief pick-up he wanted, then, to be driven straight to the airport.

Reasonably anticipating a lucrative fare, the driver smiled his pleasure at hearing the directives. "Yes sir," he answered happily pulling onto Commerce Street. As the cabbie noted casually, the time was now 1:16.

From a discreet position in the back of the cab, *Fleety* Waco smiled also. As the vehicle crossed Elm at Commerce, he just barely caught the retreating image of a sprinting, thin-jacketed Frenchman. In one hand he clutched tightly a small bag of items. Money for payment of bills included, they were of a type most people would hate to lose in the wrong place and environment.

That which began as a phone conversation between Leona Fletcher and her mother underwent the desired changes of participants. In time it expanded to a three-way chat, including Leona's friend, Patsy Thongler. From there the communicators changed to the party of Leona with friends Theresa Miles and Patsy. Somewhere in deep recesses of Leona's depression-agitated mind the meaning behind the changes registered. But it was only vaguely, for she was slipping minute by minute into emotional breakdown.

It was sad to listen to the evidence of Leona's fragmented state of mind. Increasingly, her speech lacked uniformity and, eventually, even logic. But help was on the way. While Theresa desperately elicited continued rattling from Leona, Patsy Thongler hurried quickly to the Fletcher home.

For sure, small gambles had been taken in the switch-ups. As before, Leona was asked on occasion to press her finger on the phone receiver and wait a few seconds for another ring. In that brief interim a call was returned, allowing different arrangements of two and three-way conversing. The "gamble" lay in the dreaded event that Leona didn't take the next call. Fortunately, that never happened, as Leona lethargically obeyed without questioning.

In a final rearrangement of the participating parties, Mother Matti was back on the line. As a new round of conversation got underway, Matti privately calculated the time that Patsy pulled onto Leona's street. With persistence, she kept her daughter talking, while she listened for sounds in the background. Believing that Leona's friend must be very near, Matti waited anxiously for the doorbell to ring, audible in the phone.

By now the gun Leona earlier held in her lap had fallen to the floor. As was reflected in the disjointed talking she had done, Leona now was oblivious of it.

The distraught and unwitting widow shifted her circuitous line of discourse back, once again, to her failed marriage. Mother Matti, along with Theresa, listened on.

"Who will take care of Nathan, now that he's left me, Mother?"

"You shouldn't worry about him, now, Leona. He'll be all right."

"He hasn't been home in two weeks."

"You've spoken to him everyday over the phone, dear. You even spoke to him this morning if you remember."

"Oh, yes. He was all the way *across the field*. But he still goes to work. He calls me from work. He'll have to come all the way *back across the field* to come home again. But he doesn't *want* to *cross* the long, long field. I can see him *way on the other side* sometimes. I wave at him and he won't wave back. Why won't he wave back? …Oh! He lost his insurance, Mother! He let it go. He let it fly away. What if something happens? He has nothing to protect him now. It's gone. He let it fly away…far away."

Mother Matti was thinking something she saw no reason to express. It was that it would take 24 hours after notice of intent to cancel life insurance for that cancellation to go into effect. That was if Nathan had cancelled at all. Having *referred* the underwriting company, and agent, issuing the policy, Matti was very familiar with its *terms*. For some policies, she knew, cancellation didn't activate until the passing of five business days. "He'll be all right, dear." she chose to report. "You needn't worry about him."

"Mother...Theresa?"

"Yes, Leona, we're still here."

"Did I tell you how Nate so loves to find his special dessert in the lunch I fix for him? But he doesn't like it too often. He says he'll get tired of cheesecake if I overdo it. So, I have to add it to his lunch at just the right times. If I add it on too many occasions he'll say I'm trying to ruin his love for it. And, Mother, if I wait too long to include it, he says I'm trying to deprive him of one his few joys in life.

" Oh, God! Now that he's *across the big field*, who will know what to do? ...Mother...what about the cheesecake?"

"You needn't worry about it, dear. People like Nathan always get their *just desserts*." Immediately after she spoke the latter, Mother Matti heard the doorbell ringing. "Oh, go answer the door, Leona. I think it's Patsy. We'll hold, while you go see for sure."

"I don't think I want to see anyone right now, Mother."

"But, it's Patsy, dear. She needs to see you—*now*. It's very important, Leona. *Very* important."

"Patsy? Isn't Patsy on the phone? How can she be here and on the phone, too?"

It was Theresa that spoke next: "Leona, we'll explain it later. Can you just trust us for now and let Patsy in. She really needs for you to let her in. Please don't make her stand outside. It's very cold out Leona...very, very cold."

Ringing downstairs, the doorbell was nevertheless audible all through the house. Leona began tending to it more. "Oh. Oh, no...we don't want her out in the cold. I hear Patsy ringing. ...I'll go--."

At 1:20 police were called to the Blyne institute. It had followed immediately the frantic rush to free Kaye Spritey from her *prison/ sanctuary*. When the law officers arrived, the distraught young woman was sitting in one of the cushioned chairs of the center's client waiting area. Beside her, Louee kneeled partially, giving consummate consolation and moral support. He had come to the center sounding the alarm of matters reportedly amiss where she was concerned. The muffled sounds of her banging on the bathroom door came just as staff rescuers, and Louee, were arriving.

Kaye sat telling her harrowing story and allowing her hand to be held gently by the deli-café owner. As she did, she was aware of the gratitude and heightened appreciation she felt toward Louee. Sprawled on the chair beside her were all the items seized from her purse by her erstwhile captor. They had, she reflected gratefully, been gallantly recovered by the owner of her favorite area eatery.

Inquiries led to the conclusion that Fletcher Lee Waco must be the man behind the furor. With a likely suspect in mind, police sent units to the address under which he was registered at the center. Also at their request, the Blyne staff scoured their records for Waco's listed relatives. He could run, the law officials knew, but hiding for long would become more and more difficult.

Amid all the report-taking it was a full nine minutes before a thorough search of the premises was begun for the absent psychotherapist. Until the decision was made at 1:32 to conduct an extensive search of BICHM, no one knew crimes beyond robbery and a brief abduction had been committed.

In due course, of course, the bodies of Nathan Fletcher and Mark Cuzdorf were discovered. Against opposite walls, each remained carefully propped up inside the counseling room closet. Within, the burgundy carpet was wet with seepage from each man's chest, with barely detectable staining. At the very time that police were cordoning off the crime scene, the Blyne clocks read 1:35. Nine minutes later, "Fleety" Lee Waco was passing through screening in the airport security area.

At 1:55 police were still rummaging through Waco's empty apartment for telltale signs of his present whereabouts. In addition, patrol units cruised over an area a mile in radius of his former home. Nearly a half hour passed before the chief of police ordered communication with the local airport. Anyone attempting to board a plane under the name Fletcher Lee Waco should be detained by airport security.

When the order was finally put in place, Waco's plane was preparing for takeoff down the runway. As it turned out, though, the name given by police did not match that of anyone scheduled for flight that day. As mentioned, Fletcher had purchased the airline ticket using the Canadian identity he employed years earlier.

After some minutes, and in accord with a plan spanning three months duration, he was headed for Canada. Snug in his window seat, *Fleety* was suddenly aware of an odd hankering he had for cheesecake.